Poisoned Ivy

LEGACIES BOOK I

AVA RANI

Copyright © 2024 and © 2025 by Ava Rani.

All rights reserved.

No part of this book may be reproduced, stored in a retrieval system, or transmitted in any form or by any means, electronic, mechanical, photocopying, recording, or otherwise, without the prior written permission of the author. Except for the use if brief quotations for the purpose of a book review.

This book is a work of fiction. Names, characters, organizations, places, events and incidents are either products of the author's imagination or are used fictitiously.

This book is protected under the copyright laws. Any unauthorized reproduction or distribution of this work is illegal and punishable by law. No part of this work may be used in any form for generative artifical intelligence.

For the daughters who grew up hearing:
"What will people say?"
instead of:
"What do you think?"

Content Warning

Please be aware that POISONED IVY is an adult romance novel that contains on-page mentions of financial, verbal, and physical abuse by a parent. Navigating a relationship with controlling parents weaves throughout the narrative.

For a full list of content warnings, please visit:
www.authoravarani.com

CHAPTER 1

Malena

I was standing on a jockstrap.

A jockstrap that smelled like laundry detergent and had been propped up on a shelf a minute ago... so at least I could assume it was clean. I sighed and pushed the sliding door to the nearly pitch-black closet closed. And I tried my best not to knock into anything else.

"Hey, Mom," I answered quietly. But casually, like I *hadn't* accidently fallen asleep at my one-night stand's place only to wake up to my phone buzzing incessantly.

"Malena, there's mail here about tutoring opportunities at the library." Her voice was coming through low on my burner, so I clicked the volume button up a few notches. My real phone was sitting on *my* nightstand, back at *my* place, dutifully transmitting its GPS location and forwarding all her calls and messages. "Are you a tutor?"

"Of course not," I lied. I *had been* a tutor for the last two years, but the schedule filled up this year and my usual time slot was taken. "I'm not tutoring anyone."

A metal hanger scraped against the rod overhead, emitting a tiny creak and making me flinch.

My mom paused. A few barely perceptible taps could be heard through the earpiece. I knew her well enough to know that she was pulling up her location-sharing app.

"You're in your room," she stated.

"Yeah," I answered. I kept my voice low but close enough to normal that she wouldn't get suspicious. And I prayed that the lacrosse player who'd kept me up all night was a heavy sleeper.

"Oh..." Papers crinkled in the background on her end. My mother didn't believe in privacy, so any mail addressed to me that went to my parents' house was fair game. "Why are you getting tutoring applications in the mail?"

I sighed and thought about the warm body a few feet away, still blissfully asleep. Meanwhile, all the stress I'd worked off last night started knotting in my back. After a long summer under her thumb in my childhood home, the start of the fall semester always promised a good unwinding.

And she was undoing it all.

"They send that to everyone with a high GPA," I lied.

I sank a bit deeper into the clothes rack, a line of haphazardly hung T-shirts and button-ups on one side of my body and some pullovers on the other. They did a decent job of muffling the sound. As far as places to take a call from my mom went—when I wasn't where she thought I was—a closet ranked solid.

"You don't need a job. Focus on school, Malena." Her voice stretched with steady frustration. "We pay for everything you need."

My parents' financial support was a double-edged sword. While I was blessed to have my education paid for, it gave them a lot of control over me. Especially when they made it known that anything they paid for, they could simply take away—which was my entire future.

"I know," I answered curtly, trying to get her off the phone so I could get the hell out of here.

I was a twenty-one-year-old college junior, but my parents still imposed their unrealistic standards on me—based off of what they thought constituted a "good" South Asian woman.

The older I got the more I wasn't allowed to partake in—no dating, no sex, no parties. A semester abroad was out of the question, as was taking trips with my friends or having virtually any freedom. And they demanded that my phone's location stay searchable at all times.

So, I got the burner phone—the same make and model as my normal one—and the secret tutoring job to pay for it.

Whenever I did anything they would not approve of, I took the burner and forwarded calls and messages from my real phone, which I left charging in my room. My parents would be satisfied to see my location—aka my bedside table—and could get in touch with me. Which they did, incessantly.

They got the daughter *they* wanted; I got to live the life *I* wanted.

"And why haven't you called in three days? I can see you're just sitting in your room, yet you can't call us? You're *that* busy?" Her voice smoothed back down from angry to her normal level of irritated. "Just because you leave home doesn't mean you can ignore your family."

It wasn't enough that I'd graduated high school at the top of my class, got into the oldest and most prestigious Ivy League school in the country (on a partial scholarship, no less), *and* was acing all my classes. No, I still had to be on-call because *God forbid* they bother my perfect older sister.

"Sorry, Mom." At this point, I'd say anything to get her off the phone.

"*Selfish*." She tsked to herself. "Call me tomorrow."

She hung up, and relief shuddered down my body.

I pushed open the closet door and crouched down,

reaching for my discarded shirt and scanning the wide polished-oak planks for my shoes. I spotted them on the other side of the bed and scurried over, my socks muffling my steps.

I loved the first week of classes; the semester wasn't hectic yet. Between my chemistry major, writing minor, and the school paper, it wouldn't be long till some of my *extracurriculars* had to take a back seat to work.

"Hey." A gravelly voice dragged across the silent room.

I rose up from the floor. Balancing on one foot at the end of the bed, I pushed my block-heeled bootie on. "Hey."

He folded an arm behind his head and watched me with a wide, dopey grin. The sheets pooled around his waist as the morning sun skimmed along his solid torso like a stone skipping over the surface of still water.

"I was just leaving," I told him, zipping up my jeans. "I have a meeting."

I glanced around the relatively neat room. There was some lacrosse equipment in the corner. A desk that was clearly only a dumping ground for clothes and other items he probably wouldn't be organizing.

"You could be late." He gave me a playful smirk and pushed a hand through his dark hair. It was *just* long enough that it fell into his eyes before he swiped it back. The perfect length for me to weave my fingers through and occasionally tug in the heat of the moment.

My kryptonite.

"Not for this one." I tucked my burner into my back pocket. I wished, hoped, *prayed* that Dillian, the editor of the school paper, liked the pitches I submitted a few days ago. I planned to enter the stronger of the two into a feature-writing contest. "But this was fun."

"Let's do it again?"

Flings, not to be confused with *actually* dating, were standard operating procedure when you had parents like mine. I'd fought tooth and nail for my freedom, so I wanted to experience as much as I could. But the cute lacrosse player with a skilled tongue and excellent stamina was worth a repeat or two.

"Mm-hmm." I tapped my back pocket where he was saved as *Jake. Lacrosse.* I pulled his door open and gave him one last look. "Text me."

I hustled through the quiet off-campus house, thankfully not running into any of Jake's roommates. I pushed the front door open and the late-summer air filled my lungs. Warm, floral, and a little salty.

As much as I loved the first few weeks here, autumn at Winchester was my favorite. The New England campus blurred into shades of red, orange, and yellow, and my favorite poorly lit bench in the back of the Amherst Building's library would be mine for the taking. I could read or study for hours with a contraband hot chocolate while the wind rattled against the patina windows.

It was bliss.

I checked the time: 8:16 a.m. Just enough to get back to my place and shower before meeting Dillian.

With tutoring no longer an option, I needed cash from somewhere. And that feature contest was looking like the perfect solution.

BARS OF SUNLIGHT streamed through the domed windows of the centuries-old Hastings Building. Despite the warm weather outside, it was chilly between the thick stone walls. They swallowed my footsteps' rapid metronome as I sped through the vaulted archways.

I turned the corner when I reached the newsroom and passed through the threshold. As my eyes adjusted to the low light, I ran headlong into someone and only just managed to stay upright.

I stumbled back a couple of steps, and two firm hands landed on my shoulders, steadying me.

"I'm... sorry," I stammered.

My brain skipped like one of those old-timey CDs. Glacial blue eyes, tawny hair, a cut-glass profile that belonged in a Ralph Lauren spread. He wore a loose-fitting crew shirt that hung on his body like cloth over marble and an amused expression on his face.

"Don't be. I'm not." His smooth drawl rolled down my body—plucking a cord deep in my stomach. "But I *am* a little surprised that anyone would be in such a rush to get to the paper."

I took a step back. His hands fell from my shoulders.

"Is..." I faltered. "Is Dillian in there?"

"Nope. Lucky me." His smile tilted up at one side, eyes locked on mine. He put out his hand and a slow static moved up my own when I shook it. "I'm Conrad Hastings."

And just like that, my brain started firing on all cylinders again.

I didn't know him. Not *personally*. We'd never been introduced. But everyone at the paper knew Conrad Hastings. He breezed into the newsroom at the start of every semester, usually with a girl or two on his arm. He'd talk to the editor and his work would get reassigned, and that would be the last any of us saw of him.

He was also one of the obscenely wealthy students who lived in my building with all the rest of the legacies. Being a prestigious Ivy League school, Winchester was filled with the children of powerful families. With a population of over five thousand undergrads, the rich ones tended to blend in.

"I'm late for a meeting." The reason I was rushing in here filled my mind, and I pulled my hand back.

Conrad looked over his shoulder to the empty newsroom.

My face heated. I glanced at the clock; I was early.

"Well, good luck." His lips painted a mocking smile, and as much as I wanted to stay unaffected, something inside me fluttered. "Seems tense in there."

This early in the semester, it was always quiet. But the first round of assignments went out in the next week, and soon it would be alive with chatter.

I crossed my arms. Some of us took the paper seriously.

"Good luck to you too. With getting your work reassigned, I mean." I feigned a sympathetic pout. That was probably why he was here. "I don't know that Dillian will be charmed by"—I waved my finger around his face, hopefully distracting from the heat that flooded mine—"that."

The dismissal did nothing but dig the smirk deeper into his cheek.

"I should get more creative." His eyes, immovable on mine, seemed to spark as he nodded. "Noted."

I walked around him and told myself not to look over my shoulder. I had to focus.

I strode over to my desk, where the source of my anxiety greeted me from its surface in bold black letters: *Keller Feature Award Guidelines*.

All of my discarded ideas were scribbled in the margins—everything from price fixing at the campus bookstore to the rapid decline in professors achieving tenure. For the next few minutes, I read through them again, tapping my foot against my chair.

I joined the paper as a freshman because I wanted to appear well-rounded in my medical school applications, but it turned out I enjoyed the work. A lot. It led to a writing minor —a decision that my parents didn't like, but since it didn't affect my grades, it never became an issue.

"Malena." Dillian walked into the newsroom, rousing my

attention. "I reviewed your pitches for your first piece. The feature."

"And?" I sat forward in my seat.

His glance landed on the papers on my desk; a knowing smile pushed up against his cheeks. "*And*, I'm assuming you're planning to submit it for the Keller Feature Award?"

Founded by the Keller family, revered Winchester alums, the feature award was a national competition open to writers at college papers. Winning got you a foot in the door at magazines, papers, and publishing houses all over the country. And the prize money...

The award was a hundred thousand dollars. That was over a *year's* tuition.

"Yeah. I am."

If I was going to live a double life—and I had to if I wanted to *live* at all—I had to fund it. Between the phone, going out, expenses for healthcare my parents didn't know about, and the occasional purchase of clothing they wouldn't approve of, I only had about four months before my private bank account was drained. The award money would keep it well funded for *years*.

"It's highly competitive, Mal." His shoulders dropped. "And the two pitches you sent were fine for a regular piece in the *Winchester Daily News* but..." He ran a hand through his curly brown hair. "The best college writers are going to be competing; I think you need something with a bigger bite."

"Right." I twined my fingers together. *Shit.*

I had a path: Ivy League undergrad, entrance to a top medical school, residency, and then my *own* life. Once I got there, I'd figure out how to make the two versions of myself merge into one.

Till then, the two-Malena system worked. But without tutoring, I was backed into a corner. My parents couldn't *know* I was working, because they'd want to know where the money was going. And defying them came with arguments, then guilt-trips, then the threats of losing their financial and familial support. It was too much baggage when I could just as easily lie and make everyone happy.

"You still have a week before I need to submit your pitch to the faculty advisor." Dillian had taken me under his wing here as a freshman when he was a sophomore. I relied on his experience; he was among the people who encouraged my writing minor last year when I was on the fence. If he didn't believe in these pitches, I needed to find something better. "Use it."

"I will," I assured him.

He checked his watch and walked back to his desk. I tapped a pen against the spiral on my notebook and scanned over the margins of the submission sheet.

Some people went their entire lives without truly living a single day. My parents seemed determined to slot me in as one of them. But at Winchester, my world was vibrant and filled with the opportunity to be myself. Not the version of me my parents wanted. Just me.

I couldn't let that go.

One way or another, I was winning that award.

CHAPTER 2
Malena

After meeting with Dillian, I made my way back to the condo I shared with my best friends Cora and Sabrina. We all moved in together last year as sophomores after having gone through the time-honored tradition of random roommate assignments as freshmen. Today, Sabrina was leaving for her semester abroad, so it was time to put on a brave face and not think about my best friend being away for a whole semester.

I walked the half-mile down from campus, along the manicured road lined with redbrick row homes, before stopping in front of my building. Locally known as "million-heir row," the Radiant Residences were one of a few mid-rise buildings in New Harbor, Connecticut. The condos inside were managed by the historic society and privately owned by wealthy parents of the students who lived here. Mine was no different. Except I didn't own anything. That was all Sabrina.

I took the elevator up to the seventh floor and unlocked the door, where I was met with Cora's singsong voice. "You missed Pilates this morning."

Summers at my parents' house in Massachusetts were

suffocating. I couldn't so much as take a phone call without an explanation. But every year when the fall semester started, I could finally breathe again.

"I was in the mood for cardio," I answered with a wide grin, hanging my keys on the little hooks next to the doorway.

Easily hidden, sex was something I could enjoy and move on from. Just because my parents were delusional and wouldn't allow it didn't mean I was going to abstain. Besides, nobody batted an eye when *guys* sowed their wild oats, or whatever other gross colloquialism people used to describe college students having sex. So, I was going to have all the orgasms I deserved.

I walked down the hallway to Sabrina's room, finding her hanging a few dresses and last-minute outfits she wasn't taking with her on her semester abroad.

"Did you figure out how you're going to supplement the lost tutoring money?" Cora Chen sat on Sabrina's made bed, with her legs primly crossed beneath her. Her pin-straight black hair danced along her chin in a sharp bob.

Cora had been the one to set up all the forwarding and response capabilities so that I could use my burner phone as an extension of my real one. Something of a tech genius, she'd written her first line of code in elementary school. She was my fairy tech mother.

My closest friends since freshman year, Cora and Sabrina alone made up the two-Malena system circle of trust.

"Outside of the Keller Award?" I sighed. Anything through the school was retrievable through the bursar's office, and my parents would find out. Tutoring through the library was the perfect pathway because it just set you up with people who needed help. I was usually paid in cash or via payment app. "Who would've thought finding under-the-table money would be this hard?"

That's why the contest was great. Winning meant a big fat

check I could deposit and then coast through the rest of my time at Winchester. I wouldn't even *need* to tutor next year when the slots became available again.

"Babysitting?" Cora suggested.

My brow crinkled. "*On* campus?"

I didn't have a license because I purposely failed my driver's test three times so my parents couldn't make me commute back and forth from Winchester.

Cora's head cocked to the side in thought. "Do you have any *other* marketable skills?"

I slumped to the floor and dropped my head to my knees. The only thing I *had* was a perfect GPA and helicopter parents.

"I can dance? But that's probably not something I should do for money," I deadpanned, then paused and thought about it. "And I can write."

Cora's shoulders fell.

Sabrina zipped her last piece of luggage before giving me her full attention. "If you don't figure something out, I can—"

"I will figure it out," I insisted. It was my own stupid fault for missing the tutoring sign-up deadline.

"Mal, I mean it. I can help with money." Concern lined Sabrina's brow. "It's not a big deal, *really*."

"It's not *just* the money." Although money was a major part of it.

Cora and Sabrina exchanged a knowing look, then turned a sympathetic one on me.

"If I win…" I never said this part out loud because I knew the path I was on wasn't open to negotiation. "If, down the line, I want to write—" I twined my fingers around the fabric of my shirt. "Awardees have their pick of grad programs, free-lance jobs, or internships. It's a way to keep my foot in writing after graduation."

This award was a sterling qualification that nobody could look past. No way would I be able to work in the field and make connections *while* in med school, so winning would be solid proof that I could do it. I'd be able to, at least, get an interview for a freelance gig or two.

"With med school and everything." I swallowed. "Obviously."

Med school had been a goal of mine for as long as I could remember. I excelled in STEM-related classes. I liked the idea of helping people, and I wasn't queasy around blood.

I just couldn't be sure whether it had started as *my* dream. Because how was I supposed to know what I wanted when I was only allowed to want one thing?

"Okay." Sabrina nodded and I released a giant exhale. She was skilled at picking up on when I'd maxed out discussing my future and was always willing to steer the attention away. "Well, that's everything. Are you going to miss me?"

Sabrina was a member of the storied Alders family. They were American political royalty and her father—Senator Alders—was making a run for the White House. He'd be the third Alders president if he succeeded, and Sabrina's semester abroad was very likely her last hurrah before she took on the role of first daughter.

"You can't leave now, Sabrina," Cora whined. "A hookup her first week back? Mal is *clearly* in heartbreak hotel."

I guffawed a laugh. "Am not."

Was I a little humiliated? Yes. Annoyed that I broke my flings-only rule for Kash, thinking maybe I'd fit in with him and his friends only for him to ghost last semester? Also yes.

But heartbroken? Far from it.

Sabrina smiled, pushed her dark brown hair over her shoulder, and outstretched her arms. "Are you sure?"

"Yes," I insisted, fitting my arms around her small frame. "Now, go to Oxford. Drink warm beer, have sex with a cute accent, and drink more beer." The reality that she would be gone all semester weighed on my chest like sandbags, but I kept my voice firm as I held her shoulders. "In that order."

"Done."

Sabrina gave Cora one last hug and made her way down the hallway. We followed a few steps behind her. "Don't miss me too much."

We said our final goodbyes and Sabrina was gone a few minutes later. Cora slipped away to her room and blasted her go-to 2000s music—a telltale sign that she was procrastinating—and I sprawled out in the living room to study for my MCATs.

Thirty minutes later, I was still nestled in the corner of our plush sectional couch when three knocks rapped against our door in quick succession.

"It doesn't inspire a lot of confidence that you already forgot something," I called toward the door as I stood and walked over, expecting Sabrina.

I swung it open to find an empty hallway. Looking both ways, I couldn't even hear a voice or footsteps. On our doormat was a small, black, perfectly wrapped box, tied artfully with a golden ribbon.

I looked around the hallway one last time and picked it up. There wasn't a note or a tag attached, but it did have our condo number written on the underside.

Curiosity getting the best of me, I opened it.

Beneath a few flimsy sheets of tissue paper sat a traditional Venetian mask. Macrame lace covered the corners, and long satin ribbons were stitched to flow seamlessly from them. One side winged out with a black feather, and the other was gilded with gold leaf and embedded with tiny crystals.

A note lay next to it, addressed to Sabrina.

Sabrina Madeline Alders

**Scan the code
Keep the secret**

- Scroll & Ivy

Below it was a QR code and an insignia: a scroll with text embossed in Latin.

Secret societies were an Ivy League staple, like trust fund babies and admissions scandals. They had exclusive clubhouses on campus, which its private members referred to as "mausoleums." They weren't actually mausoleums—or at least, I didn't think they were. That would require me, a non-member, to have stepped foot inside one.

I ran my fingers over the smooth edges of the porcelain mask and read the note again.

Then, almost as though it magicked its way from the delicate box, an idea dawned.

My heart raced. *This could be something for the Keller submission.*

"Cora?" I yelled into the hallway, pushing the door shut with a quick swivel of my hips. "Cora! Tell me if this is crazy."

I strode straight to her room with barely a glance at my textbook splayed open on the couch.

"Tell you if what's crazy?" she said, folding a pair of leggings and dropping it into a neat pile of fresh laundry.

"Behind a mask... how long do we think I could pass as Sabrina?"

Only the children of the outrageously rich and well-connected made it into Scroll & Ivy, so it made sense Sabrina was invited.

"Behind *that* mask?" Cora clarified, pointing to my hands. I nodded and she took a step forward, running her fingers over the lace. She tilted her head in thought and gave me an upside-down grin. "One to one-and-a-half seconds."

Right. Disappointment rang in my ears.

Sabrina was white—lily white, came-over-on-the-Mayflower white. I was the daughter of two Indian immigrants and my tan complexion was two shades warmer on a pantone palette than hers. Sabrina may have been dying her naturally blond hair darker for years to look less like her own family, but it didn't really get us any closer to looking similar.

Just as quickly as Cora pointed out a hole in my plan, I found a way to patch it. "What if I go to a party and pretend to belong? You think I could pull it off?"

I'd been doing that in one way or another my whole life. How hard could it be to party crash for long enough to syphon some information?

Cora scanned the invitation. "Why would you even want to?"

They were called secret societies because, for centuries, they'd been just that: a secret. But now, with the internet and social media, everyone *knew* they existed, but only a select few stood a chance at experiencing them. The rest of us had to rely on gossip.

And there was plenty of it, the rumors stretching from moderate (lavish parties, secret traditions, and trips abroad) to ridiculous (a network of secret underground tunnels called *the catacombs*).

"I know it's a little crazy..." Like a weed, my smile grew wild. "This *could* be perfect for the Keller Award."

It would be unique; a peek inside a world that only a few would ever see. I didn't have an angle *yet,* but I could figure it out. It was a hell of a lot more than I had before.

"Yeah... a little crazy is right." Cora shrugged. "Let's just call Sabrina when she lands, figure out what she knows, and see if it's doable." She glanced back up to me and her shoulders moved down a fraction. "Although, based on that look"—she circled her finger in front of my face—"you're already plotting."

I swatted her hand. "What look?"

"Same one you wore when you bought that second phone. The 'Malena-found-a-loophole' look."

Smoothing my thumb over the mask, my heart raced.

This was how I won the Keller Award.

CHAPTER 3

Conrad

T he muted skim of saltwater as it cut along the rowing shell hummed over the sound of the music playing in my ears. I gripped against the wooden oars, and with a coordinated push with my feet and steady pull from my arms, the boat sliced through the water like steel through silk.

My heart raced. Fueled by the tabloid gossip I was bombarded with when I woke up this morning, I pushed harder. On top of being the reason for my calluses and the curious glances I'd surely be met with later, my dad was scheduled to visit me on campus, and that was never good news.

I was exhausted, but I moved past the soreness that crowded my arms and back and kept going.

"Jesus, Con. Look out!" A loud warning cut through the blaring bass line, yanking me from my thoughts a couple of seconds too late. I looked up, spotted James, and then came a swift smack against my torso from the oars, pushing all the air out of my lungs as I nearly ran aground. The boat rocked violently.

"Shit," I cursed, steadying the shell with my oars. *Just what*

I need. I yanked my earbuds out and called to my best friend, "Is it bad?"

I pushed to the pier a few feet away where he and Ishani stood. I got out of the shell and James picked up the end. He clicked his tongue when we put it down and gave it a quick inspection.

"No, you're fine," he answered.

"I'm guessing you're out here because of your father?" Concern laced Ishani's proper British accent. She tucked a lock of her long black hair behind her ear, crossed her arms, and arched a brow as she watched us.

James and I pulled the shell up and hauled it onto our shoulders to walk it back to the outdoor rack outside the shell house. "Yeah. He's going to be here next weekend."

He orchestrated his appearances when he needed to levy threats, and he always made good on them.

A fact I learned the hard way as a seven-year-old, when my mom and I stumbled upon his first mistress in Newport one summer. After that, I started acting out and spent the remainder of elementary school in some form of trouble or another. He got frustrated and decided to ship me off to Swiss boarding school so I wouldn't damage the family name. It was how I met James and Isha; we all went to Le Rosey together.

"You'll have to behave for Scroll & Ivy's first event." Ishani Roy, heiress to the Roy family dynasty, loved a party. And the society we'd all gained entrance to last year was *always* a good time. "Masks went out last night."

Now that we were seniors, we were in charge of operations. "Yeah, I'll be careful."

"Any idea why he's visiting?" James asked as we placed the shell on the rack and secured it.

I couldn't be sure, but it was probably some iteration of disappointment about my lack of motivation. But, I'd always found ambition to be a punishable offense in my family. My brothers were constantly at each other's throats to one day lead Hastings Media, and my mom, whose attempts to keep her marriage together were evergreen, weathered affair after affair.

Trying was a fool's errand when it never meant change.

"No," I answered.

"Don't worry, we won't give him anything to be upset about." James squinted against the bright sun. He looked out at the water, then at me. "You good?"

I knew where this was going but stayed silent.

"You're out here *again*," Isha added.

"We row crew," I pointed out.

James and I had been on the team since freshman year. Out on the water, away from public scrutiny, I could clear my head. And it was the only part in my life where racing *toward* something was a good idea.

"Two-a-days isn't enough practice for you?" James countered.

I huffed a conciliatory breath. "I'm fine."

I came out here to focus on something other than the constant stream of tabloid fodder that was my dad's latest affair. Up until now, he'd managed to keep his philandering out of the press. And so, rather than suffer in privacy, my mom was forced to navigate this affair with public scrutiny.

"After everything that happened last semester..." Isha looped an arm around mine, giving it a quick squeeze. She didn't need to finish her thought; it was rarely far from my own mind.

We turned, wandering over to the path that led away from the bay and toward the far side of campus.

"I don't need a tutor, if that's what you're asking." I headed her off, saving her from her tendency to worry.

Last semester had been a mess academically. I missed a lot of class because someone had to check on my mom and I was the only one who'd been concerned enough to do so. I took the incomplete in my Monetary Policy class knowing I'd figure a way out of it.

"How's your mum?" Isha asked.

She'd kicked my dad out of the Manhattan house, like usual. Every time he cheated, she kicked him out. Then she'd spiral, and he'd move back. Rinse and repeat, ever since that sunny July day in Newport.

It never changed.

I shrugged. "Better. You guys don't have to worry."

My friends checked in a lot last spring when things got a little out of control. My mom wasn't the best at accepting help, and it took a while before she was willing to.

"We're not worried." James mulled over the words he wanted to use. "More like, accessible. Here to help. We all are. We can check on her too."

"I'm good," I insisted. "My mom *does* seem better."

It wasn't a lie, not completely. Mom had started going out to her normal lunches with her friends and ventured out of the house more frequently. When I saw her a couple of weeks ago, right before the start of the semester, she was doing a lot better.

"Well, Lucy and Felix are waiting for us on campus." Isha glanced at her phone. "You okay to go?"

Lucy McMaster and Felix Herrera made up the rest of our tight-knit group. Although I'd known James and Isha since boarding school, the five of us had been friends since freshman year.

I had two older brothers, but they weren't my family, not like my friends were.

"Yeah," I assured her. "I'm fine."

"Great." James hooked an arm around my neck. "Let's have some fun this semester, starting with the Scroll & Ivy party."

He gave me a wolfish grin.

"Under-the-radar fun," Ishani reminded us. "Let's keep poor Conrad out of trouble."

MUCH LIKE CREW AND SCROLL & Ivy, every Hastings was involved with the *Winchester Daily News*. Unlike the other two, I found the paper tedious. However, when you were set to inherit a third of the largest media company in the world, you were expected to take an interest in the family business.

I stood waiting outside the newsroom in the humanities building because I knew James's lit class let out soon. After missing Dillian yesterday, I tracked him down when I got back on campus earlier, and I hoped after the meeting we'd had, today would be my last time stepping foot in this building.

"What did Dillian want?" James asked when he found me outside the lecture hall's doors. He jumped out of the way to avoid being trampled by a crowd of people rushing toward a couple of sheets of paper tacked on the bulletin board.

I rolled my eyes. "I swear that guy is on some power trip." He was the editor of a college paper and acted like none of us had anything better to do than bend to his whims. "He ran an audit and noticed I haven't written anything..."

"Shit." James looked at me then back at the commotion by the notice board. Neither of us was in a rush, so we were content waiting for the class to disperse. "Does that mean you're *actually* going to be a Hastings this year?"

"No," I scoffed. I saw how that was going for my mom and brothers.

He let his bag slide to the floor and leaned against the wall, a curious look on his face.

"I called Barrett," I stated. "Guess who's going to intern at Hasting International's newsroom over winter break?"

Seeing as my older brother Barrett oversaw the entire division, I had him set Dillian up with the internship, and in exchange, he was going to re-assign the work for me. Dillian wasn't happy about it, but he wasn't exactly in a position to argue.

James chuckled. "That's *one* way to handle it."

"And now I'm free all year."

We walked up to the two printed-out spreadsheets that were the center of the fuss.

"Dammit. Every time." James cursed and ran over the list of names from Professor Cromwell's American Literature class. One of the only professors who still posted names next to the grades, he was really taking the whole "tenured" thing seriously.

"Hmm?"

"She was in Cromwell's Advanced Comp tutorial last year too. She beats my score by a point or so every time there's an exam or a paper. And she's a *junior*," James complained, his brow crinkling as he read the printed spreadsheet again. James was a Rutherford—the ones behind every train, jet, and motor engine built in Europe and most of the States for the last century. And as the human embodiment of *work hard, play hard*, he hovered at the top of our class. "And we only had a week to write this one. I swear this girl is my Aaron Burr."

"I'm pretty sure getting bested at every turn makes *you* Burr." A new voice—soft but sharp—pulled our attention, and we both paused. "And *me*, Hamilton."

Awareness tingled down my body. A thin flowing blouse tucked into a skirt, long black hair pulled into a bun, legs that went on for days. Big brown eyes and an instigating smile.

It was her. The girl from the paper.

Immovably intrigued, my pulse jumped as I searched my memory for her name. I'd seen her in passing a few times but never stopped to glean anything more.

Maybe I should have.

"If it makes you feel any better..." She leaned up and tracked her finger along the rows on the spreadsheet, confirming what James had announced. I glanced at the grade list to catch it—*Malena Amin*. Her chest filled with air and a proud look overtook her face. It was gone in a flash. She turned to smile broadly at James. "You shoot me in the end."

I chuckled.

"It *does* make me feel better," James retorted, the playful bite in his tone whipping me back to reality. My eyes flicked between them. "Just tell me the time and place."

She was cute. And James was flirting with her.

"And expedite everyone forgetting who you are?" She tilted her head patronizingly. Her gaze moved to mine and paused. For that second, I was frozen. Her lips tipped to the side in a quiet acknowledgment, but the moment passed as quickly as it came, and she looked back at James. "I'd never do that to you, Burr."

She turned on her heels and walked back the way she came.

"Hamilton? Burr?" I tamped down the curiosity—or whatever it was that thrummed in my body—with a hard swallow, because that little exchange was as good as James drawing a hard line of interest in the sand. I watched as she walked down the hall toward a friend waiting for her underneath the stone archway. "*Adorable*. Are you gonna ask her out?"

"Haven't decided yet."

"You were flirting with her," I pointed out.

"I like to be on a flirtatious basis with *all* the beautiful women on campus." James looked at me and shrugged.

My face crinkled. "Since when?"

I'd known James since we were kids, and he was *always* in a relationship—loyal as a dog. After a breakup over the summer, he was determined to embrace his single status. Maybe a little too much. His weekends were starting to look a lot like mine, which was concerning.

"Since I'm single and planning to enjoy it."

"If you say so," I answered, unconvinced.

My gaze lingered on her.

I wondered if I'd see her again. If James *did* ask her out, I probably would.

And for some reason, that fact was both alluring and unsettling.

CHAPTER 4

Malena

A couple of days after finding the mask, I was still figuring out how I wanted to approach the feature—assuming my half-cocked idea of party crashing worked.

I walked out to the living room and discovered two bowls with yogurt and granola sitting next to each other on the coffee table. Morning light flooded the room, and Cora's laptop was propped on a stack of magazines. Sabrina had only been gone a few days and we'd already deduced that morning or afternoon calls worked best since she was six hours ahead of us. Cora held a mug and pointed her chin at the one waiting for me on a ceramic coaster.

I sat on the thick emerald-green carpet next to Cora and faced her laptop screen, grateful for the coffee she'd brewed us. I was in charge of cleaning since Cora had a firm grip on hostess duties.

"What's up?" Sabrina asked, smiling brightly. We hadn't planned to talk until she could properly settle in, but the mysterious invitation required a code, and I needed to run our plan by her.

"I need some help." I twisted my fingers between my hands. "And I'm sorry, I know you wanted some peace before—"

"The election?" she finished for me. "Honestly, I love not thinking about it, so go ahead."

Winchester was no stranger to the children of important families, which meant as long as Sabrina kept a low profile, she lived her life pretty normally. All of that was easier when there wasn't an Alders in the White House. A reality that might soon change, with the election in a couple of months.

But as the daughter of a chemist and an engineer, I had no idea about how any of this rich-people stuff worked. Neither did Cora, whose parents were dentists. We needed Sabrina's expertise.

"Okay, so..." I dived into my idea, unhinged details and all. I'd crash the party and find an angle.

Fancy costumes and illicit affairs were to be expected, but I was sure there was more. Traditions, maybe rituals, a secret or two. Either way, it was one night and more direction for the Keller Award than I had a few days ago.

"Go in, get what you can, and get out." Sabrina clapped her hands together on the screen. "Love it. And if there is one person who can lie themselves in and out of a situation, it's you, Mal. Do it."

I laughed and pulled the invitation out. "Great, because I scanned the invitation and a message popped up." I showed her the prompt. "I need to input a code. It only allows one attempt."

Sabrina inched her face closer to the screen. "It's the same for every branch of Scroll & Ivy. *Verbum Numquam Mori.*"

I had her spell it out for me and inputted the password, and voilà. The next page populated.

"'Outside the Radiant, tomorrow at 9:07. Black SUV, License Plate M0DP9I,'" I read aloud off my phone, scribbling the instructions down before I could forget. "Nine oh seven... That's oddly specific."

"Having everyone arrive at the same time isn't exactly inconspicuous. A private car will pick you up and take you to another location," Sabrina explained.

Everything that could possibly go wrong flashed in my mind. "They're not going to like... hurt me, right?"

Sabrina's laugh boomed from the speakers, so loud that it dissolved into static. "Oh my God, no, it's a social club. They haven't been true *secret* societies in decades. Besides, nobody goes that hard anymore with how easy it is to record things."

When Cora and I didn't say anything, Sabrina went on.

"Think fancy frat. Except there's no rush week because invitations are passed down bloodlines. Less beer in a keg, more cocktails on a yacht," Sabrina encouraged. "Worst-case scenario would be getting caught and thrown out, which you could just blame on me. Say I sent you, that'll make you untouchable."

I nodded. It was a benefit of your best friend being the closest thing America had to a princess.

"Do the clubhouses really have secret passageways?" Cora asked, echoing my thoughts from a few days ago. It was one of those rogue pieces of lore that circled these legacy kids. Most we knew were straight-up rumors, just like the one about the catacombs. That was my personal favorite.

"I don't know. My dad said the ones at Harvard were like the social clubs in Manhattan," Sabrina offered. "Alums aren't supposed to tell their kids what to expect, but my mom told me that Scroll & Ivy's mausoleum is beautiful." Sabrina looked at me. "If you go inside, I want details."

Determination laced with excitement rolled through me.

I had a plan. This was going to work. It had to.

I saluted her and grinned at Cora. "I'll report back."

CHAPTER 5
Malena

The next night, I decided to wait for the car at nine o'clock on the dot. Our building sat right on High Street, one of the central streets that ran from off-campus, through campus, and all the way into town.

The crisp breeze rattled against the kaleidoscope of colors along my dress. Delicate blue and pastel yellow hues interlocked beautifully over black lace, creating the illusion of stained glass. It ended just below my knees.

A black SUV approached the curb at the same time I spotted a familiar face. A group of about six people made their way down the road in outfits that looked ready for barhopping. It took me less than ten seconds to identify who they were and even less time to wish this driver would hurry up and park.

Alarm twisted through my muscles.

"Malena." The group stopped when one person—Sonali Shah—called my name. A kind smile bloomed on either side of her lips. Next to her were a few familiar faces, Kash's being one. His gaze lingered on my bare legs. "You look great."

My fingers traced the lace on the mask in my hands. My

heart soared and the knots in my stomach loosened slightly. Sonali had always been welcoming to me.

She and the other three girls in her friend group were some of the first people I met here at Winchester. We'd all gone through the first round of dance team auditions together.

My mom *loved* to hear about the dance team girls. In her head, they were the *good girls* I should've been friends with. By nature of their background, my mom assumed they had parents like I did—controlling—who raised children that politely conformed. The type of influences my mom wanted in my life.

For me, I just figured we'd have a lot in common as first-generation South Asians. I regaled them with stories about hookups, my other friends, what I wanted for the future, and how it differed from my parents' plan. I'd been hoping to commiserate, to carve out space to be myself, but those hopes quickly evaporated beneath a mountain of unanswered texts and whispered jabs I pretended not to hear.

When the final day of auditions rolled around, I decided not to go, and Sabrina found me hiding out in the ballet studio. She and I had been inseparable ever since.

I shook my head and smoothed a clammy palm down my dress. "Thanks," I answered curtly, hoping they'd just keep on strolling.

The SUV's driver's-side door *finally* opened and a man dressed in a suit rounded the car. I handed him my invitation and he opened the door for me.

"Where are you going?" Sonali asked, taking another step toward me.

A few mumbles from the group behind her became louder. Her attention put a giant spotlight on me, and without Cora and Sabrina as my parasols, it was a heat lamp I slowly melted under.

"It's sort of a long story." I swiveled the toe of my heel

against the pavement, nervous. A minute ago, I'd felt like a supermodel in haute couture, and now I just wanted to run back inside, take the elevator up to my floor, and eat junk food with Cora on the couch.

Thankfully, the driver chose that moment to clear his throat.

"Well, you look great," Sonali repeated.

"Thanks." I got into the car, the dull thud of the door shutting sending a shiver of relief down my body.

I was happy with who I was, but growing up in Western Massachusetts, there weren't many South Asians. The few I knew were kind, but they'd served as the only exposure to my culture outside of my family. I got to Winchester and saw the opportunity for more, naively hoping to expand my circle.

After multiple humiliating attempts with Sonali and her friends, it became easier on my heart—and ego—to stop putting myself out there.

I buckled my seat belt and stared out the window, watching them grow smaller as they headed toward town.

My mind flashed back to last semester, when Kash and I were sort of seeing each other. Those types of awkward interactions with his friends had been commonplace and only succeeded in making me feel small.

I closed my eyes as the car pulled away, wondering if it would ever happen. If I'd ever *belong*.

THE CAR PULLED up to the far side of campus, at a clearing where the old clock tower was. Lovingly nicknamed Big Ben because it resembled a scaled-down version of London's famous landmark, the square stone structure overlooked the entire campus and the bay.

I walked up the cobblestone path to the wooden doors,

pressing my hands flat and giving a slight push. Slowly, they creaked open.

Gone was the hum of a silent night on my deserted campus. In its place was the buzz of chatter, glasses clinking, raucous laughter, and the reverberations of the orchestral version of a familiar party song ricocheting off the stone walls.

Between the twinkling lights, the elegant garments I'd already spotted other guests draped in, and the general decadence, the chilly air was transformed into something entirely new. It was like something out of Fitzgerald's New York, but in the last place you'd expect.

"Where to start?" I muttered.

The steps leading up the tower were interspersed with more partygoers, all donning masks and drinking out of crystal coupes. No one seemed to notice me, which I was grateful for.

"I recommend the bar," a voice answered. I turned to find a woman with luscious blond curls smiling at me from behind her mask. She wore a gold floor-length gown that fit like it was made for her. "I got here five minutes ago, and this gimlet is divine."

"Thanks," I said, meeting her amber-colored eyes and returning her smile.

"Azalea Burton." She stuck out her hand. "I'm a junior."

I didn't expect to run into anyone I knew here, since these were the types of crowds Sabrina generally avoided, but I was glad not to have to linger by myself a minute longer.

"Hi," I answered, shaking her hand. I moved on quickly so we didn't get hung up on the fact that I was crashing. "Do you know what happens next?"

I looked around at the landing. There were about twenty-five people, if I had to guess, wandering around in merriment.

"Nope. Honestly, I'm surprised I got an invitation," she said meekly.

I nodded and reminded myself to keep a low profile, get *something* of interest, and slip out unnoticed. Preferably *before* I talked myself into a corner.

"I think I'll start with a drink."

Azalea smiled, and with a wave, I made my way up the steps of the tower, stopping occasionally to take in the view from this angle and snapping pictures discreetly as I went. From campus, the town, or the bay, Big Ben could be spotted towering over the trees—but seeing the view from the other side made my heart race.

When I finally made it to the top floor, it was just me up there. I glanced out the windows but could hardly distinguish the stars in the sky from the specks of dirt on the aged glass. I paused by a quiet alcove and opened my Notes app. Typing as quickly as I could, I jotted down every single sight and sound. The chatter, the music playing in the background, the distinctive *clack* of stilettos and dress shoes.

It was cool to experience, given how few people ever would.

But honestly, I couldn't help feeling disappointed.

I'd spent the last few days reading the previous Keller awardees' pieces. They ranged from in-depth looks at payment structures for incoming professors to poetic comparisons on how an overemphasis on STEM-only educations had harmed not only the arts but the collective critical thinking capacity of college students.

They were deep and meaningful. Scholarly.

I pressed myself against the railing and peered down at the party below before turning back toward the New Harbor expanse. If I squinted, I could make out the shops that lined the bay and make an approximation as to where my favorite bookstore was.

I let out a bored sigh.

A night at a fancy party I had no business being at, in a

building I didn't even know could house it, was cool. It just wasn't Keller-worthy.

No rituals, no traditions, no secrets. This was a letdown.

Maybe I'd put too much stock in my expectations for tonight. I took a few pictures of the view and tried to think of an angle that competed with the ones I'd read.

"No pictures." A voice, deep and familiar, filled the empty top floor.

I froze.

"You should know that," he added.

I tucked my burner phone away and checked that my mask was in place, then spun around to face him. Unsurprisingly, he was dressed like every other man I'd passed on my way up here: tailored black tuxedo, polished Oxfords. Except his mask was white, and it didn't do anything to mute the bright blue of his eyes.

A tingle moved from my toes up my legs.

"Umm... oops," I stammered.

"And you are...?" He took a few steps closer to me, and suddenly the cavernous clock tower walls seemed to press closer.

Unsteady nerves pushed out my answer. "Sabrina."

I could have said a thousand things that were marginally believable, and instead I said that. *Dammit.* I was better at lying than this.

He cocked his head. Disbelief drew lines between his brows. "Alders?"

The shaky feeling of being caught melted into something *else.*

"Mm-hmm." I chewed on my lip.

Moonlight streaked across his face as he closed the space between us.

His tawny brown hair, piercing eyes, and that deep, luxurious voice. Understanding set tiny little fires in my chest.

Behind that mask, I knew who he was. I'd seen those eyes occasionally passing in the lobby of my condo building, and more notably, the paper.

"Sabrina Alders?" he repeated. His eyes moved along my body slowly, until they met mine. And stayed fixed there.

My heart slowed a beat, and an inexplicable tension thrummed between us.

"Y-yes," I stammered.

He lowered his head until his mouth was inches from my ear.

"No, you're not." His whisper glided over me. The soft, almost velvety tone left me feeling dizzy, and I reached back to rest a hand on the windowsill, willing the draft to cool my skin.

"I..." I forced words up my dry throat. "I thought I was alone."

"*And* someone else." Amusement played on his tone. He pulled back an inch or so, still *close*. His neat aristocratic smile —the kind that came from years of etiquette and the gentle reality that life was already paved for him—tilted up in victory.

I lifted my chin, deciding to drop the pretense. "This can't be the first time someone crashed this little secret party."

"Nope." He tucked his hands into his pockets.

"And you're not going to shove me out of here," I teased, not to flirt but to keep him talking and hopefully squeeze *some* information out of this flop of a night.

"It's a secret society, not a bar. I'm a member, not a bouncer." He shrugged casually with an almost gracious cadence to his words. "You got in, I can at least admit when I've been bested."

"Really? Because I'd love to see that." I reached for his mask. I would bet it was Conrad, but I wanted to be sure.

He grabbed my wrist, gentle but firm, and inadvertently pulled me a step closer so my chest bumped against his.

"I'll show you mine if you show me yours," he taunted. The words pricked against my skin.

I pulled my arm back slowly to my side, giving my head a subtle shake.

"You didn't come here to mingle or you wouldn't be up here alone..." His tongue roamed from one cheek to the other. "So, why are you here?"

"Curiosity," I answered honestly.

"And that's been satisfied, so you should probably go."

"You just said you're not going to manhandle me out of here."

The sliver of space between us disappeared. "What if I promise to be gentle?"

My stomach flipped.

"But I haven't even gotten the next clue yet," I drawled, raising a sarcastic brow.

"Next clue?"

I was reaching, sure, but there had to be more to this whole thing, right? Or were secret parties the only thing they did? Seemed like a letdown.

"There isn't some next clue or invitation?" I goaded, propelled by the urge to stay right where I was. To bask in the hypnotic sparring. "Let me guess... it's written somewhere ridiculous, like the back of the Declaration of Independence."

A short laugh brushed against my cheek.

"You want to see what happens next?" he said, holding my gaze and dipping his head closer.

The air went thin. "Maybe."

His hand moved to my hair and I let it, fingers skimming along the ribbons of my mask. His proximity was intoxicating, *distracting*. But his eyes, like clear ocean water sparkling on a bright day—they made me want to relax into the moment and just *float*.

Chills cascaded down my neck as one of the ribbons came

loose and my mask fell into his hand. His lips were millimeters from mine as something passed through his eyes. Calm waters became stormy.

He blinked rapidly and pulled back.

"Sorry." His jaw flexed. "But you can't stay." He turned and motioned for me to follow him down the steps. "You don't belong here."

The thread suspending the moment snapped with a cold rush of reality. My muscles went rigid.

I didn't belong; *obviously*, I knew that. I didn't want entry to his ridiculous club. I needed information on it, which I'd now come to understand was a waste of time.

I set my jaw and swallowed the indignation. "Got it."

I tied my mask back on and followed him down the steps I'd taken such care to nonchalantly climb up earlier.

My mind whirled with all the things I tried to take note of, now that my only chance at peeking behind the veil was evaporating before me. I looked down as we descended and noticed almost nobody was left in the foyer or by the bar despite the music still playing.

I craned my neck, taking in my surroundings with fresh eyes.

We'd been on the top floor, so if anyone left the way I came, I'd have seen them from that vantage point.

Curiosity spiked.

"Where is everyone?" I asked.

Conrad stayed silent at my side as I peered over the railing in time to see someone disappearing through a stone-lined doorway from the bottommost steps.

The ones *below* ground level. Below the entrance.

"Where are they going?" I repeated, this time knowing there was *something* down there.

"Not important." His eyes stayed glued forward.

He knew.

It clicked in my head.

My memory raced with everything I'd gathered about this "secret society." The catacombs—an underground tunnel system beneath the school—had always been my favorite story, simply because it seemed the most far-fetched, but how did more than thirty people vanish into thin air?

"Students using the fabled Winchester catacombs to party hop...?" I injected my voice with boredom, trying to drown out the pounding of my heart in my ears.

His muscles jumped.

I'm right.

"Honestly, it seems sort of boring," I continued, hoping to maybe bait him into saying something more. "Like a waste of perfectly good lore."

A secret passageway that only the wealthy kids had access to? There wasn't a better metaphor for the myth of the meritocracy.

I had a story.

The story.

One that I knew could hold up against every other submission.

We made it to the landing, and as we approached the door, I noticed three words etched into the stone on the frame.

Verbum Numquam Mori

"Does it?" Conrad's hand pressed at the small of my back, heat spindled out from his touch. He guided me down the steps to the waiting car.

"Yeah, like passing around a candy jar filled with pills." My eyes darted around frantically as I did my best to bide my time. "Woefully unoriginal."

"Good night, Malena." He pointed over my shoulder to the black car, the driver getting out to open the back door.

I ignored the warm tingle from hearing my name exit his mouth.

I got in the car, but I wasn't defeated.

That was my angle.

I wasn't about to take a gamble on winning. Because that feeling, the one I got when I first turned on my burner phone —when the world flashed from black and white to brilliant technicolor—was only possible thanks to the two-Malena system. It bent the security bars around my life and widened them so I could pass through.

I'd learned a lot of things since I got to college, but one resonated most: I had to blur certain lines so I wouldn't cross them.

This wasn't any different.

CHAPTER 6
Conrad

Sunshine clawed my eyelids open.

With a yawn, I looked to my side to see the girl from last night still there asleep next to me. Sleeping on her stomach, her light brown hair fanned down her back and onto the pillow.

Sarah... was that her name? Or maybe Stella?

After the party, we went out to a bar in New Harbor. And since a certain set of brown eyes were stuck in my brain, I figured a hookup would help. Because Malena and James had a... *rapport*. Which meant he liked her. So, the sooner those eyes stopped appearing in my mind for no good reason, the better.

My phone buzzed on my nightstand, pulling my attention from the woman at my side.

I wiped my palm down my face slowly. My skull, heavy and throbbing, felt like it was being packed with sand.

My heart rate spiked when I saw the missed calls and text. It was my dad.

Satan: You're late.

I checked the time on the screen, my eyes shooting wide. *Fuck.*

I was supposed to meet him an hour ago. He'd probably already had his sit-down with the university provost and president by now and was irate that I missed it.

I pushed off the sheets, grabbed my towel, and rushed to get ready.

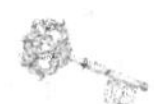

BY THE TIME I was out of the shower, last night's... *friend* had already left. I prayed it was a good omen, since I hated having the "let's keep this casual" talk.

"Sorry I'm late, I was rowing," I lied, practically sprinting into the newsroom before doing my best to appear unruffled.

My dad stood like a monument in the middle of the room, staring at the board Dillian had put together for the latest edition.

"Since its founding, every Hastings man has rowed crew at Winchester." His brow furrowed and he tucked his hands in his pockets. His dark hair, pushed to the side, stood eerily still. "You happen to be the only one without enough brain cells to both participate *and* focus on your education."

I took a breath and reminded myself not to take the bait. "Why did you want to meet me here?"

"Or is it a different extracurricular that's the problem, son?" He ignored me and continued. "Scroll & Ivy, perhaps?"

I rolled my eyes because it was just as much a Hastings legacy as crew and the *Winchester Daily News*. And Scroll & Ivy wasn't some out-of-control frat, he knew that.

"I haven't done anything—"

"Oh, that's been made abundantly clear." Deep lines pressed into his forehead when his eyebrows arched up condescendingly. "I spoke to President Packham this morning, vile woman. She told me that you took an incomplete in Monetary Policy last semester?"

Shit. That's why he was here.

"I'm retaking it now," I answered curtly, resisting the urge to add that it wasn't his concern. He didn't take well to obstinance.

The reality was that even if I provided my reason, he still wouldn't care. Monetary Policy was every Monday morning, and after his actions translated to society gossip, my mom became a shut-in. I checked in on her every weekend for months last spring, not leaving until her book club showed up for lunch on Monday. That meant missing those classes, which I tried to explain to the professor. When he refused to hear it, I sought out President Packham. Admittedly, my situation as the outrageously wealthy heir with a scheduling concern wasn't one she was overly sympathetic to.

"She also tells me that you're the only member of the paper without a single byline."

Fuck. This was getting worse by the second.

Packham used to be the faculty advisor for the paper before her promotion, and she'd never been a fan of mine. Probably because I did things like bribe the editor.

"Do you know how that looks?" he added.

My patience slipped. He was concerned about how *I was making* the family look?

"Probably better than the Hastings Media CEO being pictured with his mistress at the Gansevoort," I grumbled.

His mouth drew a tight line. Instead of a fiery warning, he let out a conciliatory breath.

"While I don't have high expectations for *you*, all future Hastings will go to Winchester. I will not allow a blemish on the legacy we've built here."

"Then stay out of the press, Dad," I bit back, bracing myself because even I knew that was a step too far.

He had *another* mistress. And this time she was splashed across Page Six. He couldn't even do my mom the decency of keeping it discreet. Yet *I* was the blemish. But Page Six didn't matter to people like him; places like *this* did.

"I'm not fucking around here, Conrad." His hand landed on my shoulder with a sharp crack. "Do you know what had to be done to repair your academic shortcomings? To ensure you *graduate* with the rest of your peers? Can you imagine how humiliating it is to find out you could have been the first Hastings to be held back?"

Could have were the operative words here because it would have never happened. He'd throw money at it, take his concerns all the way to the top, the usual. It was how he solved everything, proving it didn't matter what I did. The result was always the same.

"It's not going to happen," I said instead of all the other things I wanted to say. "Like I said, I'm retaking the class now. I'll do fine."

"And all the work for the paper you've pawned off for three years?"

"I'll handle it," I answered. It wasn't fucking rocket science; I'd find something acceptable to complete.

"Listen to me when I say this." He squeezed my shoulder hard. "You're a senior—this is the *last* year before you need to grow up. In lieu of the pieces I know you won't write, you can assist in running the paper's operations." He smiled like he was enjoying this. "The early mornings and late nights checking copy, securing advertisers, proofreading. For the *entire* semester."

My heart dropped. "Dad—"

Crew reached its offseason in November. From now, the first week of September, till then, most of my free time would go to practice or races. Any downtime outside of that I'd planned to spend with Scroll & Ivy members. Not the paper.

He was doing this on purpose, taking away the only things that mattered to me.

"I'll speak to Coach Durham, make sure you're excused from crew. I think that should be sufficient repayment to this paper in place of—"

"He's already doing an *extensive* feature." My dad and I both turned to the doorway to see Malena and Professor Fulton—the paper's new faculty advisor—standing at the threshold. "A likely contender for the Keller Feature Award."

Professor Fulton's brow dipped, apologetic for the interruption. Malena, however, looked smug.

CHAPTER 7

Malena & Conrad

MALENA

I'd found my way in.

When I caught up to Professor Fulton at the tail end of her Saturday office hours, I was originally going to ask for access to the newspaper archives. But when she said she had to cut her office hours short in order to speak to her "most important donor," it took all of two seconds to figure out who that was, seeing as the paper's building was named after the Hastings family.

That was my opening. My loophole. So, I told her Conrad and I were partnering up on a piece together. It was a win-win, even if Conrad hadn't agreed. Yet.

Conrad's jaw was tight, his eyes heavy. I felt a little bad about my outburst, because I knew that look. I lived in that look when I was at my childhood home, and I understood what it meant: he was trapped.

"Yes, Miss Amin was *just* telling me about the piece on our walk over," Professor Fulton added brightly as she walked past the warring Hastings men and set a few files on the editor's desk. "A rare insight into one of the oldest, most exclusive institutions on campus. A truly inspired idea."

Conrad *was* delinquent when it came to completing work for the paper, everyone knew that. And now, judging by the way his dad was talking to him, this would help us both.

"Thanks, but it was Conrad's actually," I chirped. If he wasn't willing to let me into his precious club, I'd force my way in.

Conrad's father looked at his son skeptically. "*You* are writing something for Keller Award consideration?"

"Yeah. You know the one. You gave it a shot when you were at Winchester, didn't you, Dad?" Conrad asked innocently. "Malena and I will keep our project quiet from the rest of the members, and the identities of anyone associated will remain anonymous."

"Right." I hiked up my shoulders with an innocent smile. "The only people who know about it are the people in this room."

I was a lot of things, but a narc wasn't one of them. I wasn't going to *expose* anyone. I just wanted to whack at the velvet embroidered drapes and see what the dust bunnies had to say.

My catacombs angle was *good*. I could twist and turn it in a bunch of different directions.

"I'm excited to read it when it's done." Professor Fulton looked at Mr. Hastings and then me. "I'm sure it'll be popular among students as well."

Professor Fulton picked up a different stack of papers on Dillian's desk and crossed the room.

"Run with it." She gave me a curt nod. "Conrad, that will satisfy your requirement to the paper as well, so the other arrangements won't be necessary. And Mr. Hastings"—she motioned to the door that led out of the newsroom and into the faculty office—"if you'll follow me, we can speak in my office."

"I'm keeping a close eye, son." He jostled Conrad's shoulder, the force of it almost causing him to lose his balance. Conrad hardly winced before regaining his composure. "One more blunder and I will ensure every moment of your free time is well-occupied."

I couldn't help but pity Conrad after watching him get berated like that. I was sure he had a hundred-foot yacht to lick his wounds on, but still, it felt like solidarity to be on the side of the college kid and not the fun-hating parent.

Mr. Hastings's tone lifted when he addressed me. Not kind or welcoming, but no longer downright hateful. "Miss Amin."

With that and a few purposeful steps out of the room, he was gone. Professor Fulton followed a few seconds later.

And I was left staring at the remaining Hastings.

CONRAD

Outmaneuvered, I took a second to run back everything that just happened over the ongoing hangover that pummeled my brain.

"He's... charming," Malena said wryly, looking over her shoulder as the door closed. The irritating bravado dropped for a second, as did the corners of her mouth when she looked back at me. "Are you okay?"

"Nothing a pill from a candy jar can't fix," I retorted, rolling my shoulder a few times. If she wanted to believe I was just a rich kid with nothing better to do than party, then who was I to interfere? "So, what? Didn't have enough fun party-crashing last night?"

Malena shrugged unapologetically. "I saw an opening and I took it."

"You just happened upon Professor Fulton and knew I was—"

"The only member of the paper who hasn't written anything?" she finished with a scoff, walking over to her desk. "Yeah, everyone knows that."

An odd heaviness weighed on me for a minute. All these years, and I could honestly say I'd never thought about *who* covered the pieces I didn't. I cleared my throat, not wanting her to see me falter. "And that was your way of leveling the playing field?"

"You're welcome to go back and tell your dad that I was lying. That you haven't done a single thing for the paper and don't have any plans to. He doesn't seem like the 'hear you out' type, but let me know how that goes." She cocked her head to the side. "And either way, it worked, didn't it?"

"I guess," I murmured, rounding her desk and waiting for some sort of explanation. With the chair pulled out, I had a clear view of the underside. It was riddled with Post-it notes. "Jesus, is this a bunker?"

She pushed the center drawer back and tucked the chair into place, huffing quietly.

"Look, this helps both of us," she said, sidestepping my comment. "I *know* people have written about secret societies in the past, all I want is some access. It won't take long, and I won't write anything salacious or include anything you don't want me to."

My dad would make good on his threat. He'd turn my world upside down just to prove he could. A few parties with her seemed like an easy trade-off. And having my name on a Keller Award submission would probably piss him off because he'd never come close to winning it.

"It's simple, no big deal," she added.

I didn't know what it was about her, but she was... compelling.

In the same way a grenade was.

Dressed in a thin sweater tucked into her skirt and a pair of dark black tights that wrapped around those impossibly long legs, she looked put together. Spoke like she was too. But I could practically see all of it waiting to come undone.

"If it weren't a big deal, you wouldn't need *me* to do it." My eyes drifted along her neatly organized desk. At the top of a stack of papers sat a résumé with a few red marks and scribbled comments. I picked it up. "But I see your point."

She mumbled something as she made herself busy emptying her bag. Different colored pens, a few more of those square notepads.

I scanned the paper in my hand line by line. "Wow."

What *didn't* this girl do?

A chem major. The paper. Tutoring. A twenty-credit course load. I didn't know if she had a social life, but her willingness to insert herself into mine told me that she wasn't averse to the idea.

"I know." She grinned and crossed her arms over her chest.

"And humble," I quipped back.

"Doctors tend to be accomplished." She plucked the paper from my hands. The ridiculously long résumé made more sense now: she was on the med school track. "And there's nothing wrong with being highly motivated."

"Tell that to all the dead bodies on Mt. Everest. They were all *highly motivated* too."

She stared blankly at me. "Cheeriness runs in the family, I see."

"I don't think I have one," I mumbled to myself, still a little dumbfounded. It was impressive but read like a person who loved *everything*.

I liked crew. And socializing. And sex. But the last two didn't seem like things you would put on a résumé.

"I'm assuming you mean a résumé..." A look of repugnance-stained disbelief skated along her face. *Interesting*. She'd managed to hide all of that so well when my dad and Professor Fulton were in the room.

"This may surprise you," I retorted, voice low, "but I plan to work at Hastings Media." I wasn't dumb. I did well enough in school and took my extracurriculars seriously.

"Shocking," she deadpanned. I wasn't sure why it bothered me that she was making the same assumptions most people did. But I wasn't some moron who couldn't write a simple piece for the paper. I could be more; I chose not to be —because it didn't fucking matter. If I was going to be ignored, and on occasion reviled, I was going to do it while having fun with my friends.

Not that I needed to explain myself to her. She didn't even know me.

And that brought me right back to what *I* needed to know.

"What's your angle?" I asked sharply.

"I was thinking of covering an event or party or *gathering* —whatever you guys call it. And I definitely need to see the catacombs. That's it." Her cheeks lifted and she motioned her hands around directionless in front of her. "I'll tie it together as an exploration into why it's so widely accepted that certain students have access to a path others can't even see." She looked at me and dropped her hands. "It's a metaphor," she added, like she was explaining the sky to a toddler.

"I know what a metaphor is." I rolled my eyes. My headache making its presence known and thinning my patience. "Just like I know that a commentary on wealth and privilege isn't exactly groundbreaking."

"And until meritocracies become reality, the allure never

gets old." She crossed her arms. "Look, as you so astutely pointed out last night, I'm not Sabrina Alders. But she *is* my roommate and best friend, and she's at Oxford all semester. Let me attend in her place. Say it's on her orders. I attend a couple of events, see the catacombs. That's all. I won't disparage or name *anyone*."

Despite the hangover, a puzzle piece fell into place. That's how she got Sabrina's invitation. She lived with her, coincidently in the same building as me.

"Wouldn't you be more comfortable writing about something... tamer?" If I had to write something with her, I would. But I wasn't guiding her along on a fishing expedition. "Wandering around centuries-old tunnels is a little off-color for the teacher's pet."

Her shoulders hiked up.

"I need something compelling for the Keller Award, so don't you worry, I'll be just fine." She walked over to Dillian's desk and dropped a stack of marked-up pages in one of his baskets.

I was going to ask her what the motivation was behind winning, but judging by the length of that résumé, she needed something else to put on her fridge at home.

"But call me *pet* again..." She walked back to her desk, narrowing her eyes and dropping her fake smile into a scowl. "And you can deal with the claws."

My skin tingled. "Don't threaten me with a good time."

She crossed her arms. "Do we have a deal?"

This was probably a terrible idea, but she was right: if I had to tell my dad about this elaborate ruse, I was fucked. "We share both bylines—the paper and the submission—and you're only there until the article is written."

Her face brightened.

"Try not to sound so glum," she encouraged sweetly. "This will be your *first* byline, you should enjoy it."

I rolled my eyes.

"And don't worry..." She rocked forward onto her tiptoes and patted my head like a good dog. Her voice lowered to a whisper. "I'll be gentle."

My stomach flipped.

She dropped back down and held out her hand. "Give me your phone."

"Why?" I asked, but my brain took a few seconds to catch up to my body—which seemed perfectly content doing what she wanted because I pulled my phone out of my pocket.

She rolled her eyes. "I know finding things on the first try is hard for some guys, so I'm going to put my number in it."

My cheek twitched and I handed her my phone.

"Let me know when the next event is." She tapped her fingers along the screen, then handed it back to me.

Before I could say anything else, she turned and walked out the door. I stood there and ran back every thing I'd just agreed to.

CHAPTER 8

Conrad

I told James about Malena's idea the next day. Mostly because I was a terrible liar, but also because I needed to run this harebrained scheme by someone.

And James had always been the responsible one among us.

"No way." James chuckled as we stopped in front of our building. "I got the sense that Hamilton was a little nuts."

I leaned against our building's arched doorway. Despite our hour already spent on the water, James wanted to go for a run in the nice weather. I was just as happy to go upstairs, shower, and pass out. "You think it's funny that a reporter wants to write about Scroll & Ivy?"

Three hundred years ago when it was founded, secret societies were an *actual* secret. Now, people knew they were around because it was impossible to keep things under wraps in a digital age. There was always the occasional post about a trip or party that one of the members would upload without thinking and then promptly take down.

We tried to keep what we could contained. Which was why inviting an amateur reporter seemed like a terrible fucking idea. One that I'd agreed to.

I blamed the whiskey hangover.

"No, I think the methods she used to back you into a corner and get you to agree is funny." He grinned. When I didn't say anything, James's smile fell. "Getting your dad out of your hair this semester and maybe spiting him if you actually win? It's not a *bad* deal. Besides, Scroll & Ivy isn't going to bring us up on charges for breaking a measly rule."

He had a point. The only rule at Scroll & Ivy was that the stories stayed with it. It was ambiguous and up for interpretation by every set of students that passed through. Malena wasn't planning on writing about the people, but rather the place. And even then, it would be framed around a larger conversation about privilege. I had to admit, it was a good idea.

"You think anyone's going to buy that she's there in Sabrina's place?"

"Who's going to care enough to ask? Or press us on it if they do, knowing they'd be challenging an Alders?" James rebutted. "The incoming juniors are just happy to be there, they're not going to jeopardize that."

That left the fifteen of us who were seniors. "And everyone else?"

"They can be threatened or bribed," James added glibly. "So, what's the problem?"

Something about it all was unsettling. Maybe it was that she assumed I was the rich kid that life simply happened to. And, okay, she wasn't *wrong*, but the assumption was rude.

"I guess there isn't a real one. I'll read what she writes beforehand." I huffed a sigh and considered asking the other thing that was buzzing in my mind. "Do *you* want her around?"

"Cute, a little crazy, but mostly harmless. It could be worse," James mused as he looked past my shoulder. "Speaking of your new shadow."

I followed his gaze and spotted Malena, dark hair billowing around her like she was walking a runway when what she had on was a tight spandex tennis dress. Her attention was fixed on her phone and her purposeful stride made me stand up a little straighter.

The shadows from the trees she walked under streaked along the fabric, wrapping her thin frame in a moving pattern. When she finally looked up, a few steps from the ornately carved keystone entrance, her smile fell.

"Oh." She stopped in front of us. "Hi."

James coughed on a laugh.

"I'm going for a run." He threw a collegial pat on my shoulder. "See you guys later."

Malena gave James a polite wave as he took off in a slow jog. When I didn't move, she looked around, then at me. "Do you need something?"

"We should talk about that article."

"I don't need your help *writing* it." She waved her hand dismissively and looked back down at her phone. "You can focus on... rowing your little boat. Crew, right?"

"A fan?" I tilted my head to the side. If I was going to agree to this, which I guess I already had, the least she could do was pay attention. "And I meant ground rules."

"Oh." Her eyes shifted around again, to The Radiant's empty lobby on one side and the sidewalk with the occasional pedestrian on the other. A light breeze drifted past us. "You want to talk about it here?"

"If you want to be alone with me, that's fine too." We probably *should've* been somewhere less public for this. But perfect-student types were always so straitlaced, I wondered if that comment might keep her attention. "You're welcome to come up to my place."

"Hard pass." Her eyes swept over my shirt and lingered a moment before she blinked a couple of times and fidgeted with her fingers. "Besides, you smell." She scrunched her nose. "Like saltwater. Have you even showered?"

A thrill whirled through me, returning every quip she served. "Another excellent reason to head to my place."

She didn't seem to like me, but fucking with her was fun.

"We can go to mine." She notched her head to the side, motioning toward the elevators. She turned and walked a step ahead of me, patting the side of her bag where she'd stored her phone, as though it'd pulled a Houdini in the last five seconds. "Cora's in her room studying, so inside voices."

The pliant fabric of her dress hugged her hips as they gently swayed. Frustratingly beautiful, lemon scented, with a sharp wit.

She had to be some kind of karmic punishment.

Either way, I followed.

THE FRONT DOOR to Malena's condo thudded behind us as we stepped inside. It was laid out pretty similarly to my own. A kitchen island overlooked a living area with a sectional couch flanked by a couple of tall brass floor lamps. A giant coffee table sat in the middle, with a stack of magazines on top of what looked like boxes of board games. A view of New Harbor stretched out past the gabled windows.

"So, these rules?" A couple of steps ahead, Malena placed her bag on the marble countertop. She paused. "I'm not doing some creepy blood oath."

"What?" My attention boomeranged back to her. "Nobody is interested in your bodily fluids."

"*Stop*, you'll make a girl blush." She turned back around to face me, leaning against the island. "And just because we're submitting this for the Keller Award *doesn't* mean I'm splitting the prize with you. The byline is the only thing I intend to share."

"Determined *and* gracious?" I drawled sarcastically. "Lucky me."

"Snarky and overprivileged. Lucky *me*."

I took a few steps closer to her. "You can keep the award money."

All I needed was the requirement checked off for the paper. And if we won, the added benefit of seeing my dad's face fall when I told him.

"Great."

"No pictures. No identifying locations. You can't take anything from any of the events. And you have to stick by my side—no running off on your own." I waited until she gave me a curt nod before continuing. "And, most importantly, I get a final read on anything you write."

Her eyes moved over me slowly.

"Fine." She pushed off the counter. "But I want to attend three events."

"One," I countered. "Since you were already at the clock tower."

She crossed her arms. "Three."

"One."

"Three." She rose to her toes, her face inches from mine. Her voice dropped to a whisper and my pulse ratcheted up. "I could do this for hours."

"Fine." I tipped my head back and blew out a breath. "Two."

She cocked a brow, waiting.

"*Malena*." Frustration propelled her name out of my mouth sterner than I meant to.

Her throat bobbed, eyes widening with indignation and something else I couldn't identify.

"Okay..." she said quietly. "Two."

A door creaking open down the hall jostled us back to reality.

Malena seemed to remember her roommate was home and took an unsteady step back.

"Out of curiosity..." Her voice lifted like she was about to kick off another headache for me. "If I were to break one of the rules..."

This little menace was going to kill me.

And a part of me didn't hate it.

I cleared my throat and pinned her with a warning stare. "Don't."

"I won't." She put her hands up in surrender, her lips arched at the corners. "I was just curious."

"At each event, I am your shadow," I stated. It felt like that rule bore repeating, but still I waited with a bizarre anticipation, wondering if she'd fight me on that one too.

"You don't trust me?" she asked, eyes shining with mirth. Her attention was a tiny hit of dopamine every time it landed on me, and I couldn't help but note the amusement ringing through each syllable.

"The worst imposter in history?" I cocked a brow. "Not even a little."

Her smile fell and the muscles along her arms flexed.

Admittedly, it wasn't the nicest thing to say, but a part of me thought we were trading barbs. "Look, I'm sorr—"

"Don't worry, I'm not trying to blend in or belong with *you*," she snapped with disdain. When she looked up, emotion flared in her irises so bright it nearly cast a glare. "Are we done here?"

"Yeah..." I thought back through what I said, every word coming under rapid-fire review. I took a step back, and with a curt wave, I turned. "Next weekend is the next event."

CHAPTER 9

Malena

I stacked *Winchester: A Student Anthology* on top of the pile I'd gotten through.

The back of the Amherst Building was my favorite place to study. Its west wing was a library and the rest of the building was dedicated to workspaces for the arts. Between the wooden beams that stretched up the high ceilings, the smell of old books, and the muted amber light that shone through the stained-glass windows, the cathedral-like building was the right mix of cozy and uncomfortable to get solid studying done.

"Malena." A voice lifted me from the stack. I looked up.

In a neatly ironed pencil skirt and matching merlot-colored blazer, President Packham's presence cast a dim shadow over my study cubicle.

"Oh, hi." Delight and surprise pulled my whisper up an octave.

Before her promotion last semester, Caroline Packham was the faculty advisor for the paper. She'd become a bit of a mentor to me, she'd also been the one to suggest my writing minor. I was used to seeing her at the paper, not in her new role as president.

"I'm here to finalize the plans for the president's annual fundraising dinner in the atrium," she explained, probably noting the confusion lining my forehead. "The job of a university president is becoming increasingly less academic, I'm afraid." She observed my stack of books with a look of pride. "Research for the paper?"

"Yeah, working on my next feature." I sat up a little straighter.

Since I'd already gone through the newspaper archives, I came here to look at historical texts. I had a clearer picture of the different secret societies on campus. There was Cloak & Dagger, which had a bizarre fascination with death. Snake & Raven was all about nature, with one article from the eighties speculating that their mausoleum was actually a seed bank. Scroll & Ivy, however, wasn't well-documented.

She smiled warmly. "I hope you've considered that writer's workshop this summer. I think you'd get a lot out of it."

"I'm hoping to get a spot at the New York Lightning's training facility," I told her. "It's a research position exploring orthopedic injuries in college athletes."

Her polite smile dipped at the corners. Maybe because as much as she steered me toward something I enjoyed—writing—I steered myself back to something I was *allowed* to enjoy.

"You know, I was a chemist at a lab for years before I went back to school for my master's." She'd told me the same story last year, but I smiled and nodded all the same. "Just keep your mind open."

"I will." I *wanted* to. The workshop seemed like a great opportunity, and *when* I won the Keller Award, it could be another stone on a path I'd forge one day. But now, my summers were owned by my pursuit of med school. "I'll think about it."

"Good, and why don't you come to the president's annual fundraising dinner here next week?" She tapped her fingers along the wrap-around bench that encapsulated the tiny study cubby. The event was a big night for nepo babies and their rich parents. "Meet some people in the writing world, just in case."

While it sounded boring, if I'd learned one thing being at an Ivy League as a regular person: connections were everything.

"Absolutely," I agreed. "Thank you."

President Packham dipped her chin and made her way out between the shelves.

My phone rattled on the solid wood desk, and I pressed stop on the timer I'd set to let me know Cora was done with class. Our building wasn't far, but with the days getting shorter, we made an effort to walk home together as much as possible.

I gathered my things and made a beeline toward the exit. I pushed the heavy door open and waved at Cora, who stood at the bottom of the stone steps, waiting for me.

"These are pretty cool," Cora said as she flipped through the clock tower photos. I'd sent them to my regular phone from my burner. "And don't worry, my lips are sealed."

I'd let Cora in about the article because she already knew it was my plan before Conrad and I hatched our latest one. Besides, she was a vault.

"Hopefully I can turn it into something good. I'd love to retire from tutoring." I sighed. It would be nice to have one semester where I didn't have to overextend myself.

"I think you'll turn it into something great," Cora encouraged. "What did Dillian think?"

"He was actually a little annoyed when Professor Fulton and I told him," I admitted. "I *did* jump the chain of command and go right to the faculty advisor instead of the editor though. I should probably offer to proof something for him to smooth things over."

"Well, I think this is cool."

"Me too." I smiled. I couldn't place what had me fizzing about this article, but my fingers were itching to write it.

"Oh." Cora's voice dropped a few octaves and she handed my phone back. "Your mom is calling."

That sinking feeling, like hearing your name over the loudspeaker in grade school, slammed into me whenever my mom called unexpectedly. The countless secrets I kept whipped past my vision as I swiped to pick up the call and held the phone to my ear. "Hi, Mom."

"What time will you be home this weekend?"

"I have to study," I lied, looking at Cora and miming running into traffic. She giggled quietly and yanked my arm away from the road.

"Pinky Auntie just called to say she's coming over. You can spend time with her daughter Asha." My mom said it like it was all the explanation she needed to overrule me. "What will she think if you're not here?"

Who cares? I sure as hell didn't, but I knew my mom did. So deeply that she was willing to berate me about it.

"Tell her I have to study," I repeated.

"You can study *here*." Her voice strained. "Avani *always* came home when we hosted family friends."

Not counting the extra year it took her to get into medical school, my sister was perfect. Avani was six years older than me, and we weren't all that close. Because growing up, dutiful Avani made the friends they wanted her to make. Now, she dated the guy they wanted her to date, and generally did everything she was *supposed* to do. Her unquestioning acceptance of their rules made my reluctance look like the problem. That didn't exactly foster sisterly bonds.

"Pinky Auntie's daughter is a *good girl...*" my mom

continued. "And you need to try harder to make better frien—"

"No, I don't." I huffed. I had friends. Great ones. And I wasn't going to listen to her make a jab at whatever nonsense she didn't approve of: Cora's choice to change her hair color on a whim, Sabrina's tendency to state her opinions loud and proud, often unsolicited. My mom picked it all apart because she didn't like that Cora and Sabrina weren't tightly controlled. "And I have a mountain of work to get started on for the semester with the paper."

I winced, knowing I'd just given her an opening.

"You're wasting your time with that newspaper." She switched from English to Hindi, a sure-fire sign she was annoyed. "We pay for your *education*, not a hobby."

Over the years, they explained away their obsession with my grades, my social life, my *everything* with wanting me to be "safe." And it wasn't just my parents, it was a lot of their friends too. Having control over every aspect of our lives ensured predictable results.

Good jobs, carefully chosen friends, and respectable marriages.

That was their end game, because those three things provided stability in an ever-changing world. I understood it; I just didn't agree with it. Not that it mattered.

"It'll look good on my applications next year. And I need to study," I repeated firmly, *for the third time*. Translation: I wasn't going to miss my first Scroll & Ivy event.

A long sigh came through the line, an indicator that I hadn't heard the end of her grievances. "Okay."

She hung up.

Cora looked at me with a pitying smile. "Everything all right?"

I knew seeing my struggle made her thankful for her

parents. They were the "what do you think?" kind of parents, while mine were the "what will people say?" kind.

"Just my mom being my mom." I shrugged.

I handed my phone back to Cora and she swiped through more of the slightly blurry pictures I got from that night. "So, the catacombs are a real thing?"

"Wild, right?"

The warm September air gave way to a crisp breeze that whipped past us, and I took a deep, settling breath. Despite the phone call and my academic responsibilities piling up, I couldn't wait for whatever came next.

CHAPTER 10

Malena

After successfully completing three MCAT practice tests, I decided that I deserved one of the lemon drops I eyed Cora making when I took my last study break.

"Oh, she's *definitely* gonna have sex with him," I overheard her say as I walked into the living room. She sat on the couch with her laptop open next to her, grinning wide.

"Who's having sex?" I asked and took a seat on the sectional, pulling the throw blanket over my legs.

"You are, with Conrad Hastings," Cora answered, handing me a glass. She looked at the screen and Sabrina smiled. "She invited him over."

"Mal invited a guy back to our place?" Sabrina screeched.

I never invited guys over. Too much potential for evidence.

Apparently Sabrina's semester abroad wasn't going to stop Cora from filling her in on *everything*.

"Not for *that*." My face scrunched. Although, there was *something* there. Probably best to ignore it though, since he was right. I was an imposter in his world. And while I didn't know if he'd meant it the way I heard it, it wasn't any less true. And I hated the feeling of sticking out. I would get what I needed and get out, write the piece, and win my award. "We needed to lay down ground rules for the article. You know, the one I wasn't supposed to tell either of you about?"

"We aren't going to say a word." Cora gestured as if locking her lips.

"Be careful with him, Mal. Conrad has a... reputation," Sabrina warned from the other end of the screen.

"Good-looking, rich, and sleeps around? *Shocking*."

"So you *do* think he's good-looking?" Cora gave me a wolfish smile.

I ignored the question. My eyes narrowed on Sabrina; it was late over there, and if I did the math correctly, her classes would be starting in just a few hours. What was she doing up? "Don't you have class soon, Sabrina? Everything okay?"

Sabrina had struggled with nightmares for as long as I'd known her. Cora and I used to stay up all night with her when she couldn't sleep, taking turns making tea and choosing what movie to watch on one of our laptops. But over the last year, it'd seemed like they were getting better.

"I couldn't sleep." Sabrina shrugged off my question and looked at Cora. "Were they flirting?"

"Oh yeah..." Cora drawled.

"I flirt with everyone," I dismissed. It was a victimless crime and flirting was fun. It kept me on my toes, and occasionally I'd find a half-decent sparring partner.

"All I'm saying is that I know these kinds of guys," Sabrina added. "They're charming and witty. But for them, they have the girls they marry and the ones they screw."

"Careful, Sabrina, I might swoon," I teased.

Sabrina's face crinkled in thought. "You're sort of like a

perfected version of them, Mal. You have the guys you screw and the guys you... well, I guess that's it."

"Oh." Cora snapped her fingers, standing up in a flash and making her way down the hall. "You should add him to your bracket."

Sabrina craned her neck and watched Cora wheel an easel out from her room.

One side was a vision board, but when you flipped it over, it was the remnants of our annual March Madness bracket. Some names were crossed out in red and others remained—the ones we never got to since Cora came in as a dark horse and won the whole thing week one.

"It's a little early for that, don't you think?" I asked. "Spring is months away."

We did it a little differently than sports fans. We each made a list of three guys, and whoever had sex with everyone on their list first, won. Things got interesting when there was overlap—like in the case of last year's hot biochemistry TA. Whoever had sex with him first won the whole thing, hence Cora's victory.

"It's never too early," Cora added with a grin. She took another sip, her eyes moving across the couch as she raised her index finger in the air to pause the conversation. "Speaking of bracket potential. Your burner just got a text."

She leaned over and reached for my phones. While I studied, I tended to leave both my actual phone and burner on the couch. It was my attempt at trying to remain disciplined, but as I sat here drinking a cocktail and laughing with my friends, I realized my strategy probably needed work.

She handed me both—the two were nearly indistinguishable aside from a star sticker on my burner phone's case.

Conrad: You have plans tonight at 8

Conrad: Meet me in front of our building

I checked the time and sprang up; I had forty minutes.

I could practically hear the sarcasm. A skitter ran down my fingers, anxious to type something back. Before I could, another text came through.

Ignoring the teasing from Sabrina and Cora, I disappeared to get ready.

A HALF HOUR LATER, I passed through the lobby doors, coming face-to-face with a butterfly-inducing tableau.

Dark pants with a light brown crewneck sweater that fit just right. A light breeze moved through his brown hair that was just long enough to get in his eyes when he didn't swipe it back.

He leaned against a motorcycle, casual, like it didn't short-circuit my brain.

Ugh. Why did he have to be hot? It was a distraction when I needed nothing more than to focus.

I walked to the curb. "A gentleman knocks at the door."

"For a date," he said with dry amusement. His lips slid together and curved for a moment. "Not *blackmail.*"

"You see being forced to do your own work as blackmail?" The sudden urge to spar ignited. "That's a touch dramatic."

His jaw tightened and he shoved a helmet in front of me, whatever brief playfulness I registered gone. *Okay then, no more jokes. Noted.* "Let's go."

"I'm not getting on that thing." I took a step back. I was all about new experiences, so much so that I'd crafted a perfectly stable web of lies to ensure I could have them, but this felt like the fast track to an early grave.

"Why?"

"There are piles of data correlating motorcycle injuries to lasting traumatic brain injury," I pointed out like it should have been obvious.

"You must be a *riot* at parties," he drawled. "Is that why you have to crash them?"

My molars ground together. "Interesting word choice."

He sighed. "It's perfectly safe."

"Easy to say for someone who—" I stopped myself before I said something unnecessarily mean.

He took a step closer, his eyes narrowed. "Who what?"

My pulse flickered.

Something about his smugness made me want to twist the knife, but I bit back the urge. "Nothing."

He shifted his eyes as if strategizing what to say next. His shoulder dropped a bit. "Figures, teachers' pets are always so—"

"Easy to say for someone whose future isn't contingent on functioning brainwaves." The words rushed out of my mouth.

A satisfied smirk dug into the side of his cheek.

"That wasn't so hard, was it?" he cooed mockingly. "And again, it's perfectly safe." The polite tone wore thinner. "It's a short ride—"

"Then let's walk."

His jaw flexed. He leaned in closer, his face just a few inches from mine, and lowered his voice.

"Either stay here..." His piercing blue eyes pinned me in place. "Or get on the bike, Malena."

The words hardened to metal and sank to the bottom of my stomach.

I got on the bike.

"Fine." I pushed the helmet on. "But if I die, Sabrina Alders will have you killed."

His response was muffled when he put his own helmet on. I skimmed both arms around him and held his unreasonably solid body tight.

To his credit, Conrad wasn't lying. He took it easy, and it was a quick ride. I wasn't sure if that was meant to placate my anxiety, but it was... nice. Away from campus and about a mile down High Street, we came upon our destination.

At the end of a line of Victorian-style homes was Scroll & Ivy's mausoleum. Their "clubhouse" of sorts.

With five towering columns, each supporting an archway, it stood proud on the corner of the block. The structure looked like a smaller version of the Pantheon and was partially covered in vines that spindled their way up the veined marble columns and bricks. A wrought-iron fence ran along the perfectly manicured lawn, standing tall and ominous.

Conrad got off first, removed his helmet, and then helped me down. I swung a leg over the bike and steadied myself against him for a quick second, then pulled off the helmet and gave my hair a gentle shake, hoping it wasn't matted down.

As I handed the helmet back to him, he looked frozen.

"What?" I asked.

The cords along his throat shifted, and he blinked a few times.

"Nothing," he grumbled. "Are you done with your slow-motion hair flip?"

"You see me in slow motion?" I taunted, tapping him on the chest. "You should probably get that checked out."

A dimple screwed into his cheek. "Let's go."

Walking inside the quiet—and empty—foyer was like walking into a Dickens novel. A stark difference from the exterior, it had wood-paneled walls extending up two floors, with paintings neatly arranged on them. Everything from stern oil portraits to lush landscapes.

My eyes followed the carved wooden moldings to the grand doorway in front of us. The sound of chatter could be heard from between the heavy double doors that were slightly propped open. Flanked by a staircase on either side, my attention was drawn to the words etched above the threshold.

"'*Verbum numquam mori,*'" I read aloud. I'd looked up the meaning after it worked to unlock the first invitation, and its translation from Latin was "Stories never die."

From my sleuthing in the archives, I knew each secret society on campus had a clubhouse, or a *mausoleum.* They all looked a little like this one from the outside and were interspersed throughout campus, but Scroll & Ivy's dated back to the late 1700s.

"What's the goal here?" I asked.

"Tell a good story." Conrad stepped forward and skimmed a hand on the staircase. It gleamed, polished after centuries of hands doing precisely the same thing.

I hummed and followed Conrad through the double doors. They revealed a large room lit with gilded sconces. It boasted wall-to-wall bookshelves that spanned the two-story height of the salon. Members were interspersed in conversation.

We took a few more steps inside and the realization paged through my mind.

"Your mausoleum is a library..." I could have fallen over in delight.

"The people leave this place, but the stories stay," Conrad

explained, his lips moving up his cheek. Whatever irritation thorned at his words earlier was gone. "And they never die."

The walls of floor-to-ceiling shelves, the ladders that would swing along them, the plush furniture at the center of the room—I could get lost here.

Everything I wanted to ask filled my lungs at once.

I took in the room, turning in a full circle. On the center-most wall—the only one without a bookshelf—was a grand painting that spanned almost the entirety of it. Blues and greens wisped around what looked like a Renaissance-era goddess.

"You're gawking." Two fingers pushed up against my open jaw.

"Or..." I shooed away his hand. "Am I living out my *Beauty and the Beast* fantasy?"

A brow jumped up. "*Fantasy?*"

"I meant the bookshelves." We took a few more steps into the library. Everyone in there was dressed pretty casually. The gentle hum of conversation and music drifted through the room, occasionally broken with a loud laugh. There was a fully stocked bar, dusty old bottles of wine that I could only assume cost more than a semester at Winchester, round silver trays being passed around with the smallest snacks I'd ever seen. It was... unreal. "Although... the beast got significantly less attractive after he became a man."

"I'll take your word for it," he said from a step behind me.

I straightened my cashmere cardigan that sat on top of a flowing satin tank top. I paired it with my favorite pair of jeans, and even though I didn't *look* out of place, I felt it. A few passing glances and then a whisper or two—nothing out of the ordinary when witnessing a new person in a familiar space—was all it took to throw me back to my time with Kash's and Sonali's friends all over again.

That feeling of wanting to disappear into the air became

stronger. The members of Scroll & Ivy knew I wasn't supposed to be here, I was a fill-in for Sabrina. Her name had enough weight to allow me space here tonight, but only because it was temporary.

I decided to focus on the task at hand. "How does all this work? Keeping things private on campus, I mean."

Everyone on campus knew *something* about a secret society, mostly thanks to social media. But since they were the only private clubs that were allowed property on campus—heavily secured property, by the looks of that towering structure along the perimeter—nobody actually got much insight unless they were invited in and, well, that only came alongside an old-money bloodline.

"Scroll & Ivy owned most of the land the campus is on now. They donated it with the stipulation that only members have access to its buildings."

"Who monitors all this?" I scanned the shelves, hoping to keep him from noticing how intimidated I felt. Information was armor when I felt out of place, and the sheer absence of any relating to Scroll & Ivy made that impossible.

He looked at me. "Planning a heist?"

Three words cracked some of the tension. I smiled for a millisecond before taming it.

"I *did* break in pretty easily," I mused. "Literally—I walked through the front door."

His lips arched up, and something about that filled me with satisfaction.

"A security firm does it all. Cameras and facial recognition at the front entrance. Everything is handled by alums." He said it nonchalantly, as if it were information us mere mortals were privy to. "They vet everyone from the groundskeepers to the cleaning staff that comes in occasionally."

"Ahh yes, they covered that in Bizarre Rich People Shit

205." I moved along the length of the room, passing the rows and rows of bookshelves.

He didn't answer, but he followed.

"Upstairs are a dozen more salons. The library takes up two floors, obviously." He motioned to the walls. "Downstairs is a wine cellar."

My body screamed to get downstairs and confirm the catacombs existed. The fabled underground tunnels were, obviously, underground, so the cellar was probably my best bet if I planned to see where they led. Also, down there, I wouldn't feel so out of place, but I needed to play it cool. Ignoring the sweat forming at the back of my neck, I stopped at a swath of shelves that carried books with similar-looking spines. All crimson red and leather bound; with names engraved next to a year. "And all of these books?"

"Journals. Every member submits their story at the end of their time at Winchester."

Stories never die.

In these walls, between all those pages, was an entire history that *nobody* but members knew about. "Where's yours?"

He pointed to the shelf where newer-looking spines sat. A quick scan of the year listed on each spine confirmed that fifteen members were added annually. **Alders, 2026** was etched into one, waiting for Sabrina.

I stopped at the **Hastings, 2025** spine.

I pulled it out, but he pushed it back in line with the others before I could read it. "It's blank, but I'll write something along the lines of *drinking and traveling*."

I snapped my fingers. "And this little deal."

A boyish smile pushed through his prickly demeanor. It sent a round of goose bumps down my body. "That's probably worth a sentence or two."

I cleared my throat and remembered all the other questions I had. "Do the seniors decide who gets in?"

"No, alums do. The journals show up day one of the school year. Incoming seniors send out the invitations."

"Okay, you got me." I scanned the opulent setting before me. "This is *slightly* more than just rich kids and fancy parties."

He shrugged. "Welcome to Scroll & Ivy."

CHAPTER 11
Conrad

Tonight's party was supposed to be a way for the newest members to familiarize themselves with Scroll & Ivy's clubhouse. I left Malena to her own devices for a couple of minutes to find my friends. The mausoleum's main floor was mostly its library, so I assumed she'd hang around James, seeing as they were already acquainted and had *adorable* nicknames for each other.

I figured he would thank me, wingman and all.

But I wasn't in the mood to watch, so I got caught up talking to Lucy about the Head of the Charles races happening in October. It shouldn't have surprised me that in those few minutes, Malena had disappeared.

"What part of 'no running off' was difficult for you?" I called when I eventually found her in the hallway outside the double doors, on her way down the steps to the basement.

She stopped with one foot on the landing but didn't turn around. "I didn't want to bother you if you were trying to sleep with the cute blond."

"What?" I grimaced. Did she mean Lucy? "I wasn't trying to *sleep* with Lucy."

"No judgment." She put her hands up defensively, clearly not understanding why that statement was so off-putting. "And, also, not my business who you take home."

Moving past her, I took the steps down and opened the basement door. There was no point in trying to turn her around; her one-track mind was fixed on the catacombs.

"And *yet* you can't seem to help but sound a little judgmental," I said.

I didn't aspire to things I knew I'd be terrible at, and being someone's boyfriend fell into that category. Like most things, I knew how relationships ended. Besides, if I wanted to watch one fall apart in real-time, I'd go home to the Upper East Side and visit my parents.

"Oh." Her voice jumped an octave. "I didn't mean to come across that way. I'm sorry, I really *wasn't* judging," she said from behind me. It actually sounded genuine, and it made me pause on the cool stone floor for a brief moment. "And it's not like I'm one to talk, I have my own flings-only rule."

Wow, an apology *and* a self-deprecating comment in a single breath?

Huh. I didn't expect that.

She was a litany of contradictions. The by-the-book type who impersonated her best friend to crash a party. An overachieving student who seemingly had no issues breaking rules —case in point: our current location.

In a depressingly predictable world, Malena was an anomaly.

She stopped ahead of me when the domed walls of the wine cellar reached a dead end and looked over her shoulder at me, eyes glinting. All that was left was a single door. Which she promptly began attempting to pry open, making the correct assumption that it led to the catacombs.

"You know, for someone who prides themselves on functioning brainwaves"—I held up my key patronizingly—"you miss some pretty obvious things."

I unlocked it and she rushed through like she was worried I'd change my mind and lead us back up to the party. I shut the door behind me, and we were exactly where she'd been gunning to be.

The catacombs consisted of musty and damp stonewalled tunnels that were scarcely lit with electric lanterns. There were a few entry points into them, all of which were from basements of old buildings on campus. The doorways were still there but had been sealed for years.

"So... who knows about the catacombs?" Malena asked, her head on a swivel as she peered down the dark tunnel. I sidled up next to her and used my phone's flashlight to light the path. The walls were wide enough to allow about four people to walk side by side, but she stayed close.

"There are hundreds of stories about them," I reminded her.

"I mean who *knows*." She threw me an unamused look. "Stories are one thing, but who *knows* how to get in here?"

"Nobody knows." What part of *secret* did she not understand?

"So where does the tunnel go?"

We'd just left the mausoleum by way of its wine cellar, so it would probably be another forty-five minutes before we got to one end. "Walking in this direction"—I pointed ahead of us— "we'll be at the bay in about an hour. If we turned around, we'd be at the clock tower in ten minutes."

She nodded, and for a couple of minutes, a quiet passed between us as we walked.

Maybe she'd get bored and we could head back soon.

"And these doors?" She stopped and pointed to the first door we came across. A thick wooden door with an iron handle, sealed all around its frame with what was probably mortar. She flicked an annoyed look at me. "Way to bury the lede."

I sighed. "It's not that interesting. The catacombs were once accessible from half a dozen or so campus buildings. With the exception of the clock tower and our mausoleum, the doors have been sealed since the Eisenhower administration."

"So you're telling me no students have snuck down here in the centuries they've been around?"

"No, they have, but wandering around the catacombs is pretty useless since all these doors are sealed and only members of Scroll & Ivy have keys to get in."

"Do these tunnels eventually lead to crypts?"

"No."

"They're called *catacombs*," she pointed out. "Have you checked?"

"There are no crypts." I let out another long sigh. This was going to be how I spent my night. Maybe if I answered all of her questions, I could wrap this up. I had a social life to get back to. "The tunnels are called catacombs because the clubhouses are called mausoleums."

She stopped and her face scrunched with disappointment. "That's all?"

"People in the sixteenth century were weird about death; what do you want me to say?"

"Something more interesting, for starters," she mumbled to herself. She paused and pursed her lips, inching a step toward the doorway, eyeing the iron handle with palpable curiosity. "How do you know that all those doors are sealed?"

"Every so often a member tests the theory." James and I drunkenly stumbled through here last year ourselves, come to think of it. In the low light, I watched her perk up. *Great.* This little menace was going to give it her best shot. "And, as expected, they didn't open."

"Who *could* access them?" she asked.

"Nobody. Because *they are sealed.*" My patience was wearing thin, but I did my best to head off what I predicted—no, what I *knew*—was about to happen.

She yanked at the door that led to the old theater. Then shoved her shoulder against it, as if that was going to open it. When she had no luck opening the door, she moved back to my side.

"So which building do these doors lead to?" She went on like she hadn't even registered what I said. When I didn't answer, she looked up at me. Standing this close, I could trace the delicate curve of her cheek and the way her smirking lips made her look utterly devious. "If you help me with this, I'll be out of your way sooner."

The statement knocked the gears back into full speed in my head. "The old theater." I motioned to the door in front of us. "Then the Amherst Building, the old lab building, and then one of the shell houses at the bay."

"Why those spots?" She started moving farther down the tunnel and I followed a step behind her.

"They were the first buildings on campus," I guessed, but curiosity sprouted in my head. "These tunnels were used during Prohibition to get booze in from the bay."

She stopped abruptly, whipping around with wide eyes. The cream-colored sweater she wore slipped a bit off her shoulder, and my eyes momentarily traced up the line of her collar bone. "No way."

I blinked a couple of times and couldn't help but chuckle. Her unfiltered delight was infectious, and as I stood there in the damp tunnel, knowing we'd make our way toward the next sealed door that she'd undoubtedly try to open, I realized it *was* a pretty cool story. "Yeah, the old science lab was a distillery too. I came across a story about it in one of the journals in the mausoleum last year."

A grin grew like a weed across her face, and I bit my lip to leash my own.

Sometimes—especially when my family life was circling the drain—those journals were a way to get me out of my head. And they were one of the things I loved about Scroll & Ivy. Inside of each was an entire unknown history.

We kept walking along and she moved a bit closer.

The next doorway came into view a few minutes later. "Feel silly for questioning the lore?" I goaded.

"Jury's still out on that." She walked up to the threshold at the next door, the frame looking like the last but dustier.

As she crouched down to inspect the prehistoric-looking hinges, I tapped my phone to wake up the screen. I didn't have service, but I wanted to check the time. We'd been down here a while, and it was nearly eleven at night.

A loud thud sounded and I startled, almost dropping my phone.

A cloud of dust and debris and the sound of coughing assaulted my senses, and when it settled, the door was wide open. Malena, who must've fallen forward, sprang up.

With wide eyes and hair askew like a mad scientist, she looked at the open door then to me, then back to the open door.

"Well, don't just stand there." She turned and poked her head into the dark room. "Let's go."

An unfamiliar feeling, warm and jittery, danced down every nerve ending. She flicked her hair back and swatted at the air in front of a door that should have never opened.

A rogue smile took control of my face.

Maybe not *everything* was as it seemed.

CHAPTER 12

Malena

My heart beat violently against each rib.

I stared through the halfway open threshold.

I didn't know what any of this meant, but I wasn't about to waste any more time.

Conrad's presence loomed at my back as I tracked a beam of moonlight that peaked through a tiny window. It showed us we were very much still below ground-level, because the twelve-inch window sat right where the wall met the ceiling and was partially obstructed by dirt on its outside face.

Excitement gave way to apprehension, and it cemented me to the floor.

"Age before beauty." With a flourish, I swept a hand toward the room.

I'd seen enough horror movies to know that I, the ambitious brown girl, would *not* be going in first. Besides, nobody killed off the cute white boy. He was perfectly safe.

"Just admit you're scared," he said when it became clear I wouldn't be moving.

"I'm not scared." I scoffed despite him being correct, then angled my body so he could step past me and through the threshold. He closed the door behind us and did just that. "I'm trying to figure out where we are."

I drew up a mental map of our location. We left the Scroll & Ivy's clubhouse through its cellar, entered the catacomb tunnels, walked for a bit, passed that first sealed door—which I now knew led to the old theater—only to end up *here*.

Now that my eyes had adjusted, I could make out book-shelves along one cinder-block wall. They were covered in a thick layer of undisturbed dust. Another bookshelf seemed to be a storage site for woodworking equipment.

"Amherst Building," he answered curtly. His arm stretched back to maneuver me behind him. We took a few steps forward and his palm slid down to grab my hand.

My already erratic pulse jumped.

"This... this its cellar," I stammered. This time, the creepy surroundings weren't what made me falter. It was the fact that we were ten feet below one of my favorite places—the Amherst Building. It housed the rare book library and archives that I always studied in.

When I trailed behind a couple of paces, his grip tightened and he pulled me in until I just grazed against his back.

"Yeah, and there's a stairwell," he answered. We passed the window and reached the center of the room and he notched his head toward the stairwell in the corner.

"What do you think this room was used for?" I stumbled forward again, bumping into his back.

"A dusty old basement?" Conrad's palm pressed tighter against mine. "I don't know."

I hummed and nudged an old table saw with my foot.

Conrad continued guiding us toward the stairwell. "What are we looking for?"

"I don't know, but I don't think we're going to have much luck with any of those other doors"—my palms and shoulder still ached from trying to bodily shove them open—"so we should make the most of it."

As I spoke my last word, we came upon a painting leaning against the railing. The thing was massive, at least six feet wide and the same if not more in length. It boasted a landscape with a deep blue ocean and a shoreline in the distance.

Staring, I tripped over my feet and nearly took us both down.

"Be careful," Conrad hushed under his breath.

"I wasn't *trying* to fall," I whispered back. My bejeweled flats were good for walking but not *exploring*, thank you very much. I brushed lightly against the painting and followed his lead as we traversed past rows of posterboard carriers, books, catalogues, and oak filing cabinets. We stopped at the landing.

Releasing Conrad's hand, I craned my neck and sized up the stairwell. If the basement wasn't the destination, maybe it was a part of the journey and there was something up there? I pushed my shoulders back and started the ascent.

The Amherst Building wasn't as popular to study in because there was a bigger, more well-appointed library in the center of campus, so I was under no illusions that it would be open now, at midnight.

When I got to the top of the stairwell, I reached for the door before stopping with my hand in midair.

"There's probably an alarm," I said under my breath.

"If there was, it would've gone off on whoever unsealed the door to the catacombs in the first place." He grinned and clicked his tongue when I looked confused. "You didn't think you managed to open it through sheer force of will, did you?"

I didn't even have time to huff out a reply before he looked up at the door jamb, drew his eyes back to meet mine, and pushed it open.

I braced, but after a second or two of silence, the realization that we were in the clear settled.

He tilted his head, a smug grin plastered on his face.

"What if there had been an alarm?" I whisper-shouted as I followed him, brushing any residual dust off my shoulder and shutting the door in question.

"We'd go back the way we came," he stated plainly as we found ourselves in the office attached to the stairwell. Conrad shut the door behind us. "We're in New Harbor, Connecticut, Malena. They probably never even turn on the alarm."

I scanned my surroundings in the moonlit space. My eyes floated along the familiar frames lining the walls, at the stray cart half filled with books that'd probably be re-shelved tomorrow.

"Or someone shut it off," I argued. This was all too much to be coincidence, right? "An entry point to the catacombs that *should* be sealed is open. And this door, leading to said catacombs, is conveniently alarm-free?" I could hear myself sounding like a conspiracy theorist, but I kept going, my heart racing with the new information. "Lightning doesn't strike twice."

Not to mention I'd been in here before.

It was where the Amherst Building's head librarian and archivist, Abby, worked. This was her office, off in a remote corner where the rare-book archive was located, not far from my favorite study cubicle. Her desk stood by the single window; the doorway we'd just walked through was one I'd passed countless times and always assumed was a closet.

"That's not true at all." He ran his hand along a shelf, pushing a bit of dust into the air. "Lightning *famously* strikes twice." He took a few more unhurried steps, like it wasn't against all sorts of rules that we were in this office to begin with. "It's why skyscrapers have grounding beams."

I blinked. Something about that threw me. Admittedly, I'd expected him to be a little more air-headed.

"How oddly jaded," I noted.

There wasn't much in the office. The gabled window had a clear view of the quad in the distance, and I once again wondered how many times I'd walked past, oblivious to all that hid below.

"Realistic," he corrected.

"If you say so..."

I rounded the desk and took a second to think about what lines I was willing to cross. I shrugged it off and knew I'd rationalize my choices later. I bent slightly and began trying the drawers, only to find them all locked.

"This was anticlimactic," I said through a long sigh.

I glanced up to Conrad, whose gaze was fixed on my attempts at ransacking the librarian's desk. The corners of his eyes softened when I planted my hands on my hips and gave him a look like *Are you just going to stand there?*

"Maybe they host a rave between the shelves when we aren't around. We should check, for good measure." He shrugged and made for the door.

I couldn't tell if he was joking, but I blinked at his back and quickly moved my feet, because for the first time since we started, he seemed on board.

This section of the library was small and cramped, with the bookshelves spaced no more than a couple of feet apart. Bronze wall sconces did enough to illuminate our path, but I'd walked this floor so many times, I could probably do it with my eyes closed.

But I kept them open and tried to remember everything in case it was important. Since *clearly*, there was a lot more than met the eye.

We walked ahead another couple of steps, down the last aisle. I didn't know what I was expecting to find, but there wasn't anything here.

The thrill I'd felt walking up those stone steps waned. There was probably a reasonable explanation that I just wasn't seeing. I turned and looked at Conrad, who wore a divot between his brows. Like he felt bad that all my excitement ended the way he probably predicted—with nothing.

Humiliation swept over me.

"Is someone there?" a new, unfamiliar voice filled the quiet.

My pulse spiked.

"Shit," I hissed.

After three years of perfecting all the many lies of Malena Amin, *this* was what threatened to bring me down?

Flustered, I wondered why Conrad stood unmoving. I looked around in panic. "They're going to find us."

He looked over his shoulder then back at me.

"Relax." His voice lowered but remained calm, washing over my nerves. He closed the space between us and gripped my waist.

I sucked in a startled breath. This close, the pine and musk in his cologne managed to knock the remainder of my panic down, replacing it with *something* else.

"What are you—"

"We need an alibi." His controlled tone fanned across my skin as he dragged his hands up and laced his fingers around the back of my neck, tilting my chin up. My ribs rattled around my frantic heart. "Play along."

Without further explanation, he walked us backward and pressed his lips against mine. I tensed for a millisecond, just long enough for a burst of electricity to shoot down my body.

My hands curled around his collar, my lips parted, and then *everything* melted together.

With a gruff groan, he deepened the kiss.

His body molded against mine. He raked his fingers into my hair, and just like the expensive whiskey he'd been drinking at the party that I could taste on his lips, he was intoxicating.

The heat from his body, the commanding pressure of his

lips, the subversive feeling of having a need be sated... it was addictive.

Pushing me harder against the bookshelves, he groaned again. This time, the sound reverberated down my throat and arrowed itself right between my thighs.

Fuck. Who knew being pressed between a dusty bookshelf and a marble slab of a torso would feel so good. I rolled my hips against his, chasing the high, desperate to pull that sound from his throat one more time.

A glaring light shining onto our intertwined bodies broke the spell.

"What are you doing in here?"

Conrad pulled away, his eyes connecting with mine. Unfocused and gorgeous. For a moment, he looked completely lost.

Then, he cleared his throat.

"I think that's pretty obvious," he mumbled between heavy breaths as he turned to face the security guard.

"I'm so sorry." I took a step forward. "We..."

"Conrad Hastings." Conrad outstretched his hand and introduced himself in a smooth and warm tone that reminded me of the night of the masquerade party. And maybe it was the rush I'd just experienced or the dim light, but I was sure I saw something in his palm. "Apologies, we lost track of time. We didn't mean to interrupt your work."

The security guard's eyes darted down as he cautiously shook Conrad's hand.

I bit back a scoff.

"Don't let me catch you in here again," he warned, stepping to the side as he shoved his own hand into his pocket.

With that, we were escorted out the main entrance.

WE RUSHED DOWN the stone path that led off campus, away from the Amherst Building. It was only a couple of blocks until we approached Radiant, and with our time running out, I had to know. "Did you bribe him?"

"We're walking out of there scot-free, aren't we?"

"And that usually works?"

He shrugged. "I'm Conrad Hastings."

He didn't *need* to lie, in fact throwing around the truth—like his name—was pretty useful for him. All while I had to set up a fake identity in order to scrape by with a normal college experience.

He looked down at me as we turned the corner in front of our building, like he was waiting at the other side of a tennis court to return a serve. "I know how that sounds, so you can spare me the moral high ground."

"I *am* blackmailing you." I reminded him of his gross exaggeration of our agreement, breathing out a chuckle as I stepped inside the lobby. "I don't have any moral high ground here."

A full-blown smile broke out across the steep cut of his jaw. A *real* one that came alongside a tiny roll of his shoulders and a subdued laugh.

The notes rang deep and rich.

Our eyes caught, and I stilled.

"You have..." Conrad leaned in and brushed something off my shoulder. His breath skated across my cheek, goose bumps prickling every inch it touched. His palm smoothed over the nape of my neck. "Paint?"

Cloudy and warm, a familiar tension returned.

"You... do too." I pressed closer, my mind blanked.

And then, a tapping along my thigh yanked me out of the moment.

My heart raced, even faster now.

It was my burner phone. The hurricane-force wind that

was reality smacked me in the face. I hadn't checked my phone all night, and I definitely didn't have service for most of it.

Shit.

I took a step back and fumbled for it. Five missed calls. My mom didn't do well with feeling ignored. She got anxious then angry, and then it was up to me to do damage control. "I should probably go."

He blinked a couple of times, his jaw flexing. "Yeah."

"Thanks for the tour." I pushed my phone back into my pants. "The article won't take long at this rate."

"Yeah... You're welcome." His brow furrowed as he muttered something I didn't catch.

I turned and walked quickly to the elevators.

CHAPTER 13

Conrad

"You slept with Azalea?" I asked, my voice curved up hopefully.

The cool morning air skimmed over the water. James had been waiting for me on the porch at the shell house and caught me just as I was leaving to get back to campus after rowing all morning.

"No, I had sex with her," James clarified impassively with a grin, after he explained where he ended up last night.

I came out here around sunrise because I couldn't sleep. A feeling of pins and needles had bothered me all night, and this was my futile attempt to clear my head. After everything that happened at the Amherst Building, I'd returned to the mausoleum for my bike and came home to an empty place. I figured Felix and James were still out, and instead of sleep, all I did was toss and turn in bed. Maybe it was simply being down in the catacombs and finding that open door, or maybe it was almost getting caught by security.

I knew two things for sure: For the first time in years, I *wanted* to do something for the paper. And I couldn't stop replaying that kiss.

I never got a straight answer from James about Malena, and now she was living rent-free in my mind. That was a sign of a guilty conscience, right?

"You like her?" I asked as we walked down the steps from the shell house. "Because I think that's the only loophole in the *don't fuck your friends* rule."

We didn't live by many, but that one and *don't fuck anyone over* were the only two rules we ever held each other accountable for. I never aspired to be the kind of guy who fucked people over.

I wasn't my dad.

"She's not *my* friend," James defended, nodding his head in the direction of campus. I checked my phone for the time—close to nine.

"She's Scroll & Ivy," I reminded him.

"Azalea Burton is a big girl, she'll be just fine," James said, a little sharper this time.

But Azalea was different. She was a new member, equal parts old and new money. Her mom was an Amherst, and her dad was Wall Street tycoon Clark Burton. James would run in those circles for the rest of his life, and given that he was the Rutherford heir, he needed to keep those relationships tidy.

"Is that why you're all moody?" he drawled, and I looked past his shoulder at the bay. "Azalea?"

"I'm not—"

"You were out here before sunrise. Conrad on the water *this* early in the morning is a distress signal."

"I kissed her," I blurted, and stopped on the path.

There, I admitted it. He could punch me and we could all move on. The incessant overthinking and pins and needles could fucking cease.

"Who?" James looked around at the empty bay. "Azalea?"

"Malena."

We never went after the same girl. If we happened to be

interested in the same one, I backed down because—aside from these past few weeks—James was the "bring her home to Mom and Dad" type of guy. I wasn't.

"Oh..." He stilled and blinked a couple of times.

Shit.

"It didn't mean anything," I insisted, trying to sound disinterested, because why would I be interested? I *wasn't.* She'd inserted herself into my life, I had to work with her, James maybe liked her, and I kissed her. End of story. "We ended up in the Amherst Building's library after we left the mausoleum, got caught, and it was the first thing I thought of."

He nodded. The next ten seconds felt like hours as he processed.

"It's fine," he answered, studying me like he was looking for something. "Really, it is."

"You were going to ask her out," I stated instead of asking if he still wanted to.

"Honestly... yeah, I *was.* But I hardly know her." He paused. "She's hot. And, if given the opportunity, I'd have slep—"

"You're not mad?" I interrupted, because I *really* didn't need to hear the rest.

"Nope." He slapped a supportive hand on my shoulder. "But, if it makes you feel better, we can duel at dawn."

I chuckled, relieved. Maybe now I could forget it ever happened.

"If *you* like her..."

"I don't," I answered reflexively.

It probably didn't matter, given how fast the moment between us had evaporated when she got that call. The one that made her disappear without a word.

It certainly wasn't her *mother* calling after midnight.

James's eyes narrowed. "Okay."

"I wanted to tell you, that's all."

"Uh-huh."

I did not like the grin he was giving me. But before I could say anything, I noticed a few messages on my phone. My pulse jumped.

Then, my shoulders sank with a disappointed exhale. It was my dad.

> Satan: I will be at the president's annual fundraiser dinner next week.

> Satan: I expect you there on time.

Not sure who I was expecting to text me, but it sure as hell wasn't him.

> Me: See you then, Dad.

Even though James and I were good, the pins and needles remained.

CHAPTER 14

Malena

The flood of calls last night was my mom telling me, in no uncertain terms, that I needed to be at home today.

So, first thing this morning, I got on the train and did as told. Because I knew better than to play chicken with them when summoned. It was the same old story: answer her calls, come when she demanded, listen when she spoke. I toed the line, I skipped rope with it, but I never crossed it if there was even a *chance* of getting caught.

"I heard that the Gupta's daughter—that one who had the perfect SAT score..." My mom shook her head, her voice lowered like she was delivering grave news on a natural disaster. "Well, she works at some restaurant as a *cook* after she ran off to Portland with *that boy*." She scooped a mound of spiced potatoes from the bowl between us. We stood side by side a few feet apart, each of us making our way through giant heaps of dough and masala filling, and I'd been dutifully nodding along as she gossiped about her so-called friends.

After our two-hour lunch where I served the chai like a "good daughter," Pinky Auntie left, and I'd been in the kitchen ever since, assisting my mom in one of her cooking marathons. Today we were preparing a care package that would be shipped overnight to my older sister.

"Isn't she a sought-after pastry chef?" I asked, even though I *knew* the Gupta's daughter—Neha—was. I hadn't seen her in years, but I'd started following her on social media after her family gave her an ultimatum and then stopped all contact with her.

My mom's eyes flashed. "You think that's what her parents left their homes and started all over in a new country for? So she could cook for strangers like a servant?"

"I guess not," I murmured, knowing this was not the time to make a point.

"Her family is humiliated. She's alone. When her life falls apart, nobody will be there to help her," she added. "She did this to herself."

That reminder felt like a warning.

I sighed and decided to change the subject, glancing down at the massive stack of parathas I was making for my sister. "Did Avani ask for *all* of this?"

"No." My mom didn't look up.

Irritation pricked me. Then why was I wasting a Sunday doing this? "Did she ask for *any* of it?"

My mom doted on my perfect older sister even more now that she lived across the country. Making me help gave my mom the fringe benefit of telling her friends that Malena was *so dutiful* and made *all this food* for her sister.

"No." A hard smack with her palm cracked against my skull, and a ringing bounced between my ears. "Why do you *always* need to argue? Avani never argues."

"*Mom.*" I grabbed the back of my throbbing head.

I didn't say anything because *good* kids didn't bring up the occasional smack from their parents. We pretended we deserved it, learned whatever lesson it was meant to instill, and moved on.

"Family doesn't have to ask, family just does." She pointed her spatula at me. "Imagine what people would think of you if they heard you speak like that..." She shook her head. "*Selfish*."

"Sorry," I mumbled, and went back to my work quietly.

"I remind you of these things to *help* you," my mom emphasized. "Nobody wants to deal with someone who's strong-willed and self-centered."

I bit back the urge to defend myself, because I'd just be proving her point.

"Sorry," I repeated. I finished the last paratha and brushed the flour and ghee off my hands. "I need to go; I should study for the MCAT."

"You didn't study this weekend?" My mom threw a look at my class schedule that she'd printed and tacked onto the fridge. "Your Fridays are open and you were at school all of yesterday. You should have been studying."

"I *was* studying," I lied. "But I want them to be perfect." *That* was true, but I wasn't worried. School came pretty easy to me, and I'd studied for the MCATs all summer.

My mom's face paled, lines drawing a valley on her forehead. It was the same look she had when Avani didn't get into med school on her first try. While some parents would feel dejected *for* their children, you would have thought Avani did it *to* them. But all was set right again when she got in the following year, apologized profusely, and lived her life exactly as they prescribed. "Are you having trouble with school?"

"Of course not," I answered firmly. "No harm in being overprepared."

Her shoulders relaxed.

"We don't need to worry about our Malena in school." She grasped my chin proudly. "So smart." The flip from menacing to motherly happened at breakneck speed, and I could've sworn the gesture eased the ringing in my head.

I washed a couple of spoons in the sink, then my hands, when Dad stepped through the threshold into the kitchen. "I'll drive you back."

"No, the train is fine," I answered immediately. "I want to get some reading done."

"No." My mom walked to the fridge. Inside were containers filled with some of my favorite foods—sambar and aloo bindi. Everything I missed when I was in New Harbor. "There's jalebi at the top, everything else goes in the fridge."

"Oh." I smiled. The warm feeling of being cared for wrapped around me. I pulled a linen tote off the old wooden hook in the pantry and began filling it, my cheeks heating.

Lying wasn't great, but things could be worse.

My parents cared for me. I had everything I needed and a lot of the things that I wanted—as long as they were pre-approved, of course.

I was lucky.

I wasn't sure if my parents were the disowning kind, but my mom's ease when sharing cautionary tales made me think they were. Either way, I was too scared to find out, because I wouldn't just lose them and the luxuries they paid for. I'd lose *everyone*. Cousins, aunts, uncles. My connection to my culture. All of it.

I'd be treated like a contagion. I wasn't ready for that.

The two-Malena system wasn't perfect, but it worked.

I GOT BACK to our condo and slumped onto the couch, a giant pitcher of margaritas staring me down from our coffee table.

"I figured you could use this," Cora explained as she

brought in a bowl of chips and a few dips on a slotted platter. "The tequila was stashed in my room, waiting for your dad to leave."

I smiled at how well-rehearsed we were. I always gave Cora and Sabrina a heads-up when I was coming back to campus because if my parents were dropping me off, they'd come upstairs, and my mom would snoop. She'd look for everything from alcohol to clothes she deemed risqué.

"Five hours of cooking." I sighed into the well-salted rim and took a giant gulp. "Thank you."

I folded my legs beneath me and wrapped myself in the chunky knitted blanket that Cora bought on a trip to Sweden last year.

"Oh, I meant to ask, what were you and Conrad doing it against?" Cora turned my cashmere sweater over in her hands, giving it a final look.

When I got back from the library last night, I gave Cora the run-down on my night—everything from the ride on Conrad's motorcycle to navigating through the catacombs and stumbling upon the unsealed door.

"It was just a kiss," I reminded her, and took my sweater back. A vibrant dark blue patch was smeared across the sleeve. That same paint was along my jeans too, lengthwise.

It must have happened in the basement, where I was knocking into about a dozen things.

"And it was against the books," I added quickly, holding my sweater up to hide my blush.

A sly smile curled up Cora's cheeks. "I approve."

With the freedom of being away from home and an endless supply of random hookups at my disposal, sex was generally good, sometimes great. But rarely was it the toe-curling kind I showed up to college expecting from having secretly read romance novels growing up. Except for last night, and that was just a *kiss*. I didn't have to fantasize or force my imagination to concoct some steamy scenario in my mind to get my heart racing. Conrad had done that all on his own.

"Painted books?" Cora asked, snapping me out of my runaway thoughts.

I cleared my throat, reminding myself that I needed this award. And Conrad was already reluctant about our deal, so it was on me to keep this fragile alliance from breaking. This campus was riddled with hot guys; if I wanted a fling, I'd use one of them. "It must have been from the basement," I told her. "There was a painting down there that was the same color pattern."

She hummed and took a generous gulp of her margarita.

"There was paint on his clothes too," I added, almost as an afterthought. Last night, between the kiss and my mom's summons, our adventures in the catacombs and the Amherst Building's library had been quick to fall to the back of my mind.

Cora looked up with a Cheshire cat's smile. "Yeah, I bet there was."

"It was a good kiss, but it was a fake one. So, stop that."

"Stop what?" She peered at the fabric again and ran her fingers on the smeared colors.

"Whatever you're thinking."

"If you knew what I was thinking, you'd know that I was wondering how the hell a dusty old painting smudged your clothes."

My ears perked up.

"Huh." I hadn't actually given it any thought while I was at my parents'. I was too busy being "good Malena," planning my study schedule for this week and thinking about when I'd proof a piece for Dillian. I was trying to be overly helpful since he was a little miffed about my jumping the chain of command with the feature. "What do you mean?"

"It's still a little wet." Cora pinched at the fabric and

showed me her fingertip. It came away blue, and still a little glossy. "I'm trying to understand how the paint still hasn't dried when it's been almost twenty-four hours since you bumped into it."

"That's weird... The painting was in a frame and everything."

"No way it's smearing off like that on your clothes unless it was painted recently. And..." She rubbed her fingers together as she stood up and walked to the kitchen. Moments later, she was back with a paper towel, wiping at her hand. She neatly placed my sweater, paint side up, on the coffee table. "It's an oil-based paint and all commercial oil-based paints have desiccants in them, so they dry in a couple of hours. Nobody's used desiccant-free paint since, I dunno, the nineteen-thirties?"

Cora, on top of being a fine arts major, was a fellow chemistry minor. A brilliant one too, with her perfect grade point average and the offers she already had coming in for graduate school.

"Someone bought desiccant-free paint?"

"Which can't be easy because it's not shelf-stable for very long. The ingredients separate," Cora pointed out. "It would be a giant waste of money, and that's *if* you can find an arts supply store that stocks it. The more likely story is that they made it."

"Why make oil paint?"

"Beats me." Cora shrugged. "But it's weird, right?"

My heart soared. There was a story somewhere in all of this, all I had to do was find it. And that was the most thrilling part. "Yeah."

That, mixed with the door that should've been sealed... something was up. I should have taken a picture of that damn painting.

Maybe I could go back.

Or find where it was painted, and by who.

My mind raced, but before I could say anything else, my phone rattled against the coffee table.

Kash: Hey

Kash: I know it's been a while

Kash: Wanna go out next weekend?

Cora's eyes flicked up to me. "No."

Cora was like an Olympic sprinter's sports bra. Strong, flexible, and supportive. She was my biggest cheerleader when I decided on something, but, like a good friend, was the first to bring up concerns.

"What's the harm?"

"He asked to date you, pretended like he wanted to, then ghosted." Cora's mouth twisted to the side. "Not to mention how rude his friends are to you. And you know about the data on completely homogenous friend groups."

I sighed. "I know."

Cora already gave me the lecture after last year's Diwali party. She and Sabrina went with me and I left early, choosing to retreat rather than feel alone in a place I thought I'd fit into.

That night, back in our apartment, eating spicy ramen, Cora recounted how she'd had trouble finding her place here on campus as a freshman. And how, when she confided in her mom, she'd ended up with pages and pages of research on the characteristics of racially, socioeconomically, or sexually homogenous friend groups—her way of telling her daughter that she was better off without people who weren't accepting of her as she was.

I envied Cora for having a mom like that.

"They are insular, excessively judgmental, less creative as a whole, and more likely to encourage patriarchal values." Cora listed off the main components, having memorized it by now. That last part was definitely true, Sonali and her friends did not find our man-bracket as empowering as we did. They practically recoiled when I told them about my sexual escapades. It only got worse when I began sort-of-dating Kash. "*And* you broke your flings-only rule for that little punk."

"I wasn't going to say yes," I defended, my phone forgotten. "But that doesn't mean I can't be nice."

Cora's face scrunched with discontentment. "Why not?"

I laughed and finished off my margarita. "I dunno..." Sometimes I felt like if I could just make myself fit in with them, it would be proof that I belonged. Then maybe it would translate to approval from my mom, to being more like the good daughter Avani was.

"I'm not going out with him. I need to study anyway," I said.

Plus, I had the annual fundraising dinner on Saturday night. I'd probably spend this week catching up on everything I'd ignored with getting so wrapped up with Scroll & Ivy. I wasn't one to let my obligations fall to the wayside, but this article proved anything was possible.

The feeling was disorienting and sort of fantastic.

"Got it." Cora squeezed my hand and graciously took the hint, pivoting to a new conversation topic. "But first, let's finish these margs. I do my best studying a little buzzed."

CHAPTER 15

Conrad

A week after the kiss I couldn't stop replaying in my head, I was back to the scene of the crime.

The annual fundraising dinner was always held in the Amherst Building—an early 1800s cathedral-like structure that was dedicated to two things: housing the university's extensive rare-literature collection on the west end and providing open studio spaces for students to pursue painting, sculpting, and the like on the east end. And every year, the Amherst Initiative made a giant donation, so the president held a dinner here in their honor and all of the significant donors—legacy families, for the most part—got to show up and make their demands known.

I took a long sip from my glass of whiskey, standing next to my father and nodding politely at anyone who made a bid for his time.

"Looks like we'll get that incomplete removed from your academic record." My father let out a long sigh, the glow from the delicate bronze chandelier at the center of the main atrium's dome accentuating the lines in his forehead. "And the

Hastings astronomy tower will begin construction in two years."

"All's well that ends well," I said, half baiting and half sincere.

He was being a little more patient than usual. It happened every time Mom kicked him out and threatened a divorce. It wouldn't last; it never did.

But in the months between her empty threats and him going back to his philandering ways, he was relatively congenial.

"One day, when you grow the hell up, you'll have responsibilities that extend beyond your team and your friends." He tilted his glass of scotch back and forth. "You're a Hastings, start acting like one. That incomplete is the last mess of yours I clean up."

I wasn't dumb, just highly unmotivated. But now that I *had* to keep an eye on my Monetary Policy grade, I would. And Malena would probably have that article written soon, since she was already halfway to getting what she wanted.

"Understood," I said curtly, glancing around for a distraction.

And beyond the smile that was beginning to hurt my face and the polite one-upmanship that was common amongst society parents as it pertained to their children's accomplishments, I found one.

Dressed in a black silk dress with blooming sleeves, a form-hugging bodice, and a flowing skirt, Malena pulled all of my attention. Her long hair, curled at the ends, bounced as she made a determined stride away from the party. I followed her line of sight and landed on a hallway that led down to some old art studios.

Chalking it up to boredom and *nothing* else, I followed.

She continued down the narrow hallway, oblivious to my presence, before stopping at a door marked with caution tape.

I propped a shoulder against a trophy cabinet and glanced behind me, confirming the space was deserted, before whispering, "Malena."

She jolted in her skin and paused with her hand on the doorknob.

She whipped around to meet my gaze, and her tight frame loosened. "Conrad. Of course you're here."

I pushed off the wall and closed the distance between us, trying to suppress my grin. What was she up to?

She tipped her head back and muttered something I couldn't decipher, then grabbed me by the lapel. Without thought or reason, consumed by her tantalizing citrus scent, I let her pull me into the art studio.

"I'd say I'm surprised, but breaking and entering seems to be a pattern." I turned to the side and shuffled in, trying not to disturb the haphazardly placed tape.

The small studio smelled of paint and dust, and as I scoped out the place, I counted five easels, each draped with a heavy tarp, and one that stood uncovered in the center of the room in front of a singular arched window. Without any additional lights, the room's golden hue began to dwindle with the sunset.

Malena didn't say anything. Rather, she took care to close the door silently, turning the knob all the way down to ensure even the lock wouldn't sound. From there, she went straight to the rows of paint tubes that lined the side wall.

"For the record, I never broke into Scroll & Ivy's parties. I was invited." She began picking up each bottle of paint, reading the label before replacing it in its spot. "And this door wasn't locked."

"It was taped off," I noted, choosing not to correct that she was only "invited" because she stole Sabrina's invitation.

"Oh, that." She waved her hand casually, still not giving

me her full attention. "Everyone out there is a couple of drinks in, nobody is going to notice me here."

"And if someone did? You'd need an alibi."

It was probably reckless to remind her of the last time we got caught somewhere we weren't supposed to be, but a part of me wanted to see her reaction.

She paused with a tube of paint in her hand. "Now that you're here, I just might throw you under the bus."

"How kind of you."

"You'd be fine." She threw a haughty look over her shoulder. "You're *Conrad Hastings*"—she mimicked my shrug from a week ago, the irony that we were back in that same building not lost on me—"it's not like the rules apply to you."

Fair point, I *was* disciplinary Teflon.

"So, why are you in here? This studio is closed for repairs." I pushed my hands into my pockets.

I didn't bother explaining that there was a much larger set of studios on the other side of campus, because I vaguely recalled her telling me her roommate Cora studied art. Which meant she'd be well aware.

"The paint that was on my sweater..." She paused again, tapping her finger on the paint bottle. "It was some home-made oil paint. It's not commercially available."

"How do you know?"

"I spent hours online searching for answers, and the only places to buy oil paint that doesn't have a drying agent in it are artisanal paint stores."

"Why would anyone make their own paint?"

"Right." Her voice nearly squeaked with excitement. She held the small jar in her hand—it was the same vibrant blue that was on her sweater that night. "Who would go to the effort to make paint like Picasso used to?"

The enthusiasm practically poured out of her.

"Pretentious art student?" I supplied.

"Exactly." She snapped her fingers and spun on her heels to face me.

"To what end?"

"No idea," she admitted, her shoulders lowering half an inch. She dropped the paint back into its spot on the shelf. "But if I can place the paint from the basement to this studio..."

My lips curved up. "We may have a more interesting angle."

Fuck, could we actually win this thing? The Keller Award was huge, and at first, Malena's optimism had made her seem mildly delusional, but the more we found, the deeper I was pulled in.

I wanted to know more. I *wanted* to figure this out.

The tops of her cheeks rose with her grin.

"There's a ton of art all around campus..." She lowered her voice. "Imagine an art student making their own versions of some of these paintings." Her smile turned crooked and uncertain. "*This* is a story."

A jitter ran down my sternum because she *was* right, there was something off about it all. And it was compelling.

She was compelling.

Just as I opened my mouth to tell her that we should probably hurry it up, a crinkling sound traveled our way from behind the closed door.

An exchange followed, and I homed in on a couple of irritated voices.

My smile dropped.

"Shit." Malena's head swiveled as she searched for places to hide in the abandoned studio. Wide eyes met mine.

Before I could react, she crowded my space and walked me back a few steps, the door behind me whooshing open before she pushed me through and shut it.

Inside the makeshift storage closet, we were sandwiched

between the wall and easel stands. There was barely enough space for one person, let alone two.

"Shhh," she said under her breath, her body flush against mine.

I could feel every inch of her. Her hands held onto me a little tighter as she stumbled over what looked like poster tubes littering the ground. I slid a palm along each of her hips to steady her, trying to focus on anything other than the warm prickle her breath left against my neck.

Malena raised her eyes to mine slowly. Beneath the thick sweep of her dark lashes, she held my attention there. For an extended breath, one I could feel my heart in my ears for, I let the static draw my head down, closer to her. Back against those pillowy lips I couldn't stop thinking about.

No matter how hard I tried, every annoying part of her—her brashness, her flippant sarcasm, her haughty upturned nose when she bested me with some convoluted logic that I couldn't fucking figure out—all of it was imprinted in my brain.

I leaned a little closer, my vision finally adjusting to the dark, and saw the delicate outlines of her face with clarity.

She let out a tiny sigh, opened her mouth, and—

"Workers will begin restoration tomorrow." A woman's voice, one I couldn't quite place, resonated on the other side of the door. "Are the students still using this studio?"

Malena's head whipped to the side, and I could see her eyeing the sliver of light on the tile floor, trying to place it too.

"Advanced composition students sometimes come in here..." a different voice answered, and the rest became inaudible because Malena turned her frame a bit. "...a case of senioritis making them bold."

All it did was press her against me tighter.

Fuck.

She needed to stop moving.

"The Amherst endowment was *very* specific..." That part came through clear from the first voice, along with a frustrated sigh. The rest was once again lost, replaced by the blood roaring through my ears. "...have someone clear this out so we can begin construction."

I hoped Malena couldn't feel how fast my heart was racing.

It was the circumstances, that was all. A boring, predictable night turned into something noteworthy for once. A delightful phenomenon that always seemed to happen around her.

CHAPTER 16

Malena

We strained to listen as the footsteps roamed the studio and the conversation became completely inaudible. Time warped in that cramped closet, like every passing second was an hour.

"I wonder what's in the poster carriers," I whispered, my breath bouncing against his skin and warming my own.

With every inhale, that rigid body pressed harder against mine.

I tried to think of *anything* else.

Who knew rowing a boat honed a body into what felt like a marble statue chiseled by Donatello himself? I had to start mentally listing off all the US presidents in alphabetical order so I wouldn't think about how it might feel to have *that* body on top of mine.

He didn't answer, so I settled on yammering quietly until he stopped feeling... *good*. "Probably works by an—"

"Stop talking." His rough command faltered in its hushed whisper.

His jaw flexed and he looked up at the ceiling as he pressed his hands into my hips and turned me slightly to the side. It put a fraction of space between us—not nearly enough.

"Right," I squeaked. We should've been listening. "In a closet, inside a studio we shouldn't be in, we—"

"Malena," he warned. The deep, gravelly sound ricocheted between my thighs.

I closed my eyes and thanked whoever was listening for the dark, because I was blushing up to my hairline. I took a deep breath, sure that I was a second away from passing out.

After what felt like hours, the voices subsided. I shifted to open the door, but Conrad yanked me back.

"Wait," he ordered, keeping me tight to his chest.

My stomach dipped. *God*, he needed to stop talking to me like *that*.

I looked up at him and mouthed, *For what?*

"Make sure they're down the hall first."

I counted to three in my head before bursting out, sighing as the cool air rushed against my face.

"Well, that was convenient," I said matter-of-factly. I turned around and made myself busy by picking up all the poster canisters I displaced.

"Shoving me in a closet?" Conrad knelt down next to me and helped.

"Yeah..." I tried to focus on the fact that I needed more evidence. I opened one of the poster cannisters and out popped around twelve neatly stacked and rolled pieces of paper. I carded through them. Each was the same landscape of the same ocean waves crashing against a stony shore.

"Maybe it's a reprint?" Conrad speculated from over my shoulder.

"Dozens of them? That all look slightly different?" I tilted my head in thought.

Based on the conversation we'd just heard parts of, whoever these belonged to wasn't supposed to be in here.

"Practice makes perfect." Conrad opened another poster cannister. And just like mine, it was a stack of near-identical painted works rolled together. The same ocean and shoreline there too.

The painting styles were similar. Light and wispy brush strokes juxtaposed against the color scheme that was deep and practically exploding with emotion. All landscapes too. I took out my phone and tried to snap as many pictures as I could. "Yeah, but why?"

It looked as though someone was attempting to master this one specific painting style and these forgotten canvases showcased their efforts in improving the technique. The version Conrad held up looked to have fluffier brush strokes in the cresting waves, while the two I'd just taken shots of were a *bit* sleeker, more refined, with the rocks appearing hyper-realistic.

"A few of them are signed," Conrad said as my mind began to wander. I couldn't make out the signature, but I zoomed in with my camera and took a few pictures anyway. "Maybe they're meant to be forgeries."

"I wonder..." I stood and heard him rolling up and sliding the works back to where we'd found them.

I walked to the easel that sat front and center of the room. It was positioned in front of the paned window, so I didn't need to use my phone to study it; the twilight outside was already doing the heavy lifting. It was a landscape that resembled the works splayed out on the studio floor behind me, only this one had a cottage beside a river at sunset. No waves. But similar blues and purples.

Conrad approached and he waited for me to capture what I needed.

Then, he stepped forward, ran his finger over a blotch of the inky blue and showed me the pad with a cocked brow. The paint hadn't dried despite it being at least six or seven hours since anyone had been in here—no one would be so reckless with the dinner's preparations underway.

"I think you're onto something, Watson." He smiled.

The air between us shifted. Not as heavy as it had been *in* the storage closet and not awkward like it was directly *after* the storage closet. It was light but enthralling. Like every breath was laced with something hallucinogenic.

"You can call me Mal. Everyone else does."

"Oh." His brows arched. "Sorry."

"I don't mind," I added offhandedly. "But why am I Watson? I'm doing the heavy lifting here."

"Watson was the smarter one." The innocent look plastered all over his face felt like friendly fire.

"I am *no* sidekick." I took one last picture and tucked my burner back into the pocket of my dress. I raised one hand in the air and held it flat like a line. "Me." My other hand came up to float a few inches below it. "You. Got it?"

He rolled his tongue from one cheek to the other, a smirk tugging at the side of his jaw.

Butterflies. Everywhere. Flapping their wings in dizzying unison.

"You want to be on top of me?" He shrugged. "Got it."

And with that, he crossed the distance of the small studio back to the door. He opened it and tipped his head out into the hallway, his eyes shining with mischief.

WE MADE our way back down the narrow hallway and into the atrium. The twenty or so dinner tables, each perfectly set with crystal stemware and crisp white tablecloths, were spread concentrically around the circulation desk. Covered by towering floral arrangements, I could hardly recognize the same desk that I often used to locate old literature.

Just to the left of the entrance was the bar, and as we made our way to it, we were met with a hushed voice. One that did not sound the least bit impressed. "Where have you been?"

I caught Conrad's flinch before he masked it and braced myself for what Mr. Hastings would say next.

"Reading? Half of this building is a library." A knowing smile inched up one side of his mouth. The side closest to me. "Dad, you remember Malena."

His father bristled, skating a hand through his salt-and-pepper hair as he glanced around. "Conrad. I brought you here to speak to some of the other important families, not run around with—"

"You'll have to excuse my father," Conrad cut in sharply, shooting a glare at his dad. "He's not normally so rude."

I knew I should have been a little offended, but more than anything, I envied the courage. I hardly ever had the guts to be *that* flippant with my parents, and when I was, it didn't end well.

"Yes." His dad cleared his throat. "You'll have to excuse me, my wife is the social—"

"Your *wife* is considering a divorce," Conrad interrupted with a satisfied smile. He put a supportive hand on his dad's shoulder. "Don't worry, I'm here as emotional support."

My jaw hung open. This would be the part of the movie where I got smacked.

"Oh. Good for her," was what popped out of my mouth. My eyes went wide and I brought my fingers up to brush my lips.

While I did my best to stay away from it, I had a general sense of campus gossip. And I'd read the newspaper every day since I was a kid. When a media magnate had a public affair, it tended to make waves.

"Good for everyone," I corrected, my pulse thrumming. I wasn't Conrad Hastings; I wasn't allowed to be flippant.

Mr. Hastings's face remained stone-cold serious, but Conrad chuckled under his breath.

I didn't know what it was about Conrad, but I kept forgetting to put up the appropriate facade around him.

Mr. Hastings smiled tightly at me then nodded at his son before walking away with a tense "We'll talk later."

"I should apologize." I looked to Conrad when it was just the two of us again. "*You* should apologize."

"Nah. My mom kicked him out, so I've got a few weeks of him *trying* to be half decent before she inevitably takes him back." He gave me an appraising look. "Besides, that was awesome. Some people need to hear the bitter truth, so let's consider it a public service and move on."

"Well, I meant it. Good for your mom." My mind snagged on that, reminding me that he hadn't actually told me anything about his family's situation. The last thing I needed was Conrad thinking I kept tabs on him. "Not that I know your mom, but like, good for *both* of them."

Heat scalded my cheeks, and I cleared my throat. What the hell was happening?

He blinked a couple of times.

"I mean..." I faltered. *Get a grip, Mal.* "Two people who don't want to be together shouldn't be." My voice jumped an octave, but I ran with the pivot. "Like my parents. They'd be better off without each other."

He tilted his head and watched me for a beat. "Huh. I thought rooting for your own parents' divorce was strictly an Upper East Side thing."

The nervous energy evaporated, like walking in to air conditioning after being out in the hot sun.

"Trust me, it's not." I was sure there were plenty of first-generation kids like me whose parents' social mores were stuck in the year they left their home country. For my parents, that was 1980s India. "They won't get divorced because of how it would look. They're white-knuckling it to the grave."

"Impressive," he noted lightly.

It illustrated what they wanted for me: the stability and social check mark that came with marriage, not the happiness that came with love. I tried not to dwell on it—the fact that my happiness never really factored into the equation for them.

"Oh definitely. Their screaming matches are the stuff of legend." Oddly, it felt like telling a story. It felt *easy*, like talking to Cora or Sabrina. I found myself relaxing, and I didn't bother questioning the revelation before I continued. "I used to have to do my schoolwork in my closet, tucked away with a little lamp plugged into an extension cord. The clothes did a pretty good job of muffling the yelling."

Before I invested in a pair of noise-canceling headphones, it was my go-to spot. Eventually, I retreated in there when I needed some quiet, even if it wasn't to study.

"My parents aren't really the yelling kind," he stated, eyeing a platter or hors d'oeuvres as a waiter passed us by. "Dad cheated. Mom ignored it. It was all very civil."

"Lucky bastard," I said through a laugh, unsure when this conversation had turned so dark. "Quiet is hard to come by."

"Wait." He turned completely to face me. "Is that why you have that little cave under your desk in the newsroom?"

I stood up straighter. "No."

"Oh my God, it is," he reeled. "Do you study under the desk?"

"It's surprisingly effective," I argued. "And I have a perfect GPA, so maybe trust the process instead of making fun?"

He chuckled and smiled so warmly my stomach did pirouettes. "You're a little weird, Holmes."

I tilted my head and studied him, my lips quirking up at the sides despite my best efforts.

I learned long ago that being myself was only safe around

select people, so to be standing here in a thousand-dollar dress I borrowed from Sabrina's closet, surrounded by influential people and feeling at ease? Not feeling that reflexive need to cover my identity in half-truths? Well, that was rare.

I told myself that it was because Conrad was low-stakes. He didn't expect me to be anything, so there was no *need* to be anyone other than myself.

And, *God*, that felt good.

CHAPTER 17

Malena

The weekend after the fundraising event, I was riding on a wave of optimism because I'd been hyper-productive all week. I proofed two pieces for Dillian, studied for both my upcoming biochem exam and the MCATs, and helped Cora with what was a Winchester tradition: juniors v. seniors for the Armistice Games.

So, today, on a bright and sunny Sunday morning, I decided to take Kash up on his invitation.

But, when I arrived at Biscuits on the Bay, one of my favorite weekend brunch spots, it became immediately clear that I'd been invited out with his entire friend group.

Not on a date.

If anything, it was an audition. And instead of leaving like I knew Cora would have yelled at me to do, I sat there and tried to make conversation. That old desire to be friends with them hadn't just vanished when Kash and I broke up, I just stopped trying to claw my way into fitting in.

"Hasn't that been a stalemate for the last... I dunno, century?" Nara Desai, a friend of Kash's and one of the girls I'd tried to befriend and struck out with freshman year, asked with a bored sigh.

She and Sonali sat at one end of the table with me while Kash and his two guy friends were deep in conversation on the other.

"Yeah... That's what makes it cool," I insisted, my chair squeaking as I shifted in it. I had trouble containing my excitement about the plans for the Armistice Games on Tuesday. I was just about to explain how Cora and I and a few other juniors were planning to win them this year.

Given that Winchester was the original Ivy League school, it preceded even the American Revolution. Armistice Day was when defeated British soldiers were allowed safe passage through our campus, since they'd laid down their arms. Now it was commemorated with a friendly game of capture the flag —or in Winchester's case, a pennant—between the junior and senior classes. Each class hid their flag and was tasked with finding the other's.

Nara shrugged and looked at her nails. "Maybe we have different definitions of *cool*."

That feeling of not being enough was back and whispering in my ear *go, get up, leave.*

Trying to ignore the awkwardness, I looked at Sonali. "Cora has been helping us figure out its location ahead of the games."

"Oh." Sonali smiled warmly. "She's a programmer, right?"

"Cora's a genius, she's good at everything," I confirmed proudly, a weight lifting off my lungs. Campus traditions were fun, and I intended to enjoy my time here as much as I could, no matter how "uncool" it was to others. "She's running an algorithm on class schedules for persons of interest against a campus map. It should help."

"Cora's the one who had purple hair last semester, yeah?"

Nara's tone dripped judgement. She flicked an expectant look up to Sonali, then turned her attention back to her nails.

Sonali didn't meet her gaze, instead looking down at the polished wood table.

Indignation made my muscles go rigid.

"Cora changes it when she feels like it," I snapped.

"So, who do you think knows where the senior pennant is?" Sonali cut in.

I wanted to leave, but the mental image of Mom's genuine —if a little prideful—smile when I talked about making friends with Sonali and the dance team girls kept me firmly planted in my seat. Maybe I was the problem. Maybe I was too sensitive.

I swallowed the anger that pushed up my throat and welled behind my eyes. "We aren't sure..."

"Oh, maybe that lacrosse player I saw you with a few weeks ago knows?" Nara jumped into the conversation again, her voice carrying across the packed dining area. "Or was he just one of the guys on your brack—"

I pushed my chair back, the squeak barreling over the conversation.

Kash looked over to our end of the table, bewildered.

Don't cry. Don't cry. Don't cry.

"I think I'm gonna go." Leaving behind the pancakes I only picked at and the hot chocolate I hadn't even touched, I stood. Frankly, I was a little embarrassed with myself for not leaving when Cora was brought up and the conversation turned judgmental.

I threw a few bills on the table and threaded around the booths, not stopping when Sonali called my name, likely trying to smooth over the prickliness. The most annoying part was that Kash stayed seated, not even attempting to check that I was all right.

I STEPPED out onto the sidewalk and sucked in a deep breath of the crisp air that whipped off the bay.

Glancing into my bag, I realized that I brought both my phones by accident. I sighed and shoved them to the side, pulling out the paper bag with *Bardam Books* stamped on the side. Brunch was a bust, but at least it gave me an excuse to stop in at the bookstore down the road beforehand.

Making my way down the tree-lined sidewalk, with October a few days away, their leaves had started to burst with color. I took a few more steps until awareness struck me and I looked up, stopping in my tracks.

Broad shoulders. Sharp jaw. Intrigued glint in his eyes.

Conrad.

Dressed in a crew shirt and quilted brown jacket with a tartan lining, he looked... well, he looked *good*. A brown paper bag with the Bardam stamp was tucked under his arm and he had an athletic backpack slung over his shoulder. A casual smile crested on his lips as he dipped his chin. "Holmes."

I blinked away the momentary surprise and I smoothed a hand down my hair, realizing it was probably messy because I'd been nervously running my fingers through it. "Watson."

He craned his neck and looked past me inside the restaurant. "Rough morning?"

Did I look *that* bad?

"Oh, no," I sputtered.

The Biscuits on the Bay door opened with the jingle of a bell, and nerves filled my gut. I blinked a few times and cleared my throat.

"I was getting coffee and ran into my ex," I lied. That was a much less humiliating way to explain what just happened.

"Ex?" He quirked a brow.

"Yeah..."

Conrad's mouth curved into a tight smile and he acknowledged someone. I looked over my shoulder to find Kash and a couple of his friends waving politely.

He hummed, drawing my attention back, and nodded slowly. "Makes sense."

After the morning I'd had, that was all the excuse I needed to go from frazzled to annoyed. What the hell did that mean? "I'm sorry?"

"Nothing," he noted plainly.

"No..." I demanded, planting a hand on my hip and cocking it to the side. "What?"

"Let me guess. He broke your heart, so no more relationships for Malena?"

My shoulders relaxed. Right. My flings-only rule. I forgot I told him about that. "Took Psych 101, did you?"

He chuckled. "Some things are pretty predictable."

My nerves cooled.

"*He's* not the reason for it," I admitted softly, although whenever a guy questioned me on it, they all assumed the same thing: I'd had my heart broken and was wary. I didn't correct them because *mommy and daddy won't let me date* felt infantile and embarrassing.

"An exception to the rule." He crossed his arms. "I'm intrigued."

I rolled my eyes. I knew he was teasing to be charming or whatever, but I wasn't in the mood to talk about Kash.

"What are you doing in town?" I asked instead.

"I was rowing my little boat." He cocked his head to the side, toward the end of the street that led down to the water. If you followed the shoreline north, you'd pass campus and reach the shell houses for the men's and women's teams. "And grabbing a book." He held the brown bag up like a prize, then notched his chin toward my bag, the one currently spitting out Post-its and page tabs. "Stocking up for the bunker?"

A laugh bubbled out of me.

For the first time all day, it felt like the perpetual state of auditioning was behind me and I could simply *be*. I tucked my book back inside my bag and crouched to pick up the pieces of paper that must've flown out during my earlier rummaging.

Conrad picked up a yellow sticky note I must've missed and I took it from his fingers, tucking it inside the pocket of my jacket.

"All a part of the studying process," I said with a nod. "Although, most of these are to annotate my books."

Of the three books I'd purchased, two were romance novels from my favorite author because I loved the peace of a happy ending. The other was a fictional memoir of a dressmaker living through the French Revolution that sounded interesting.

"Turning a hobby into an assignment?" he teased.

Maybe it was the distance between the crowd inside or maybe it was the earthy, damp air that always blanketed New England this time of year, but relief washed over me. I grinned and looked around at the storefronts, each boasting a little stoop decorated with kitschy flair. A couple of benches lined the curbs and the occasional black trash receptacle cleverly shaped like a flower in bloom sat beside them.

"The tabs are a *part* of the hobby," I corrected, then looked up at the tinted windows bracketing the entrance to Bardam Books—a little stunned we had a hobby in common.

"You look surprised," he ventured, like he knew what I was thinking. "I *can*, in fact, read."

"Mhm." My toes and fingers tingled. I *loved* reading, it was a way to escape into a world that wasn't my own. Before the burner phone, it'd been my only way out. "What did you get?"

He handed me the bag and I pulled the paperback out. The black cover illustrated a man facing a large lake house with lights on in a few of the windows. *Dark and eerie,* the cover seemed to scream.

"A mystery?" I asked, passing it back to him. "A little on the nose, no?"

"What kind of sidekick would I be if I didn't study my craft?"

My lips burst into a wide smile and I heard myself let out a snort-giggle.

He had enough grace to step right over my fumble as he said, "I showed you mine. It's only fair."

I shrugged and gave in, pulling out one of the books at random to reveal an illustrated cover with a race car on an empty track and two people looking very annoyed with each other under a checkered banner. A woman with a microphone in her hand and the man, presumably the racer, with his arms crossed.

"F1 fan?" he said, and softly lifted it from my hand.

"Yeah, I guess," I answered. F1 on its own was cool, sure: high-performance cars, strategy and data analysis, championship points... but I liked the books because of all the travel. "It's like a trip around the world in every book."

"All the Scroll & Ivy initiates went to the Sao Paolo grand prix last year." Conrad paged through the first chapter.

"Damn, I picked the wrong year to—"

"Steal your best friend's spot?" He looked up and handed it back to me.

A skitter ran across my nerves. "It was *one* time."

His lips formed a mocking slant. "By my count, it's at least two."

"You know..." All my newfound energy funneled down to my foot as it tapped eagerly against the pavement. "You make it very hard to be nice to you."

"You say that like you've tried."

His eyes caught mine in a hold I didn't want to break. I

sort of liked that he could catch me off guard. Hit a shot that I'd miss.

It was a novel feeling.

A quiet moment passed between us, filled only with the distant sound of the bay and the occasional rustle of leaves.

He moved a step closer. "Speaking of Scroll & Ivy, the next event is in a week."

"Oh yeah?" My voice lowered now that he stood only a few inches away.

"It's tradition to have a game and a trip every semester."

"Like the Armistice Games?" My ears perked up.

I loved games of all kinds. Hell, every birthday party I was allowed to have growing up was at laser tag. And after spending the better part of a half hour explaining my plans for the Armistice Games to disinterested ears, this felt like a reward.

"Sort of... This one's more Scroll & Ivy specific. Ishani suggested our own version of *The Most Dangerous Game* on the Rutherford family estate," he said offhandedly. "With paintball guns, obviously."

"Obviously," I drawled.

"But James has something else in mind. It's a scavenger hunt all over campus. It sounds sort of lame..." He rubbed the back of his neck. "I swear it'll be fun though. And these games can be—"

"I love a game," I blurted, finding a surprising thrill in knowing we had another thing in common.

His eyes brightened then flicked up to over my shoulder to where Kash and his friends had been moments ago. "Great. It'll finish up on a boat in the harbor. It's an all-day thing, so you might miss a date."

"I'll live."

He took another step closer. "Good." His eyes moved along the street and then anywhere but me when I caught the implication. "I mean…" he stammered, his laugh choppy as he took a step back. "Isha takes games very seriously. Full roster and all."

The mention of Ishani sparked something in my head. I kept circling back to the idea that someone who knew about all the catacombs had to be involved in this painting mystery we'd yet to uncover. How else would they be so sure about where to enter and where they led?

The assumption cut the student body down to a very manageable list: all thirty current members of the Scroll & Ivy.

"Well, I *could* always use some fodder in case that forgery idea of yours falls through," I teasingly excused, like I wasn't interested.

Maybe it was a bit of cover so he wouldn't notice the delight that had to be plastered all over my face. Because the parts of me he knew were *me*, the real Malena. That simple fact was oddly thrilling.

I couldn't put words to the feeling, but it was like slipping out of a too-snug dress after a long night of carefully maneuvering in it. My constantly code-switching mind reveled in the ease. It was an addicting feeling.

"Text me the details?" I asked.

He gave me a playful salute and passed me on the sidewalk, calling over his shoulder, "You got it, Holmes."

I grinned and made my way over to a wrought-iron bench, deciding to crack open my book and spend the rest of the morning in the sun. The optimism that brunch drained had been refilled, and I didn't want to question it. Not when it felt this good.

CHAPTER 18

Conrad

Keiran's Irish Pub was every bit a raucous as I'd expected, given that the highly anticipated Armistice Games were back on.

More correctly, they were already won.

Through the crowds of people, I spotted her across the room. Five-seven, bright brown eyes, impossibly shiny hair I wanted to run my fingers through. Mal stood at the bar, a thin knit sweater over a dark skirt, her head craned up between the two guys vying for her attention. It'd been all of two days since I last saw her in town—looking a little frazzled but completely adorable—and she was all I'd thought about.

"Apparently the juniors had a group chat monitoring the persons of interest," Sage explained. We'd slept together a few times, usually when I needed to clear my head, and she seemed cool with the arrangement, so I was hoping that was all this was. She'd just spent ten minutes practically gushing about how the juniors had managed to pull off a victory this year. And I'd spent that time trying not to stare at Malena. "A few of the fraternity presidents, some athletes, the student body president, all were being surveilled. Can you believe it?" she said, sounding awestruck. "The juniors knew their class schedules and texted each other whenever they spotted them at any particular spot. All of that data got run through some algorithm and popped out the most likely locations for where the pennant was hidden."

Mal leaned her back against the bar while one of the guys hovered a little *too* close to her.

"Really..." I droned, hoping she wasn't expecting more of my input.

"Yeah, the overlapping locations led them to the Arthur Winchester statue. The senior pennant was curled into his hand, completely hidden."

The only rule when hiding the pennant was that it had to be somewhere on campus where any student could retrieve it. Given how large the campus was, most years, nobody found it. The games ended in a stalemate, and everyone partied just the same.

Except this year. And Mal was involved because of *course* she was. I was finding myself anticipating the next delightfully surprising thing I'd learn about her. She wasn't kidding the other day when she said she liked games.

A frustrated huff cut across my thoughts as Sage bobbed her head in my line of vision. I met her gaze and smiled apologetically.

"Unbelievable, right?" she added.

"Yeah." I tried to keep my focus on Sage. I really did. But the guy standing next to Mal was crowding her space, and his hand was moving down her back as he leaned in to say something in her ear. "Unbelievable."

Mal smiled at him.

My molars ground together and I rolled a shoulder to loosen the uncomfortable tightness in my chest.

A brief shuffling pulled me back to the booth just in time to see Sage leaving. Good for her, honestly.

I stood, making no attempt to stop her, instead searching my mind for a good excuse to interrupt whatever flirting was happening at the bar. But my legs were moving before I could think of one.

I closed the space, weaving between hordes of mostly drunk juniors until I finally got to her. "Holmes."

Her eyes raked over me, the corners of her mouth tipping up. "Watson."

I relished that feeling—her eyes on me.

"'Holmes'? 'Watson'?" the guy—who was probably an athlete if the Winchester Athletics jacket draped over his shoulders was any indication—said in an impossibly slow drawl.

My gaze stayed fixed on Malena, ignoring the guy who I'd decided wasn't worthy of her time. "I hear congratulations are in order."

"My condolences to your class." She feigned an apologetic pout. "Outmatched and outmanned. A shame."

"You were finding a pennant," I said dryly, "not performing a craniotomy."

"And where is the junior class's pennant, hmm? Since, apparently, it's so easy to find, why didn't the seniors find it?" She notched her chin up and looked around the crowded bar patronizingly. "Oh, right."

I chuckled, and that familiar unsettling feeling I'd become used to in her presence was back, tapping rapidly alongside my heartbeat. "Did you ever stop to think that maybe we didn't bother looking for the junior pennant in the first place? It was a nice little tradition we had going, a century of stalemates."

The seniors did look, and like every other year, they'd come up empty. Everyone assumed the juniors would too.

And I wasn't going to admit to her just how fucking cool it was that she found it.

She gave me a hard look.

"*Tradition* is a very nice way to phrase *cycle of mediocrity*." She was shoved to the side a little from the moving crowd, and it brought her body even closer to mine. "Besides, games are fun and they make for a good story."

"They do." I leaned in a fraction of an inch, but just as I opened my mouth, the delicate tension snapped at the sound of a throat clearing.

Right. That guy.

"Oh. You're still here." I flicked a glance over to him for a millisecond before landing it back on her. "Sorry, was I interrupting?"

Her eyes narrowed in amusement and bounced between us. She crossed her arms. "No, you're not."

Dismissed, the guy huffed and walked off, leaving me to my delightful menace.

"And I don't think you're sorry either," she added.

"You're right," I conceded. "But you don't seem particularly devastated."

"He was cute. Tall," she stated, tilting her head to look past me in whatever direction he went. Indifference clung to her words, like she was explaining a math problem. "Plays rugby, probably has pretty decent—"

"Head injuries?"

Her lips curved up, and my pulse thrummed in anticipation.

"Not every sport is as *tame* as rowing."

"Tame?" Excitement popped down my nerves. "The racing part? Or the strong current part?"

"How about the sitting down part?" She cocked her head to the side, leaning in a fraction.

"What we lack in cerebral trauma we make up for in stamina." I could practically feel her breath on my lips we were so close. "I'd be happy to prove it to you."

Crimson warmed the tops of her cheeks. She opened her mouth only to close it, and her eyes flickered, searching.

The realization hit me with the same shot of adrenaline I got every time I raced. I caught her off guard—whatever sparring match this was, I'd won.

I basked in the novelty.

"I was thinking about you the other day." She took a half step back and hopped on the barstool that'd just freed up. The lines along the column of her throat shifted as she busied herself ordering a drink. "After seeing you outside the bookstore in town."

"Oh yeah?"

It was only fair that I crossed her mind since she'd taken up residence in mine.

"Yeah, I wanted to ask you. That painting in the center of the mausoleum? It's a Van Holden, right?"

By *you* she'd actually meant *us*. Scroll & Ivy.

Disappointment curdled in my stomach. "Yeah... I think so."

I did know that, mostly because I'd been a little curious after all the evidence in front of me. An unsealed door in the catacombs. Rare paint that someone was using to make dozens of the same painting...

Those facts were more interesting than my paper on the effects of inflation on price stabilization in global markets. And they served as the perfect distraction. I'd spent an hour last night on a reverse image search hunting for information on any of those paintings we saw in the studio the night of the president's dinner.

Nothing concrete, but Nicolas Van Holden's work had come up as a potential match. I didn't think much of it.

"How did it get there?" Malena asked.

"I dunno." That painting was massive, spanning what was easily a twenty-foot wall. "The front doors?" I guessed, but the look on her face told me she was back to fixating. "You can't seriously believe someone brought that giant painting in from the catacombs."

"Maybe." She chewed on her lip, and I tried not to stare. "I don't know why they would go through the effort..." She sighed. "Or maybe I'm biased because I've always thought they were this cool myth and I've just discovered they're very much real. Either way, I'm going to go to the Amherst Building's archives tomorrow to see if there's a record of his pieces. A lot of art from that time is lost and—"

"You didn't have any luck matching the pieces we found in the studio on a reverse image search either?"

"No, I didn't..." Her cheeks lifted in a teasing smirk. "Were you... helping?"

"My name's on it too, remember? I'll come with you and we can get through the archives faster."

"You don't have to, I know it's boring," she said, like she was trying to convince me of her disinterest. Which was impossible to believe because she practically glowed whenever it came up. "Filling in the missing pieces is the least interesting part of all this."

No, it was quickly becoming the *most* interesting part.

A lifetime of having my last name and generally pleasing face be all I needed to gain entry to anything I wanted, *this* was new. I had to work for this—*wanted* to work for this.

"I want to help," I answered plainly.

I could have pushed for her to finish the piece and call it a day. I could have insisted that we be done with this partnership and returned to focusing on crew and getting through my last year of undergrad.

But I wanted something else.

I wanted *more*.

The story, the work, the playful sniping, that candied lemon scent, the smile I couldn't stop seeing in my head.

The only thing I knew for sure was that I wanted *more* of everything.

CHAPTER 19
Malena

The next day, I set myself up in my usual secluded corner in the library.

Sunlight streamed through the stained-glass windows and colorful bars lit the otherwise dull timber-framed wall. Here, in the back, behind rows of mahogany bookcases, a few glossy wooden tables were made available.

My fingers ran over the foil-lettered invitation to the annual Diwali party being hosted on campus. I pushed it into a book when I heard movement coming my way and settled back into the rigid seat, breathing in the scent of old paper.

"Holmes." I closed my eyes briefly. His voice felt like the gentle pinches from the derma roller Cora bought me for my birthday last year. "Any luck?"

I looked over my shoulder and the warm gleam in his cerulean eyes *almost* held my complete attention. And they would have, had it not been for the way his dark gray crew-neck sweater fit him *just* right. Slightly loose except in certain spots, like the way it snagged on his sleeves and strained with his every move. Or when the fabric grew taut against his chest when it filled with air.

Like right now, as he smiled at me.

My lungs burned.

"No, not yet." I scooted over to make space for him on the bench. "But I only started a few minutes ago."

"Oh yeah?" He sat down and the space between us disappeared. He paged through a book titled *American Impressionists* he must've just pulled from a shelf. "I was sure that you'd be here early."

He settled in and pulled a folded sheet of paper from his backpack, laying it open. My eyes moved down the list and I made out familiar names. The few I recognized were of painters. With my brain trying to catch up, I managed to spit out, "What's that?"

"After seeing that piece in the studio, I did a little digging and figured it was meant to resemble an impressionist painting." He flipped through a few more pages then reached toward my stack from the archives, running his fingers over the spines of both before he nodded and pulled one open. "I made a list of painters from the late 1800s who had *some* prominence, then cross-checked their works with what I remembered from the piece in the hazard-taped studio."

I watched him riffle through the pages, noting how long the list was. At least twenty-five names, which told me he'd likely been working on this since we went our separate ways in town last weekend.

My mouth hung open. "You did all this in five days?"

"Yeah." He didn't look up, just kept bouncing his eyes over the pages and scribbling in a leatherbound notebook he'd pulled from his bag. "I was curious."

Regardless of whether he was helping out of obligation or because he was genuinely interested in the article, it was... *ugh*. It was cute. And he had no business being cute while looking like *that*.

"What's this?" Conrad asked a few minutes later, holding

up the invitation to the Diwali event. He flipped from the English side to the one with *The Festival of Lights* written in various languages. At the bottom of the back side, announced in Hindi, was the date and venue—which Conrad appeared to be mouthing. He looked up after a minute and said, "I went a few years ago."

"You can read that?"

"I thought we already established that I can, in fact, read," he noted offhandedly, then grinned to himself in confirmation that what he'd read was translated in his head correctly. When I didn't answer, an unreasonably charming smile pinched his cheek. "Not just a pretty face."

"You... can read Hindi?" I amended, still sounding incredulous to my own ears.

"Not well." He shrugged, attention back on his ancient book, now flipped to a chapter on the early 1900s. "Isha and I made a bet back at Le Rosey. She bet that I couldn't make it to the top of the mountain and ski back before class one morning." His eyes took on a faraway look, and I noted the fondness in them. "If she won, I had to learn Hindi. If I did, she had to learn the Viennese Waltz."

"So, you lost?"

He shook his head.

"She cheated. She had James stop the ski lift I was on." He thumbed another page and kept reading as though this story wasn't *wild*. "Anyway, we called a draw. I learned basic, conversational Hindi, and she learned the stuffy dance. If anything, I'm the real winner here. I learned *some* of a language and she learned a skill only useful in 1700s Vienna."

He said it all simply, like the fact that bopping around world-class ski slopes at his boarding school in *Switzerland* was a regular occurrence. "You went to boarding school with all your friends?"

Was I the only one who showed up to college without a

built-in group of friends? I shook my head. Thank God for Cora and Sabrina, or I'd be alone.

"No, just me, Isha, and James. Felix and Lucy we met here. So..." He lifted the card between his fingers. "Are you going?"

"Oh." I wasn't planning on it. Cora wouldn't be around and Sabrina was thousands of miles away. When I was with them, my world felt full and vibrant, but without them, it felt like... like a reminder that there was a flaw in my code. That I didn't belong. And as much as I loved Diwali, I hated the reminder. "I... um, I'm..."

He looked up from the book and his striking blue eyes managed to once again pull a bizarre stream of consciousness from me. "I love the holiday. When I was a kid, we used to have a big party with all my cousins. We'd get dressed up and dance for most of the night," I began. "I always ended up eating so much jalebi that I got sick..." His mouth curved up in a smile, inviting me to go on. This time, I blinked it away. "But, no. I probably won't go."

His smile fell. "Why not?"

"I usually go with my friends, but the party is right before fall break and they won't be around."

"So *you* can't go?"

"It's..." Irritation crinkled between my eyes.

"Don't tell me you're scared to go by yourself." A light, disbelieving chuckle moved through his lips. "The same person who would have wandered around probably haunted catacombs alone?"

"No," I retorted, my voice getting louder in the quiet space. "I just... don't feel like it."

He wouldn't understand what it felt like to discover that all the places you *should* have fit in were in fact inhospitable. "*You* wouldn't get it."

"I was only saying—"

"I don't fit there." The words flew out of my mouth, and

even though they caused my pulse to hike in embarrassment, I hoped they at least warranted an exit to this conversation. "Drop it, okay?"

"I'm sorry." The sincerity in his voice made my heart stumble, but I focused my attention on the books in front of me.

"It's fine." I swallowed the emotion that clogged the back of my throat and gestured to the table. "We still have a stack of these to get through."

"Right."

The tense air dissipated, but we spent the next thirty minutes or so paging through the archives in silence.

After getting through a stack of American impressionists, Conrad leaned back against the bench and stretched an arm out. This close, the cedary scent in his cologne clouded around me, giving me what I was sure was a contact high, because I was suddenly dizzy.

Maybe it was that downright slutty sweater.

He blew out a long breath and pinched the bridge of his nose. "They *look* like Van Holden pieces, but not a single one ticks all the boxes. Matching color palette, slightly different subject. Right subject, slightly different background. Nothing matches *exactly*."

"So much for forgeries." My voice faltered because at that moment, his thumb drew a tiny line up and down along the soft wool fabric of my sweater that hung over my shoulder. I kept my attention ahead. "Why forge something that never existed? Maybe it's an elaborate prank?"

My stomach see-sawed. Did he realize what he was doing? Either way, I didn't want it to stop.

I stayed completely still, reveling in the feeling. When Conrad didn't say anything, I turned my head to look at him. Under the warm yellow glow from our study cubby's Edison lamp, I could see the exhaustion beginning to line the corners of his eyes as he closed them. "Are you okay?"

"Tired is all," he answered as his head tilted back against the wall. "We're training for the Head of the Charles race. Two-a-days. I'm beat."

"See?" I teased. "Motivation *isn't* just for people who plan to die on Everest."

He shook with a silent laugh, his thumb continuing its up-and-back movement. "Don't ruin my reputation with all that motivation talk. It's only for the race."

A gentle stroke moved along my collarbone, and my breath caught.

"Right." I nodded, my pulse thrummed. "Boats and paddles and such."

Bright blue peeked out from beneath his eyelids and he smiled. He sat up and my shoulder immediately missed the light touch.

"Yup. Rowing and oars and such," he corrected gently. "The Head of the Charles is over in Boston. It's two days of races. The biggest regatta of the season, and people tend to fly from all over to spectate. Every year around this time is exhausting."

"That's pretty cool. Will your family be there?" His dad didn't seem like the cheering type, but surely there was more to his family. I thought back to his mention of brothers, of his mother who lived in the city.

Conrad chuckled again, but he looked down at my face, entirely serious, and his smile fell. "Oh. No," he answered indifferently. "But Isha and Lucy always tag along. Some years my mom comes too."

My brow furrowed. How neglected did you have to be to hear that question and assume it was a joke? Despite how often I felt suffocated, trapped, and perpetually misunderstood by my parents, at least I could never say I was *ignored.*

"Is she coming this year?"

He opened his mouth then closed it, his eyes dropping to the table. "Probably not."

"When is it?" I asked, then mentally scolded myself because now I felt like I was prying. We weren't exactly friends.

Though, maybe we were. Either way, my heart squeezed seeing the downright sullen look flash across his face.

I didn't have time to spiral too deep before he cleared his throat. "Two weeks, right before fall break. First race kicks off on the second Friday in October and goes all weekend."

"That's the day of the MCATs! My mom says it's an auspicious day," I stated brightly, unable to fight the urge to tell him something to make him feel better, even though he didn't seem to care that his family had no plans of showing up.

"Well, auspicious or not, I'll still have to train for two hours later today," he said through a short yawn.

"Yikes. I'll take studying in a dark cubby over cardio in freezing water any day."

"Oh." He blinked a couple of times. "Speaking of studying in a dark cubby."

He maneuvered on the bench and reached into his pocket, his chest momentarily pressing against me. An armada of tingles set sail along my skin.

He pulled out a key and dropped it in my hand.

"What's this?" I registered its weight and closed my fingers around the cool metal. It looked like the one he had in the catacombs that night.

"It's a key," he answered flatly. "You know, breaking into things isn't the only way—"

"And *this* key unlocks...?" I interrupted, the jitters making it all the way to my fingers.

"The mausoleum's back entrance. It's mostly empty when there isn't a party. May be a good spot to study if hiding under a desk like you're waiting out an earthquake isn't working for you."

My body fizzed. I ran my fingers over the bronze carvings. "This is Sabrina's?"

"Yeah." He leaned an arm on the back of the bench again, the already limited space between us disappearing. "Make sure she gets it?"

"Is that breaking a rule?"

He lowered his voice to a whisper. "I won't tell if you don't."

My stomach tumbled at the glimpse behind the impossibly charming smile or the reserved, sometimes biting humor. He was sweet. *This* was sweet. "I can go alone?"

"Don't take anyone with you and don't steal anything." His mouth curved, inching closer. "And *don't* go into the catacombs."

My heart beat erratically. "Can I read the books in the mausoleum?"

"Sure." His fingers played with the hem at my shirt's collar, and my skin pebbled beneath.

The Amherst Building had some strange power over us because it drew us into the same loop over and over again. At first, it was that night after discovering the unsealed door, coming up here to this section and then... that kiss. The one I couldn't help but replay at all the wrong times. Then a week later, on the other side of this exact building, shoved in a closet with professors and alumni and his *father* down the hall.

The familiar feeling—like mild electrocution—kept sparking between us. And all I wanted to do was let it.

"Careful..." My face warmed and I bit my cheek to tamp down the nerves swirling in my stomach. "Someone might think you're enjoying my company."

"I've never cared much for what other people think," he replied quietly. His fingers brushed a loose strand of hair behind my ear. The playfulness faded, and the look in his eye concentrated into something different. His lips, just inches from mine, pulled up on one side in a smirk. His voice lowered. "But... they'd be right."

A need blossomed between my thighs at the same moment his lips brushed over mine.

I leaned forward, chasing the feeling, and closed my ey—

"Gloves," barked a voice behind the bookshelf.

With a sharp inhale, I jolted in my seat, my nose knocking against his mouth. I scrambled to gather my things together on the desk, letting my hair fall over my shoulder to hide the furious blush on my cheeks.

Eyes dilated and unfocused, Conrad shook his head slightly, like he was snapping out of a dream.

"Sorry, Abby." I swallowed against the desert in my throat. Abigail, the hawkish librarian, crossed her arms and pushed her glasses—the ones attached to a beaded gold chain around her neck—up the bridge of her nose. "I'll put them on."

"I don't think so," she said in a huff, gloved hands grabbing the two rare books off our desk. "I expect better from you, Malena."

"Sorry." The reprimand yanked me back to reality as something I struggled to name crested over me. "I forgot, honestly."

I didn't know what I was feeling—hazy and lustful, sure, but there was more. The warmth that blanketed my chest was *new*.

And I didn't have a game plan for that.

"Well, thanks." I tapped Conrad's shoulder, motioning for him to move so I could get the hell out of here. Maybe douse myself with cold water while I was at it. "For the help."

"Oh." His chest caved with a sigh as he slid over and got up. "I... uh..."

"I have to get to class, I'll see you later." I hurried away, gaze pinned to the floor, and navigated between the narrow bookshelves that fortressed the study cubby in seclusion.

Not letting myself look back, I beelined out through the airy atrium. It flooded my mind with memories from the president's fundraiser—not the hallucinogenic kind from the storage closet, but the fun ones out here when this space was transformed for a posh dinner. I replayed the light banter. The relaxed smiles. The hypnotic ease.

I sped to the exit, my lungs begging for fresh air.

It was this building. That was all.

Reactive ingredients, proximity, and a catalyst. This building was our proximity and maybe everything we found in common, the catalyst.

I pushed the heavy doors open. The crisp autumn air moved through my nostrils and filled my lungs. I brushed off the tightness in my chest as nothing more than a fluke.

It was chemistry. Plain and simple.

Nothing more.

It *couldn't* be anything more.

CHAPTER 20

Malena

I made my way out of my American Lit class, deciding to spend the rest of the day and probably most of the night catching up on the semester's reading. Since we came up empty at the library yesterday, I reminded myself that the Keller Award wasn't the only thing at the top of my to-do list. Winning was a priority, but so was my rigorous course load—the one that would get me into medical school.

Waiting by the doors where I planned to meet Cora, one hand tucked into his joggers as he leaned against the wall and scrolled on his phone, was Kash. His brows jumped when he looked up and saw me coming. "Mal."

I stopped and gave him an expectant look. "Kash, what's up?"

It had been less than a week since our not-date at Biscuits on the Bay, and with how busy my days were at the moment, I'd forgotten all about it. Plus, I was having trouble thinking of anyone other than Conrad, which was its own new kind of problem.

"I wanted to apologize." He shifted his weight between his

legs, looking at the ground and then over my shoulder. "That probably wasn't what you'd been expecting."

"To be honest, I've hardly given it any thought." I gripped my books against my chest.

Even after Conrad managed to flip my mood, it took hours of binge-watching a juicy Korean drama to pull me out of my humiliated funk. But I wasn't going to let him know that.

"Nara..." He looked around. "She's a friend, and she can be protective, that's all."

"Got it," I said curtly. This was feeling less like an apology and more a justification, but whatever. "Anything else?"

"Wanna try again? Just you and me?" he asked. "Casual, like last semester."

It would appear that I failed at whatever ass-backward test brunch was, just as I'd thought. And yet, relief eased down my body.

"Maybe," I answered instead of the *no* I wanted to say. Because saying no felt like locking myself out of something. I wasn't sure what, exactly, but I didn't want to take that risk.

He opened his mouth, but we were interrupted when Cora barreled over.

"Mal!" She looped her arm in mine and didn't even acknowledge Kash. "We have fifteen minutes."

"I'll text you," he called as we hurried out the door.

I gave him a lazy wave over my shoulder, not bothering to look back.

Cora didn't ask me about Kash on our walk home even though I was sure she was curious. But we were both pretty excited for our weekly call with Sabrina.

When we walked in, she scurried into the kitchen for snacks while I set up my laptop.

"Did he at least apologize?" Sabrina asked five minutes later, after Cora finished summarizing her version of my conversation with Kash. Every friend group needed one person who wasn't afraid to make waves for the good of the group, and for me and Sabrina, that was Cora.

"Sort of." The words came out more like a question. "He asked me out again, *casual* this time. His words."

Cora froze and her mouth hung open. "What a little bitch."

"Honestly, I don't even care," I admitted. Flings-only had always been fine with me. "Either way, I don't have time right now between school, the MCATs, and my article."

"The one that has her playing some game with the other rich kids all over campus on Saturday," Cora cut in with a wolfish grin. "And, of course, the cute guy Mal is *definitely* not into."

Sabrina's eyebrows waggled. "What did I miss?"

"There's nothing going on," I insisted, regretting telling Cora about my weekend plans. The game that would *not* be their rendition of *The Most Dangerous Game*. Technically I still had one more event he agreed to let me go to. "Really, nothing."

"Cora?" Sabrina looked at her for confirmation.

"They may not have fucked, but she wants to," Cora reported.

"So... sleep with Conrad and get it out of your system..." Sabrina answered from the other side of the screen, like it was obvious. "You may not even be compatible. Sexually, I mean."

Thoughts of his hands on my waist and his lips pressing against mine flashed through my mind. "It's just a crush. Chemistry. A base-level attraction that'll pass in a week. Anyway, he's a deeply unserious trust fund baby."

The words were bitter as they left my mouth, because I knew he was more.

"A sexy one," Cora supplied unhelpfully.

I pushed a frustrated breath out through my nose. I could

use some sex. I hadn't had any since that night I went home with Jake the lacrosse player earlier this semester. Between my school work and the article, my sex life had dwindled. And the vibrator under the false bottom in my nightstand was putting in too many hours.

"Once the article is submitted, I'll sleep with him," I decided, slapping my hands together resolutely. I *could* fuck away whatever this feeling was. It'd never sprung up before, but I was sure a physical release would satiate it. "No mess. Neat and orderly."

The two-Malena system worked because I was organized. A fling followed by a clean break kept the lines clearly drawn.

"Hot," Cora drawled.

"Anyway..." I took a deep breath.

"I met a guy," Sabrina interjected, giving me a sympathetic look and the reprieve I needed.

Cora looked at me then Sabrina and shrugged, just as happy to move on to the next juicy topic. "Have sex with a cute accent." It was an item on Sabrina's semester abroad to-do list. She winked at the laptop screen and added, "Check?"

"Not yet," Sabrina answered. "We can talk about that *after* we hear about your leafing trip plans."

Cora's parents always took her on a trip for fall break. This year, they were going to Vermont to see the leaves change. It was sweet, and I envied the relationship she had with them. They knew *everything* about her, and I knew she confided in them almost as much as she did Sabrina and me.

I wondered what that was like. As far as my parents knew, I walked the straight and narrow, stayed in on the weekends, and aced all my classes. And they *still* found a variety of things to be upset about.

"You joke now, but we'll see who's laughing when I'm up to my ears in fresh maple syrup," Cora shot back, dipping a popcorn kernel in hot sauce and throwing it into her mouth with a laugh.

ON SATURDAY MORNING, I met the Scroll & Ivy members at the base of the clock tower for their game. The one Conrad had given me no real information on and I hadn't asked about because I was trying to keep some distance after that almost kiss a few days ago.

I stood alone because even though everyone knew I was there in Sabrina's place under her orders, I was still met with a healthy bout of skepticism. This being the only other event I was actually invited to—again, in Sabrina's place—it was also the only one where I'd be around members the whole time. When Conrad brought me to the mausoleum, we'd left the party within an hour and embarked on our catacomb adventure.

So, I kept to myself.

After James explained the task at hand, I carded through the set of hints. The game was actually pretty simple—a scavenger hunt, like Conrad mentioned at the pub. The senior members hid an object of some importance, and James gave the juniors a series of hints to find said object.

"What's the prize?" I asked aloud to myself as I walked the path that led back to campus. I kept my eyes on my sealed stack of cards so as to not catch Conrad's, because that kept happening.

He'd offered to drive me over to the tower earlier, but given that I was one motorcycle trip from mounting *him*, I figured it was best I come on my own and take notes quietly.

"I think it's more a glory thing," Azalea Burton, the junior I'd been introduced to briefly at the first Scroll & Ivy party, said. She was dressed in a cashmere sweater dress, black tights, and leather boots. She was seemingly one of the few others taking this game seriously.

I only spoke to her for a few minutes that night at the clock tower, but it'd left me curious. Azalea was from a notable enough family that she had relatives with journals on the Scroll & Ivy bookshelves. I might've been on high alert in my futile attempts not to get caught, but her words—*I'm surprised I got an invitation*—stuck with me.

I read the riddle on our first card and traced my finger on the image below it.

"It's an anagram," I announced to Azalea. The high noon sun shone bright overhead and I held the card closer, casting a shadow on the paper I tried to decipher. "Winner and garment?"

With very little in the way of progress with the mystery, there was a decent chance that my feature was going to be more in line with my original outline. Which was still great, and this scavenger hunt would only add to the narrative about the rift between the privileged students at Winchester and the regular ones. The legacies had their own everything: clubhouses; parties; hell, even their own campus traditions.

"*The Button.*" Azalea snapped her fingers and looked up at me. "On campus."

"The sculpture?" I asked.

It was a giant crimson button commissioned by the school years ago. That sculpture, along with a dozen others, made up the Artist's Walk on the west side of campus. Along a circuitous cobblestone path that connected the different arts buildings, the sculptures ranged from bronzed statues to modern abstract works, like *The Button.*

"Yeah, The Button," she said, like I should know what she meant. When I stared blankly, she continued. "It's society tradition: the first person to have sex there without getting caught wins." She looked back down at the next riddle. "We need to go there next... I'm an arts major, so I'm sure of it."

Azalea tore the next card open.

"Sex under *The Button*?" I grimaced; I was all for trying new things, but that couldn't be hygienic.

"Under, around..." Azalea's head bobbed. "It's more of a dare, but the first one to do it wins."

"Wins what?"

"Nothing. But it's a good story for the journals."

It made a lot of sense the longer I was around. "Seems to be the case with most of these games and excursions."

Each member would document them in their journal. And those stories would probably bond them together when they went out into the real world and needed the connections.

It all proved my point. Meritocracy was ultimately a myth too. And probably not one that would become real like the catacombs had.

"I have a question for you."

"Mm-hmm." She studied the next note.

Conrad glanced over from where he was talking to James and Ishani and I quickly looked away. Until he was no longer filed in the "cannot fuck yet" column, I needed to steer clear of him and those autumn sweaters he favored.

"What did you mean when you said you were surprised that you got an invitation?" I looked back to Azalea.

"Oh." She paused for a second as we reached the smaller quad where the sculpture was located.

"Sorry, I-I didn't mean to pry, I was just curious."

The Scroll & Ivy members thought I was here as a personal request by Sabrina. It wasn't as though I interacted with any of the other members at Winchester, so I understood her wariness at my presence... unless it was something else?

Her eyes flickered around the yellows and reds that

painted the trees as we resumed our slow crawl down the cobblestone path. "We've been in the papers. My dad has…"

"Oh. Sorry," I said quickly, immediately regretful. How had I already stepped on a landmine? I really needed to get some more background from Sabrina on these people before I put my foot in it again.

"It's fine, it involves his company, but when the FBI started seizing assets, I assumed the alumni committee might go the way of the country club board and revoke my membership."

I winced. As an outside observer to their world, it seemed as though some scandals—like cheating—were perfectly fine or at least tolerated. But losing money? Why did it not surprise me that a line would be drawn there.

"My grandparents, my mom's parents, they've been really nice," she chirped with levity, like she was trying to cheer *me* up. To assure *me* that she was fine. "They're helpful with tuition and stuff."

"That sounds tough," I empathized. Nobody should pity an old-money heiress, but I recognized the sound in her voice down to my bones. It was the unique melancholy of being outside of a world you thought you'd be welcome in. "I assumed admission to secret societies went down bloodlines, like heirlooms and IBS."

She squeaked a laugh. "You don't have to do that."

"Do what?"

"Be nice about it. I know how lucky I am."

"It's not being nice," I lied, but this time it was an attempt at a good deed. I linked my arm in hers. "I'm great with puzzles. You're an art major," I parroted her earlier credential. "And you're great with the lore. I propose a strategic alliance."

"For glory." She notched her chin up and smiled. "Can you stay once Sabrina gets back?"

I laughed. "I think the rules say every class is capped at

fifteen people." I pulled my arm back and held both hands up, gesturing a scale balancing back and forth. "Fifteen juniors, fifteen seniors."

"Well..." She sighed. "We make the rules, right? Why not change them?"

I smiled at the absurdity of it.

Rules were rigid, but that didn't mean I couldn't enjoy the occasional loophole.

CHAPTER 21

Conrad

Malena was avoiding me.

Successfully.

Which was impressive because we were on a boat.

After what had to be a record time of two hours, Malena and Azalea marched onto the dock with the first edition Walter Hugo novel that was hidden around one of the historic sculptures on campus.

Now, standing out on the deck wrapped in a blanket, she was deep in conversation with Alex Scott. And had been ever since Azalea went down to the galley awhile ago.

The thorny grip around my chest tightened and I knew, strangely, that it wasn't envy. It was confusion. I had no idea what I did to make her start avoiding me.

"Holmes," I interrupted. After a brief flash of what looked like concern, her shoulders rolled down. "Alex, you mind?"

He shot me a glare but kept moving, and Malena's eye skated up to meet mine.

"What the hell is a coxswain?" she asked quietly as Alex walked off to the larger sun deck at the bow of the boat where there were about fifteen people draped in blankets. Several members were seated around the bar, and the rest of the group had gone down to the galley.

Here, at the stern's more intimate sundeck, it was just Mal and me left.

I handed her a warm cider from inside. "The first position on the rowing team. They steer the rudder from their seat at the front, facing the rowers."

"That's a crew thing?" Her voice lowered with understanding. "I thought he was being disgusting."

With that, the awkward tension melted away and I wondered if she was actually avoiding me or if I'd been in my head this whole time for nothing. Something about her had every instinct scrambled. She was a flirt, which never bothered me until I saw it directed at another person.

"No, Alexander Scott really takes it seriously," I assured her. "His whole family is like that. They call his dad *The Captain*."

Malena winced. "Yikes." She turned and leaned her arms on the railing.

I chuckled to myself. "You know you really pissed off James by finishing that game so quickly."

A smile touched her lips. "My sister and I never missed an episode of *White Collar*. That has to count for something."

"I didn't know you had a sister."

"We're not close," she answered curtly, her smile falling to a straight line. "We used to be, when we were kids."

"If it makes you feel better..." Something about seeing that spark in her eyes dim made me want to light a new one. "Sitting in the same room to watch a TV show is a hell of a lot more than I'd ever get out of my brothers."

A corner of her mouth tilted up. "Oh yeah?"

"Most days I'm just waiting for the news that one poisoned the other," I admitted, and she laughed. The sound warmed every inch of skin it touched. "My money's on Tripp."

"And where do you fall into the mix?"

"I avoid it. I'd rather be the ne'er-do-well Hastings than anywhere near *that* murder mystery."

Her smile grew. I'd do anything to hold on to that feeling—the one of pulling away whatever was weighing her down.

"Is your sister trying to poison you?" I added dryly.

"I guess not. We're not nearly as ridiculous," she conceded. "Avani is..." She paused, and her eyes flickered back and forth. "She's perfect in all the ways that matter."

Talking to Malena was like walking through a hedge maze. I kept hitting dead ends, but I was determined to keep going. "And those are..."

She opened her mouth and took an inhale, like she was going to explain, then closed it again.

This time, I waited.

"We're different, I guess," she said finally. "It makes sense that we're not close anymore. She's a lot older. Already in residency."

"Smart and a doctor," I deadpanned. "It's like night and day."

Her shoulders rumbled with a tiny laugh. "We *are* different. But back when we were little, she used to humor me and read some of my kids' mystery books with me. Then we'd compete on who could solve the mystery first."

"Let me guess. You won?"

She pressed her lips together for a moment. "*Sometimes* I'd skip to the end of the book first."

I leaned in. "That's cheating."

"Only cheating myself, so it doesn't count." She held her hand up like it made more sense that way.

"You realize that sucks the fun out of finding out."

"Maybe, but it's peaceful." She smiled wistfully at the sun as it melted along the horizon.

I leaned my hips against the railing and turned to face her, inching closer. "So, it turns out that the best reporter at Winchester is on the pre-med track. Seems like a shame."

"I'll be a great doctor *and* a great writer. Two things can be true at once," she pointed out. "And this is going to sound conceited..."

I grinned. "Don't keep me in suspense."

"I'm smart. Top of my class, perfect GPA, flawless extracurricular record," she listed off. "It all comes naturally to me. It's stressful sometimes, but I can't waste that."

"Writing would be wasting it?"

Her brow lifted. "Have you ever compared the salary difference or job stability of a critical care physician to a writer?"

I lifted my hands. "Point taken."

"My parents had advanced degrees before they immigrated to the States. They had to redo all of it—it cost them time and money, years of sacrifice. They were incredibly intelligent but didn't have a lot of opportunities. And I..."

Her eyes flicked around the water.

"You have both."

She nodded.

"Stability is safety," she said, like she was repeating an earworm marketing campaign she'd heard a thousand times. "I like to write, so I do." She sighed. "I don't know, why shut any doors now?"

There was an optimism in her words that practically bathed her in a glow. Brilliant and impossible to look away from.

"That's why you want the Keller win," I surmised. "So you can keep writing too?"

It was prestigious and a big deal in the writing world. One

that had begun as a fun way to needle my dad, who was so sure I'd be a disappointment.

But all of that had changed over the last few weeks.

Now, I wanted to know what was going on with those paintings. And I wanted to figure it out with her.

"Part of it." Her voice swung up. "The money would—" She looked down at her glass.

The Keller Award was prized at a hundred thousand dollars. It wasn't nothing, that was for sure.

"It would help?" I offered.

"Yeah." She drew in a breath and turned the glass in her hand before looking me square in the eye. "You know... sad little rich boy is trite. *You* have a world of opportunities."

I wasn't *sad*, I just knew what it looked like when none of your effort mattered. It was plastered on my mom's face every time she learned of a new affair. "And only one correct answer."

I was well aware that I was lucky to live the way I did. But I envied Malena, because all of that ambition was going somewhere. She had control over what happened next, and not knowing the ending to a story made it a hell of a lot more compelling than one whose ending was unavoidable.

A judgmental divot carved between her brows.

"So?" she questioned with enough withheld disbelief I wasn't sure if she was actually confused.

"So..." I laughed nervously. The weight of her full attention was *heavy*.

But so fucking addicting.

"I mean, do both." She threw her hand up like it was obvious. "You're a business and English major, right?" she asked, and I nodded. "Great, then go to B-school, work at Hastings Media, and figure out what you want while you do it." She counted off on her fingers. "Being the ne'er-do-well Hastings is beneath you."

Mean and commanding—if I wasn't mistaken, that was her version of a compliment.

"And what, leave after that?" I drawled. It wasn't exactly an option, but just saying it aloud was exciting.

A warm buzz surrounded us, different than in the library. This time, it was like a magnet, pulling me closer to her.

"Or stay, if *God forbid* you enjoy the work." A tiny giggle cut through the seriousness. "Either way, make sure the trust fund clears first."

I barked a laugh. The idea was *almost* underhanded, yet another surprise out of Malena Amin.

Her voice lowered a bit, softer and more serious. "Seems unfair to give up what you want before you ever learn what it is."

"Yeah..."

She took a long breath, and in that millisecond, something shifted in the air between us.

She took a step back.

"Besides." She smacked my chest with the back of her hand—*friendly* and not at all flirtatious. "Ambition isn't *just* for people who plan to die on Everest."

I took the hint and stepped back myself.

She smiled, and I couldn't help but do the same.

Uncovering all of her many talents made me wonder because underneath all of that ambition was a measure of hopefulness. One she hung on to for some reason. Like she wasn't sure she'd get what she aspired for but would fight like hell anyway.

Which only confused me more, because if there was one person who was well-equipped to get everything they wanted, it was Malena.

CHAPTER 22

Malena

I was never going to get what I wanted. Not when what my parents wanted always came first.

I let out a sigh and spoke into my burner phone's mouthpiece. "I'm busy today—"

"Malena, it's a quick lunch. Naina Auntie and her family are coming over," my mom interrupted. "Her daughter is your age."

The phone call rained on the perfectly productive morning I was having the day after the scavenger hunt, where I'd set myself up to work in the middle of the Scroll & Ivy's mausoleum. Conrad was right, it was deserted.

"Maybe some other time," I answered quietly. "The MCATs are *next week*."

In the daytime, the brass sconces affixed between each shelf reflected the light passing through the arched windows. That combined with the reflective nature of the gilded chandeliers strung to the high ceiling, and there was no shortage of brightness between the floor-to-ceiling bookshelves.

"It's two hours. Dad will drive you right back to school,"

my mom countered, the sound of pots and pans clanging in the background.

She always sprang this on me: last-minute playdates so she could have a say in my friend group too.

"I have to study," I repeated more firmly. "I *can't* come home."

"You need to *try* to spend some time making *good* friends."

"I have—"

"Ones who don't run around with weird-colored hair for a whole semester," she added.

The words cracked down my sternum. "Cora *is* a good friend."

She sighed. "*Good* friends were all the support we had when we moved here, they are the backbone of a full life."

I could tell she believed she was delivering well-meaning advice. That controlling this aspect of my life had a purpose, some deeper way to make sure anyone I was in proximity to was "good" by her standards.

But all it succeeded in doing was making me more adept at eluding her will.

"I have good friends, Mom," I repeated. They weren't the ones she wanted me to make so it didn't matter that they were the only people I ever really felt like myself around.

"Fine, believe what you want." She huffed a breath. "Dad will be there in—"

"I'm not coming," I cut in. My independence was always two steps forward, one step back. For now, I was going to take what I could get. "I mean it, Mom. I'm staying on campus until next weekend, and I'll be here during fall break the week after too."

Fall break at Winchester was always the third week of October. The only other break in the semester was Thanksgiving, and that wasn't until the end of November. My parents tended to fill my free time if I didn't get ahead of it, so I'd been dropping hints since I was last home. No way was I getting stuck with them for an entire week.

There was some shuffling, then I could hear my mom speaking a mile a minute, scolding the other person in the room. It was probably my dad. Eventually, he picked up the phone.

"Are you sure you can't just come home for a little bit?"

"Dad." My shoulders relaxed a little. He was no better; he excused my mom when she acted the way she did, but it was still nice to hear his voice. "I have to study, and I need some time to relax after. Okay?"

"You can't do that at home?" he negotiated in a soft, tired voice.

"Do you know what people will say?" my mom's voice erupted in the background. "She doesn't come home even though she's close by. Doesn't make an effort with family friends. They'll think she's..." The rest got lost in a mumble.

"I'm staying. I need to study today," I answered firmly. I was allowed to do so little; I wasn't going to budge on my peace today. "Sabrina is visiting for fall break, and we're planning to spend the week on campus together."

The truth was, Sabrina wouldn't be back until the end of the semester and Cora had her trip to Vermont. I didn't *want* to be alone, but I had a stack of books I wanted to read, and it would be quiet. That was always better than going back to the chaos at home.

"Okay," my dad conceded with a long sigh. "You stay at school."

My mom let out a frustrated huff. "Weeks without visiting her *family*. I'll be happy when the semester is over and she returns."

The line clicked off and a reminder reverberated in my head.

I'd only be this distant from their expectations while at Winchester.

Once I hit the "med school milestone," their expectations would recalibrate. I saw Avani go through them all. In childhood, she was compliant and never talked back. As an adolescent, she befriended everyone my parents told her to and fit in with ease. As a college student, she *eventually* got into med school. And then, she dated who *they* liked. Hell, she'd probably marry him.

I was expected to do the same. The two Malenas had to fuse into one if I was going to keep them at bay.

In my mind, I hoped it would be smooth, like a zipper coming together. But the more those two parts diverged, the more I was sure that it would be like an earthquake. The kind that lifted mountains in its path of destruction.

The real me on one side. The one I had to be on the other.

The sound of a throat clearing pulled me from the paralyzing reminder.

I looked up and found Conrad shifting awkwardly a few feet away. His navy crew neck sweater was speckled with the multicolored light being bottlenecked through the mausoleum's stained-glass windows. "You okay?"

"Oh... hi." I put my phone down and tried to reset from that conversation. I looked back up at him and a few lines appeared on his forehead. "Depends, how much did you hear?"

"Nothing." Conrad took a seat in the high-backed velvet upholstered chair across from me. "Just a lot of huffing and puffing."

"I'm fine." I swallowed the heavy reality I'd just been contemplating and pressed my palms against the soft leather tuxedo sofa I sat on. I looked around at the vacant couches interspersed with end tables. I'd chosen a spot in the middle of the room, where the four seats surrounded a single mahogany coffee table. "Is it always like this?"

Conrad shrugged. "I guess members found something else to do this semester."

"Except you?"

"I, uhhh…" He rubbed the back of his neck, then pulled a couple of books out from his backpack. "Monetary Policy's midterm is a few days before fall break and I can't really skate by on this one."

"Oh no." I leaned forward and smacked a dramatic hand on my chest, thankful for the distraction. "Is Conrad Hastings going to have to study?"

"I am." His words carried a playful indignation that made my stomach tumble. "And I'll have you know that I could be solving the campus mystery right now. Instead, I'm here."

"With me, *studying*," I drawled. "Tragic."

The weight of his gaze pushed the unwelcome shadows to the back of my mind. He leaned forward, his elbows braced on either leg and his arms folded lazily over his lap. "I guess it could be worse."

The chemistry that we both knew was there bubbled quietly in the background, getting louder with every second.

I reveled in the way his voice put me at ease. It was like a blissful state of drowning and I never wanted to come up for air. "It might ruin that carefree reputation."

He gave me a nonchalant shrug, but a smile crept through. "I'll take my chances."

His eyes moved from mine and down to the lists of names from the university archives. He looked back to me and picked up the papers.

"Looking for Van Holdens at Winchester?" Fascination colored his face. It was adorable; the unambitious Conrad Hastings was invested in this.

And that did something completely unfamiliar to me. Something I wasn't sure I was ready to face.

"It's a dead end." I sighed. The school records were well kept and no Van Holdens came up. And while I hadn't yet searched for a family tree, I was beginning to think it was best to put this caper to bed and go with my original feature idea. The myth of meritocracy was a good angle. "Another one."

My phone buzzed in my pocket. I pulled it out to read the forwarded texts.

> Mom: You need to come home a day early for Thanksgiving break next month
>
> Mom: We are making food and Pinky Auntie is coming over.
>
> Mom: No excuses or I will have Dad get you.

Like the walls were closing in, I had to find an exit. A way back to what I could rely on: two Malenas. Neither life was so completely perfect that I would fall apart without it.

"Maybe there's no connection to him. Maybe it's random that he's the artist this person chose to imitate," Conrad theorized. He tapped his pen along the edge of the table. He stood and rounded it, taking a seat next to me with his entire focus on the lists.

"We don't even know if that's what they're doing." I pushed my burner back in my bag, then shifted in my seat with a hard swallow.

"No, but we have a lot of different leads. Something is bound to stand out."

"I think we're stuck," I announced louder than I expected to. He looked up from the papers, bewildered. "And I need to get moving with the submission."

I reminded myself why I was doing all of this in the first

place. A path to writing later, when I *could*. And my own money—a way to stem the tide. Because the second I was wholly financially dependent on my parents would be the same one that college-Malena disappeared. And I wasn't ready to let her go.

But the system didn't account for *this*.

It was the feeling that'd first surfaced in the tight study cubical. And now, it glared directly in my eyes, making it impossible to ignore. The feeling of getting wound tighter and tighter, binding me to something. And some*one*.

"We still have weeks," he rightly pointed out.

Yes, the feature wasn't due until December. But, I had what I *needed*. Like all things I experienced here, this had to end. And staring into those crystalline eyes made me want to prolong it. It made me want to search for an answer when there probably wasn't one.

"I have what I need for the article," I went on. "I'm spending fall break on campus. I'll write it then." I closed the folder and grabbed the few notebooks I brought along with me, stacking them neatly.

"We haven't figured anything out."

"It's a feature." My tone jumped an octave. I dodged his gaze but managed to catch the disappointment. Seeing that light—the excitement that'd been like looking at the sun only a few seconds ago—dim a bit... It *hurt*. "The first idea I had, before we found out about the rest. It was solid."

"Yeah, but the unsealed door, the paintings." Confusion laced through his words. "That's definitely better."

I stood and shouldered my bag. "We can't wait on something that may never work itself out. I can't lose the good in search of the perfect."

"I can help—"

"No need," I interrupted. An ache swelled in my chest and I *had* to get the hell out of here. "I promised you a read before it goes out, and I'll honor that. Besides, you've got those races, right? The regatta?"

"Yeah..." He scrambled to stand, almost stumbling as he moved to follow me. "I'll drive you back."

My phone vibrated with another text message against the books in my bag.

"It's a nice day, I'll walk." I took another step back. "The article was easier than expected, see? Not so bad."

I should have slept with him and moved along. I wouldn't be feeling this way if I had. Instead, I ambled around in his life, getting to know it and understand it. And him.

"No, it wasn't," he said, so quiet it was almost a whisper.

"I'll keep Sabrina's key safe and give it to her the next time I see her."

He nodded and I turned on my heels.

"See ya around, Malena," he called as I made my way down the corridor toward the exit.

Disappointment became cement in my lungs.

Stupidly, I'd let myself get used to him calling me Holmes.

CHAPTER 23

Conrad

"Conrad's races begin tomorrow," I heard my mom say from down the hallway.

It was early Thursday evening when I walked from my childhood bedroom down a grand spiral staircase to the living area. The four-story brownstone on the Upper East Side had been in the Hastings family since the 1800s.

I got back home this morning. An hour after my midterm, I left campus and made my way to Manhattan. I was excused from my Friday classes for the start of the regatta, so I swapped out the motorcycle for my Aston Martin and drove here before I made the journey to Boston tomorrow.

I hadn't wanted to sit around campus feeling whatever I was feeling. So, I decided to ignore it—as was the Hastings way.

"Oh, I remember those days," Beatrice Amari, the paragon of Upper East Side mothers, said back as I stepped around the corner, passing painting after painting that lined the walls.

Inside the sun-filled salon, both women looked up from their glasses of what was probably a pre-dinner drink. I smiled; my mom was going out. And then winced when I looked around the room and saw that I'd left a few of my art books open.

They reflected the last-ditch effort I decided to put in this afternoon to find anything I might've missed in the books I'd checked out from the library. Because Malena might have been done with what was going on, but I wasn't.

Unsurprisingly, I came up short.

The intrusion in my social life was over now, so I should've been using my time for other matters—like focusing on the race tomorrow. But ever since Malena ended our arrangement, I was finding that rather difficult.

"Sorry about the mess."

I'd come to see my mom, since I gathered that she was still shutting my dad out. I also knew my brothers, Barrett and Tripp, were too busy plotting against each other to concern themselves with visiting.

"Don't bother yourself, dear." Beatrice waved her hands in front of the books and pointed to the Bergère chair across from them. "Come here, let me look at you."

Having these friends was crucial for my mom; I'd sit still and behave for her.

Beatrice folded her hands neatly on her lap when I sat down. "Tell me, are you ready for this race?"

My mom's eyes dropped to her glass, her neatly styled brown hair falling forward. "I'm sorry I can't be there, Conrad."

"Don't worry about it, Mom." I reached over and squeezed her hand. She had enough going on, and that race would be bursting with society mothers who thrived on this gossip. "It's just a race," I assured her. She hated letting me down, so I never let her believe she was.

She tended to lose track of herself around this time of year. Summers were her reprieve, and every year she retreated to that house in Newport, even after Dad ruined it.

"Well." She took a deep breath and stood, running her hands over her skirt. "I need to get something from the study. Why don't you show Beatrice what you were looking at before you forgot your manners and left your things strewn around the living room."

Beatrice glanced down at the art books that were opened to the known Van Holden works.

"Sorry, Mom," I called, but she was already down the hallway.

Confused at the abrupt change in subject, I eyed Beatrice, who didn't look surprised at all. In fact, she was already paging through the textbook on early impressionists I had left open.

"Are these from the Van Holden collection?" Beatrice asked.

My interest spiked.

"Are you a collector?" I leaned forward with my elbows on my knees.

"Sit up straight!" she commanded, which I did immediately, because Beatrice Amari was a little scary. "And no, I'm not a collector, but my daughter-in-law has a discerning eye. Photography mostly, but she dabbles in early twentieth century paintings," she stated proudly. "I've been to more art auctions than I can count, but this series caused quite the stir."

We'd done everything to try to identify them. He'd come up alongside a few matches, but there were only a couple of pieces to compare, and while the styles matched, none were exact.

What was the point of making forgeries of paintings that didn't exist?

"Why did it cause a stir?" I asked, knowing that *caused a stir* meant it was some degree of gossip she'd willingly share.

"It's all very messy, dear." She took a tiny sip from her martini glass then placed it on the end table with all the grace of the queen. "Van Holden was a painter during World War I.

During World War II, his paintings were largely seized by the axis. It's rumored they were destroyed during an allied attack. But a piece will resurface every decade or so. Now, two in the course of a year..."

She raised her brows and shuffled her shoulders.

"Suspicious?"

"Well." She lowered her voice like she was making a show of what she happened to know. "Rumor has it that some oligarch out of Moscow came upon them during the post-war chaos and has been hoarding them for *decades*. He passed, and his pernicious children have been selling off his art. Allegedly, of course." She winked at me. "Two previously never-before-shown pieces have sold at the Modiste Gallery this year."

"Really?"

"All a colorful story to drive up the price, I'm sure." She nodded. "Every gallery in the city was hoping to get the sale of the next ones, but it looks like the Modiste has the ultimate connection. Who knows how many they have left, but it was rumored he painted at least twenty in the *Blue* collection alone."

"Lucky, I guess." My heart raced. "But wouldn't there be some record of these pieces having been painted?"

"The family kept a record, I'm sure. It's probably with the gallery now. Paintings that were previously lost to the world, suddenly found. It certainly makes for a good story." She tilted her head. "I had no idea you were so interested in the arts, Conrad."

If there was a list of his pieces rumored to have been lost, then we'd have a map—a way to connect what we found to what was being sold.

"Neither did I." My mom walked back into the room and handed Beatrice a piece of paper.

The two exchanged a look. One that I took to mean *Not in front of the boy*, but I had an idea.

A smile crested against my cheeks. Maybe she was doing something for herself. And if that something was a divorce, having all of high society take my mom's side would mean having a chance at facing off against my father.

"Something going on?" I asked. For as long as I could remember, she'd been resigned to the reality in front of her. Maybe now she'd finally decided to change it...

"Nothing to concern yourself with." My mom placed a hand on my cheek and moved her thumb back and forth. "Now..." She sat back down next to Beatrice. "Is this a newfound interest in the arts or a young lady who's interested in the arts?"

I chuckled and stood.

"Just curious." I put my hands up. "That's all."

Beatrice's eyes narrowed on me. "Yes, well, Modiste Gallery has quite a few Winchester alumni working in the curation department... Could be something a date might be interested in. Who am I to say?"

"You should take her there, Conrad," my mom added, perking up.

"I was only curious," I repeated.

The pieces were being sold. There was a list of them, a way to uncover what was actually going on. And Malena would definitely want to know more now... right?

It was worth a shot.

CHAPTER 24

Conrad

I drove back to New Harbor right after talking to my mom and Beatrice. By the time I was knocking on Malena's door, I had no idea how I was going to start, but *fuck*, I didn't care.

"Cora, I told you, I was fine when you called ten minutes ago," I heard her call as footsteps got closer to the doorway. "You didn't have to come back and check on—"

Finally, it swung open.

She was dressed in polka dotted pajama pants and a crimson oversized Winchester University sweatshirt; her hair plopped at the top of her head and held together by one giant clip.

My heart tripped.

By some unfair law of nature, she always looked beautiful. My mind wandered to how she'd look waking up. If she'd look this... perfect.

Probably.

"Conrad—" She stilled in the doorway. "Don't you have your races starting tomorrow?"

"I have to talk to you."

"O-okay," she stammered, twisting her fingers around the hem of her sweatshirt. "About what?"

So many fucking things, I thought. But for now, I'd keep it simple: "The story."

She moved aside and opened the door a little wider.

"I have the MCATs on Saturday, but I was going to write the article after that," she told me in what sounded like a stream of consciousness. "I have what I need..."

I took a couple of steps into their living room and noticed a dress laid out on the couch. A sparkling navy-blue skirt with a bejeweled bodice.

"You're going?" My chest filled with something warm and pleasant.

I wasn't surprised, charging ahead despite totally valid concerns was a very Malena thing to do. Which made her choice to pivot from the painting angle so frustrating.

The Malena I was getting to know wouldn't do that.

"Still deciding," she said, and I turned to her. "Cora and Sabrina aren't here..." she murmured. "The dress doesn't fit. It's too big, or maybe I put it on wrong, but I can't seem to get the pins in correctly..."

My smile fell. Was she finding excuses to not go?

She wrapped her arms around her waist and looked at the floor. "What's up, Conrad?"

My mind kicked back on with why I was there, even though all I wanted to do was curl my arms around her. Something was wrong and I wanted to fix it.

"I need to tell you something." Without hesitating, I took her through everything I'd learned at home that afternoon.

With every new piece of information, she stood a little straighter. Like a weight was slowly being lifted off her shoulders. The crumpled look of defeat unwound with excitement.

"If someone is selling pieces that *could be* Van Holdens,

ones that were previously thought to be destroyed..." I trailed off at the end of the story.

"Maybe the pieces that were in those poster carriers *were* practice," she surmised brightly. I didn't know where she'd been since she ran from this—and me—on Sunday, but she was back now. "Do you think that's one of the two that were sold?"

"I checked the gallery website, and the latest sales aren't listed." I took a step closer to her. "But they have to have that information at the gallery, right?"

"Someone has a list of his unshown pieces, the ones that've been lost to the world. They figure out how to forge one and they can forge them all." She started pacing back and forth in front of the coffee table, and I stood still. The bun atop her head bobbed precariously, the clip barely holding it together, and I couldn't help but grin. I liked this unkempt version of Malena. "And probably use the same art dealer. If they're using the same gallery, that is."

"So, we find the art dealer, or whoever is selling them..."

Another spark lit in her eyes.

She crossed the span of the coffee table that cradled a few bowls filled with snacks and candies. A couple of knit blankets were strewn across the couch. Suddenly I was *very* aware that I was at her place and that her room was just down the hall. And that, unlike the last time, we were alone.

"And we find the forger." She pressed her lips together and tugged at my shirt, rising to her tiptoes. "We have something here."

"Yeah... We do," I said quietly under the sound of my heart slamming against my chest. "Better than rich kids and predictable parties?"

"That part wasn't *so* bad," she whispered with a lilt in her voice. "We need to go to that gallery. Or at least get an idea of what's being sold next."

"Isha can probably set up a meeting with the curator," I told her. Beatrice offered as well, but I was sure Ishani would ask fewer questions. "She's been known to go on shopping sprees that include rare art, so she'll jump at the chance."

Mal nodded. "You think she'll agree?"

"I might have to tell her why, but Isha can keep a secret."

"I guess that's okay."

"She's not our culprit, that much I know," I assured her. Isha had more money than God and absolutely no reason to be in on this. "And she won't risk us losing the Keller Award—she knows how important it is to me."

Mal's brow jumped. "To you?"

My face heated. "Maybe."

I wanted so much more than I'd ever expected to want. Maybe, out of spite, I'd avoided the paper all this time. But this story was pulling my attention, and I loved it. And whatever attention remained was Mal's.

"Okay." Her breath wisped across my cheek. She still hadn't moved, and I tried to keep perfectly still so she wouldn't.

Through the haze she had me in, I managed to remember that she had her MCATs in a couple of days. "I'll ask Isha at the regatta this weekend."

"Right. The races." She dropped to her heels, but the electricity that encircled us kept her close. "Good luck."

"You too." My hands moved to her hips. I took a step forward and she matched it with a step back.

"Con..." She laid her hand on my chest but left it there, not pushing or pulling. Her eyes got lost in thought.

"Let me try, Mal," I whispered into the column of her neck.

She let out a tiny whimper; the sound burrowed down my spine. I stepped her backward until she pressed against the wall.

"Con..." Her breathy moan puffed against my skin.

Fuck.

I held her chin and made her look at me. Indecision warred in her eyes.

"My test is in two days." The delicate lines along her throat shifted around a hard swallow. "I have to focus."

I nodded, trying to remember that I had to get going soon too, but my body *really* wanted to stay. "Where are you during fall break?"

"I'll be here."

"Yeah?" I breathed against her lips. "Scroll & Ivy always goes on a trip. This year the whole thing is on the Roy family's dime. We're taking the Rutherford jet to Paris and staying at the McMaster house. You can come in Sabrina's place..."

"Oh." Her eyes fell to the ground. "I don't..."

"Think about it," I encouraged. I pushed myself off the wall because if I stayed another second, I'd be waking up here and skipping the race. "Either way, I'll see you after the races, Mal."

If she didn't want to go, I'd skip the damn trip if it meant spending a week here with her.

Her teeth scraped over her bottom lip and she nodded.

I left with the electric excitement of knowing that none of this was over. It was just getting started.

CHAPTER 25

Malena

After my MCATs, I spent an entire afternoon preparing for a trip to Paris that I wasn't even sure I was going to take. The fact that the travel and accommodations were taken care of did help push me in the direction I *wanted* to go. It could work.

But, when everything was packed, I was still no closer to a decision.

"There was a difficult set of k-type questions for a feedback loop about apoptosis." I rattled off some thoughts about the test to Cora and Sabrina, who shared a split screen on my phone. They'd called just as I finished packing. "Otherwise, it went well."

I let them know about the whole Conrad-trip thing seconds after he left the other night, and they were thirsty for an update.

"And aren't we glad," Cora chirped. "But the reason we waited until *after* your exam to call was because you needed to focus."

"And now that it's over..." Sabrina segued. "The trip?"

My passport and secret bank card were tucked inside a

vintage Hermès bag that Sabrina gifted me for my last birthday. When I tried to thank her, she told me that money for people who had it was never an obstacle, so they shouldn't get any credit for spending it. Like Cora, Sabrina was the type to show up, and *that* was why I loved her.

Either way, it was the chicest thing I owned, and suddenly I was considering my greatest lie yet. A trip my parents didn't know about.

"I dunno." I sighed. I curled my legs under me on the couch and gazed out the window, watching as the sun set over New Harbor. "It might be a step too far."

"You can check in with me if you're worried," Cora offered.

"And I'll have the State Department monitor your plane," Sabrina added. "You'll be safe."

"Think about it," Cora encouraged.

"Yeah, I will." Just as I was about to say my goodbyes, a knock at the door startled my already erratic heart. I looked at the door then back at the screen. "I gotta go."

The girls gave me twin wolfish looks and then hung up.

I all but ran to the door and swung it open.

My hopes barely had the chance to fall before they were picked up off the ground by curiosity.

Ishani Roy and Lucy McMaster stood on the other side of my doorway, dressed head to toe in stunning lenghas. Ishani's was a pastel blush while Lucy's was a deep and rich gold.

"She's not dressed," Lucy announced with a blank expression, then looked over to Ishani. "She's not dressed."

"Yes, I see that, Lucy." Ishani cocked her head to the side. The diamond encrusted tikka sitting on her hairline stayed remarkably still. "Good thing we came prepared."

"Umm..." I failed to understand what was happening, so I simply stood there. "What are you—"

"Conrad *randomly* needs a kurta on one day's notice and

needs me to call Mahesh Malhotra to whip one up at his atelier," Ishani began as she gently placed both hands on my shoulders and moved me aside in the doorway.

Lucy followed her in, carrying a garment bag. "It was adorable."

"What?" My mouth gaped open, but I managed to shut the door behind my surprise guests.

"I mean, Mahesh *does* owe me a favor, but that level of handstitched work in twenty-four hours? The man is a fashion genius, not a magician," Ishani clarified, though that wasn't the part I was confused about.

"But... sorry, what did you mean about Conrad?"

"Oh." A slow grin stretched across her lips. "Yes, he tried to be sly about it like he just *happened* to need one." Ishani laughed. "James tried to cover for him, made something up about how he was planning ahead for the Roy family Holi dinner in the spring."

"Boys are dumb..." Lucy laughed with a hearty roll of her shoulders, then poked her head into my room, the only bedroom door that was open. She walked in, put the garment bag down, and took a seat on the ottoman in front of my vanity. She looked over and patted the seat in front of her. "Sit, I'll get you ready."

Still flustered, I did as told, Ishani trailing behind.

"Although, you need next to nothing. Excellent features." Ishani took hold of my chin and turned it both directions. "Have you done stills? You might be a little clumsy to walk."

I squeezed my eyes shut for a second, trying to catch up. "What's going on?"

"We're going to the Diwali party with you." Ishani blinked a few times, as if the last five minutes made any sense. "Obviously."

"You can go alone. Girl power, and all," Lucy said as she

riffled through my drawer in search of brushes, "but we have Rahul Mishra's latest line, so why waste it?"

"You're wearing Rahul Mishra?" My mouth dropped open, and I looked at the black garment bag hanging off my bed.

"Well, I happened to have a couple of dresses from the September shows at my house in Manhattan," Ishani explained.

"So, Conrad sent you because..." I pieced it together.

"For the same reason Scroll & Ivy members with personal access to the mausoleum's library were either threatened or bribed to keep clear of it during the day." Ishani smiled. "So *someone* could study."

My heart stumbled. *That's* why it was always empty. "Wait..."

"He likes you." Lucy guided my chin to face her and prepared to apply eyeshadow. "So much so that he drove to Manhattan, picked these dresses up, drove back here to give them to us, and then made his way to Boston for the race."

"Oh..." The realization fizzed up my body.

"Suffice it to say, it was clearly important to him that you not go alone, so here we are," Ishani added. "Don't worry, we're plenty of fun."

My heart dipped again. Two of the only people who'd ever shown up to his races were here with me. On his request.

He was alone so *I* wouldn't be.

SONALI'S KIND smile greeted me when I got separated from Ishani and Lucy a short while later. Her thick wavy hair was curled at the ends, her deep, almost burgundy lipstick popped against her tanned skin. "You look amazing."

"You too," I said, my fingers tangling in on themselves. I

glanced at my reflection in the window that looked out at the dark quad. My hair cascaded down my sparkling red bodice. I had the perfect golden jhumkas and armor in the form of Ishani Roy and Lucille McMaster. But I still felt the overwhelming urge to hide.

"I'm glad you're here." She looked around the auditorium decorated with colorful garlands and electric tea lights. A low orchestral rendition of a popular song floated in the space between us. At the center of the room were a series of towering floral arrangements—marigolds, lilies, and jasmine. A rangoli design crafted with sand painted the floor around the base of the flowers. Even with the hundred-plus guests in attendance, each one dressed in an array of colors that reminded me of the Diwali parties of my childhood, the large space wasn't any less daunting. "I wanted to apologize, about that day at brunch—"

"It's fine." I didn't want to relive it, and was perfectly content pretending it never happened.

"No, it's not." She played with her golden bangle. "Nara shouldn't have said that to you. And *I* should have said something to her."

"It's okay," I repeated.

My eyes skated over the pleated silk saris that were draped over the folded bleachers in an attempt to make them blend in. They did a pretty good job.

"And, for the record, I think the Armistice Day thing was really cool."

I smiled. "Thanks."

A silence fell between us, broken a moment later by a few calls from behind Sonali. Her friends, waiting to take pictures by the canopied floral arrangements that hung above the entrance. Sonali glanced over her shoulder, her smile falling at the corners.

"I should go, but it was great seeing you." Sonali paused

mid-turn. "You and I should hang out, maybe with Cora and Sabrina next time?"

"Yeah..." It felt like an olive branch. Maybe one I'd take if my battered ego wasn't screaming to simply go home because I'd tried and failed and was sick of feeling like a misshapen puzzle piece. "Maybe."

Sonali walked back to her group, and I took a few steps closer to the wall.

Not long after, Ishani found me. She handed me one of the drinks she was carrying.

"I know we don't *really* know each other, but based off what Conrad has said about you—" She glanced at me and stopped.

My face warmed.

The corners of her mouth tipped up. "It's sweet, really. I don't think he realizes he's doing it. But he talks about you *all* the time."

Delighted but also a little flustered, I was the shade of ruby red to match my dress.

"Anyway..." I cleared my throat, not sure how to react.

"*Anyway.*" Ishani took the hint and kept going. "Based on how he describes you, you don't seem like a 'stand in the corner' type of person."

"I..." I failed to put into words why it was easier to hide. "Once bitten, twice shy, I guess."

Her brows arched.

"When I first got to Winchester, I tried to make friends with some of the other students here tonight." I motioned toward the dance floor. "I guess we didn't have a lot in common, and I sort of gave up." The words shot out of my mouth because maybe it would be less humiliating if I said it quickly. "I try every now and then, but I feel like I'm some other version of myself."

And honestly, it was exhausting.

"If it makes you feel any better, I had a similar experience. When I was a freshman, I'd never felt more out of place than here."

"Seriously?" I struggled to believe that.

Ishani Roy *oozed* cool. A posh British accent, a Brazilian supermodel mom and heiress in the Mumbai-based Roy family. Her paternal aunt was former Miss Universe, Amani Roy. In the time it took to get me ready, she'd recited the story of her dating a prince, breaking his heart, and then hours later walking in fashion week like it was a regular Tuesday.

"Well, to be fair..." She shrugged, plucking a samosa from a circulating waiter. She took a bite and as she chewed, her eyes narrowed like she was thinking something over. "I'm the half-Indian, half-Brazilian British socialite whose highly publicized relationship with the future king of England was splashed across global tabloids for months." She gave me a knowing look. "I'm a bit of a spectacle."

"A fun one." I smiled sympathetically.

Based on past experience, she was right to be a *little* cautious. Ishani colored outside the lines, publicly and proudly. That wasn't always welcome, and rejection was painful. Especially from a place you weren't expecting it.

She popped the tiny bit of samosa that was left in her mouth and sighed happily. "I tried to find common ground, and when it didn't stick, I gave up. Probably sooner than I should have."

"I get that." My eyes moved across the room. In the small clusters of people talking amongst themselves, I spotted familiar faces. A girl from my biochem class, a few people from my differential equations lectures. I *could* find a lull in conversation and use that as an opening to join in on whatever they were talking about. But past wounds made the task even more unappealing.

Ishani shrugged, dropping her napkin on a nearby tray. "I

chose Winchester over Oxford because my best friends were here. I stayed in my own bubble. It was easier, but sometimes hard things are worth it."

"Yeah..." I glanced around. There were plenty of other people here, plenty of other chances to find a place. Speaking to Ishani now, I had a renewed hope that I would.

"And..." She sucked in a deep breath like she was about to launch into a dramatic soliloquy. "There's no one way to *be* anything." She jutted her chin up defiantly and looked around the room. "Nobody can simply kick you out of the diaspora because you don't run in the same circles or like the same things."

A chronic ache in my chest lightened.

"I guess you're right." Outside of Cora and Sabrina, this was the most *seen* I'd felt in a long time. Thanks to her.

"You know." She looped an arm through mine. "I've never been to Carnival, but my mother *loved* it. Certainly doesn't make me any less Brazilian. Having celebrated Holi in Mumbai the last few years doesn't make me any more Indian. Being the one that got away for a certain prince most definitely doesn't make me *any* more British."

I laughed.

She was right.

For so long, my connection to my culture was mainly through my family. But their way of relating to the diaspora was a tiny facet. And in front of me were a million more.

"Thank you."

"Don't mention it, really. Now come on, let's be brave, no more hiding in a corner." Ishani nodded her head toward the party. "We are wearing couture Mishra. These dresses were meant to be seen."

I smiled and followed.

I wasn't brave, but I wanted to be.

Maybe I could finally take a step in that direction.

CHAPTER 26

Conrad

The starting gun blared into the dissipating morning fog, and for the next fifteen minutes, my mind was completely clear.

The salty mist from the oars, the water rushing against them, the muted sound from the crowds as we neared the three-mile finish line—all of it filled my ears and narrowed my focus to this moment.

I loved rowing.

You could change the outcome of a race. You pushed harder, moved faster, trained more. It was completely within your control. There was a high that came along with knowing that I could eke out a win when a loss seemed inevitable.

We crossed the final finish marker, and everything went from moving in frames to full speed. I glanced up to the time.

After our performance yesterday and today's time, we won.

I grinned as everything else I was thinking before the race flooded into my mind.

Pinpoint taps cascaded along my fingers, waiting to get back to the dock so I could look at my phone. Mal hadn't texted, but I got a militant call from Sabrina Alders early this morning.

I didn't even know how she got my number, but she said *You will end up in an unsanctioned black ops facility if anything happens to Mal*, and then refused to tell me if Malena had made her decision about Paris.

Either way, I was seeing her. On the trip or on campus.

James's hand slapping down on my shoulder yanked me back to the present. "Hey, look up at the dock on the north end."

"Huh?"

"I think you should look," James called again, giving my shoulder a shove this time as we waited on the water for our signal to row to the dock.

My brow crinkled against the sun as I looked over to the newly constructed stands along the water. There was Isha and Lucy, which was unexpected, since I figured they'd stay the night on campus after the Diwali party.

But it was when I looked at the person next to Lucy that my heart skipped.

In a crimson sweater, with a Winchester Rowing pennant in her hand, stood Malena. Her entire face brightened when my eyes caught hers, and she waved *almost* sheepishly.

My lips stretched unabashedly across my face and I lifted a hand to wave back.

Growing up, spending so much time away at boarding school, I didn't let myself rely on many people showing up. And while a part of me half expected she'd text me today or call to tell me her answer regarding the trip, I was so stunned to see her there that I stopped rowing.

She's here. For me.

"Jeez, Con," James shouted from behind me. "Pick up the pace, you can't *finally* close unless we get to shore."

EVERYTHING after I got to shore was a blur. It only cleared as I jogged up the wooden walk where some of the spectators still lingered.

She was *here*.

I finally spotted her at the corner of the walk, in front of a tall post. The breeze off the bay tossed at her hair gently. She fidgeted with her fingers and stood, waiting for me.

My heart slammed against my ribs with every step until I was finally in front of her.

"You're here." The high from winning, from seeing her in the stands and knowing this was just the start—all of it made my muscles tremble.

I skimmed a hand over her hip. The other ran up the column of her neck, my thumb pushing her chin up until her eyes met mine. Her hands smoothed over the shirt I'd thrown on in my rush to get to her.

"People might think you enjoy my company." I added, dropping my forehead to hers.

My thumb brushed over the skin just above the waistband of her skirt. I let it dip below, barely grazing lace.

Her breath hitched.

"I'm actually here for the race," she whispered, and her breath wisped across my cheek.

Goose bumps waved down my back.

"Liar." I stepped her back until she was up against the post. My heart roared in my ears.

The air between us thinned.

She grinned, her cheeks flushed, and yanked on my collar. "Then call my bluff."

I *finally* pressed my lips against hers, and she melted into it with a tiny gasp. Her hands closed into fists around my shirt.

My nerves cracked and popped. Pins and fucking needles

that I never wanted to end. Her lips, soft and sweet, parted for me.

A contented sigh sailed up her throat and I kissed her deeper.

My arm tightened around her, pressing into her body that was flush against mine. Her hand spanned up my chest and carded through my hair at the base of my neck. My fingers dug into the skin that was as soft as I remembered it.

The world around us muted. All I could hear, think, *feel* was her.

Then, like thunder cracking through a storm, an airgun's boom shook us apart.

She pulled back, and the early afternoon light brightened her irises so they were almost amber.

"Con..." Her lips were a little red and swollen, and the sight unlocked a new thrill. I stayed close, our breaths tangling. She looked down at my shirt and asked, "Why did you send Isha and Lucy?"

My heart stumbled seeing her like that. Was she nervous?

"You know, they're pretty difficult to steer. *Sending* them anywhere is—"

"Conrad." She looked up, her tone serious but her eyes soft.

The Mal I was getting to know was fearless. Even still, I'd recognized that reluctance in her eyes when I showed up at her apartment the other day. Not from my own experience, but from Isha's. There was a reason she transferred to Winchester after only one semester at Oxford. I couldn't help Malena with that feeling, but I knew Ishani could.

"They're a push in the right direction if you're looking for one," I tried to explain. Lucy and Ishani were a kind of supportive that didn't smother. James, when concerned, tended to be direct. We Hastings men didn't talk about *anything*. But Isha and Lucy had a way of nudging you in the right direction. All while being a little ridiculous. "Seemed like you wanted one, and I thought Isha would be better for it than me."

"She was. They both were." Malena rocked forward and pressed another short kiss against my lips. Her fingers tapped down my chest, stopping at my waist. "And she came bearing Rahul Mishra."

I smiled and kissed her again. Dizzy and unable to think of anything else, I wanted to get her alone.

This time what pulled us apart was my phone. It buzzed a few times in my pocket and Mal pulled away, motioning for me to answer.

"It's nothing," I whispered, leaning back into her, but she bobbed her head back.

"It could be important."

I checked the screen and tucked it back in my pocket. "It's the midterm."

Her eyes widened. "And..."

"I'm sure I aced it." When she dodged me a third time, I finally gave up, tipping my head back with a groan. "And I don't know that it matters."

"It does. Regardless of the Hastings legacy on standby to sweep in and save the day."

Without another word, her hand slipped into my pocket.

"Careful." Startled—and avoiding thinking about how good she felt *that* close—I cleared my throat. "Malena, we're in public."

Undeterred, she shook her head, pulled out my phone, and held it to my face to unlock it. "I can tell you or you can tell me."

When I didn't answer, she took it upon herself to look. My pulse picked right back up, and this time it wasn't the beautiful girl in front of me but rather her fingers flying over my phone, the results she was about to reveal.

Her lips arched as she looked up at me. "I'm sorry to be the one to tell you this, but it turns out you might not be ne'er-do-well material."

Relief ran down my body. "Yeah?"

"You *unfortunately* have potential."

"Oh no," I teased, glancing down at the screen and seeing the bold *B+* listed beneath my name. A foreign feeling warmed me. I was a little proud of myself.

"A life of ambition and maybe... achievements."

"Stop." I brushed my lips over hers. "You'll ruin my reputation."

She giggled and I kissed her again.

We stayed like that, delirious and caught in our own bubble, until the grating sound of Ishani and Lucy clamoring a few feet away broke through.

Interrupted once again, I gave up on kissing her until I could finally get her alone.

"So, you're coming to Paris with us?" I asked, hoping what I'd planned for over there wouldn't be for nothing.

I was sure Ishani had already taken over and done more than I asked anyway.

All the excitement deflated when she took a step back though, her slightly dilated eyes returning to a clear focus and cutting away the high we were floating on.

CHAPTER 27

Malena

Staring into those deep blue eyes made everything very real, and all the bravery I'd mustered last night loosened.

I always figured that one day Good Malena, real phone-Malena, the Malena my parents wanted, would take over and I'd figure out how to bridge the divide.

"We don't have to go." Conrad watched as I internally debated. His hands gently gripped either side of my waist. "Let's head back to campus."

The problem was that Good Malena never existed in the first place. She was a lie, a series of them, all constructed for someone else's comfort at the expense of my own.

If I wanted something, I had to take it.

I shook my head. "We're there till Wednesday, right?"

My parents worked during the week, so the only chance of a surprise visit was on weekends. We'd be back by then.

An unsteady smile pushed against his cheeks—boyish and completely adorable. "Yeah."

That day in the mausoleum when I told Conrad I'd finish the article without figuring out what was going on with the paintings, I did have what I *needed*. For the feature. For the Keller Award submission.

But I *wanted* more. Of everything.

I sucked in a deep breath and nodded again, more assured this time. "Let's go."

My hands found his shirt and I pulled him close again for a kiss. The feeling of calm he always seemed to inject me with spiraled together with the newfound thrill of being completely enveloped in him.

He groaned, kissing me a little deeper. Fireworks went off in my stomach like I'd swallowed Pop Rocks.

"I should probably tell you that Sabrina called." He pulled away. "And threatened me."

"She's serious," I warned. "Precious cargo."

"Don't I know it." He threw an arm around my shoulder and notched his head to the left, down the path where a few feet away, his friends—the ones who'd all been an unfamiliar and unexpected type of kind to me—were waiting.

It was nice. Like playing house. And right now, I didn't want to think about anything past the *playing* part.

We joined them by the lineup of cars where Lucy began detailing the plans. The jets we'd take, the house along the Seine that we were staying in—the McMaster family property. The nights out and the dinners, everything.

"And, as a reminder, this year's excursion is on me, so don't you boys try to be gentlemen about it again," Ishani added after Lucy finished, pinning James with a warning look before her eyes softened and moved to Conrad. Her lips pressed into a straight line but wavered at the corners. "Well, except that little surprise Conrad planned—"

"Got it, Isha," Conrad interrupted.

I turned a raised brow to Conrad and tried to get a handle on whatever I was feeling. Excitement, anxiety, dread. But more than anything, freedom.

"I'm not giving you any spoilers." He pressed a kiss on my head, sweet and familiar like he'd been doing it for years. My stomach did somersaults.

He and James left us to get showered and organized, and we'd all reconvene at the private hangar. I was left marginally dumbfounded and more than a little dizzy.

So, I texted the people who always managed to ground me.

Me: I'm going to Paris

Me: Do either of you know what these surprises are?

Cora: Maybe.

Sabrina: It's above your security clearance, sorry.

Cora: Burner with you? Calls and text forwarded?

I smiled.

Me: Check and check. Real phone is at the condo charging.

Cora: Look at that, Sabrina, our little girl is growing up.

Sabrina: I'm so proud, I could cry.

A FEW HOURS LATER, we boarded a flight.

On the plush leather seat, next to Conrad, I dozed in and out of sleep, waking to find him either reading or listening to whatever played through his headphones.

I shuffled and stretched my legs under the blanket he must've thrown over our laps.

"What are you listening to?" I asked through a yawn. Sitting up, I glanced at the screen at the front of the cabin—we were almost there.

"I just got through a great scene." He clicked the side of his headphones and took them off. "You should listen to it."

"Oh, what book is it?" I asked.

"You'll see." He lifted them off and placed them over my ears.

He hit play and my face warmed.

It was the book I'd been reading. The F1 romance novel, the one he saw in my bag that day in town.

Specifically, he was at the scene in the pit when they were alone and...

Conrad leaned in and moved one of the headphones off my ear. "I'm gonna need to see where those sticky bookmark tabs of yours ended up."

His breath lit tiny sparks that danced down my neck. Beneath the blanket, he ran his fingers along my side, pebbling my skin with goose bumps.

I laid my hand over his and pushed the headphone back over my ear. "Probably better I show you."

He let the audiobook play, his eyes occasionally moving from mine to my lips or along my collar.

A hard swallow shifted the tense column of his throat.

A plane full of people that had no idea what I was listening to, except for him, who watched me with the uninterrupted focus of a lion surveilling prey.

The tension that stretched between us became impossibly thin.

"What in the hell are you doing?" Isha's voice cut through the noise-canceling headphones, and Conrad startled, turning and sitting forward in his seat. "*Sharing*?" Her lips curled into a teasing smirk.

"What do you want, Isha?" Conrad's voice twisted in frustration.

"We're landing soon," she announced, her eyes moving between us. "Seat belts, if you can manage it."

She spun on her heels and went back to her seat next to Lucy with all the polite efficiency of a flight attendant.

CHAPTER 28

Malena

I chewed on my lip, staring at the heavy oak door in front of me.

Tucked behind a neatly laid white stone facade, the sprawling McMaster mansion in Auteuil, Paris was lavish. A pool, a courtyard, a turret that winded up three stories and overlooked the entire right bank.

We landed in the middle of the night Paris time. The new Scroll & Ivy members were at a five-star hotel a few blocks away, while everyone else was here, sleeping off the jet lag.

Except for me, because *I* was indecisively pacing in my guestroom. I'd slept on the plane, so I wasn't tired in the slightest. And all I wanted was one thing.

But when we arrived, Conrad gave me a polite forehead kiss and said good night. It *was* cute and gentlemanly, and that didn't seem like the right time to tell him that I was wide awake and wanted to be fucked up and down this bedroom until I *was* too tired to move.

So, I was here, pacing in the moonlight that spilled through the curtains.

A knock on the door stopped me. I waited a second so as not to seem too eager even though I definitely was.

I opened the door, and his blue eyes locked onto mine. His hair was a little messy, like he'd been raking his hands through it.

"I can't sleep." The confession fell out of his mouth like he was startled that I answered the door.

"Me neither. Want to not sleep together?"

"Yes." Relief mixed with desire, the word settling like metal at the bottom of my stomach.

The nervous energy distilled down to something infinitely more combustible. I took a few steps backward and he followed, closing the door behind him.

"You *did* ask where all those tabs ended up…"

His gaze, slow and smooth like molten caramel, moved down my body. The corners of his mouth tipped up and my heart skipped a few beats. "And *you* promised to show me."

Heat rushed into my cheeks then diffused down my body, meeting between my thighs.

My back hit one of the bed's towering posts. He followed, smoothing his hands onto my hips and dipping his head down to the nape of my neck.

He dragged his fingertips up and down my waist, beneath my satin camisole. "Mal…" he whispered. "You have no idea how bad I want this."

I pushed my fingers through his hair, gently running the tips of my nails against his scalp. He groaned, tilting his head against my touch.

I let out a shuddering breath. "Then take it."

His throat shifted as he pulled back to look at me, an unmistakable heat lighting his eyes.

With a resolute, almost pleading sigh, I reached for the nape of his neck and pulled him in.

Like our kiss in the library, it was tentative at first. But when a tiny moan slipped from between my lips, it cracked open to an almost delirious race to kiss, touch, *feel* everything.

Hands, tongues, teeth.

His body molded to mine. Heat and expertly crafted muscle pinned me to the bedpost. He palmed my thighs, my ass, then moved up my waist. I ran my fingers down the divots of his sculpted back.

We broke away long enough for him to peel off his shirt, and mine soon followed. I slid my satin shorts down my legs and he pushed his joggers off, giving me a preview of the rigid dick I was aching to feel inside of me.

A few seconds later, his lips were back on mine, and he once again pressed me against the wooden bedpost.

My hands traversed over his plate-glass chest and I reveled in the delicious carving of muscle on his stomach.

Unhooking my bra, he flung it off to the side as he stepped me back to the bed without breaking the kiss. His palm, warm and big, gently cupped my breast and he brushed the pad of his thumb over my puckered nipple.

I pulled away to suck in a breath. "Con..."

He let out a beleaguered pant. "I like the sound of my name out of your mouth."

Without another word, he pulled me into another searing kiss.

He nudged me down and followed, and the next thing I knew, my bare back was on the sheets and he was on top of me. He bucked his hips against mine, his rock-hard erection between my legs filling me with impatience.

He pulled away and paused, running his eyes over my body with a look of reverence. He licked his lips, lust weighing on his eyelids. "Fuck, Mal."

A slickness gathered between my thighs as my pulse raced out of control.

He kissed and grazed his teeth down my neck, moving lower to my chest. His tongue dragged along a nipple.

My fingers curled into his hair.

"Patience." He kissed down the line of my sternum.

This was when I'd usually take charge. I'd ask for what I wanted, or I'd take control.

I never did *this*. Moving at a pace that wasn't mine, my pleasure at someone else's mercy... and it sent a thrill whirling through me. Vulnerability, but in the hands of someone I trusted. My stomach dipped and bowed as he moved south, kiss by kiss. One landed just below my belly button. My clit pulsed, waiting for more.

I yanked at his hair in warning.

"Let me *savor* you." Reaching the apex of my thighs, he let out a deep, hungry groan between them. The vibrations coiled my desire tighter, and he grazed his teeth over my panties.

My hips jerked, and as though it was all the encouragement he needed, he yanked them clean off.

He rolled gentle strokes over my clit with the pad of his thumb, and my face crumpled under a deep moan.

"Con..." I begged, electricity sparking down my legs and back up.

A low chuckle warmed my thighs. "You like that, Mal?"

"Yes," I breathed. I pressed my head back against the pillow and curved my hips into him.

He pushed two fingers inside, and I gasped at the gratifying stretch. I dripped along his hand. At the same time, he continued the slow strokes against my clit with his tongue.

My vision went blurry. A string of unintelligible sounds fell out of my mouth.

He moved faster and with more intention, twisting and curling his fingers, pushing me closer and closer.

Heat moved down my spine. Every muscle grew taut. My nerves tangled together, tighter and tighter, until it all burst together and I arched up from the bed, an orchestral crescendo ringing in my ears.

I slammed my eyelids shut, writhing beneath him as my climax moved through me in waves. A cold sweat misted off my skin.

Moments later, his lips were back on mine in a deep kiss, and the fog began to lift. He shifted out of bed and my eyes opened, my sated gaze roaming up his sculpted body.

"It's impolite to stare," he teased as he slid a condom on.

I ran my teeth over my lower lip. "Oops."

Despite still being in the afterglow, I was hungry for more.

He got back in bed and pushed my legs apart, lining himself up at my core. He dragged his erection over me, watching as I squirmed, waiting.

"I sort of like teasing you."

I rolled my hips against him, chasing the friction, and closed my eyes. I needed him *now*.

After weeks of banter and foreplay, long stares, and too many dreams that had me reaching for my vibrator in the middle of the night, it was finally happening.

"*Please*." In a nearly broken sob, impatience stretched my words.

"Look at me," he said roughly, and my eyes fluttered open.

Our gazes clashed and he pushed into me slowly. He watched as I took him, inch by inch, stretching me with satisfying tension, until he finally bottomed out inside me.

"That's it, Mal," he said through a pleasure-filled groan. I let out a tiny moan as my body adjusted to him. "You okay?"

I swung a leg over his hip. "*Yes*."

With a low chuckle and a satisfied smirk, he slowly withdrew. His hand moved to pin mine above my head and the other clamped on my hip. He leaned forward and eased into me before picking up the tempo, and with every thrust, he pushed the oxygen from my lungs and the patience from my body.

"More," I begged.

Not waiting an extra second, he took me harder.

His gaze was transfixed on where our bodies met before it passed languidly over my own. A new erotic sensation unlocked in that moment, knowing how much he enjoyed the *sight* of being inside of me.

"You look so fucking good like that, Mal," he murmured. I sank my fingernails into his back, hanging on as he snapped his hips with abandon. "Full of me."

Completely lost in all of it, all I could sense was him. The way he filled me, how his weight pushed against my body, his heavy breaths quickening as we neared the same place.

My mouth fell open with a splintered cry as I barreled toward another climax. This time it ripped through me, white-hot and all-consuming, setting fire to every last nerve ending and pushing a few tears out of the corners of my eyes.

A few more deep thrusts before a shudder overtook his body, and he jerked forward with a heavy groan.

What came next happened in flashes as I came down from it all. He got out of bed and disappeared into the en suite, then came back and pulled me to him. His thumb stroked my shoulder, and I relished the feeling similar to gently rocking in a hammock.

I wasn't thinking about my next move or anything at all, really. And that was new.

"You okay?" Conrad whispered against my forehead, our legs intertwined.

I hummed and nodded. My eyelids became heavy as the exertion combined with the jetlag caught up to me.

Sex was one thing; it was easy. It was figuring out what turned me on and what didn't. I tried not to put too much emotional stock in it because there was no point. These were my college years—my only chance to figure it all out.

But that...

He slid his palm down to the small of my back, his fingers slowly curling out and pulling in against my skin. Wrapped in his arms with the reverent way he gently stroked me, I drifted to sleep, bathed in a different feeling entirely.

A feeling akin to floating, because I was safe. There was no pretense weighing me down. With him, I didn't have to conform to some idea of what I was supposed to be.

It was subversive.

Because now that I'd felt it, I never wanted it to stop.

CHAPTER 29

Conrad

I woke to the mattress shifting.

I groaned, rolled over, and stretched my arm out to the other side of the bed to find it empty. My eyes opened and a foot away, the sheets at her waist, Malena was checking her phone. She'd look at it, click the screen off, only to check it again seconds later.

"You alright?" I asked through a yawn, running a finger down her bare back. I folded my other arm onto the pillow, tucking my hand behind my head and watching her. We'd only slept a handful of hours, but I felt refreshed after spending the night tangled in the sheets with her.

"Yeah." Her voice almost squeaked. She clicked her phone screen off again and placed it back on the nightstand. "I was just thinking."

"About?"

She paused, then looked over her shoulder at me. She opened her mouth, her eyes moving along the comforter, only to close it again.

Concern rattled between my ribs. "Mal..."

"I..." She looked back ahead. Another pause. "Someone

has a list of these Van Holden pieces... They're making them and then selling them through the Modiste Gallery."

Surprise, or confusion, or *something* pushed my voice up an octave. "What?"

"I've been turning over everything we talked about the other day. Someone is forging Van Holden paintings that were thought to be destroyed in World War II. And they're selling them through this gallery." Malena twisted her fingers around the sheets. "That's the most likely scenario, right?"

My jaw slackened. She was talking about the paintings? *That's* what was on her mind? Fuck, I thought she was having second thoughts about whatever this was between us. Because after last night, I was sure I didn't want it to end.

I nodded, relieved, and curled a hand around her waist, tugging gently. As much as I liked the view of her hair cascading down her bare back, I wanted to see that smile. "Probably..."

"Then what does that have to do with the catacombs?" she continued, looking straight ahead. "Why not rent a studio in midtown Manhattan?"

"Cheaper rent?" I sat up and pushed her hair over her shoulder, hoping to get her mind back to where mine was. "Or maybe the catacombs are an incidental finding." I slowly kissed up the nape of her neck. "A red herring."

I snaked a hand between her thighs and splayed my other just below the swell of her breasts, my thumb running a few firm swipes over her puckered nipple.

"Con..." The firmness in her warning wavered under a tiny yip.

"Mal." I brushed my fingers against her clit and her body jerked. "You're naked and you expect me to focus?"

"*Con*," she repeated, more serious this time. And despite how good my name sounded falling out from between her lips, I knew my trying was a lost cause.

I cleared my throat, trying to shift gears. "The student doing this needs the supplies that they're obviously making on campus. Remember? The paint and that time you shoved me in a closet?"

She hummed and leaned back against me. Just as I was beginning to think her curiosity was sated and we could get back to other things, she pulled her legs beneath her and turned to me.

"And the paint takes a long time to dry..." she added. My eyes wandered down the body I'd spent the last few hours touching, kissing, and fucking every inch of. "So, they probably have to move the pieces already framed, which would definitely draw unwanted attention." She snapped her fingers. "Hence the catacombs."

"Makes sense." I blinked a few times. "So they're probably going to the clock tower to move it off campus."

"And you said the catacombs are never used by Scroll & Ivy members? Right?"

"Only for the first party of the year, the one at the clock tower." I nodded, remembering the night well. "You seem to be the only person who finds the catacombs interesting."

Mal shook her head. "Having the world as your playground makes *everything* boring. You have a warped sense of reality."

I chuckled.

"That narrows it down," she went on. "It has to be someone with a history or some knowledge about Scroll & Ivy and an inside track on Van Holden. Maybe a relative or someone close to his family." She shifted a bit in bed, pushing the covers farther to the side and throwing a leg over mine so she was straddling my lap. "It's a lot more than we knew before." With a contented sigh, she put both hands on my chest. A playful smile inched up her cheeks. "Now... back to what you were doing."

I glanced at the clock over her shoulder. The light peeking through the drawn curtains was dim and kept the ornate room draped in darkness, but it was almost noon.

"*Now* you're on board?"

"What can I say? Sex is great for mental clarity." She rolled her hips purposefully. "How about we get some more?"

"Too late." I put a hand on either thigh and nudged her back to her side. We had to get moving.

"Are you kicking me out of bed?"

"Never." I held her chin and pressed a kiss against her lips. For a second I paused there, negotiating how late we could be, then pulled away with a soft shake of my head. "We have plans."

WE WERE LATE.

We got distracted in the shower. Twice.

"No way." Malena gasped as our private car pulled up to the Geroux Raceway.

My chest filled with air seeing the delight in her eyes.

Lines of fans began to file in through the main gates while we were driven to a separate entrance. It was the one closest to the Rutherford box.

"F1 fan?" I asked. "What a coincidence."

"You just *happened* to want to catch a race?" She smiled ear to ear.

"James's family has a permanent lounge at all F1 events." I threw an arm over her shoulders as we were escorted in.

While they didn't own an F1 team, Rutherford Motors made the engines that populated most of the grid. In addition to making jet engines, Rutherford engines were second to none in formula one racing.

Her wide eyes narrowed when she looked up at me. "Conrad. Did you..."

My heart rate picked up.

"We needed to pick a place to go. The Paris GP got rescheduled from this past summer for the Olympics," I told her nonchalantly, even though this was entirely my idea. "Isha and Lucy come to Paris sometime before fall break every year anyway, figured it would..."

"Save jet fuel?"

"Exactly." We entered near the end of the hall and walked into the exclusive lounge. Our seats overlooked the entire circuit but sat just above the hairpin turn. I looked for James, but he was probably at ground level in Mercury Racing's pit, being greeted by drivers.

Malena took the glass of champagne one of the waiters offered her and we walked to the line of seats directly in front of the glass-paned safety divider. She sat down ahead of what would be a perfect, unobstructed view. "How efficient."

I smiled as one thing became undeniably clear: I liked her. I liked seeing her smile. I liked hearing her laugh. I liked it when she was mean to me. I liked kissing her, touching her, fucking her. I liked everything about her.

And that hadn't happened to me before.

I wasn't sure how to proceed, and seeing as I'd never been the one to bring it up, I thought it better not to disrupt what was developing between us. For now, anyway.

"I was hoping to do a trip to Brazil before medical school, time it with the GP in Sao Paulo." Malena took a sip of champagne and leaned forward, looking out to where the drivers would take their positions. Isha and Lucy were buzzing around, making note of which racers they were keeping an eye on. Most of the other members had already taken their seats in the box. "It's on a long list of places I want to go."

"Where else is on the list?"

"Everywhere." Her voice petered off, still looking ahead but her eyes seemingly lost in thought.

"So... trips around the world," I began. "You never did that with Sabrina?"

I knew the Alders family peripherally and that Mal lived with her at one of their many properties. So it stood to reason that she'd have been invited on the occasional trip—winters in Zermatt or Saint Moritz, summers in Newport.

"Sabrina always invites me, but I can't go..." She paused. "Long breaks from school are usually filled with internships or studying."

I nodded.

"Right, that résumé." A slight commotion at the door drew my attention and I smiled. The reason I didn't want to be too late had arrived. "Speaking of Sabrina..."

Mal looked over her shoulder and was across the room throwing her arms around her best friend before I could say another word. The next five minutes descended into a string of high-pitched squeals, and all the while, I sat back, trying to rein in my own excitement.

I'd texted Sabrina while we were on the jet to see if she'd be able to join us. I figured if she was willing to threaten my bodily safety to ensure Malena's, then she'd probably jump at the chance to see her.

Besides, she was a member of Scroll & Ivy. This was a Scroll & Ivy event. It made sense that she be here.

And I liked seeing Mal smile.

More than that, I liked *making* her smile.

CHAPTER 30

Malena

I didn't want to let her go.

I squeezed my best friend, not realizing just how much I'd missed her over the last few weeks.

"I can't believe you're here." I looked past her to the stern, tower of a man who seemed to be trying for a blank expression but whose piercing gray eyes watched the room closely. "Hello..."

He gave me a slight nod then resumed scanning the room.

"What happened to Ridley?" I whispered.

Sabrina traveling with a security team wasn't anything new, but I was expecting Ridley, the private security she'd had since she was a kid who was with her when she started at Winchester. He'd only hung around through the first semester of freshman year, at which point her father gave the green light to scale back her team on campus. Sabrina still had security protocols in place that other students wouldn't even begin to comprehend, but it was all fairly standard.

"Ridley's not Secret Service." She tipped her head to the staunch-looking man standing five feet away. "And Secret Service protection protocol starts one-hundred and twenty days prior to any Presidential election," she rattled off in a tone imitating her dad. "So, I have Agent Emerson."

"Oh..." My voice jumped up an octave because this new guy was... well, hot, to put it bluntly.

Chiseled jaw, dark brown hair, broad shoulders.

Basically, the polar opposite to Ridley, who'd always come across like a "fit dad." He was kind and treated Sabrina like his own daughter. The significantly younger man with an earpiece and a scowl gave off a completely different vibe. And I didn't miss just *how* he'd been looking at Sabrina since they arrived. Cora and I would need to bring up the new development next time we had her alone.

"He seems nice," I added.

"I'm stuck with him for the next while." Sabrina cast a passing glance over her shoulder. "Now come on, let's enjoy the race..." Sabrina looped her arm in mine, and we took a few steps back to our seats. She looked directly at Conrad even though she was talking to me. "And then after the race, I'm stealing you for the rest of the day."

"Fine." He held my chin, tilted it up, and pressed a kiss on my lips. Tingles spread down my body, curling my toes. "But we're going out tonight."

"Dancing!" Ishani called from behind him. "You're *both* joining us," she added sternly.

Not that I ever needed an excuse to party.

AT A SMALL CAFÉ along the Champs-Élysées, Sabrina and I settled at a table in front of a pair of closed French doors. Outside, in front of the buildings with pale brick faces, tinned roofs, and iron-wrought balconies, was a steady stream of tourists enjoying the less crowded autumn season. Checkered among them were locals hurrying past, dressed in chic wool coats with understated handbags.

"How are things on your own?" I asked just as we received our drinks and pastries.

Sabrina didn't talk about her past a lot, but being the closest thing America had to a princess came with a price. Hers was a kidnapping when she was six. It made the national news for months even though she was recovered safe and sound in a day. While a lot of people in her family learned to thrive in that spotlight, Sabrina avoided it.

"Good, I've even been going out," she reported, momentarily dragging her fingers along the lip of the marble table and doing a little shoulder shimmy.

When I walked onto campus as a freshman, I was determined to try *everything*. Sabrina was the opposite; she relied on me and Cora to coax her out of her shell, so this semester abroad was a big step for her.

I beamed. "You look good."

"So do you." Her lips stretched with the last syllable. "So..."

"I'm having fun," I explained as I stirred some sugar into my cappuccino. "Finally managed a trip without my parents knowing."

The "safety" that my parents' rigid standards provided also kept my view on the world pretty narrow. With every broken rule was a slightly more vivid future, a bigger canvas to paint on. More possibilities than I was allowed to imagine.

I looked up and Sabrina's brows pulled in. "Sabrina?"

"I know this trip is a sweet gesture..." She fussed with her mug, now looking at it while she turned it on the table. "But just remember, taking you to Paris and a Grand Prix doesn't prove anything. And, for the record, I could have done both."

I smiled. She'd already extended a similar warning, but

Sabrina was protective, and I'd been waiting for another one—delivered in person this time.

"Sabrina Madeline Alders, you are swoonier than any man." I put one hand up like I was taking an oath. "I promise."

My eyes were wide open. I knew about Conrad's reputation and I planned on enjoying it. Because if anything, it gave me some solace. We both fell squarely in the "people you screw" category for each other. I wouldn't fit in his world, and he couldn't exist in mine. This was the perfect setup, a way to have it all, for now.

She laughed. "I only mean, this is sort of different than your usual hookup, and I don't want you falling for some guy who—"

"Don't worry, I'm not planning for the future."

It wasn't like I could, even *if* I wanted to. And I told myself I didn't want to.

The gorgeous, cavalier, lily white legacy with no real plans for the future was *not* what my parents had in mind for me. Maybe it was a fling, maybe it was a little more, but it would end. Just like everything else.

"Good." Sabrina's face fell a bit as she agreed. "You don't have to be pessimistic though. Just vigilant."

I shook my head, putting her at ease with a playful grin. "I'll be fine."

I wasn't going to let it bother me, because I'd finally stolen a little freedom.

When the Winchester diploma landed in my hand at the end of my senior year, all of this would settle like sparkling grains at the bottom of my memory's hourglass. I was going to enjoy them while they were at the top.

CHAPTER 31

Conrad

Syncopated beats pushed through the club between sparkling lights and muted chatter.

Hours into the night at a club in Paris, everyone had dispersed. Isha and Lucy were dancing, Felix and James were sipping whiskey by the VIP bar. Sabrina called it an early night an hour ago, taking her broody bodyguard with her.

That left Mal and me, off to the side in the private lounge that overlooked the dance floor, her body swaying gently as she sipped from her glass.

"Do you want to dance?" I murmured in her ear.

She leaned into me and craned her neck back, resting her head on my shoulder. She pushed onto her toes and I looped both arms around her waist. "Can we go somewhere quiet?"

I smirked. *Fuck*, of course we could.

"Let's get out of here." My arms tightened around her waist. I'd been wanting to take her home since she met us here wearing that silver sequined dress.

Ending just below her thighs, I watched those long legs move all night and I'd been waiting to get her back in bed. And see that dress on the floor.

She dropped back to her heels, turned around, and shook her head. "Quiet, not *that* quiet." She looked down at the ice cubes in her glass then back up at me. Her teeth scraped over her bottom lip. "Private."

Understanding burrowed all the way down my spine as she sauntered past me.

"Mal..." I followed, weaving our fingers together.

A security guard stood in front of a secluded hallway draped closed by a heavy curtain. Malena began to pull me through, and I gave him a quick glance, stopping briefly to make sure he heard me when I said, "Privacy."

He nodded. The swish of a heavy curtain closing the space off lowered the volume of the music to a distant hum, the thumping through the walls becoming gentle taps.

"Sabrina left through here earlier," Mal explained, turning around. The dimly lit corridor was short and ended at the emergency door that presumably led out on the street. She tugged my arm and pulled me into her, then tilted her now empty drink up to her lips.

"How much have you—"

"Sparkling water all night," she said, low and soft, pressing her palm into my chest and backing me into the wall. Before I could say anything, she picked up an ice cube from the empty glass. "Relax."

She popped it into her mouth and let it move from one cheek to the other. Eyes on me, she undid my pants and stroked my length.

"Mal..." I groaned.

A devious smile tugged at her cheek, and as far as I could tell, the ice had melted. She gripped my dick a little more purposefully, stroking me with intention.

"Mal..." I repeated, and this time my breathing faltered. My heart slammed against my sternum as she dropped to her knees. "What are you doing?"

She ran the pad of her thumb over the tip of my dick. It throbbed, waiting to see what came next.

Eyes locked on mine, she set her glass on the floor and pulled another ice cube out. This time she ran it over her lips before dropping it back in her glass. "Whatever I want."

She ran the tip of her tongue and her lips—both frosted from the ice—along my shaft.

Electricity shot up my spine.

Then she slowly swallowed me down.

The cold snap from her lips. The soaking heat of her mouth.

The sensation punched all the air out of my lungs.

The icy prickle melted into a mind-altering heat. She hollowed out her cheeks, tightening her hold on me, and my skin broke out in a cold sweat as I tried so fucking hard not to come.

My head rolled back against the wall. My vision began to blur.

Sex with Mal was something else, but a blowjob, here? Like *this*? *Fuck*.

My fingers tangled into her hair. I looked back down at her as she bobbed along my shaft, her hand stroking my balls and her hair swishing along her bare shoulders.

"That's it, Mal." A pleasure-filled groan moved up my chest.

She sucked, licked, even grazed me lightly with her teeth, sputtering as she continued to take my entire length.

She tilted her head up to meet my stare and take me deeper.

The club, her stunning eyes, the fact that she was constantly surprising me, and the tableau of her lips wrapped around my dick as it slid down her throat... All of it was too much.

My heart raced out of control.

"Babe," I warned, unable to keep my hips from bucking into her. Tingles curled my toes and moved up my legs, concentrating at my hips.

I was getting too close to the edge.

Her pace increased wildly and she let out a long moan along my length, the vibrations doing me in. Every nerve ending in my body erupted.

"Mal," I grunted loudly in warning.

She didn't pull away.

I released hard in her mouth, and she coaxed every last drop from me, the slide of her tongue torturous. Moments later, I looked down to find an expression of victory sparkling in her eyes as her throat shifted around a swallow.

"We need to leave," I demanded hastily between heavy breaths.

My vision cleared, and she pulled away as I got myself together.

"I'm not done dancing."

I pinned her with a stare. "Don't worry. Those hips *will* move."

CHAPTER 32

Malena

T hursday afternoon, a day after getting back from Paris, I felt invincible.

I sat in the newsroom and basked in the quiet. Now that the MCATs were behind me, I was focusing on some of the work I'd put on the back burner. Today, that meant prepping my notes for my advanced biochem lab practical.

"Malena." Dillian's voice lifted me from my work and I found him standing there in a baller cap and tweed jacket, looking quite literally like a 1930s newsie. "What are you doing here?"

Conrad dropped me off before heading to his family's house in Manhattan, where he'd spend the last bit of fall break. Since Cora wouldn't be back till Sunday, I spent last night alone, recharging my social battery and letting pride fill me at the step I'd taken in the right direction. It was different to sneaking out for a party in high school or even toeing the line of normal life here in college.

I'd finally done something *real* for myself.

My parents would never know, but still, it was a step.

"I got back to campus early. The building was open, so I figured I'd get some work done." I looked around, and it hit me that I'd never actually asked if I could use the room. "That's okay, right?"

"Yeah. Of course," he assured me. "While I have you, have you given any thought to that writing seminar over the summer? You were recommended for it."

I chewed on my lip. There was no harm in getting more information... Maybe I'd fill out the interest form anyway. I'd have to figure out how to schedule it around my planned internship with the NY Lightning's medical team, but it was *possible*. "Still figuring that out..."

He nodded. "Great. And how's your feature?"

"Good, I got plenty of material for the 'meritocracy is a sham' angle." I figured it was best to keep my suspicions quiet until I knew more. Especially since he was averse to the idea when I first pitched it. "I saw a couple parties, got some interesting lore."

"Oh." His eyes brightened. "That's all?"

I paused. "I thought it was pretty interesting..."

"It is. That sounds great, piercing. Definitely the kind of thing the Keller Award committee looks for," he insisted. "If you have some time..." He knocked on my desk a couple of times, his head tilted up in thought before he walked over to his own desk. "I need that piece on the Astor donation proofed."

I stood and walked over, glancing at his screen from the other side of his desk.

"No need," Conrad answered from the doorway. "It's done."

"What?" Dillian and I said in unison, turning toward the door.

In a dark blue quilted jacket with one of those distracting crew neck sweaters underneath, Conrad walked into the newsroom, a boyish grin on his face that made my stomach flip.

He never came to the paper.

"Yeah, I got that email asking for a volunteer too," Conrad drawled sarcastically. He pointed to Dillian's computer and ran his hand up my back before resting it right above the curve of my ass. "Turns out, I *can* read."

"Oh..." Dillian stammered, clicking around on his desktop. "It's..." He looked up at the two of us incredulously. "Thank you."

Conrad stroked his fingers back and forth, pushing electricity up and down my spine. Keeping a perfectly straight face and his attention squarely on Dillian, the corner of his mouth quirked.

"Need anything else?" he asked.

"No..." Dillian rubbed his forehead.

I turned, taking a few steps to my desk, and Conrad followed. Once we were out of earshot, his fingers curled around my elbow. "Can I talk to you?" His breath skated down the nape of my neck. "Privately."

All thoughts about finishing my lab practical notes evaporated as I followed Conrad out.

"You're back early." Curiosity skittered along my arm and his hand slid down my back as he led me through the stone corridor.

"I had some work to catch up on." He stared straight ahead.

"Like the piece Dillian wanted proofread?"

"There's this cute girl at the paper," he explained. "I'm trying to impress her."

I looked up at him inquisitively. "By catching typos?"

"Go easy on me." An adorable nervous laugh rumbled up his chest as he pushed the doors to the old building wide open. "I'm new at this."

The piney scent of the cool fall day filled my lungs and before I knew it, his heavy coat was being draped around my shoulders. We walked down the steps, and he led me to the side of them.

"I don't grade on curves, I ruin them," I said, sidestepping his mention of "this," seeing as we hadn't discussed any labels formally. I looked around, wondering why I was here. "And... you needed to tell me that outside?"

His eyes glimmered in the afternoon sun.

At first, I thought it was easy to be around him because he was so carefree and that it'd rubbed off on me. In actuality, I was realizing it was how he looked at me when I was unabashedly myself. It was always with this wonder or curiosity—like all he wanted was to know more.

Never with expectation or judgment. It was refreshing.

"No." With his eyes glued to mine and his hand smoothing over my hips, he backed me up against the cool gray stone. "I *needed* to do this."

He dropped his lips to mine and pulled me into a slow kiss. Like sipping a spiked hot chocolate, it was warm and intoxicating. A few ivy leaves brushed against my skin, and I closed my eyes, sinking into the feeling.

"You look so fucking good in these." His hands spanned over my soft leggings, gripping my thighs, and need flourished between my legs.

He pulled away and pressed a few pecks along my chin and one on my collar. My teeth scraped over my lower lip, and I tipped my head back.

"Con..." I warned.

"Sorry, I couldn't wait." He kept going, leaving a trail of goose bumps behind as he kissed down my neck. "But I figured you didn't want Dillian to see me feel you up."

His navy wool coat smelled like him, fresh and woodsy and something uniquely Conrad. The rich silk lining brushed against my skin and the length of it provided cover now that my leg was all but swung over his waist.

"We should probably take this inside." My fingers played with a button on his sweater's collar.

"One more." He leaned back in and his lips connected with mine.

Another shot of adrenaline pushed through my veins.

It wasn't until the sound of someone clearing their throat cut through the tension that we stopped. In a puffer jacket with a pantsuit underneath, President Packham crossed her arms, her mouth arched down.

I took a sharp inhale, then pushed Conrad back a step. "Ummm..."

My brain, foggy from the kiss and completely suffocated under the weight of President Packham's stare, refused to form words.

"Let's try to keep these spaces reserved for more *appropriate* activities." She looked directly at Conrad, sparing me the humiliation.

"Sorry." He rubbed the back of his neck.

She didn't say anything else, just shook her head and walked past.

"We *should* take this inside," Conrad whispered in my ear, unfazed and playful.

I was frozen. While it might not be a big deal for *him*, I had to be cautious.

"Hey." Conrad put both hands on my shoulders, dipping his head down and trying to catch my eyes. "I'm sorry."

"No, it's okay." My cheeks warmed.

What could I say? *My mommy and daddy don't let me talk to boys, and President Packham knows them, so that's why I'm nervous that we got caught?* It was ridiculous, but the fact remained that the whole situation left me embarrassed and feeling like a child.

I hadn't told him about my parents because I enjoyed the illusion of independence that simply being around him offered. He was allowed to have this full and interesting life, and I had to do that from the confines of the cage I was occasionally able to sneak out of. How did you explain that to someone who had all the freedom in the world? It would be like explaining air to a fish.

"I *may* have given you an impression about my taste for public displays in Paris," I added.

For those blissful days across the pond, reality had ceased to exist. I'd enjoyed not having to be two versions of the same person, but it was proving to be a high that preceded one hell of a comedown.

His warm smile chased away the uneasiness. His fingers pressed against my hips a little tighter, but he kept the space between us. "You're a moving target, Mal."

"Sorry."

"Don't be, I'm having fun keeping up." He dropped a chaste kiss on my lips before pulling away. "I'll keep my hands to myself around faculty."

"Thanks." I curled my fingers around his sweater. "Let's go back to your place."

CHAPTER 33

Conrad

The Tuesday of the first week back to class after fall break, I leaned against an iron-framed window waiting for James and Malena's American Lit lecture to finish. The chill circulating in the drafty hall fought a losing battle against the heated air pushing through the building's vents.

"Here you go," said Ishani, appearing out of thin air and handing me a card, a wide grin splayed across her face.

It was simple, a blank note with the words: **Benedict Lancaster, May 2024** neatly written in Ishani's handwriting.

"What's this?"

"Well, you said you wanted information on the Modiste Gallery's latest Van Holden sale." She tapped on the card. "That's the seller."

My interest spiked and I pushed off the frosty window frame. "And they just shared it with you?"

"I am Ishani Gabriella Roy." Her shoulders rose with feigned offense and she brought her hand to the center of her chest. "If I wanted the curator to paint himself in the Pop-art style, he'd ask for my color preference."

I rolled my eyes at the hyperbole. "And how did you *actually* get this?"

She grinned. "I purchased a few pieces and told them I was interested in one of the Van Holdens they'd already sold."

"What did they say?"

"That they'd contact the buyer and see if they could broker another sale."

I smiled. A master at getting what she wanted, Ishani knew how to play anyone's motives against them.

"And the gallery will get paid twice if they broker two sales," I surmised.

"Exactly, but this…" She circled back to her point and tapped the card. "They let the original seller's name slip in conversation. At least the account name, anyway."

"Lancaster,'" I read aloud.

"Are you going to tell me why you need it?"

"I already told you." I ran a hand down the back of my head. Mal said I could tell Isha, and I was sure she'd keep it quiet, but at the same time, I liked sharing this secret with Mal.

"You want me to believe you plan to gift it to your mother?" She gave me a knowing look. "Next you'll tell me that Malena is in Scroll & Ivy in Sabrina's place and that's *all*."

I winced. "It's that unbelievable?"

"Don't worry, I think everyone assumes she's blackmailing you. Honestly, I did too until I saw you all googly eyed for her. Either way, you're a terrible liar." She pinched my cheek. "It's why we let you act like a complete man-whore. We *know* you won't lead those girls on. You're incapable of telling a good lie."

"Thanks, I guess." I shooed away her hand. Then, I lowered my voice and looped back to the question she'd originally asked. "We think the paintings might be fakes."

"Oh," she said in an exaggerated drawl, like it was obvious.

"Well, then all anyone *needs* to do is request additional authentication."

"Why would they oblige? The gallery has their own in-house authenticator, right?"

"They do." Ishani shrugged. "Although, I could include it in the terms if the owner agrees to sell."

"And the gallery would do that?"

"They would if I paid a few hundred thousand extra for it."

"If it got past one authentication, it'll get past another," I reasoned.

"Not if I ask for it to be radiocarbon dated," Isha suggested. "Paint used prior to the nineteen-forties doesn't have radioactive carbon. The process is terribly expensive, is at the owner's expense, and *will* require damaging the piece a bit to remove paint samples. Ultimately hurts its resale value, but if the new owner insists..."

My mouth hung open a bit. Isha lived a glamorous life; she knew her way around an art gallery, a fashion house, and a cosmetics lab. It was easy to forget how many hats she wore when I was so used to seeing her as Isha Roy, longtime friend and occasional instigator of trouble.

"You do realize you attend a university with the best fine arts program in the world, right?" She cocked her head to the side. "Not to mention the Roy home in Kensington houses three Picassos, four Vermeers, and seven Degas..." she listed off. "Spend your childhood amongst gallerists and glitterati, you learn a few things."

"Isha..." I teased. This was incredibly helpful information and she seemed excited to share it. "Are you invested in my assignment?"

"Not at all." She craned her neck to the side to look into the lecture hall as the first few students began to exit. "She's lovely. Headstrong. I like her." I didn't have to ask to know she was referring to Mal.

"Me too," I answered quietly, leaning back against the windowsill, the wind rattling against the old tempered glass.

"I made a new acquaintance in my Advanced Linguistics class, she's organizing this year's Holi Festival," Isha went on. "The Diwali party with Malena gave me the push I needed, I think."

"She has a way of doing that."

"Yes, well…" She released a contented breath. "I'll see you later. Lucy and I have plans, but happy sleuthing."

With that, she walked down the hall and out of the building while I waited for the doors to open again, because I was sure Malena would take her time leaving class. She had this adorable need to check all of her belongings five times, like her phone was going to disappear if she didn't.

A minute later, the doors opened again, this time propped open by a student, and the rest filed out.

My eyes flew to where I knew she sat. In jeans and a soft-looking sweater today, her hair fell around her shoulders as she stood and talked to a tall, dark-haired guy.

Concern swirled in my gut, then became a cement block when I realized who it was.

The one who'd waved at her as he exited the brunch spot that day in town.

The ex.

The exception to her no-relationships rule.

My legs moved for exactly two steps before I was stopped.

James stood in my way, brow quirked. "Oh no… is that… *jealousy?*"

I craned my neck to look past him. "No."

Malena didn't date; she told me that weeks ago. Except she did. She'd dated *him*.

I flicked a glance at the guy in question. "Do they sit together?"

I felt like a toddler asking that question. She could sit with whomever she wanted, I knew that.

"They used to." He glanced at them over his shoulder. "Last semester in Advanced Comp. Based on how they were acting, I assumed they were dating."

My jaw flexed and I took a step back.

"Based on how they were acting?" The image of them *together* twisted in my mind. Surprisingly, it wasn't all the things we'd been doing for the last week... but were they cuddly together? I liked to think she was only that way with me. "What does that mean? Were they noticeable?"

"No, it's nothing like that. It's just... I mean," he sputtered, and my eyes stayed glued to the pair as they continued to talk. "Come on, Con." He clasped a supportive hand on my shoulder as he glanced over to Malena. *My* Malena. "She's... hard to miss."

My head whipped back to glare at him.

"Not that I was aiming." His smirk straightened and he threw his hands up. "Jeez, redirect that look, I'm not the ex."

I rubbed the back of my neck, hoping to loosen the uncomfortable tightness that ran down my sternum. It wasn't *only* that I was jealous...

She looked different. Bored. Polite. Not like herself.

Maybe I was biased because next to me she felt warm and bright. But from my vantage point, it was like hanging a Degas in an attic. Her normally proud stance was slightly crumpled and her shoulders sagged.

"Look, we need to talk about Mal." James drew my attention back to him. "We don't fuck people over, remember?"

"I know..." I trailed off. Understanding what he meant, shame whistled in my ear. Based on my track record, if I got into a relationship, I wouldn't be any better than my dad or my brothers, I knew that.

And, apparently, James did too. Hence the warning.

For the first time, I felt the harsh sting of being categorized as the kind of guy James would keep from Isha or Lucy.

I couldn't fuck it up if I didn't try. Only... Mal made me want to try.

"I like her," I admitted quietly. "A lot."

"And she knows that?"

Why wouldn't she? We were together all the time. If I was an outsider looking in, I'd think we were fucking nauseating. "What do you mean?"

James's mouth hung ajar. "You've talked to her about it?"

"No." I winced. We Hastings were the "sweep it under the rug" types. We didn't *talk* about anything. "We're together all the time, do we *need* to?"

"Jesus, Con." James wiped a hand down his face. "That guy has been sniffing around her all semester and she's still a free agent?"

A flame lit in my chest.

"You said it wasn't that bad," I whisper-shouted at him.

"I lied," he rebutted. "I wasn't sure if you were actually going to date her, so I was sort of on Hamilton's side for this one."

"Stop calling my girlfriend by a nickname." It didn't bother me. It was... annoying. That's all. Besides, she had a nickname. The one only *I* called her by.

"So she *is* your girlfriend?" James crossed his arms and gave me a shit-eating grin. "You should tell her that."

"I will." I let out a frustrated breath. "Do *you* need the reminder?"

He gave me an unamused look and brought us right back to the point we were circling. "No, but that guy might."

Fuck. I glanced back at them. "What do I do?"

"It's pretty simple." James waved Mal over. "First, make sure you're not *gonna* be a piece of shit to her, and then don't be."

He went quiet just as Mal approached.

"Hey." Her eyes bounced between me and James.

"I wanted to see something in the mausoleum," I told her. "Come with me?"

"Sure." We took a few steps out of the lecture hall together.

James was gone before I could ask him how the hell I was supposed to "make sure" I wasn't going to be a piece of shit.

I didn't plan to be. I'd never cheat. I didn't lie...

But I didn't want to make promises I couldn't keep. All of this was new to me, but fumbling this thing with Mal was out of the question.

"'LANCASTER, LONDON.'" Malena ran her thumb over the notecard Isha had scribbled on. I told her about what Isha was able to devise on her own when we walked over here. Mal was fizzing with excitement with the news. "Does her family know them?"

We walked through the carved wooden doorway and into the mausoleum's library. I put her bag down on the couches and she headed toward the far side wall. "Not as far as she knows."

"You think they were members?" she speculated, tucking the notecard in her back pocket.

"Only one way to find out." I looked up at the shelves holding members' journals.

"There's no list of members?" Malena followed my gaze. "Considering the wealth among those granted entry to this place, I feel like hiring someone to make a spreadsheet wouldn't be that big of a deal. A drop in their billionaire buckets, you could say."

I chuckled. "Not that I know of, but don't worry, they're in chronological order, so it shouldn't be too hard. I'll look."

"And let *you* live out *my Beauty and the Beast* fantasy? I don't think so." She smacked the back of her hand against my chest and walked over to the ladder.

I followed a step behind her, waiting as she put a foot on the bottom rung, a hand on each rail.

"I know we're hot on the trail of a lead." I held it still and pushed the brakes on either side. "But that's the second time you've—"

"I meant the bookshelves," she called with a laugh as she moved up a couple of rungs, and I watched while she scanned through names. "There are journals by the Lancasters here."

"Really?"

"1915." She reached forward and pulled it out, dropping down a few steps to hand it to me before climbing back up. "And another from 1919, then one more in 1932." She scanned the shelves through the 40s and 50s. "That's it."

She rejoined me and we began paging through some of them.

Silence descended over us as Mal started with the one from the 20s and I dived into the one from the 30s.

"Look." She pointed to a passage, nudging my arm. She read it again and her eyes flicked back and forth to the painting in the center of the room. "Nicolas Van Holden donated *The Dawn* to Scroll & Ivy in the thirties."

"So, Van Holden knew someone at Winchester," I surmised.

"Or had a connection to the school." Malena nodded and walked closer to the painting. It was enormous, at least twenty feet in height, and spanned the entire wall. "And invitations to Scroll & Ivy run down bloodlines."

"So... the Lancasters would have his list or some idea of the lost works." Malena's eyes flickered, gaming out what we knew. "They don't appear again after the thirties, maybe the family lost prominence and didn't make the Scroll & Ivy cut."

Mal pulled a notebook from her bag and walked back to the ladder. Silently, she began scouring the shelves where she'd pulled the journal, murmuring various names and scribbling them down.

"What are you doing?"

"Since the Lancasters stop appearing here after the thirties, we probably won't find a Lancaster in the Winchester student body, but maybe one of the other families here has a connection." She went spine by spine, getting every name. "Anyone during that time period might."

"True."

She stepped onto solid ground again once she'd completed her inventory, chewing her lip.

"I should probably get back, I forgot something at my place." She turned her phone in her hand and pushed it into her bag. Closing the space between us, she looked up at me. "I'm gonna see what I can find on these families. Thank you for coming through with another clue "

"This one was Isha."

"Either way." Her hands curled around my shirt, then she rocked onto her toes and pressed a kiss against my lips. "We have a lead."

She turned to leave but I caught her wrist. "Mal?" James was right, I had to tell her what I wanted. "What are we doing?"

"You mean with the feature?"

My heart beat furiously against my ribs. "I mean..."

"Oh." She paused and made herself busy buttoning her coat, cutting down all the confidence I'd built up in the last hour. "We're having fun, right?" She looked up and smiled.

"You don't have to freak out, I haven't gone starry-eyed after our trip to Paris. Casual is fine with me." She patted my chest in that way that she did when she wanted to change the subject. "Sabrina already spoils me, I'm immune."

"Yeah..." I stammered, swallowing against a hollow throat. "Great."

CHAPTER 34

Malena

I got to my American Lit class early on Thursday, hoping to catch up on some last-minute reading.

The lecture hall was like an amphitheater—a semicircle with a giant chalkboard at the center and long curved tables that swept around it. When I walked in, the chair next to mine—the one Kash occasionally filled—was taken.

James Rutherford tapped his pen on his notebook as he scrolled his phone, wearing an expensive-looking wool sweater and a bored expression.

"Burr." Skepticism laced around my monotone as I set my bag down at the table. I kept my coat on because despite the heating, the century-old gray stone structure was constantly chilly.

Dark hair and dark eyes looked up at me above a pleased smile. "Hamilton."

"What are you doing here?"

"I'm in this class," he stated matter-of-factly. "In case you weren't aware."

"James," I repeated.

I'd seen him in the last row, studiously taking notes, but he always kept to himself. Today, he was bright-eyed and early, and had apparently decided to change his seating arrangement nine weeks into the semester.

"This spot is closer to the front, less drafty…"

"So you got here ten minutes early to claim it?" I sat down next to him.

"Company's not bad either."

"You'll make a girl blush."

"All right…" He tapped my head with his pen, then used it to point to the board in front of the lecture hall. "I know I'm the better looking one, but you need to stop flirting with me. You're gonna get me killed."

A delightful, if not slightly indignant, buzz skittered along my skin at the idea of Conrad sending James to act as his loyal watchdog.

I stacked my hands neatly on top of each other. "Are you going to pee on me next?"

"Listen." James turned to his laptop. "What you and Conrad do in the privacy of—"

"Please stop. Forget I said anything." I squeezed my eyes closed.

I pulled out my notebook, watching him from the corner of my eye.

"Conrad asked you to do this?" I dragged my pen along the metal spiral, then the blank pages.

"No, of course not," he answered with a firm sincerity. "But I figured this seat was empty and *maybe* that was giving people the wrong idea."

"Wrong idea?"

"That this seat is *available*." He cocked his head to the side and motioned his hands over himself. "When *clearly*, it is not."

It was so adorably wrapped in double-speak I almost didn't see the concern flash through his eyes. James was a good friend. A protective one. And I knew this was him warning me as much as it was him welcoming me. Honestly, it felt like something Cora would do.

"Are we still talking about chairs?"

James leaned back in his and linked his fingers behind his head. "Nope."

Conrad and I had yet to have the exclusivity talk, because I was actively dodging it. Most recently: my hasty retreat two days ago in the mausoleum. The sooner we had the talk, the sooner it became real, and then I'd have to start making choices I wasn't prepared for. I'd tell him about my parents and Conrad would assume the same thing Cora and Sabrina did: their "overprotective" habits would eventually give way to acceptance.

Cora and Sabrina, as well-intentioned as they were, *couldn't* understand the simple truth that if—*when*—it came down to it, I'd choose my family. Because otherwise, I would be out on my ass. Alone.

It was why flings were a necessity; anything more boxed me into a corner.

"Understood." I dipped my chin in agreement. "Make yourself comfortable, Burr."

He chuckled.

"The whole Hamilton/Burr thing really drives him crazy." James shoved my shoulder with his. "Now that he isn't scowling all the time, pissing him off is fun again."

LATER THAT AFTERNOON, I put my water bottle down next to my reformer at the Pilates studio in town. The low-lit room, filled with a subdued syncopated beat and neon blue lights, was the exact vibe for the mental and physical torment we were about to willingly submit to.

I loved Cora, but her Pilates addiction was going to kill me. She did this class three days a week; I only managed to make it to one, at best. These weren't women working out, these were sleeper agents training for combat.

"If I can't walk after this..." I began with no real threat in mind.

"I guess Conrad will have to do some work and get on top." Cora shrugged.

I laughed and made my way to the end of the machine, adjusting the handlebars to my height.

"Oh, by the way," Cora called from her reformer next to mine. "My mom told me that I got a letter for the Autumn Awards ceremony in the mail, so your parents probably got the same one."

I froze.

Shit.

I hadn't visited home in a few weeks, which meant that I couldn't intercept mail. The Autumn Awards ceremony was held for juniors who maintained excellent academic records. The letter would go to the address listed on my file, where my parents would definitely open it.

The only benefit to these events was that they gave my parents reason to dote on me. And I knew it was partially because they *loved* being my parents when I was being celebrated academically. But either way, it was nice.

Except now things were complicated.

"I forgot about that," I admitted softly. The ceremony usually fell on a weeknight, so I could only hope it would be too much of a hassle for them to make it here after work. Maybe they wouldn't come. "When is it?"

I let out a resigned sigh, knowing that regardless, my mom would make time. Being that it was an accolade she could brag about to her friends, of course.

"Next Thursday, but don't worry, we'll do what we always

do." Cora tested the different resistance bands and started stretching her calves. "I'll make sure anything controversial is out of sight. And you steer them off campus as soon as possible."

The news gave me whiplash as I mentally calculated the additional loose ends. I had to make sure Conrad and anyone in his circle kept a wide berth, had to avoid any mention of the paper, and I certainly couldn't risk them finding out about my trip overseas. The careful web I'd constructed was beginning to resemble a net slowly trapping me.

"Yeah..." I laid my body flat on the machine's cushion and stared at the ceiling.

A week wasn't enough time to think of a suitable way to keep them off campus. The thought alone made surviving this class feel easy in comparison to an evening juggling two lives.

CHAPTER 35

Conrad

Trying to date Malena was impossible.

"Here we are," I announced. We looked up at the grand white marble columns of the Manhattan District Records Hall. A week after Isha slipped us the name, we were here.

We parked my car a block away—even I could admit the motorcycle seemed impractical—and had walked here hand in hand, bundled up against the November evening chill.

But it was all for nothing, really. I brought Mal into the city, hoping we could have dinner. But not just any dinner, one at the Morgan Library. It was a gilded-age donation to the city and the type of place I was sure she'd love. I could almost see her eyes lighting up the way they had when she first walked into the mausoleum.

"Why so glum?" Malena's voice pulled me from my thoughts.

I cleared my throat. "Nothing."

I figured I'd take James's advice and *show* Mal I could be the kind of guy you date. But, in an attempt to be romantic, I hadn't been clear.

I'd been cryptic last night when I texted her about why we needed to go to Manhattan, mentioning a library, which was where our plans diverged, if I had to guess. We hadn't even left campus when she'd begun to rattle off all she wanted to figure out about Benedict Lancaster, and I wasn't about to put a pin in all that excitement.

"The Lancaster family immigrated to the States from Germany and were naturalized at the turn of the twentieth century." I climbed the steps, nodding along as she rattled off the facts she'd gathered, and linked my arm with hers. "Their family records, and any Van Holden ones, should be here."

Watching her light up as she spoke, I made my decision. No way would I let her go from practically buzzing to disappointed when she learned this was my attempt at a date—it sounded like more humiliation than I cared to experience.

We entered the sparse and bland lobby that led to a stairway and then another depressingly mundane record room. It was a far cry from my gilded library plans.

She took a seat at one of the long rectangular tables that sat in between the aisles of perfectly lined-up file boxes.

"These are all the families that are in the mausoleum's journals from that time period." Malena handed me a sheet with a list of names. "You look for relation to the Lancasters on the first half of the list and I'll start from the second half?"

"Great." I sighed.

A couple of hours into sifting through the housing records, I crossed off the last set of names on my list. "I've only got the Carringtons." I crossed off the final name.

"I have the Amhersts," Mal answered.

"So..." I leaned forward and added their names and all relevant dates to the piece of paper Malena was taking notes on, where she'd also drawn up a fairly impressive family tree. "That's the last of the relatives in the records."

While this wasn't the plan for the night, it was still thrilling.

"Two families have government records that connect them to the Lancasters: the Carringtons and the Amhersts." Her finger tapped on the last one. "The Amhersts, those are the same ones with their names carved into all those campus buildings, I'm assuming?"

"One and the same," I confirmed.

"Are there a lot of Amhersts?"

"Tons. You can't throw a cufflink in Manhattan without hitting one."

"Right." She chewed on her bottom lip. "What if it's someone you know?"

"Like Azalea?" She was an art history major, which alone put her under suspicion.

"It would make sense." Mal stood and carefully picked up a record box she'd signed out, placing it gingerly back on the shelf.

"If she's connected to it..." I took a deep inhale and released it through my nose.

I wanted to figure this out because for the first time in a very long time, I was determined to see something through. Even if the end result was simply proving to myself that I could.

Mal had been right that day on the boat, I could be more. I wanted to solve this thing. But that didn't mean I was comfortable putting someone I knew in the line of fire.

"I'm not throwing her name in the mix," I finished, looking over my shoulder and watching as she returned to the table.

Malena sat down next to me and smiled. "I happen to agree."

That answer pushed relief down my body. "Yeah?"

"The truth comes with too much collateral damage," she said offhandedly, like it was a fact of nature that everyone knew.

My body stiffened.

Was that why she was so reluctant to date me? Was she worried she'd be lied to, since the truth was, apparently, damaging? The realization cracked against my skull. Of course she'd think that about me.

I wasn't James, I wasn't the guy who had relationships. And whether I liked it or not, I had a reputation at Winchester.

"The *truth* doesn't come with damage. Lies do." My voice was firm; I needed her to know that I knew the difference. "I don't lie. But *I* also don't want to be the person who gets Azalea in trouble."

Malena paused, wide-eyed.

"Right." She nodded resolutely. "If it *is* her, we'll keep her out of the submission. Have it end on a cliffhanger, and then that'll be Azalea's hint to stop." Mal closed the folder with the family tree we'd hobbled together. "Honestly, I think that makes it even more compelling."

"Me too. I feel good about this, Mal." I tapped the folder. She smiled.

"I'll check for these three last names in the Winchester student archives this week. Maybe some current students or recent grads are related. In which case, we figure out if it was plausible that they were involved." She pulled her shoulders up with a breath, looking pleased. "Thank you for getting that name."

I stood and took her bag before she could stubbornly

insist on carrying it. The thing easily weighed as much as she did.

"That part was easy."

"But important." She leaned in and kissed me. Sweet and short. "You can't fool me, Conrad Hastings. You're invested in this."

In this. In her. Correct on all fronts.

She pulled away, but her hands lingered on my sweater, moving up to my collar then running flat down my chest. Was she staring?

Not that I minded.

"You look nice." Her tongue poked to the side of her cheek.

"Uhh..." I smiled despite myself; I had put more thought into my appearance than usual tonight. And Mal always looked pretty, as evidenced by her trademark skirt and leggings. The only thing that should have tipped me off sooner about her obliviousness was her bag filled with books. "I like to think I always look nice."

Her face filled with the realization. "Oh."

"It's nothing."

She bared her teeth in a nervous grin, trying and failing miserably to look anything but pitying. "You had other plans today," she said slowly. "For us."

God, now I felt even worse. At least before, the humiliation was only mine to know. "It's not a big deal."

"I didn't even ask." She closed both eyes and winced. "Sorry. I took over your night with work."

"It's nothing we can't do some other time." I took a step forward and put both hands on her waist.

And the reality was, I'd had a good time. I liked working with Malena. Talking to Malena. Being next to Malena. Having sex with her. Kissing her. Seeing her eyes widen and her entire frame practically float when she got excited about something.

I liked everything about her.

And fuck, I knew she liked me more than just this casual thing we were doing. We'd been back from Paris for a couple of weeks now. She woke up in my bed most mornings, and when she wasn't in class or with Cora, our time was spent together. I knew she wasn't seeing anyone else, so why was it so hard to talk about it?

"You don't have to do that," she said. "Plan elaborate dates or anything. What we're doing now is just fine."

Mal dodged the relationship subject like a boxer in the ring. I couldn't imagine that my reputation helped. Maybe she'd been hurt at some point, and then she saw me and made her judgments. And I couldn't even blame her, I *was* a walking red flag.

Till her.

"*Just fine* is beneath you, Mal."

"No, I mean..." Her eyes dropped and darted around my shirt. "I'm only saying, I like doing *this* with you." She looked up, eyes meeting mine. "I know it's boring for most people, but I'm having a good time."

A smile touched my lips as she fidgeted with her fingers. I'd never seen her look *this* unsure or self-conscious before.

"It's not boring," I insisted. Against all odds, I was enjoying work that was uncomfortably close to my family business. I loved that it was something we shared. "I like doing *this* with you too."

"It's not a total wash..." She looped her fingers in the fabric of my sweater. "We made some progress."

"We're a good team."

"We are." She looked up at me impishly. "It's a weeknight, we should probably get back to campus?"

I nodded.

After a few steps forward and several more back, it felt like tonight had me leaping in the right direction.

I'd figure her out.

I was a Hastings. I was the exception to *every* fucking rule.

And one way or another, I was going to show her that.

CHAPTER 36
Malena

Winchester's annual Crimson Day races had been tradition for over a hundred years.

Freshmen vs. sophomores and juniors vs. seniors.

On the first weekend in November, the different classes' crew teams raced in the bay. And tradition dictated that they race in three-piece suits. It was a raucous day that usually bled into the night with parties at the outrageously well-appointed boat houses, if you were able to secure an invitation.

It was the world Sabrina avoided, so we tended to go home or to a bar afterward.

"I have to say, I prefer the wet suits." Cora craned her neck and looked out at the water where the first set of races for the underclassmen were starting.

"Yeah, Cora, we all do."

I laughed, mostly because we only ever spectated the rowing races that took place in New Harbor or Cambridge. And before a month ago, we only went to those because they were a Winchester tradition.

Early in the afternoon, students started popping up along

the shore, giving the event a festival feeling. Stands with hot cider that everyone spiked, snacks and food trucks at the end of the walk, tents and picnics dotting the shoreline up to the row houses where relevant groups converged.

My phone buzzed in my hand and my heart immediately jumped. I looked at the screen and it fell back down, disappointed.

Mom: Why are you at the bay?

I let out a frustrated huff and typed into my real phone.

Me: It's a campus event. The boat races.

Mom: Oh, okay. Don't stay out late.

"I should have just brought the burner." I tucked my phone in my pocket.

"You have to take the real one out some time," Cora reminded me as we walked up the now yellowed grass. "You being locked in your room every moment you're not in class is unbelievable."

"Yeah. That's true," I conceded.

My parents knew me to be a little headstrong, so I pushed their boundaries in ways they wouldn't like but also wouldn't care about.

It was a fine balance.

"So... what exactly is going on with your guy?" Cora stopped us just past the hot cider stand so she could pour some bourbon into both of our cups from her flask.

"I dunno..." I glanced at my phone again and realized *why* I hadn't gotten a text from Conrad yet.

Since it was subject to inspection, flings never got added to my real phone. Conrad and every other hookup lived in my burner. Kash was the one exception because on some level, I knew he was the only one who could traverse both worlds. If my mom discovered *his* texts, she'd be pissed, but it would be a bump, not an earthquake.

"You don't know what's going on between you and Conrad?" Cora turned to me, tucking the flask back into her jacket pocket "You sleep there almost every night. You got back here after Paris practically giddy, and you've stayed that way."

Anxiety curled in my stomach because I knew I was getting way too attached to him. The other night at the Manhattan Records was proof—I felt so at ease that I never wanted it to end. But it had to, since I couldn't keep dodging the relationship question.

"I'm excited about the article." I tried to skirt around her question with a truth. Between the records Conrad and I found and those I was able to locate about the Lancaster family over the last week in the Connecticut public records, my confidence was at an all-time high. "The families I told you about, the Lancasters and Carringtons, they immigrated to the states and grew to some prosperity. Looks like they owned quite a few homes around New Harbor."

Cora's brows and lips flattened.

"And I am pretty sure they're connected to the painter," I went on. "The original immigration record stated they were from the same region of Germany that Nicolas Van Holden was from, which is too wild to be a coincidence. Oh! *And* they went to Winchester."

"Okay." Cora blinked, then crossed her arms and cocked her hip. "And the article is why you wore *that*?"

"What?" I looked down innocently at my shirt even though I knew that wasn't what she was pointing out.

"You decided this was the year you'd wear a rowing shirt?"

Each class had specific long-sleeved crew necks that

students were encouraged to wear to the races to show support. There were half a dozen juniors whose names were printed on the onyx-colored shirts that we could choose from, but mine had *SCOTT* written on it for Alexander Scott, who was always a top pick among our year.

"I happen to have school spirit," I defended.

Conrad kept showing up for me in ways I never expected. He *listened* to me. After a lifetime of not verbalizing my needs, he heard every one and found ways to fulfill them. My being here today was a way to show up for him.

And I knew that meant I was probably in too deep, but I didn't want to think about that.

"As much as I believe that monogamy only *really* benefits men," Cora pointed out, "I've never seen you like this, it's sweet. I think you should embrace it." She had always been my most ardent supporter when it came to "flings only," believing that my quest to experience as much as I could was a noble one.

"Yeah..." I *wanted* to embrace it.

Cora ducked her head to the side and looked behind me, a smile on her face.

"Malena," Conrad called. I glanced over my shoulder and there he was, wearing a suit reminiscent of the masquerade party in the clock tower. This time his jaw sat on edge, and his eyes didn't move from mine.

I turned back around to Cora, who blurted, "Oh look," and then pointed to nowhere in particular. "Bye," she whispered, squeezing my arm before slipping away.

Two hands smoothed along my waist and yanked me back. His towering frame loomed behind me and he lowered his mouth to my ear. "What the hell are you wearing?"

A delightful set of sparks ran down my neck with his breath. "A shirt?"

He turned me around to face him. Brown hair a little

messy, piercing blue eyes staring straight through me, I grinned. He pressed his lips against mine for a moment.

"If I knew that you wanted to wear one of these..." His fingers snuck under my shirt and I wiggled at the cool touch. "I'd have given you one of mine."

While rowing crew was a pretty niche sport, at the Ivies, it was one of the longest-standing. So, there were a lot of traditions around them. And like a lot of traditions, these were aimed at friendly competition between the different classes.

"This may come as a surprise, but I like wearing *my* own clothes."

A smirk slid up one of his cheeks. "You woke up in my clothes this morning. Yesterday morning. The morning before that..."

"That's different." I squirmed as his thumb stroked the bare skin at my navel, making my stomach dip and bow. "I'm in an altered head space after an orgasm."

"If that's the case..." His eyes flicked up and he looked over his shoulder to the clock on the facade of one of the boat houses. "I have some time before the race."

"You're cute when you're a little jealous." I rolled my teeth over my lower lip.

"I'm glad you think so." His voice lowered and he brushed his lips against my ear. "Now, take it off. Or I'll take it off for you."

His stern tone rippled down my body.

"You first." I ran my fingers along his crisp button-up. It sat perfectly over each rigid muscle on his abdomen. "I prefer the wet suit, but this is nice."

He groaned. "Mal."

"I'm cheering for my class." I pointed to all the junior rowers who were beginning to gather at the shoreline as the freshman vs. sophomore races finished. "Rules are rules."

He didn't say anything, only watched me. Everything fell

quiet under the blaring sound of my heart in my ears and the inescapable tingle between my thighs. He tightened his arms around me, his lips hovering over mine.

Just as the space between us closed to nothing, I jerked back at the sound of an air horn. The tension snapped and fell away, and the world came rushing back.

"This conversation isn't over," he warned in my ear before pressing a kiss just below it.

THE TASTE of cider and saltwater mixed in my mouth as Conrad pressed me against the wall in the Hastings boat house. At the back corner of the room where lines of brand-new shells were neatly stacked, Conrad kissed me deeply.

Soft and playful at first, the kiss escalated so fast that now every part of my body was involved.

"Con..." I broke away, gasping for air.

"Let's go back to my place," he repeated for the third time since he pulled me in here.

I scrunched my nose playfully, pushing my fingers up the back of his neck, through his hair. "What's the rush?"

"I won. I got dressed. I got *you*." Immobilized in a heavy stare, every syllable plucked a string deep in my stomach. "Let's go."

A rivulet of water ran from his wet hair to an eyelash, falling to his cheek before moving over his lips. Unable to help myself, I leaned forward and licked it. Salty and sinful, an ache flourished between my legs.

"Or..." I rolled my hips against him and looked around the immaculate, and very empty, shell house.

He cleared his throat and pulled back. "Here?"

Being with him made me want to chase the things I wanted, and right now, I wanted him.

"Are we alone?" I asked through shallow breaths.

Not even twenty minutes after the last race had finished, everyone was out on the shoreline, where the party would continue for the rest of the afternoon.

"For now." His voice wavered alongside his restraint. "You want me to fuck you here?"

The throbbing in my core refused to be ignored. "Yes."

A sly grin slanted up along his lips. He unbuttoned my jeans, bunched the fabric in his hands, and slid it a few inches down my thighs. The cool air swept against my skin, teasing my already jittery nerves.

He gently passed his thumb over my clit, barely grazing it.

I arched back against the wall and he leaned in, pressing kisses down my neck in time with his thumb running progressively firmer strokes.

A moan slipped out of my mouth.

He paused for a moment and brought his lips to mine.

"I don't mind taking credit, but I think that's your phone," he whispered against my lips.

"Hmmm?" Dazed, it took a second, but the faint buzz persisted against my thigh. He took a step away and leaned in to grab it.

My eyes fluttered open.

Just as he tilted the lock screen to me, he caught the message previews. Conrad's brows knit together as he read the messages that popped up on the screen.

Kash: Hey.

Kash: I just saw Cora, are you around?

Kash: We could get a drink

With the false reality I floated in yanked from under me, I was relieved this was all it was. Just Kash.

"Should I tell him you're busy right now?" Still inches

from me, his eyes pinned mine. He dropped the phone in my hand and I let it slip limply to the floor as he pressed me against the wall once more.

The tension between us shifted from the tantalizing prospect of a public hookup to something else. Now it was closer to a match dangling over a tank of gasoline.

"Con..."

"*Or* do you want to tell him..." The controlled cadence betrayed the way jealousy carved streaks over his hard-set jawline. "That you're a little preoccupied getting fucked against the wall with half the student body on the other side of it?"

He yanked my jeans and panties the rest of the way down. My breath hitched and I stepped out of them, unable to break his commanding stare.

He moved his hand back to where it had been between my legs.

"It's not what you think." The words fell out of my mouth alongside a shaky breath, waiting—aching—for more.

He pushed a finger inside, and I let out a moan as pleasure struck through me.

"I think he's delusional." His fingers stroked while he massaged my clit with the heel of his palm. "Because I fuck you *every* night." Tingles moved through every muscle fiber. "*I* watch you come."

Everything in my head scrambled. All I could think was how good he felt and how badly I wanted more.

I ground against him shamelessly, his erection pressing against my thigh as he pushed me closer and closer to the edge.

"I know exactly where you want to be," he whispered, almost tauntingly, in my ear.

"Con..." I faintly grabbed at the waistband of his joggers.

"What do you want, Mal?" he demanded in my ear. "Say it."

I couldn't deny how I felt any more than I could bear another second of being teased. "*Fuck*," I breathed. "Con, I want you."

He took a step back, and my surroundings had gone so hazy I kept my eyes closed. My body knew what came next anyway. The crinkle of foil. The low groan. His warm touch on my skin.

"Yeah..." His hands spanned over each hip and he lifted me. "I know."

On instinct, my legs wrapped around his waist at the same moment he pushed himself completely into me.

My body bucked and struggled to accommodate him as his lips slammed onto mine.

The momentary flash of pain was drowned out by over-whelming pleasure. Heat fanned down my skin. His teeth, mouth, hands, dick; everything working in concert to claim me. I kissed him back.

I rolled my hips against him as he began to thrust into me, and an incoherent string of noises and pleas fell out of my mouth, getting louder with each stroke.

"That's it, baby," he encouraged, slow and smooth against my lips. The words were cut apart by pleasure-filled grunts. "Cheer for me."

My arms wound around his neck. With each increasingly rough thrust, my hips moved in time with his and tension coiled at the base of my spine.

"Con..." I rasped, my toes curling. "Oh... *yes*."

I spiraled higher and higher.

The neatly stacked boat shells a few feet away rattled against the wall as he mercilessly fucked me against it. I held on to his body for dear life and called for him again.

Completely untethered, he drove into me. Harder. Faster.

With one last stroke against my clit, he pushed me over the

edge. My gaze went unfocused and the room became a blur. I bit down on my lip as the orgasm crashed over me.

His movements became more erratic until finally he grunted through clenched teeth. His muscles went taut and he came with a groan.

After a few seconds of stillness, Conrad leaned his head on mine and my heavy breaths began to subside.

I hummed softly, riding along the warm amnesia that was the afterglow. My arms dropped limply to my sides and the sounds of the room began to filter back in. I slipped back into my jeans and he pulled away and took care of the condom. Then, just as I was about to tug my jeans up, he did it for me. And, with care, he buttoned them.

"Mal." His voice dropped low and stern despite how gently he touched me now. A thumb caressed my hip, his other hand fanning along the column of my neck, and he tilted my chin up. "I've never shared a damn thing in my life, and I don't intend to start now."

I bit the inside of my cheek, not letting myself enjoy this jealous side too much. "I've only spoken to him to say hi in passing. That's all."

"Okay." He pressed a kiss against my lips. "Your past is just that, your past, but I *know* you want to be with me now. Just like I know your no-dating rule, like all rules, doesn't apply to me. So cut the shit."

My stomach flipped.

Whether it was from the fact that he could see right through me or the dominating way he made it known, I liked it too much to care.

"Okay," I murmured, fighting a grin.

The guy known for skirting his responsibilities and academic expectations had changed right before my eyes over the last two months. The same guy who was a notorious womanizer—no judgment, obviously—was trying *so hard* to be a good boyfriend.

I couldn't pretend not to see it. And I couldn't ignore how it made me feel cared for in a way I wasn't used to: with no conditions attached.

I would deal with the inevitable fallout later; I wanted to enjoy the temporary bliss of being his.

"And for the record I'm not seeing anyone else, and I don't want to," I added, leaning into him.

"I sort of figured that out when we got back from Paris and you started spending every night in my bed." He chuckled and pressed a kiss right at my hairline.

Both arms wrapped tight around me, my body relaxed into his. That blissful feeling of floating blanketed over me.

I let out a slow sigh, not wanting to move but knowing we should. "We should probably get back out there."

"One more second," he whispered. "Please."

My heart skipped.

"Okay." I didn't want this to end either. So, for now, I was choosing not to think about what came next.

CHAPTER 37

Conrad

The smell of old books filled the air as Malena led me through the shelves in the Amherst building's library. We got all the way to the back, to the office we snuck into on the night of the mausoleum party. The night —and the kiss—that changed everything.

"Abby had to run out. She found me in the rare book room and told me to leave the key on her desk and lock the door on my way out." Malena led me into the librarian's office and shut the door behind us. "I figured there was no harm in looking..."

The office hadn't changed. A few book carts filled to the top, some paper folders scattered on the wide mahogany desk, towering shelves that spanned the walls.

"*That's* why I'm in the library first thing on a Monday morning?" I asked dejectedly. After the Crimson Day races this past weekend, I was thinking that maybe she wanted another semi-public tryst.

The apples of her cheeks rolled up.

"I found something." She walked over to the door we

knew opened to a staircase. "I snuck downstairs to the cellar to see if anything had changed."

"Next time, invite me *before* you commit a crime." I held the door open and checked the back handle to make sure it would still open from the inside like it had before. And just like last time, no alarm. "It's our thing."

"What do you think I'm doing now?" she whispered, pointing with her chin toward where the original painting had once stood. I moved ahead of her as we both dropped down a few more steps into the dark and damp stone cellar. "It's gone. The one whose paint transferred onto my clothes."

I smiled against the pleasing sparks her warm breath sent down my spine. "I remember."

In its place was another painting, already framed. A landscape of a cottage next to a deep blue riverbank. Rich purples and bright pinks depicted a sunset.

I recognized it from the art studio. Someone had completed it, framed it, and moved it down here. Were they planning on transporting it through the catacombs?

"I'm guessing this is the next one to be sold." I squinted in the low light, glancing over to the door we'd stumbled through all those weeks ago. It was closed, but I couldn't tell if anyone had altered the locks.

Malena's fingers settled around my shoulders and tapped frantically. "Someone paints them in the studios on the other side of the building, moves them through the catacombs, then sells them."

"So it would seem."

She pulled on my shoulder and motioned for us to head back, and I followed her up the steps and through the doorway. I shut it behind me. "Do you think we could catch them in the act?"

I chuckled at her unfiltered elation, but I was just as

excited about this new development. "Are we staking it out? Will you wear a catsuit?"

She stopped, halfway across the office now, and gave me an unamused look.

"Sorry. I like seeing you like this. That's all. I'll see if Isha can get us a heads-up from the gallery about whether they list this one. At the very least, they'll probably invite her to an auction."

She smiled and turned around. "Thank you."

"That's really the only reason you brought me here?" I asked as we left the office and weaved between the rows of shelves.

I took hold of her wrist and pulled her back to me. We stopped in the narrow aisle.

"Yes." A spark lit in her eyes. "Get your head out of the gutter."

"Only if I can put it between your legs." I stepped her backward until there was nowhere left to go. I wondered if she realized this was the same spot I kissed her when we'd needed a quick out with the campus guard.

I pulled her into a kiss, slow and teasing, until her body melted against mine.

I groaned and ran my hands up her buttery-smooth leggings.

"Con..." She broke away. Leaning her forehead against mine, she smiled. "I have to get to class."

"Fine. But tonight..." I told her as I pulled away. "We have a date."

"A date?"

"Yeah... No article work. No studying," I explained. The day that I saw her outside Bardam Books, after she'd been out with her ex, was stuck in my head. She mentioned that he wasn't *specifically* the reason she chose not to date. But someone had to be. And I was going to prove to her that whoever fucked it up before was just that: a fuckup from her past. I wasn't going to lie or treat her poorly or do whatever the fuck he did to lose her. "You're my girlfriend, and I'm taking you on a date."

"Okay." Her cheeks, crimson at the top, rose with a wide smile. "Cora and I are checking in on Sabrina this afternoon since the election is tomorrow. I'll be free after four."

"Perfect." I leaned in to kiss her, but she reared back and narrowed her eyes.

"Did you vote—"

"Mailed my ballot in a week ago," I cut in. One thing most people could agree on was that Fitzgerald Alders would be a great president. One we needed. "From what you've told me, Sabrina's feelings may be mixed, but her dad has my vote."

She smiled. "Mine too. Pick me up later?"

I nodded.

"I THOUGHT we *weren't* doing anything article-related," Malena pointed out as we passed through the entrance of Scroll & Ivy's mausoleum. The heavy doors made a thudding sound as I closed them behind us.

"We aren't." We walked down the hallway to the two grandstanding doors that opened up to the library.

I wanted to take her back to Manhattan, but she had an early start on Tuesday mornings so I didn't want to keep her out late.

"I figured doing something on campus would give us more time," I reasoned.

The library, already beautiful on its own, was a little domineering in its Gothic style. Tonight, tapered candles on brass candelabras were scattered around the room, casting it in a light golden glow. The tuxedo couches in the center of the library were draped in cashmere blankets, and a fire that I'd never actually seen lit before was roaring in the hearth.

Her mouth opened to say something, but she stopped, mouth agape as she took it all in. "What's this?"

Malena didn't talk a lot about what she wanted. She kept those parts of her close, like she was afraid someone might steal them if she ever put them out into the world. But she'd lit up the first time she saw this place.

"Cora told me you like that Thai place in town," I explained, and her eyes went to the takeout containers that sat on the antique wooden table.

"Is a picnic in the mausoleum allowed?"

"Suddenly *so* concerned for the rules," I drawled.

"How did you set all of this up?" She sucked in another disbelieving breath.

"I had a little help." I rubbed the back of my neck. "Isha and Lucy are... invested."

And they were both surprisingly handy. Ishani had taken orienteering at Le Rosey; she could navigate herself out of the Andes mountains using the stars and wind patterns. And Lucy, she could MacGyver just about anything. This was an easy favor, one they'd taken on with so much poorly withheld glee I knew I'd be hearing about it for years.

"Is this safe?" she asked, and my fingers weaved between hers as I led her to the couch. She gestured at the candles. "Open flames around all these books?"

"Probably not. And your limbs *do* have a tendency to flail." I arched a teasing brow. "Don't knock one over."

She leaned forward on the couch, a hair's distance from my face. "Don't give my limbs a reason."

She leaned back and took in the ambience around us, and as I began opening the cartons of pad Thai and green curry, I watched her relax. Malena was endlessly fascinating when she was willing to open up.

Not about school or her grades or her future. Just *herself*.

I spent so much time with her but hardly got to those parts. And when I did, I hoarded them like a dragon with treasure.

"Ishani told me about why the mausoleum is always empty." Malena looked up from her container. "You were the reason nobody's been in here all semester?

My face heated a little, and I shrugged. "Nobody but you studies here anyway."

"You do."

"Because the pretty girl I like studies here," I admitted, and her lips twitched. She busied herself with grabbing a dumpling with her chopsticks. "And, I like being around her."

A blush painted her face. My chest filled with pride.

"Did you spend a lot of time at the library growing up?" I asked.

She loved this place, and even though I was going to save the Morgan library for another date, maybe in the spring, I knew she'd love it there too.

She shook her head. "No, I mostly read in my room."

"Right." I snapped my fingers. "In the closet."

She grinned.

"It was peaceful, and I had a book light." Her eyes spanned along the shelves filled with first editions, classics, obscure works. "I like being around books." She took a deep inhale. "It's like peeking through a keyhole. I can't *be* in that world, but I can *see* it. Right here, I'm in the middle of a million different places. With a million different people."

Her eyes dropped a bit at the corners and her expression changed. It became almost gloomy.

"Holing up in your closet must have been lonely."

She seemed to relish being around people, while at the same time, she had that desk cave thing.

"Unbearably." A melancholic smile arched up her cheeks.

"My parents were strict growing up and I didn't go to friends' houses very often. I like the quiet, but I don't *like* being on my own. If that makes sense."

"It does." I pushed a few stray hairs behind her ear.

She had her best friends who, from a cursory understanding, were as close as James and Isha were to me. She had her places to bask in the quiet and all the opportunities she wanted to live raucously when the quiet was too still.

We weren't all that different. Aside from GPAs, probably.

The moment broke away into pieces at the sound of my phone buzzing against the table.

"Sorry." I went to swipe away whatever it was when I got a glimpse of the headline.

My heart sank. **Hastings Mistress Enjoys Another Lavish Vacation with Philandering CEO.**

I opted for alerts from all the trashy tabloids for one reason: I wanted to get ahead of anything my mom might see. And this one wasn't great. Page Six was uncovering new details to show that my dad hadn't stopped seeing the other woman.

Great.

Seconds later, three texts came in.

> Ishani: James is in Manhattan with his father tonight, I'll have them check in on her.

> Ishani: Don't worry.

> Ishani: Enjoy your night, we have it handled.

"Are you okay?" Malena's voice yanked me back to the present, and then she was tucked closer to my side, eyes running over the headline.

"Yeah." I clicked the screen off and tried not to let it bother me. I finally had Malena on a date, I wasn't going to ruin it. "Looks like the press knew where they were going this time." Concern etched over her flawless face. I sighed. "I only read them so I know if it's something—"

"That your mom will see."

"Yeah..." I huffed. And this one was bad.

Usually, right before Thanksgiving, whatever fighting my mom and dad had going on would evaporate and we'd all be forced to endure a "happy" family dinner. That was going to be tough now, seeing as we were all being reminded that my father was absolute garbage.

"Wanna talk about it?"

"No," I said quickly, trying to salvage the mood, but Malena's encouraging smile pulled at my restraint. "I wish she would just..."

"Leave him for good?" Malena looped her arm around mine.

I nodded.

"I'm sure it's not *simple* to walk away from her whole life." She leaned her head on my shoulder. "Your mom deserves better, but better can be complicated."

I hadn't realized till that moment just how unfair I was being to my mom. I hated how my dad treated her, but that didn't mean I had a right to judge her for how she handled it. But watching the same scene play out year after year didn't make it any easier to digest. "I was hoping she'd leave him and we'd do Thanksgiving in Newport this year. My mom hates the city."

"The beach in the autumn sounds nice."

"It is." I thought about all the time we'd spent there, summers at the house where I learned to swim. The one place I looked forward to going every year. "She loved it there, really let her worries fall away. It was where I first started rowing."

"*Loved.*" Of course Malena noted my use of the past tense. We were here because she caught all the details. "What happened?"

"She still loves it there." I shrugged at the banality of the story—it was practically a cliché. But once again, the encouraging look on Mal's face pushed me forward. "I was seven when we went there for an impromptu beach trip. Turns out, my dad's mistress had been there all summer since we were supposed to be in St. Barts. So..."

That day was imprinted in my memory. The salty smell of the ocean whipping through the kitchen. The broken glass all over the floor. My mom dropped the lemonade she made for me when my dad's mistress at the time came down the steps, calling for him.

I'd been sitting at the kitchen counter, completely unaware of what this strange woman's presence meant. But a part of my mom—the one that was bright and vivacious—vanished that day. And I hadn't seen it since.

"Con..." Malena sat up and weaved her fingers back through mine. "I'm sorry."

At least now he was open about it. He wasn't actively trying to hide how terrible he was. That had always been the worst part: when he lied and played pretend that he was a good guy. There was no denying who he was anymore.

"He has everything, but nothing is good enough." I stared into the crackling fire. I'd spent the following ten years watching my brothers become him in every way and be praised for it. Falling in line felt like betraying my mom and I'd rather be the ne'er-do-well Hastings than a replica of my father. "My brothers are just like him."

"You're not," Malena stated, so quickly it sounded like reflex.

The words resonated through my chest. "I..."

Sometimes I wondered about that woman—the mistress, the first one I ever clocked anyway. Now, thinking back to that day, I couldn't help feeling bad for her. My mom had to be the humiliated and betrayed spouse, but she was the dirty little secret. She didn't even get the dignity of existing in reality.

"You're not like that in the slightest," she repeated firmly, turning my chin to look her in the eye. Behind a cocked brow that told me she was not going to entertain an argument, was protectiveness. "I have tons of proof, so don't argue with me."

Her unfettered belief in me clogged the back of my throat.

I didn't *allow* myself ambition because I knew what it led to. I was fine fading into the background if it meant avoiding that. But Malena refused to let me go unnoticed. Seeing every part of me, she made me want more.

"Careful, Mal…" I brushed a kiss against her hair. "You've got me motivated."

She looked up at me, the firelight dancing in her eyes. "I'll start to feel worried when you buy climbing equipment."

CHAPTER 38

Malena

The Autumn Awards ceremony was like a marathon for me.

A couple of days after that amazing date with Conrad, I didn't want to make it look like he didn't exist in my life. But I had to. Especially since my parents showed up an hour early at my condo instead of the Gibbs theater on campus like we agreed. But Cora and I had expected it. They came by, my mom snooped, and then we made our way over to campus together.

After the ceremony, there was a reception being held in the atrium outside of the theater. I spotted my parents speaking to President Packham and was grateful for the momentary reprieve.

I decided to hang back, realizing too late I was standing next to Kash. I blew out an uncomfortable breath and racked my brain for an exit strategy.

"My parents are talking to Professor Crane," he reported awkwardly.

I nodded.

When the silence got too loud, he went on. "How was the MCAT?"

"Good. I'm pretty sure I nailed it." I pushed my toes against the hard floor, wondering what we could talk about. Kash sure had a cute face, but he could be such a dud when it came to conversation. "Congrats on the chemistry award."

"Thanks." He looked at the folder tucked under his arm. "You too."

I nodded. The awards were checkmarks on a résumé to the same end. In the time we spent together last year, I'd learned that his parents were similar to mine. They had a very specific plan for their son: college, medical school, marry a nice Indian woman, have babies, never question said plan. And he seemed to be very much on board.

"The election went great." Kash filled the awkwardness with truly unnecessary small talk; although, I guessed for anyone who didn't know Sabrina, it was pretty cool news. "Hell of a landslide, it was called before midnight. Sabrina must be excited."

I sighed.

Cora and I checked in on Sabrina yesterday, but she didn't really want to talk. So, we were following her lead and would wait till she brought it up.

It was probably a good thing Sabrina wasn't on campus because it was alive with excitement. The Alders family produced presidents who invested in public education and healthcare, expanded the American ultra-rapid railway, and took aim at climate revival. Fitzgerald Alders was expected to continue that legacy, and the hope was palpable.

"Yeah, she's super excited," I drawled. All you had to do was listen to me talk about Sabrina for more than a couple of minutes to know she was anxious about the development.

The Alders win meant a lot of great things for the country,

but it was a complete and utter loss of normalcy for Sabrina. Not that she'd ever been normal.

Kash looked around and I was tempted to walk away, but that would be rude, right? I'd texted him that day after the races that I was seeing someone and he never responded—he'd probably seen Conrad waiting for me after American Lit and put the pieces together. Plus, James had inhabited his occasional seat like the good watchdog that he was.

"Can I ask you something?" I ventured, both because I was curious and because he didn't appear to be taking the hint and moving on.

He gave me an upside-down smile. "Sure."

While Conrad did everything under the sun to try to date me, Kash had only ever been interested in keeping me hidden. A part of me knew why, and a separate, spiteful part of me wanted to make him *say it* after he had me sit through that humiliating brunch.

Something about being treated so well by Conrad made me viscerally angry that I ever let anyone treat me the way Kash had.

"Why did you even want to date me?" If all he wanted was to hook up, why put me through the humiliation he did?

"I liked you." He blew out a long breath and looked around, avoiding my eyes. "After that brunch, I got to thinking about dating, and that I should probably be with someone who..." He moved the file folder from one hand to another. "I figured we could go back to hooking up since you didn't really date anyway."

"You put me through that 'does she fit' test and realized that I'm the girl you screw, not the girl you date," I summarized bluntly. "Is that what you mean?"

There was a cruel irony in that those words were meant to warn me away from Conrad.

He blanched.

"I apologized for that." Kash huffed in defeat. "And you're... you do what you want and that's great. But we're different. *I'm* not judging you, but other people..."

With Kash, my past wasn't just my past. It was a record to be judged against.

That was the thing. I may have been hiding the real Mal from my family, but I wasn't ashamed of her. Socially, sexually, academically... I was free. I loved running headfirst into new things. I wanted to see, try, experience *everything*. I wanted to color outside the lines, and I wasn't ashamed of that.

But Kash was. And it was further proof that I *had* to hide her, because she'd get an even worse reaction from my family.

I nodded and rolled my jaw, suppressing a sigh.

"We're different. I get it," I conceded, and I *did* get it. If I was being honest with myself, the only reason I'd dated him was to chase some sort of validation. The Malena that fit with him, that could make herself fall for him despite how he treated her—*that* Malena was one my mom would like.

"Yeah..." He began to turn and walk away. "I'll see you around, I guess."

I smiled mirthlessly, thinking of Ishani's words. Nobody got to tell me about my place in the world—I'd find it eventually. I just wished it ached less. "See you around."

I turned then, and my mom whipped into my vision. "Who was that?"

At once irritated and inquisitive, her brows hooked inward.

"Nobody," I answered, smiling as my dad wandered over. "How was President Packham?"

"She says you're working diligently with the paper," Dad stated proudly, patting me on the head. Never great with displays of affections, that was his version of a hug.

"Who was that boy?" my mom pressed.

"Nobody, we're in a few classes together."

"Do you talk to him?"

I wasn't allowed to date by their standards, and my focus was to remain firmly on school. Yet I could already see my mom spinning up a few loopholes.

"Not really. I know how you get when I *socialize* too much."

My mom's face turned to stone.

"Nobody likes an instigator, Malena." She leaned in with a menacing stare and gave my arm a warning pinch. Short but painful, I yanked my arm back, rubbing it for a second but not saying anything.

She peered around, in search of Kash. "What is he going to do after college?"

"He wants to be an actor, actually," I lied.

I bit back a grin as my mom's face dropped. The idea she'd constructed of him being a nice Indian boy disintegrated at the thought of anyone pursuing something as unstable as acting. Because *what* would people think?

"Oh," she mumbled to herself quietly, then looked up at my dad. "See, Vijay? This is what happens when you don't have control of your children. His poor parents." Her lip curled and she turned her head to look squarely at me. "Don't talk to that boy."

I stood up a little straighter. "I *don't*."

At least in that moment, I didn't have to lie.

"Good." She let out a pleased sigh. "All those hours working late, redoing our education, struggling for years when we came here..." Her gaze moved along the names listed on an overhead banner, likely searching for mine, which was there among the high achievers. Her shoulders relaxed and her eyes softened as they met mine again, the corners of her mouth tilting up. "All of our sacrifices were worth it when we see how well you do in school." Her voice was warm and maternal as she closed the space between us.

Before I knew it, I was wrapped in a hug. "You never make us worry."

My body sagged into hers, not realizing how much I'd yearned for this. For her to be proud of *me*. To like *me*. I didn't think about the fact that it was the version of me that I kept perfectly in line for her. All I did was smile and hug her back.

Because in moments like these, I found myself *wanting* to color inside the lines she'd drawn, even if the resulting portrait didn't resemble me in the slightest.

She pulled back and held my shoulders.

"Just watch that mouth." Her hand moved to my chin, grasping it with a gentle firmness. Like she was doling out well-intentioned motherly advice. "We put up with it, but other people will think that *honesty* is disrespectful. Just listen, that's all, and be like Avani."

"Okay, Mom," I said quietly.

"We should get on the road." She looked at her watch then at me, and I nearly slumped in relief. "We left all of your favorites on the kitchen counter. I made some jalebi, too."

I nodded.

Sometimes, I wondered if the version of myself that my mom wanted would be all that bad. I hated feeling like a marionette with her pulling the strings, but she *did* care for me. They both did.

They were my family.

And you only got one.

I PUSHED the door open to my condo and stopped when I realized we had company. I stayed frozen and tried to make sense of what I was looking at.

"You mean to tell me, there's a way to play this game

where nobody wins?" Ishani's bewildered question to Cora greeted me as I closed the door. She held her hand to her chest. "Nobody ends up crying?"

"Yeah..." Cora carefully set four martini glasses onto the table. Each on a ceramic coaster that she made in pottery class as a freshman. "It's about prolonging the game rather than anyone winning."

Ishani tilted her head to the side. "What's the point?"

"You'll have to excuse her." Lucy held a multicolored stack of Monopoly cash in her hand. "She was raised inside an episode of *Succession*."

"Umm." I looked around. "Hey?"

"Hey, Mal." Cora looked up as she downed half her cocktail.

She and I had planned to have a game night after the excitement of my parents' visit and the awards ceremony. When we weren't in the mood to go out, the three of us girls would swap out gin and tonics at the bars for Cora's specialty cocktails and we'd play a game or binge watch a TV show.

"I saw Lucy and Ishani at the quad and they invited us for a movie, but I told them we were gonna spend the night in."

"So, we invited ourselves," Ishani explained, carefully setting her perfectly organized money aside. "But we brought snacks."

I blinked a couple times. "Oh." I hooked my keys on the rack and put my bag down next to the kitchen island as I made my way over.

For some reason, I pictured Ishani and Lucy spending their spare time doing insanely cool things like going to fashion shows or restaurant openings. Although, both of those things were in short supply in New Harbor.

"Is Sabrina still calling in?" I asked, knowing that she probably wasn't feeling particularly social right now.

"No, she has an International Policy paper due." Cora gave

me an unsure look, like she was confirming that we'd check in on her again in a few days. "But she said nobody is allowed to be the thimble."

I sat down on the rug by the coffee table and reached for my martini, blowing a kiss to Cora in thanks.

"Done." Ishani picked up the race car and turned it between her fingers. "I'm more of a vintage car gal, anyway." She set it down on the board and looked up at me. "Oh, and I was chatting with a girl in my advanced linguistics class, and she's organizing the Holi festival next semester."

"Oh yeah?" I brought the back of my hand up to wipe my mouth, my attention piqued.

Ishani looked at Cora and back to me. I imagined there weren't many people who saw Ishani Roy look nervous, so I pretended not to notice.

"Mm-hmm." She looked down at the board and shifted a bit. "We usually go to Mumbai, but it might be nice to stick around."

"And we could all go together," I suggested. "I'll invite Sonali, she might like to join us."

Becoming less and less bothered by *how* I'd fit and more concerned with wanting to do something I loved—and I loved Holi—putting myself out there didn't feel as enormous as it had in the past. Finding my place was constant work, and hiding wouldn't help.

"Can't wait." Cora grinned and took the dice.

Something about the scene in front of me was a vision of what perfect might look like: my version of a zipper neatly coming together.

CHAPTER 39

Conrad

The last of the bright red and orange autumn leaves trembled on their branches and rustled to the ground with every burst of air, setting the scene for the much-anticipated Winchester vs Harvard game. Every year, the two football teams would face off, and alums were known to tailgate. Some did it with a Hollywood-style trailer and others with demure tents and catering.

Eleanor and Christian Rutherford did both, hosting what was essentially a gala outside the stadium.

I spotted James and his dad tossing a football back and forth on the green beyond the catering tent, and James's little sister and his mom sipped hot cider as they flipped through some magazines that previewed the next year's spring lines.

My vision suddenly went black when a pair of hands covered my eyes from behind and the scent of candied lemons wisped past me.

In the run-up to winter, she smelled like summertime. "Are they always that..."

"Nauseatingly perfect?" I finished for her. The Rutherfords were like a family pulled out of a catalogue, except it wasn't fake. They all genuinely enjoyed each other's company. "Yes."

Malena laughed and whispered in my ear. "You're going to love the sweater I'm wearing."

I curled my fingers around her wrist and pulled her in front of me, wrapping my other arm around her waist and taking in the stitching on her crewneck.

RUTHERFORD.

My smile fell. "Take it off."

"It's a Lora Piana custom sweater." Malena's mouth hung open, like that was a perfectly reasonable excuse for any name but mine to be scrawled across her chest. "And actually, remind me to ask James's mom how they got Lora Piana to make a—"

"Take it off, or I take it off of you." I'd told her the same thing the last time she did this. I took a step forward and pushed my hands beneath it. "I swear you do this on purpose."

Malena giggled and squirmed in my grasp, then looped her arms around my neck.

"Eleanor got it made for James's little sister. But then *she* gave it to Ishani and Ishani looked so uncomfortable that I just grabbed it." Malena waggled her brows. "I'm guessing there's a story there?"

"Yeah..." I let out a slow breath. "I'm gonna have to tell you that story at some point. For now, ignore it."

Malena pulled the sweatshirt off and folded it neatly in her arms. "Will do."

"Speaking of Isha..." I tried to segue, because the Isha/James topic was one I didn't even know if I was allowed to bring up. "The buyer of that Van Holden doesn't want to sell, so that's not an option now. But Isha's keeping an eye out for anything that comes up at the gallery."

Ishani told me this morning, but I didn't want to dampen

the mood because Mal was having a nice time at the tailgate. And maybe I was avoiding disappointing her.

"Oh." Mal set the sweater down on the linen-covered picnic table next to us. "We'll figure something out. We have time."

"Oh yeah?" The tension loosened, and I yanked her close.

"Besides, it's the weekend, and I'd like to enjoy it with you. Especially with how crazy this week has been."

"How is Sabrina doing anyway?" I asked, knowing she was worried about how Sabrina was handling the scrutiny following the election.

"Okay..." Mal sighed. "She's been too busy to chat, but we're calling her again in a few days to see if we can coax her into talking about it. Or about anything, honestly."

A frown wisped along her lips.

"Maybe she just needs a little time," I offered.

Just before I could lean in to give her a reassuring kiss, a voice cut between us.

"Conrad?"

Malena's head turned first, and her eyes landed on a petite blond in a navy-blue sweatshirt, her hands neatly folded in front of her.

"Gemma." I rubbed the back of my neck.

Malena looked at me for an explanation, but before I could say anything, Gemma strode over and spoke directly to me.

"My mom is saying hello to Eleanor." Gemma pointed off to the side where her parents were speaking to James's. Lucy stood in the middle of the group with narrowed eyes, looking between them like she was monitoring a tennis match. "We all might be in Moritz together this winter break. She—"

"Gemma, this is my girlfriend, Malena," I interrupted, knowing she was attempting to make Mal feel invisible, or make herself seem important. My palm floated down to the small of Malena's back and I looked down at her. "Babe, this is Gemma, she goes to Harvard."

Malena's brows pulled together for a moment. She opened her mouth, but Gemma continued.

"Gemma DuBois," she said, and stuck out her hand. "Conrad and I go way back." She looked at me with a knowing smile and I sighed. Gemma and I used to slept together on occasion, but I hadn't even seen her since last year. Which solidified my suspicion that she was here to stake territory that was never hers to begin with. "And we circle each other from time to time." She laughed, and when met with silence, her eyes locked onto Mal's. "Teasing, of course."

"Of course," Mal answered with the same voice she used around faculty.

Gemma adjusted her headband before speaking again. "I come to this game every year; I've never seen you here before."

"Malena took some convincing," I shot back, more indignant than anything. Mal could hold her own, but this line of questioning or intimidation or whatever it was... I wasn't about to let it happen.

"Not a fan of the pre-game tailgate?" Gemma cocked her head to the side. "It isn't for everyone."

"Conrad made it sound appealing," Malena answered nonchalantly, but her muscles tightened beneath my palm.

"He does that, doesn't he?"

I prayed James could read my thoughts and would take the opportunity to *accidently* aim the football in our direction.

"Yeah." Malena's voice perked up. "Just look at you, surprisingly at ease for someone on enemy ground."

"Oh." Gemma's polite smile straightened and she scrunched her nose patronizingly. "I didn't realize I was in danger."

"Whether you are or not is entirely up to you." Malena

crossed her arms, and I stifled a laugh. "I'm only teasing," Malena added. "Of course."

"It was nice to see you, Gemma," I lied, dismissing her in the nicest way I could.

Honestly, it was for Gemma's own good—I was sure Ishani would make creative use of her perfectly manicured fingernails if she caught wind of any of that. Gemma walked back to her parents, and with a few polite waves, they were gone. I looked down at Mal.

"Ex-girlfriend?" Mal asked, her tone disinterested. "I didn't think you had those."

"We slept together a few times," I confessed. "Last year. That's all."

"Okay." She looked away, her eyes moving over the steady stream of students and alumni passing by.

"Are *we* okay?" The realization knocked against me like a smack in the head. She wasn't annoyed or offended.

She was jealous.

And it was *adorable*.

"Yeah." Malena's eyes refused to meet mine. "She doesn't seem to like me."

"Who cares?" I sure as hell didn't.

"Right." She looked down at her fingers. "Your *friend* doesn't like me. I'm pointing it out, that's all."

"She's *not* my friend. She's—"

"Protective?" Malena offered.

"Psychotic," I corrected. Whoever thought that type of behavior was appropriate needed their head examined. "I'm sorry she spoke to you like that."

"It's okay," she said curtly.

"Malena…" I tsked. My heart made a strange leap and my lips couldn't help but tug at the sides. "Are you jealous?"

"No." Her mouth pulled in an exaggerated oval.

"My family knows hers and so does James's, that's all."

"Okay." Her voice climbed up half an octave.

"Mal..."

"I get it." She waved me off, and when she tried to take another step away, I looped an arm around her waist. "You've known each other awhile. That's all, not a big deal." If her voice pitched any higher we were going to have to watch for broken glass. "Your families are friends, that's sweet."

I watched the endearing fidgeting because the envy was useless. Malena *had* me. That smile and sharp wit had me pinned for months.

She blew out a frustrated breath through loose lips and took a step back when I didn't say anything. "What?"

Now I had a full-blown grin. A toothpaste commercial smile. "I'm just waiting to see how much higher your voice can get."

She smacked my shoulder. "Shut up."

"Look around, Mal, *this* is my family." I jutted my chin in the direction of the green where James and Felix were now tossing the ball, James's parents off being social on the other side of the tent. "They've spent all day with *you*," I added, looking over to Isha and Lucy—both going over what I assumed was the spring line with James's little sister. "As much as I like seeing you get jealous, there is really no need."

"I'm not jealous," she insisted, and I swore I saw her stomp her foot in the corner of my eye.

"Well, in case you were..." I pulled my arm around her shoulders and dropped a kiss on her hairline. Eleanor was so taken with her that I was sure she was texting my mom about having met Mal first. I kind of liked that idea, Mal being a part of... *this*. "They are the only people who matter, and you fit perfectly."

She finally looked up at me, her cheeks lifted but her lips still stretched in a line. For a millisecond I was sure her expression glazed over before she blinked it away.

"You okay?"

She looked down. "Yeah."

"Mal..."

When she looked up again, her cheeks crested so high they pushed up against the bottoms of her eyes. Her lashes fluttered with a few more rapid blinks, but then she finally met my eye. "I'm more than okay."

CHAPTER 40

Malena

I let out a long sigh in my kitchen, standing before the bowls I just filled—one with popcorn and the other Doritos. I reluctantly swiped up on the incoming call. "Hey, M—"

"What is this summer writing seminar packet that came in the mail?" My mom's irate voice was loud enough to hear without my ear to the phone. "You can write at home if you have time after your internship."

I squeezed my eyes closed, trying to figure out what she meant. "What?"

"There's a packet about housing too?" I heard pages ruffling in the background. "Absolutely not."

The writing seminar. Right.

After Paris, riding on the freedom high, I submitted my details as per Dillian's insistence.

"I told President Packham I'd consider it." The longer this semester dragged on, the messier I was getting. "I was trying to be nice."

I looked over the kitchen island and into the living room where Cora gave me a wave to indicate Sabrina had logged into our call. We'd finally gotten her on the phone, a full week after the election. I flicked a glance at the clock on the wall. It was four in the afternoon here, meaning it was already late in the UK, another reason to get my mom off the phone.

"That writing minor is a nuisance," she countered. "You need to focus on the sciences and drop it."

"Dropping a minor would look terrible on med school applications. Besides, I..." I paused and began to pace in the kitchen. I was trying to be more open and not let past experiences taint future ones. Maybe I could try again with her too. I took a breath. "I took on the minor because writing makes me happy. I like it."

A hopeful silence floated through the line.

"You also *like* candy, but that doesn't mean you can eat it all the time," she retorted. "Not everything is about *you* being happy. You're not doing this seminar."

It was stupid to be disappointed, but I was. "I wasn't planning on it."

All the will to argue evaporated because she'd been so happy with me at the awards ceremony a couple of weeks ago. Things were peaceful, and I hated that something dumb like the seminar shook loose the tension.

"You need to come home more and tell us these things before I find out about them, because I will always find out, Malena," she bit back, scrambling to tighten her hold on her delinquent daughter. "We'll talk about it later."

She hung up.

I shoved my phone into my back pocket and walked back to the living room.

"I'll probably spend winter break with my mom going to a few sculpture exhibitions..." Cora rattled off her plans as I took a seat next to her on the couch.

"How's it going?" I asked.

Sabrina's last few months of seclusion would end soon,

and she'd be thrown into the public spotlight once her dad was inaugurated.

"I'm okay, really," Sabrina said firmly. "But can we talk about *anything* else?"

"Oh," I stammered, wishing I'd thought of something fun to share since I knew Sabrina well enough to know she'd probably need some more time to unpack all of her anxiety. "Sure... I—"

"They had sex in that boat house." The words flew out of Cora's mouth.

Sabrina's eyes went wide. She leaned in closer to the screen. "Which one?"

My face heated. "Technically it was the shell house *next* to the boat house."

"I can't wait till you get back and see them together," Cora teased. "It's nauseatingly adorable."

Sabrina blew out a sigh. "I can't believe I missed Mal settling down with a boyfriend."

The joke, meant to be light, made the room go quiet with the stale truth. My flings-only rule was primarily because I wanted to experience everything I could. But the flip side of it was that they knew my parents wouldn't approve. They just didn't know what it was like to have to weigh your own needs against potentially losing your entire family. And why would they? They had great parents who were concerned with their happiness, first and foremost.

"Before I know it"—Sabrina's unsure gaze met Cora's—"I'll get back and Cora *won't* drag me to Pilates."

Cora released a short, nervous laugh.

"If you need more time to figure this out with him, we can keep this thing quiet over the summer too," Cora pivoted. She took hold of my hand. "Especially if you get that orthopedic internship in the city."

They always assumed my parents would eventually come

around if I chose to defy them. And I didn't correct them because the truth felt too awful to admit even to myself. I didn't want to be disowned and I didn't want to have parents who did that sort of thing.

So, I skirted around it, hoping one day I'd be the daughter they wanted. And this wouldn't be a problem.

"Stay at the Alders house," Sabrina blurted. "Say you have long hours and traveling at night for that commute is dangerous."

"Yeah…" It was so much more than I was prepared to handle. Way more than I was allowed to want. "Maybe that'll work."

My mom just berated me about a writing seminar I wasn't even planning to take. I didn't want to imagine how telling her about Conrad would go.

"It will." Sabrina ventured into the silence that fell between us. "I have access to the Secret Service." She flicked a glance over her shoulder to someone off screen and then back to us. "We'll make it work until you're ready to tell your parents."

Even if we could make it work, how was I supposed to explain any of it to Conrad? *Oh hey, you know how you've made space for me in your life? With your friends—who are practically your family? I can't do the same. In fact, nobody in my life outside of school knows you exist. And that's probably never going to change. Sorry.*

Nobody deserved to live as a secret. So, either the two-Malena system ended, or the relationship did. And it would have to happen soon.

"I KNEW I'd find you here." Conrad's voice called through the mausoleum the next morning. "I thought you were coming over to my place to study."

"I wanted to get this read," I explained from my spot on the creaky sliding ladder. I pushed Cornelis Amherst's criminally boring and generally unhelpful journal back into its spot on the shelf.

Following the Scroll & Ivy rule of nothing leaving this building, I had to speed read through every journal here. But just the timbre of Conrad's voice drove the boredom from the room.

Like it always did.

At first I chalked it up to our mutual attraction and banter. But now...

I was just as *excited* to talk to him about books, my biochemistry lab work, or this article as I was to sit in a club seat at an F1 race.

An excitement that came with the feeling of being deeply comfortable because I could let my guard down.

His plotting that kept the mausoleum empty these last few weeks so I'd have a quiet space to study, sending Isha and Lucy to drag me to the Diwali party... He *saw* me.

All the ways I felt imperfect and lacking in other parts of my life, I didn't feel around him. He'd become a safe place for me to be myself.

"I have some interesting news," Conrad called from the bottom of the ladder. "About the paper."

"Oh good. Because Cornelis Amherst definitely had a more-than-friendly relationship with his best friend and was otherwise useless." I looked down again, at his hands tucked in his pockets and his eyes trained on me.

He grinned devilishly, his eyes running down my tights and probably up my skirt. "I ran into Dillian. I've got a new assignment."

I descended three rungs and turned to him.

"Oh no." I took hold of his sweater and tugged gently.

His smile straightened a bit, and he opened then closed his mouth. Finally, he spoke. "He wanted a short piece on the Autumn Awards ceremony... He gave me a list of recipients today." He took a step back. "Why didn't you tell me you were one?"

Guilt pricked me.

"It was sort of an obligation," I answered, and it *was* true. "I went, got my award, went home. It was boring."

He leaned forward, both hands dropping gently on my shoulders. Still a rung up on the ladder, I was at eye level with him.

"Watching you shine is the *least* boring thing I can think of," he encouraged. "Besides, being your boyfriend means I get to be embarrassingly proud of you at these types of things, right?"

A flutter moved through my chest. Every time I was about to cut and run, he gave me a reason to stop. "Right."

"Can I ask you something?" His hands moved from my shoulders to my hips. This close, the cedary smell of his cologne—the one that lingered on my skin when I slept over—plucked at my senses.

I rested both palms on his chest. "Sure."

"I never really dated because, well, till you, it seemed like something I'd be terrible at." He gave me a charming smile then swiped a palm over his jaw, scratching at the light stubble. "I've sort of been guessing your reason."

I didn't want to lie, so I chose my words carefully. "Life is complicated, with lots of competing priorities. Flings are simple and easy. Relationships are..."

"Hard?" Conrad finished for me, leaning forward and pressing a reassuring kiss on my lips. Like he was hoping it would keep me talking. I nodded. "But Malena Amin isn't afraid of hard things."

I tried to look away, but his gaze held mine. Unable to hide, my voice dropped to a whisper. Honesty was terrifying when its inevitable conclusion was making a choice I wasn't ready to make. "Maybe she's afraid of this one."

I'd been naked in front of Conrad more times than I could count, yet this was the first time I felt bare. Realizing that I'd never verbalized that to anyone, my eyes went wide.

He smiled softly and ran a hand through my hair, gently stroking the back of my neck. "You don't have to be. You know that, right? Not with me."

I knew what he presumed. I let him believe that someone hurt me, and that's why I was skittish. The truth wasn't *that* far off. Someone *had* hurt me, but it wasn't a guy I'd dated.

"I know." I closed the nearly non-existent space between us and pulled him into a kiss.

At first, it was a gentle peck. Something to stem the tide, keep the overwhelming emotion at bay. But as I pulled away, he pushed forward, catching my lips again. This time, hazy from the whirlwind of feelings that took flight inside of me, I kissed him deeper.

A shudder moved down his body.

He groaned and fanned his fingers along my neck, keeping me close.

Sparks danced up my legs.

He skimmed his hands over my skirt and played with the lace of my panties through my tights.

"I want you." He lowered his voice, sounding hungry and decidedly tortured, and pleaded, "All of you."

He closed his hands into fists around my tights, and I felt moisture gather between my legs.

My breath caught, realizing what he meant. "Here?"

"Fuck, Mal." A beleaguered sigh moved through his lips, his warm breath tickling my neck. My nipples peaked inside my bra. "Everywhere."

His eyes begged for permission, jaw flexed.

I nodded.

With a quick yank, he pulled both my panties and tights down, leaving me naked under my skirt. They bunched around my ankles. "Sit on the ladder, Mal."

My face flushed.

"What?" I asked breathlessly.

He clicked the wheels with his foot to lock them in place and bracketed his arms against each side.

"I can have you?" His voice was smoke by the time it touched my ear. "Wherever I want you, right?"

Desire ached at the apex of my thighs. "Yes."

"Good." A wicked smile crested up the side of his cheek. "Then sit on the ladder. And spread your legs."

I did what I was told and came to sit at the edge of a rung.

He pressed a kiss on my neck and took his time moving down my body. My stomach dipped and bowed when he got down to my navel.

My mind went completely blank, focused only on the heat of his touch, as he parted my knees with firm hands.

He lined a few short kisses along my inner thigh before drawing my clit into his mouth, stroking it with his tongue as my head slowly tipped back.

In my relatively extensive research, I found that men my age came in two varieties: the ones who ate pussy like they were allergic to it and the ones who *devoured* it like it was their last meal.

Lucky for me, Conrad belonged to the latter category.

His thumb replaced his tongue and he slipped his fingers into me slowly, sending tendrils of pleasure moving down my body. I threaded my fingers through his hair, desperate to keep him where he was.

I bit on my lip to stifle a moan. It felt *so good*.

"Is *this* the fantasy you were talking about?" he asked

against the slickness on my inner thigh, his fingers and thumb moving in tandem.

I closed my eyes again.

"Maybe," I breathed, and his fingers pushed into me deeper. Chills ran up my back and it curved away from the rungs, into him.

"Oh yeah?" he whispered, and drew my clit into his mouth again. Another finger sank into me. Electricity shot down my spine. "Judging by how wet you are, it's more than a *maybe.*"

I whimpered, rolling my hips toward him.

His fingers moved more forcefully inside me, and the pressure at my core tightened. I trembled in the anticipation of it breaking loose.

He stopped. Right at the edge, he yanked me back.

My eyes fluttered open and looked down my body to meet his heated stare. His chest rose and fell heavily, watching me with a ravenous desire.

"Stand up, turn around."

I nodded and Conrad put his hands on my hips, helping me up and maneuvering me around.

He pressed a palm on my back, guiding me to bend over, and I wobbled as I steadied myself against the ladder.

"That's my girl." He stepped back momentarily, and the audible shuffle of his belt coming off and the sound of foil ripping open filled the airy silence before he was behind me again.

He entered me slowly, and I drowned in the gratifying sensation of his size stretching me.

"That's it, Mal." He slipped his other hand under my sweater and massaged my breast, passing my taut nipple between his fingers. "Take it all."

I panted softly, my nails digging into the weathered wood. His strokes started slow, pushing the air out of my lungs.

"Con," I moaned in a broken sob.

He thrust harder, wilder.

My arms slackened and my head knocked against the rungs, but all I knew was how completely he filled me. How roughly he fucked me. How gently he cared for me. And how *good* we felt together.

"We're the only ones here, baby," he gritted out, his hands creating a bruising vise on my hips. "Let me hear you."

I closed my eyes and my senses filled with the sound of his low grunts, the filthy echo of our bodies colliding, and the creaks along the ladder. In a building I should have never even seen the inside of, surrounded by ancient books and a dim streak of light through the gilded windows, I gave myself over completely to a guy whose touch lit up every part of me.

His hand teased my clit before giving it a pinch.

Every neuron sparked out of control, and an incoherent mix of sounds spilled from my mouth.

"Con," I cried out again, the orgasm slamming into me.

With a forceful jerk forward and a pronounced shudder down his body, his grip on my hips tightened. He grunted, his climax taking control of him too. "Fuck, Mal."

After a few moments, we stilled.

As my exhausted body began to give way, Conrad wrapped his arms around me and pulled me into him.

"Are you okay?" he whispered in my ear.

I rested my head on his shoulder, feeling the rise and fall of his chest against my back.

I nodded. "Mmm..."

I'd *tried* to keep the feelings between us at bay, but it was like a tsunami. Invisible at first, a ripple out in the open water. But in no time, it was racing toward the shore, gathering power and becoming all-consuming.

Impossible to ignore.

Waiting to crash.

He curled his fingers gently forward and back against my stomach—the same thing he did every night as I fell asleep. His touch a tender metronome, I closed my eyes.

"Everything is so perfect with you, Mal," he said softly in my ear before dropping a kiss beneath it.

I sighed and nodded again.

I could tell him everything that Cora and Sabrina already knew. I knew him well enough by now to know what he'd do. He'd fight for us. He'd try to find a way around it—thinking it was sweet or gallant—because on some level he'd operate under the same assumptions that the girls did.

That it couldn't be *that bad.*

I hoped it wasn't, but I was too much of a coward to find out.

I didn't want to lie to him anymore. But, for just a bit longer, I'd lie to myself and bask in his warmth like it was mine to keep.

CHAPTER 41

Conrad

"This is insane." I threw my arm around Mal and pulled her a little closer as we made our way down the tunnel. "I love the idea, but it's insane."

We didn't have plans when I ran into her outside our building earlier, and aside from telling James and Felix I'd meet them for a drink later, my Friday night was open. She'd just hung up from a phone call, and she looked like a different person, somehow smaller. I managed to get a few details out of her—something about not going home this weekend—but she still looked like she might cry.

"It will force them to act," Malena insisted as our footsteps clattered against the stone pavers, her voice echoing in the cavernous space. I was grateful she seemed to have shaken off her earlier gloomy mood. From the moment she grabbed my hand on the sidewalk outside our building and dragged me to the catacombs, I knew I'd go anywhere with her if it meant seeing that smile back on her face.

"We can be in control," she insisted, like she *needed* this, "instead of waiting for something to magically happen. If they already moved the painting, then Ishani would have at least heard about a sale. So it has to be in there, and if we're going to catch them, we need to light a match under their asses."

"Yeah." I rubbed the back of my neck.

"It'll force their hand," she said firmly. "I go in, pull the fire alarm in the basement. A couple of fire engines show up and leave when they find the building is empty," she rambled. "It'll garner enough attention that, at the very least, the student body will be sent an email with a warning not to mess around with alarms. And whoever's behind this will need to act because they'll know their position is compromised. They'll make a move, and we can be in control. If it *is* Azalea, she'll know to stop."

I nodded along, deciding it was best not to remind her that she'd already run me through the plan. Half a dozen times.

"You sure you're okay?" We stopped at the doorway in question in the catacombs, the one that opened out into the Amherst Building's cellar. "Mal, if something's going on, something else, you can talk to me."

"I'm fine." A smile touched her lips. "You said I had to tell you before I did anything illegal."

I sighed, knowing my attempts were futile at this point. She had that determined look on her face I knew too well. "Okay, but I'm doing it."

"No." Concern divoted between her brows.

"It's the only way. I'll pull the alarm, you wait here." I rested both hands on her shoulders and gave them a reassuring squeeze. "I'm Conrad Hastings, remember? Disciplinary Teflon."

"Conrad." Her voice wavered.

"Or we can leave right now," I said firmly.

"Fine. Set off the fire alarm, wait a bit to make sure it actually goes off, then flip it back."

"You got it, Holmes." I playfully saluted her.

I took the scarf she had loosely draped around her neck and coiled it around my hand. If I was pulling a fire alarm, I wasn't going to be stupid enough to make a rookie error like leave prints.

I shoved through the door and made my way inside. "I'll be right back."

"Be careful," she called.

A few minutes later, inside the dusty and damp cellar, I found the alarm next to the stairwell. I made quick work of setting it off, waiting with bated breath as it blared for a solid ten seconds, then rushed back toward Mal.

I closed the heavy door behind me and threw the scarf back over Mal, wrapping it tight this time.

I looked around nonchalantly and shrugged. "I think this is the part where we run."

A delirious grin pushed against either side of her cheeks, and with a tiny laugh, she turned on her toes, grabbed my hand, and we bolted back the way we came.

AFTER LEAVING THE CATACOMBS, Mal and I walked a while. So long in fact, that we'd made it to the bay near town. Huddled tight against the wind, we talked about a million things: what happened next with the article. My plans for winter break. The fact that Sabrina would be back for Thanksgiving and she'd see her in the city at some point over the holiday. It was the mention of Sabrina that I suspected had pushed her back into her own head, and she'd been quiet for the last ten minutes.

"Are you *sure* you're okay? Why don't we duck into a pub, grab a basket of fries or a drink?" I asked, nodding toward the light trickling over to us from the streetlamps.

My coat thrown over her shoulders, she pulled it closed. "I already ate. But we can do whatever you want."

I was about to suggest we sit on the bench up ahead when she let out a heavy sigh and stopped abruptly.

"Does it ever bother you that your dad doesn't like you? Or that he doesn't try to get to know you, the *real* you?"

"My dad doesn't like anyone," I admitted. "His *favorite* changes based on who can do what for him. In the past, any instances he was nice to me was out of fear that my mom might actually go through with a divorce."

Malena nodded. "How do you deal with that?"

"It's really not so bad. I have a family; it just isn't the one I was born into," I told her, running my hands up and down her arms and trying to catch her eye. "What's going on, Mal?"

"Nothing. It's dumb." She shook her head.

"Mal," I repeated, firmer. She didn't talk a lot about her parents, but it was obvious they had different ideas for her future career plans. I wasn't sure what was wrong though, because she had a clear vision of her path. One she liked. "Tell me, I *want* to know."

Her eyes skimmed over the water, and I caught facets of moonlight reflected in them.

"My mom wanted me to come home today, last minute, because they had family friends coming over. And I said no," she explained. "She dropped it, but now she's *furious* with me, so I'll get an earful when I go home next week for the holiday. I'll probably have to spend the whole weekend apologizing."

"I'm sorry," I said. I'd gathered from the way she spoke about them every now and again that they had some friction, and I assumed she'd tell me more when she was ready. Maybe tonight was the night.

"I know it sounds childish—"

"It doesn't."

"She just..." Mal blew out a breath, then pinched her eyes

closed. "She loves to remind me of everything they've sacri-ficed." She blinked rapidly, her eyelids shining, and turned her face up to the clear night sky. "Anytime I disagree, I'm selfish. She forces my hand, wields the guilt I feel about everything she gave up for me like a weapon."

"Forces your hand?" I asked.

The same three words she'd used earlier when she explained why we needed to pull that alarm.

"Yeah... My parents expect a lot from me and sometimes it doesn't feel worth it," she explained.

"What are they expecting from you?"

I assumed she meant med school. She seemed dedicated, if not resigned, to that goal, and I was sure she'd find a way to write. Malena found a way to get everything she wanted.

"To do everything the way they want it done," she answered. "To be perfect."

"Hate to be the one to tell you this." I slipped my finger under her chin, tilting it so she faced me. "You *are* perfect."

She harrumphed a laugh and shook her head. "Sometimes, I dunno, I feel like..."

Her thoughts drifted off into the night.

"If it's writing you want, then you can still do that. Maybe take some time to figure it out before you graduate," I encour-aged. "Like that writing seminar over the summer, the one you keep reading about on your phone."

I knew she loved to write; it was plain as day. And I under-stood the feeling of being pushed in one direction, but *she* had been the one to point out that it didn't have to be the endgame.

"Maybe." She looked around with a sigh. "It's just... when I try to stay in the lines that they draw, I feel like I just end up becoming *blurry*. Like nobody can see me."

"Well, I happen to see you clearly." I swung both arms around her and pulled her in. "You're unreasonably smart, unfairly beautiful, inexplicably mean when you want to be." I held her tighter. "And perfect *exactly as you are.* Trust me, Mal, everyone can see that."

She looked up at me, her mouth holding a wobbly smile.

"Come on." I pulled out my phone and sent a quick text to a car service since we were miles from campus. It would take hours to walk back and cabs never wandered this far off from town. "I should probably get you indoors. The car will be here in a few minutes."

She leaned in and brushed a kiss against my lips. "Always so concerned about keeping me warm."

"You don't dress for the weather." Despite the cold, everything felt so good I didn't want to move. I wanted to keep her there, fit perfectly against me.

Minutes later, with the sound of tires slowing to a stop, she hummed serenely as I pulled away.

Only, we quickly realized it wasn't the car service, and the warm moment shattered when a sharp "Malena!" cracked through the air.

Mal inhaled sharply, jolted a step back, and froze with wide eyes. She didn't bother looking over her shoulder to see the incensed woman rounding the front of a dark blue SUV. Mal's eyes immediately went down to her purse as she started riffling through it.

"Shit," she cursed in a panic.

A protective kick pushed me forward. My hand wrapped around her wrist. "Mal?"

She finally looked up from her bag like she registered what was going on.

Before I could ask anything else, the woman, who I'd gathered was her mom, spoke again.

"Get in the car." Her mom stomped over and yanked Mal's arm, jostling her hands and sending two phones clattering to the ground.

Completely fucking lost as to what was going on, I leaned down, and my stomach dropped. Two phones lay side by side, looking exactly the same apart from one being marked with a golden star. The one without the star—the one I'd never seen before—had a few texts from Cora and twelve missed calls, all from her mom.

The second phone was blank.

It hit me like a wave, forcing the world underwater. My brain flipped back to that sunny morning in Newport, waiting for my glass of lemonade, and every messy and painful memory my psyche wasn't equipped to understand at the age of seven made perfect sense now.

Malena stood in front of me, under the glow from the lamppost, speechless and wearing a blank expression.

CHAPTER 42
Malena

The edges of my vision blurred. Everything moved in slow motion. Frame by frame.

I knew exactly what had happened, in hindsight. After my mom reluctantly agreed to drop the topic of my visit home this weekend, I hung up and silenced my real phone like I always did when I was going to leave it at the condo. But I didn't make it inside.

I saw Conrad and got sidetracked. I was sloppy. The burner was in my purse but nothing was being forwarded because I never dropped off the real phone. My mom could see my actual location.

Fuck.

I yanked my arm away from my mom, following the few steps back Conrad had taken. "Conrad."

I watched as he picked up my phones, turning them over in his hands. Understanding slowly poured into his face.

The scene in front of me snapped back to full speed.

His wide eyes bore into me, practically begging for an explanation that wasn't the obvious one in front of him. "My dad had three. Work. Mistresses. Hastings."

The contents of my stomach thrashed. "It's not like that..."

Every single lie had fused together, and the web was nothing more than a singular, tangled string that'd wrapped around itself and then me. I was caught in it all.

He looked past me to my mom. "Then what's it like, Mal?"

A black town car pulled up a moment later. Behind me came my mother's fervent demands through gritted teeth, but I stayed put.

"I know it looks..." I sputtered. There was a way to logic out of this. A perfectly good excuse, a loophole, somewhere. I had to find it.

"Hey... it's okay." His voice lowered, calm and caring and so much more than I deserved. "Mal, just tell me what's going on."

"That's my mom, and I can't explain all of this now, but you *have* to go." I needed to contain the damage. "And so do I."

His face crinkled. "Mal..."

"This was a mistake," I finally choked out. How the hell had I let it get this far? How was I going to walk it all back?

Fuck.

"What was a mistake?" His eyes turned stormy as he tried to take my hand, but I pulled it back.

My mind whirled with everything I was going to have to explain. The mess I had to answer for. "This, us, all of it. I took it too far, and for that, I'm sorry, but you have to go."

"Mal—"

"*Please.*" My voice cracked. The cords in my throat stretched and ached, and tears welled behind my eyes. "Just go."

This time it stuck, and the confusion in his eyes mingled

with pain. His voice was just above a whisper. "Will you be okay?"

Guilt stabbed me between the ribs. I was breaking his heart, and he was still making sure mine was intact.

"Of course. She's my mom." My voice trembled as I peeled off his coat and handed it to him. "Please, go."

His jaw flexed and he nodded.

Without another word, he walked away.

Breathing around the spike in my chest instead of attempting to pull it out, I faced my mom.

Tears sheened over my eyes and distorted my vision, but a final yank on my arm shook me from the fog. It was followed by a long twisting pinch. White-hot pain shot down my arm.

"Let's go." Her cold fingers strained even harder.

I ducked my head and followed, taking one last look behind me, but he was already in the car he'd called.

THE TWO-HOUR DRIVE to Western Massachusetts was silent. My mom was never silent.

Every time I did anything she didn't like, she made sure I knew it. When I had one of the bigger slices of cake at Pinky Auntie's birthday, when I wore a tank top to a summer barbeque, anytime I was a little too honest with my opinions. Tracking me down and catching me on the street, at midnight, with a guy. *Kissing* said guy. And she said nothing.

She saved it all up for the second we got into the house.

"She was in Paris! When? What else is she doing, Vijay?" My mom shook my phone—the burner—while she paced back and forth on our living room rug. She'd gone through my wallet, found the tiny slit I cut into it to hide the credit and debit cards attached to my secret bank accounts and was waving them around frantically. "Other than kissing strangers on the street like a—"

"Nikila," my dad cut in.

Sitting on the living room couch, I rubbed my arm where she'd pinched it. It had become a deep red color, and the skin was raised.

"What is she doing in *private* with that boy? A secret phone. A secret bank account. A secret life." She whipped around. "Are you on drugs?"

I bit back the urge to ask her how exactly she thought I managed a perfect GPA, a twenty-credit course load, *and* a drug addiction. "No, Mom."

"She's coming home every weekend." My mom continued to pace. "Next year she'll commute. Nobody needs to know about *any* of this."

"It's not that big of a deal. We were taking a walk," I stated, surprised to hear my voice come out calm. It was a kiss. With a guy I was dating. But that was only a small part of why she was angry. What really got to her, I knew, was the realization that she hadn't been in control this whole time. And if I'd evaded her once, I could do it again. "I wasn't doing blow off the hood of a car."

I probably shouldn't have said that.

My mom froze, then blinked three disbelieving blinks. "If we caught you doing that, we wouldn't have a daughter anymore."

"Nikila," my dad warned again, this time leveling me with a stern look. "Don't make this worse."

"What if someone else saw you?" my mom added, her list of grievances growing by the minute.

My patience snapped.

"I'm twenty-one," I huffed. My parents could claim they had my best intentions at heart, and I was sure on some level they believed that, but it was hard to see in moments like this.

"They would think I was doing exactly what a regular twenty-one-year-old does."

My mom's frame tensed. She shot a vicious look at my dad. "It's those friends. I knew they were the problem, making her think it's okay to act like..."

"Like I'm my own person? Someone capable of making my *own* decisions?" I cut her off before she said something I couldn't unhear. I was sick of having to defend the only two people who seemed to *actually* care about me. I took a breath. "I'm doing great in school, what does it matter who—"

"You lied to us," she seethed.

"I *have* to lie." I got a little louder, losing sight of the line I knew never to cross. "So, what? I can go to college, get a degree, go to medical school, but I can't be trusted to make my own decisions?"

The image of the heartbreak painted all over Conrad's face propelled me forward. I needed to put the pain somewhere. I stood and took a menacing step toward her.

"Or is it that I can only be smart when it benefits you?" My voice cracked around the question. "When you can show me off like some trophy? That way you can remain in control of *my* life."

"After all of *that*, you want to argue instead of apologize?" Her eyes narrowed. "After everything we've sacrificed for you, this is how you choose to act?"

My mouth hung open. Did she think I liked living like this?

Something in my brain finally snapped.

If she wanted the truth, she could have it.

"What about everything I've sacrificed for *you*?" The words pulled so thin they became translucent. "Do you ever think about that? No, of course not. Well, newsflash, Mom: I go out. I *love* a party. I love writing more than anything else, and I have sex. Lots, actually, and I like to think I'm—"

A slap landed in a hot flash across my face and I stumbled back.

Pain radiated down my jawline and I brought my hand up to cover the searing sting along my cheek. My head rang for a few seconds.

"Nikila, that's *enough*." My dad stood between us, but the damage was done.

"She doesn't even care," Mom seethed through gritted teeth. "You don't think about your future. What people will say about *you*, about this family…"

The rest got lost in the static that filled my ears. I held my cheek, still in disbelief. It had been awhile since she'd slapped me like that. I blinked a few times to clear the spots in my vision, making way for some clarity.

I wondered if their sacrifices were ever *for* me. Or if it was like saving up for a nice car and then protecting it from dings so you wouldn't damage its resale value.

I was a commodity.

The realization became smoke, and I choked on it.

"I have to get back to school," I whispered, my entire body shaking.

The room was silent.

"Malena," my dad started, voice low. "Stay, and we'll talk about this. Mom didn't mean—"

"I have to get back to school," I repeated.

I didn't care how it happened, but I was returning to Winchester tonight. I picked up my keys and my wallet and made my way to the door.

THE FIRST SIGNS of dawn were already blanketing our street when I stepped into the Radiant's lobby and took the elevator up to the condo, where a humid cloud of chili and broth welcomed me.

I took a rideshare to the train station, then waited an hour for the next train to New Harbor. Took another rideshare to the condo. My dad offered to drive me, but I didn't want to talk to him. As far as I was concerned, they were in on it together—he didn't slap me, but he may as well have.

Cora's giant pink polka dot blanket was carefully placed along the back of the couch as I slipped off my lace-up sneakers. On the TV, *Gossip Girl* was paused at the scene where Blair and Serena wandered through Paris together, dressed in haute couture and swinging shopping bags in their hands. On the coffee table were two of the three matching ice cream mugs that Sabrina, Cora, and I bought at a local street festival last fall.

Each was filled to the brim with spicy ramen noodle soup. My heart bobbed in my chest.

"Your mom called me demanding that I tell you to pick up her calls," Cora admitted, her voice trickling down the hallway. She appeared a second later with an unsteady smile. "I figured whatever happened must have been bad."

It was four in the morning, but here she was, my version of wagons circling. She took one look at my puffy red eyes, tear-stained cheeks, and runny nose and she threw her arms around me.

"Whatever it is"—she put her hands on my shoulders and pushed me back so she could look me in the eyes—"remember, Serena van der Woodsen killed a guy."

I coughed on a laugh. The warm scent of my favorite snack pushed the gears in my brain back into movement.

"It all finally caught up to me."

"It'll be okay."

"Yeah?" My throat dipped and I pushed back the emotion

that threatened to break out in another loud, uncontrollable sob.

"We're young, we have plenty of mistakes left to make. Probably good your parents start getting used to it."

With how angry they were, I knew how the next few months would go. Every time I made a stand for my own independence, it all happened in order. This time was admittedly worse, but it would follow the same cycle: melodramatic meltdown, my mom justifying her actions, guilt over how I'd reacted. Then, I'd knuckle under.

We sat on the couch, wrapped in the blanket and holding searing hot ice cream mugs filled to the brim with soup, and watched toxic besties bicker onscreen.

One way or another, this was bound to happen. What I wanted and what I was expected to want were going to bump up against each other because there weren't many people who were concerned with the former.

"I love you, Cora," I whispered over the steam from my mug, leaning my head on her shoulder.

She tilted her cheek onto my head. "I love you too, Mal."

CHAPTER 43

Conrad

Instead of heading to my place in New Harbor, I instructed the driver to take me to Manhattan.

La Fleur's panoramic rooftop was constructed entirely out of glass, the ceilings and walls retracting in the summer, and it boasted an almost unbelievable view of midtown. It was the perfect place to escape the heaviness of the last few hours.

"Lucy said you were here." James sat down beside me.

I didn't know what time it was now, but it'd been close to one a.m. when I found myself at the bar ordering four fingers of whiskey neat. I wasn't sure I even wanted to be alone, I just wanted to get out of my head. And since Lucy's family owned this place, I was sure it wouldn't be long before the rest of my motley crew filed in.

"You need anything?" he asked.

The music blared, but along the private lounges that lined the wall, it was a little quieter. Not "have a conversation" quiet, which was perfect. I was here because I couldn't go back to my place. Not when my clothes, my sheets, my *everything* smelled like her.

"Another drink." I downed what was left of mine, and James's general look of concern sharpened, but he motioned for the hostess regardless.

All I'd been able to think about was how I spent so long trying to avoid being like my dad.

In some bizarre twist of fate, I wasn't him nor my mom in this situation.

I wasn't the philandering partner or the scorned one.

I was the dirty little secret. The number on the clandestine phone. I was the person who flew under the radar. And after a lifetime of being just that in my own family, I hadn't expected it to hurt like it did.

A bottle of Macallan was delivered to the table, and I sat back in the booth, feeling like it was nowhere near enough.

"All right, you're going to tell me what happened." James raised his voice over the music, pouring two shots. "School, family, Malena, crew...?"

My mind flipped back and forth between that day in Newport and the present. Every memory with Malena was suddenly under review as I tried to weed out all the things I must have missed.

I took both shots. "I'm good."

He said something, but it got lost under the bass line that ricocheted off the solarium-like walls.

Over the next hour, the process repeated with Felix, then Lucy, then James again. Surprisingly, the only one who hadn't intervened was Ishani. She watched from a distance. Occasionally, someone would sidle up to her on the dance floor and try to flirt, but she kept a keen eye on me.

The more I drank though, the less I cared that all my friends were treating me like something breakable. I was here to forget, to clear my head of all things Mal.

It wasn't until a cute blond in a miniskirt and very little else took a seat next to me that Isha intervened. We were halfway through some inane conversation about the weather when she ran a hand up my thigh.

At that moment, Ishani Gabriella Roy made her presence known.

"Absolutely not." She wedged herself between me and the girl, sloshing her drink a bit but apparently not caring about civility.

"Isha, go away," I grumbled as the girl scampered off, huffing under her breath.

"I've let you sulk through entirely too much alcohol. But *that*?"

"We were just talking."

"Fine. Talk to me." Ishani plastered on a fake smile, her voice becoming prickly. "Go on then, *speak*."

"I'm fine. I'm having a good time."

"Are you?" She grabbed my chin and forced me to look at her. "Or were you hoping to forget what's bothering you between that girl's legs when you have a *girlfriend*." She released her hold with a disgusted sneer. "Honestly, I'd—"

"We broke up," I snapped, the implication slicing into my chest. "I don't cheat."

Malena had bent over backward to keep me from being part of her life in the ways that counted. How could I explain that to my friends? That I'd been drinking in order to stop myself from wondering what was real and what was fake.

"Oh." She lowered her shoulders and the corners of her eyes softened. She looked around the bar and winced. "Then we need to be *anywhere* else."

"I want to be here."

"Well, that's too bad." She pulled at my arms, looking at James expectantly to do her bidding when she made no progress. I raised my hands in defeat and followed her, stumbling a bit.

She was quiet until we got out to the street, stopping in

front of the car she'd called. The sounds of the city—still buzzing despite it being the early hours of the morning—pierced through the muffled state I was in.

Ishani looked at me pointedly. "We need to talk about it."

"It was never serious or real, so it's not a big deal."

"Not real?"

Not to Mal anyway, but now was not the time to get into the double phone situation.

"We were working together, things happened, now it's over," I droned blankly.

"It seemed real," Ishani offered quietly.

"Yeah." My breathing faltered. "It did."

My dad taught me early on that people always found ways to disappoint you, no matter how hard you tried to keep it from happening. Conclusions were usually foregone.

This was just another example.

Her voice dropped to a whisper. "It'll be okay."

"Yeah, I know." I swallowed all the hurt.

"Would you like to wallow in alcohol a bit longer?" She smiled, trying and failing to keep the pity out of her expression.

"No." I looked up at the building next to us. What I wanted more than anything was to go back a week, when everything was perfect.

"All right, then let's go," she barked, rallying like nothing was wrong. "I am standing on a public curb like some *commuter*." Her lip curled up before it morphed into a smile. "Come on, back to the Roy townhouse. We can channel all of this"—she waved her palm in front of my face—"into something productive, or maybe cathartic. We'll watch a movie and you can cry all about it."

"I'm not going to cry," I grumbled.

"Of course you won't..." She looped her arm in mine and

sent a text. I could hardly read it, but it was to Felix. "I'm certainly *not* going to play the opening scene of *Up*."

A real, genuine laugh made its way up my chest. For a second, everything hurt a little less. "You're mean."

"And you'll be just fine." She gave my arm a squeeze. "Come on, spend the weekend being a little unhinged and then we'll regroup."

CHAPTER 44

Malena

A low hum of white noise poured out of my headphones.

I spent the early hours of Saturday morning crying and eating ramen. Saturday night, Cora made cocktails and we watched movies. And now, Sunday morning was here and I faced the prospect of returning to class tomorrow, where I'd have to act like I was fine.

So, I decided to ignore the world in exchange for a different one. A dragon rider, dark magic, a plot to avenge her slain family, and all the rage I wasn't allowed to express spilled on the pages of my paperback and let me dissociate for just long enough to finally stop crying. Between the book and the white noise, I'd been sucked into a new world.

"Mal?" A voice cut through right as I got to the part where the heroine was assembling her team.

I looked up from my book and gasped, letting it fall to the bed at my side as I scrambled to untangle myself from my sheets. "Sabrina?"

Her hair was down, and it sat a little shorter and a lot blonder than when I saw her last. I rushed to meet her in the doorway, and before I could say anything, the soft wool from her sweater encased me in a tight hug.

"You're blond." I held her shoulders, nudging her back and staring in disbelief.

For years, Sabrina had been dyeing her hair to look less like her very famous family. So this was big. Bravery, for me, was honesty. For Sabrina, it was embracing who she was: an Alders.

"It looks great," I added, running my fingers through the golden locks. "What are you doing here?"

"I had to come home a little early to sit through some press obligations with my parents. Figured I'd stay this week since it's a short one anyway. You finish up classes on Tuesday, right?" When I didn't speak, gentle lines spanned her brow and curved around the corners of her downturned lips. "Are you okay?"

She looked over her shoulder and notched her head to the side, motioning me to follow her down the hall. We walked into the bright kitchen where Cora sat on one of the barstools, a steaming cup of coffee in her hands.

"I guess." I sat down at the kitchen island and looked at my phone, the real one. I must have left it out here last night. "They're radio silent, which is new."

"What's the plan with the burner?" Sabrina asked softly.

I shook my head and accepted a mug from Cora, taking a sip of the coffee. "I can't be two Malenas anymore."

Aside from the fact that my carefully fabricated alter ego was effectively burned, I couldn't hurt anyone else. Conrad's perfect face etched with hurt was all I saw every time I closed my eyes.

"So, which one are you gonna be?" Cora asked.

I shrugged. Probably the "good" one. I wasn't ready to be disowned. Wasn't sure I ever would be.

"Well, maybe this will help." Sabrina turned to her vintage

dark leather Pourchet handbag and pulled out two files. One pink, one green. She handed me the green one.

"These are investments?" Cora asked, paging through hers.

"Sabrina." I gasped as my eyes scanned down the deposits, monthly for the last year and a half.

While Cora was looking at the graph with the rate of return, my attention was caught on the amount. Each deposit amounted to what Cora and I paid Sabrina for rent.

"I told you guys I didn't want you paying me rent. This place has been in my family for generations," Sabrina explained slowly, carefully. Cora and I looked at each other then back at her. "But since you insisted, I've been investing it. And you two have accrued some pretty good returns."

Cora handed the file back to her. "Sabrina, this is too much."

"No, what's *too much* is the number of nights you both sat up with me because of the nightmares." She swallowed and blinked back tears. "We were all sleep deprived that semester, and it couldn't have been easy."

While I went through the time-honored tradition of having a randomly assigned roommate as a freshman, Sabrina had been appointed a private room. Even after she'd requested a roommate, she struggled to keep one because she was fully nocturnal for a while. It was how we met Cora; she was the one who stuck.

"If you don't want it, take it up with my uncle Tristan, he oversaw it," Sabrina added, putting her hands up. "Cash it out, let it grow, I don't have any say in the matter."

"When?" I sputtered. "How..."

"When we were freshmen and Malena decided to open up her secret bank account... It got me thinking. Then, we all moved in together last year, and I caved and let you pay me rent. I've been putting it away ever since."

"Were you waiting for my life to implode to give this to us?" A laugh rocked against my body and it felt so good.

"No, I was going to tell you at graduation." Sabrina smiled apologetically. "I always figured the wheels would fall off the lie in medical school when your parents tried to shove the idea of marriage in your face like they did your sister. I assumed the commitment would make you crack, and in the time they'd need to come around, you'd have this."

I looked at the papers in front of me. It would be enough to cover the rest of my tuition at Winchester plus put a solid dent in at least the first year of medical school. Even more if I let it grow. "Thanks, Sabrina. I—thank you. This means..." I trailed off, voice shaky.

Instead of the instant relief something of this magnitude should've provided, my reality weighed heavy. Financial freedom was only one part; the other was my anxiety at being erased from my family the way I'd seen it happen to other kids. I wanted a family, I just wished it wanted *me* back.

"Money is easy," Sabrina said, repeating a sentiment she often shared. "If it solved *this* problem, then you wouldn't be as tangled up as you are right now."

"If I lose my family, I lose it all," I finally admitted to them, staring at all the numbers on the page. "They're my tie to everything."

My culture. The holidays I loved. My extended family. I'd have cousins who might talk to me in secret, if at all. I'd miss weddings and get-togethers, and I'd be blamed for the rift because I was "too stubborn" to just fit the mold as expected.

I'd disappear.

And just because I liked the quiet didn't mean I wanted to be alone.

"Not everything." Cora squeezed my hand; I looked up at her and then Sabrina, who gave me a sympathetic look. "We can't replace them, but just know, you'll never lose *everything*."

I nodded, summoning a grateful half smile.

Sabrina folded her hands on the counter. "Have you called him?"

"Twice. He hasn't answered." I needed to explain everything. Apologize. But I realized when the second call went to voicemail yesterday that I needed to sort myself out before I dragged him into any more of my mess.

Sabrina was right, it was more than money. I could go home, take whatever level of punishment they deemed appropriate, and move on. I could finally fall in line. I had always planned to eventually. Everything that happened with Conrad had me rethinking it all, but that was short-sighted. How could I let a guy I'd known for a few months be the catalyst for so much change?

The answer was simple: I couldn't.

I was being made to choose, and I had to be smart. And now that I sorted it out, I had to apologize and hope that everything I felt for him would eventually fade away.

Conrad

Once the weekend was over, I spent any time I wasn't in class on the water. It was the only place I could clear my mind, and the blistering chill was a welcome anesthetic.

The scent of firewood burning in the distance mixed with the salty breeze as I neared the shoreline. After an hour out on the bay, the cold had settled in my bones and I rowed back to the pier, feeling more grounded than I'd been in almost seventy-two hours.

After I heaved the dripping shell onto the outdoor stand, I rounded the path, and my heart stumbled.

Sitting on the boat house steps, wrapped in a wool coat, gloves, winter boots, and an adorable knit hat that covered the tops of her ears, was Malena. I couldn't help noting that it was the first time I'd ever seen her dressed in weather-appropriate clothing.

She watched with a cautious smile as I neared the steps. "I figured I'd find you here."

"And here I am." My muscles, regaining feeling, began to tremble. I walked around her and opened the door, motioning her in. She nodded and tucked her phone in her pocket as she passed me. "Only one?"

I hadn't picked up her calls because I was in no shape to talk to her all weekend. And a little because I was terrified of what she planned to say.

"Oh... umm. Yeah," she stammered. "Just the one, for good."

I wanted to be angry with her. Because, fuck, it hurt. But more than anything, I wanted to kiss her. I wanted an explanation, and then I wanted to take her home.

My tone softened at the edges. "Mal."

"I wrote the article. A new version." With her back to me, she walked between the two rows of neatly stacked sculls. "I sent it to you to look over before I submit it."

My heart sank realizing where this was going. And it stung worse than before. "We haven't finished."

"I know, but..." She refused to look at me. She played with her fingers and glanced up at the ceiling, her eyes following the wooden beams. "We have a deadline."

"That's three weeks away," I added. We'd had this conversation once already, so I knew where it led. But this time, I wasn't sure I could pull a random lead out of my hat like before.

She took another extended pause, then a deep breath. "I'm trying to be practical," she said resolutely, turning to me. "And I owed you that, with our deal and all."

"Of all the things you owe me, the last thing I care about is the deal." Un-fucking-believable pain swelled in my chest. She was here to tie up loose ends.

"I'm sorry." Her voice hitched. "I shouldn't have lied to you. I just... I dunno. I didn't think it would turn into what it did or that I'd..." She sucked in a swath of cool air. "I'm sorry. You deserve a lot more than I gave you."

She said it with such finality that it was clear: she didn't think *we* had a way forward.

"Yeah, I do." My jaw flexed against the soreness that'd sunk into my body.

"It was never about lying to *you*. I share my location with my parents, and as you saw for yourself on Friday night, they're not what you'd call open-minded." She rubbed her gloved hands together, and it took everything in me not to close the two feet of distance and pull her into my arms. "That's why I had two phones," she continued. "So I could live my life but also the one they expect me to. I needed the Keller win, not just because I wanted to pursue writing, but because I needed it to fund—"

"Your double life?"

Mal nodded.

"Why didn't you tell me any of that before?"

"At first, I didn't think this would go anywhere…"

"And then?" I demanded, because we were *together*. She'd been around all the people that were important to me. She'd met the Rutherfords, for Christ's sake. Eleanor hadn't stopped asking if Malena would be joining us in St. Moritz this winter, and I'd stupidly thought she might.

I never pushed the subject of her family, thinking she'd come around, open up in her own time.

"And then I knew the truth would end things because I was going to be made to choose. What they want or what I want." Her eyes became glassy, but she blinked the emotion away. "I just…" She faltered. "I wasn't ready to let you go."

I swallowed against the painful truth. "But you are now?"

I'd fallen hard for her these last few weeks. I'd been thinking about stupid things, like hoping she went to med school close by while being open to long distance if she didn't. I was painting a version of my life with her in it because I'd never felt this way before.

And the entire time, it wasn't real. And she *knew* it never would be.

"My family is…" Her eyes shuttered. "They're the only one I have."

What the hell could I say to that?

I couldn't be angry with her for choosing her family. I lived a pretty charmed life, and I'd never been put in the position she was in.

She'd made her decision. And if there was one thing I knew about Mal it was that once she committed to something, she wasn't easily swayed away. Especially not by me.

"That Mal…" She took a few steps toward the door. "The one who forced you into helping her. The one who dragged you through the catacombs. That's the real one. I just…" The lines along her slender neck shifted with a hard swallow. She looked at the floor and ran a finger under her eye. "I can't be her all the time."

For years I'd wondered how my mom stayed with my dad, let herself shrink down in the face of his disappointments. And while I could empathize with Mal's situation—and I knew she was nothing like my father—it all made a little more sense now. Because a part of me wanted to live in the lie and pretend it was the truth. Because inside the lie, things were simple. They were closer to perfect than I'd ever experienced.

"It's too bad." I nodded. The heartbreak welled behind my eyes, but I refused to let it loose. "I really liked her."

She didn't say anything else, only gave me a tiny smile and left. The door clicked behind her, and almost three months after she barged into my life, I was in the same place I started.

I meandered around the wood-paneled boat house after taking a shower and getting dressed. I tried to read, listen to music, even cracked open the economics textbook that sat in my backpack untouched for weeks. Anything to *not* think about Malena. It wasn't until James texted to tell me everyone was getting dinner that I snapped myself out of it, hoping some time with my friends would lift my spirits.

When I stepped into the lobby of my building, I half expected the guys to be waiting and ready to bodily escort me to town.

Instead, on one of the navy wingback chairs, sat my mom, paging through the campus satire magazine, her face frozen in a disapproving wince.

"Mom?"

She looked up from last month's copy of *Pastiche* and quickly set it aside. "Conrad," she said, standing and smoothing her palms over her skirt. "I needed to speak with you."

"Okay..." I put my arm out and motioned for the elevator. I mustered a smile; I already had enough people worried about me. "Do you want to come upstairs and sit—"

"I'd rather not, dear." She picked up her leather handbag. "I'm not going to mince words. I'll come out and say it."

"Okay..."

Her eyes rounded at the corners. "I called Eleanor and Christian. The Rutherfords would love to have you for Thanksgiving weekend. Or you're welcome to come with me to the chalet in Stowe."

"You're going skiing? And you drove here to tell me that we're not having a family Thanksgiving?"

Finally, something to be thankful for. Those were awful, and I'd hoped for years someone would call a spade a spade and we'd all go about our own business.

"Goodness no, I took the helicopter."

I slowly exhaled. "Is that all?"

"And I'm leaving your father," she added bluntly. "He'll be served with the divorce papers over the holiday."

My mood brightened. This generally shitty day had a silver lining after all. "Well, that's..." I tried to find the right words but failed. "Do I have to pretend to be sad?"

"Well, I'm certainly not. I'm the one who leaked his most recent indiscretions to the tabloids." She slipped the gloves she'd been holding back on. I couldn't help but feel proud. My mom was finally doing something for herself. "The pictures too. Your father is incredibly sloppy."

My grin couldn't possibly get wider. "Cold-blooded, Mom."

"Yes, well... I took Beatrice's advice and got ahead of it. With all the documentation in the papers, I shouldn't have any problem leaving this marriage unscathed. *With* that beautiful beach house in Newport."

"Mom..." I faltered, the words getting stuck. High society's motto was "Never ask uncomfortable questions," and it'd been ingrained in me since birth. *Screw it*, I thought. "Can I ask you something?"

"Of course." She tucked her handbag under her arm.

"Why do you still like that house, after everything?"

A melancholic look washed over her face and her eyes darted up toward the carved crown moldings in the lobby.

"I learned something important there, something I needed to know. It was the first time I started to question what I wanted." She let out a pleased sigh. "It took me a long while to get to this place, but I'm thankful for that day. As painful as it was, I wouldn't be here without it."

I smiled. "I'm glad you're doing better, Mom."

She took a few steps over to me and gave me a hug. Taking a momentary pause, she held my shoulders and just looked at me. "Perhaps that young lady can join us there in the summer?

Eleanor tells me she's beautiful *and* smart. Good for you, dear."

I didn't have the heart, or the physical will, to tell her what happened. She'd come to her own conclusions in June. "Yeah, maybe."

"Then I'll forgive you for having introduced her to the Rutherfords before me." She hummed, laying a hand on my cheek and tapping it gently. "Have a good week, and if you'd like to come to Stowe, I'll have the—"

"I'm good, Mom. I'll go with the Rutherfords."

She nodded, and with a wave, she was gone, happier than I'd seen her in years.

> James: We're at Salt & Shell, just ordered drinks
>
> James: Lucy's already threatened to drag you here by the hair if you don't show up

I turned on my heels and headed out before Lucy made good on the threat.

CHAPTER 46

Malena

Tuesday morning began with a strange email from President Packham's assistant to meet at her office first thing. So, at nine o'clock on the dot, I took a seat on a tufted chair outside her office.

In an effort not to spiral over what the meeting was about, I busied myself on my phone, scrolling mindlessly, when a text came in from my dad. After a rare bout of silence over the weekend, he was reminding me that I was to head home the second my classes were over today. He offered to pick me up, but I declined. My mom hadn't called or texted, probably because she was waiting for an apology from me. Even though I was sure I'd never get one from her.

A door creaked on its hinges.

"Malena." President Packham stood at her doorway and motioned me in, and I noted the deep wells under her eyes that her glasses weren't doing a good job of concealing. "Please come in."

"Is something wrong?" I murmured as I approached, twining my fingers around my tote.

"Sit." She rounded her desk and took her seat, the sunlight filtering through her office casting her shadow along the polished mahogany. "It's been a long week since the Amherst Building had that false alarm." She steepled her hands together. "It woke up half of campus."

My heart fell into my stomach. "Oh, right."

"And such a concern in a historic building is taken seriously. We may need to close it entirely just before finals. Is there anything you'd like to tell me?"

She couldn't know about it. Right?

"Like what?" I asked meekly.

"Like what you were doing in the Amherst Building's library hours after it was closed earlier this semester?"

I blanched.

"I'm the president of the university. Not much gets by me." Her lips formed a line and her eyes tracked along the desk. "I don't want to see you involved in something you can't get yourself out of."

"I'm not." The words shot out of my mouth. "That was months ago. We were working late and got... *caught up*. That's all."

"Yes, well, I have a feeling I know who pulled the alarm, but I'd like for that person to come forward before I'm forced to take next steps."

I did the mental gymnastics to figure out what she knew. If there were cameras—and there weren't any that we could see—she would have only seen Conrad. Not me.

"It wasn't me," I insisted as my heart threw a tantrum in my chest. I wasn't going to throw Conrad under the bus, but it was the truth.

Apologize. My body trembled, mind spiraling despite my best efforts. What if I got kicked out of Winchester? I was already on thin ice at home, soon I wouldn't have the privilege of walking away. I'd be expelled then disowned, and I'd have *nothing*.

My chest tightened.

"I don't think it was. But, from what Professor Fulton tells me, you're working on an article that might put you in the crosshairs."

"This is about my work at the paper?"

In that moment, I remembered that there *couldn't* have been cameras in the basement—if there were, she'd have called me in here weeks ago.

"Yes." She folded her hands on top of each other. "Given the scrutiny certain students may be under in the next few months, I don't think it's a good idea that you continue the piece."

All the anxiety washed off my body with a wave of newfound understanding. Maybe she knew about the catacombs and was drawing her own conclusions. If she knew about the catacombs, she probably knew about Scroll & Ivy and that members had access to them. If she knew all of that, then...

"Oh," I said curtly, keeping my face clear of the thoughts circling.

"It's for your own good, Malena," President Packham insisted. "Write about something else. You're very talented and you still have time this semester."

An order masquerading as a suggestion. The promise of protection by way of ignorance. After being free of such constraints for a few days, I was realizing just how oppressive it felt.

"Right." *Tell her what she wants to hear, Malena.* "Okay."

I stood and my trembling nerves made me stumble forward a bit, knocking against her desk.

As I turned, my purse bumped into hers and it spilled out onto the floor. A compact mirror, a wallet, and a few letters.

Some parts of people-pleasing Malena died hard, especially after being reprimanded, because I knelt down and picked them up.

Standing back up, I read the face of one.

Caroline C. Packham
17 Carriage Ct.
New Harbor, CT
35913

The address looked familiar, and I read over it again. A few blocks off of High Street, it had to be a historic house.

It clicked, and my heart rate skyrocketed.

"Thank you." She held the other side of the envelope and gave it a gentle tug.

"Oh." I released the envelope and repeated the address in my head over and over. "Have a nice holiday."

"You too," she called as I passed the threshold.

The second I was out of her office, I typed it into my phone.

My hands shook when it finally came together.

It was the Carrington house. I knew President Packham didn't live in town because she used to host the senior staff of the newspaper at her home for a graduation dinner, which was thirty minutes outside of campus.

Did she own the Carrington house too?

Before I realized it, I was outside, running.

PUSHING the door to the condo open, I walked in to find Sabrina paging through a magazine at the kitchen island, her blond hair tucked neatly into a French braid. Her roller bag was perched a foot away and her Secret Service agent stood to the left; his attention fixed on her.

Before I could say anything, Sabrina hopped off the stool and met me in the foyer. "Are you sure you don't want to spend the weekend with the Alders?"

"You were waiting for me?" I looked past her into the neatly organized kitchen. She'd been back from Oxford since Sunday morning; after seeing Cora off to the airport, she must have come back here instead of heading for her parents' house.

"I would love the company," she added. "A weekend at the country house. Football on the green. It could be a good distraction."

"Actually…" I tripped over every single thought rushing through my mind. I peeled off my cardigan, warm from having run all the way back here. Days of telling myself that I made the right choice fell flat when the opportunity to become what I *could* be presented itself. "I discovered some important information relating to the article."

Sabrina had been right the other day, that the real reason I needed the award was the same reason I wanted to finish this piece: I didn't want to let this go. Something I loved. The chance at autonomy. The ability to make my own decisions.

Because with every concession, I felt the real me slipping away.

Sabrina's cheeks lifted. "And…"

"And I need to find Conrad." I let out a nervous breath.

"Take this." Sabrina held up her finger and went over to her luggage with her vintage Kelly sitting on top. She reached in, walked back to me, and pressed the brass key into my hand. She closed my fingers around it. "I don't want it yet."

My heart rate—dangerously high from both my realization and practically sprinting here—began to settle. With it was the reality that always tugged me back like quicksand.

"I'm supposed to go home," I said, but it came out as a question.

I was supposed to go home and apologize. Then embark on some type of rehabilitation tour doing anything and everything to prove that I *could* be the daughter they wanted. I *could* follow President Packham's orders and write something else. I *could* fall in line.

Or I could finally stop and be a little brave.

Because no matter how hard I tried to shove the real version of myself into place when I needed to, I wouldn't stay there. I knew that.

"You were also *supposed* to be the twenty-one-year-old virgin who spent all her free time studying," Sabrina deadpanned.

An incredulous smile pushed up my cheeks. "Who are you and what have you done to Sabrina Alders?"

My rule-following best friend seemed to have finally taken Cora's and my advice while abroad.

Sabrina took a step closer; her attention went to my sleeve that ended in a ruffle at my shoulder. She ran a hand over the bruise on my arm, now visible without the cardigan. "I know you don't like talking about your family, but you can always confide in me."

An ache filled my lungs. It was one of the things I didn't burden her with because pretending everything was fine had been my MO since I learned to navigate life. I didn't like having to face how defective I felt, because how unacceptable did you have to be to need protection from your own mother?

"I figured she'd ease up when I started acting *correctly*," I admitted, knowing I didn't need to explain who *she* was. "It doesn't happen a lot."

Pretending it wasn't a big deal was a lie I told myself. But I had to stop running from the things that scared me. I had to face them or they'd never change.

"I may not be able to relate exactly, but I'll always listen." She looped her arm through mine. "And I wanted to tell *you* something. I stayed back because Cora and I were talking this morning..."

Sabrina ushered me into the kitchen and onto the stools at the island.

"About?"

"We're serious when we say you have us, it's not some platitude. We've come up with a plan." She tilted her phone screen to me then scrolled down to reveal a spreadsheet. One that I could tell Cora made. It was every break, vacation, extended weekend, and holiday for the next couple of years. "Spend winter break in California with Cora. The summer with me in Manhattan..."

"Sabrina." Emotion welled in the back of my throat, pushing a watery film over my eyes.

"You have us in the metaphysical sense, but also here, in an official capacity." Her voice was firm and reassuring. "You don't have to worry, you'll never be on your own."

I nodded, because if I spoke, I was sure I'd start sobbing.

"And, for the record, the real Mal is amazing." Her voice swung up. "She's the one who sat up with me at all hours when I couldn't sleep for *months*. Who convinced me to go out on nights I would have stayed in and tried to push me out of my comfort zone. Because, and I quote, 'We only have this bone density for a limited time.'"

I coughed out a laugh.

"People who love you don't make you choose between your happiness and theirs," she added.

I smiled. "Yeah..."

She wrapped me in a hug and squeezed tight. "Call me. I'll have a car get you if you decide to come stay with us." She pulled back and kept her hands on my shoulders. "We'll figure out the rest."

I nodded, pulled out my phone, and turned off my location settings, knowing my mom would get a notification. Then, I silenced it.

If I was going to be brave, I had to *actually* do something that required courage.

Whatever the outcome, I'd deal with it. But I'd always know it was *my* decision.

And that made it worth it.

CHAPTER 47

Conrad

Everyone was leaving New Harbor for the long weekend. Technically campus didn't close for another day, but most classes had wrapped up early—a Winchester tradition despite not every student recognizing the holiday. The streets were crowded, so I decided to walk to the mausoleum. Wasn't like I had anything better to do.

Once here, I got right to work. My laptop was opened to the shared document housing Malena's article. I'd been adding in all the parts she kept out of the narrative. I couldn't undo every way she'd pushed me to change, so I was going to see this through.

"It's your shift to check on me?" I called out after hearing some shuffling. "I can hear you, Isha."

"I'm just popping in." Isha leaned against the doorframe. "James and Lucy left for the city an hour ago. Felix flew back to Jalisco this morning."

"Uh-huh…" I flipped through the journal I'd pulled off the shelf and scribbled more notes into the makeshift family tree that we'd made weeks ago. Malena and I had already gone through all the Amherst and Lancaster journals. That left me six Carrington journals to find *something*.

"And the Rutherfords will expect you on the tarmac by tomorrow evening to head out to the country house."

"I'll be there." I didn't look up.

"And we haven't really seen much of you the past couple of days."

She said something else, but I focused on the journal.

"Right," I answered.

Dating back to the late eighteen-hundreds, the Carringtons were a wealthy family who'd made most of their fortune in shipping. Some of the journals from the 30s and 40s detailed one of the members, Charles Carrington, having a home known for its art, furniture, and troves of jewelry—all imported from Europe.

Translation: they hustled priceless goods to the States under the guise of preservation during the war. The Carringtons had homes in London as well as a couple here in New Harbor, which had been a big port city at the time.

"Conrad." She tapped my forehead with a mildly frustrated huff.

"Read through this, tell me if you find something that might be relevant to Scroll & Ivy—any mentions of paintings or Winchester." I took the last journal, the one that came directly after Charles Carrington's, and handed it to Isha. If she wasn't going to leave, she could at least help. She looked up at me incredulously. "*You* told me to do something productive, remember?"

She set the journal on her lap and began reading through it.

"I need the names of any Carrington you find," I added.

Malena was probably right. Maybe there was a student here with ties to the family. It would explain how they knew the catacombs existed, and since the Carringtons were no longer a prominent name in today's society, I surmised they'd lost their wealth and status, meaning they'd lost their admission to the club.

"So... we're just ignoring everything that happened then?" Isha asked, her focus moving line by line down the journal.

"What would you have me do?" I asked curtly, trying to keep my voice steady so Isha would move past it.

"All I know is that if I were in her shoes..." Isha looked up. "I'd have done the exact same thing. And I'd venture a guess that you and James would have been my accomplices."

"She doesn't want an accomplice." I stopped on a page and put a pen in the spine to mark my place. "So can you *please* drop it?"

Her shoulders fell a bit and she turned her attention back to the journal, quiet once more as she read.

"Ummm..." Ishani turned to me twenty minutes later. "This is the final Carrington journal, right?"

"Yeah..." I checked the spine—it was listed as 1948 and the member was Adrian Carrington. Charles's son.

"Well." Isha ran her finger along the minuscule font. "The year Adrian Carrington graduated, he attended his sister's wedding to Victor Packham."

Isha turned the book to me, where I confirmed her timeline. It stated that he left for London early in the winter semester to attend. "You think there's any relation?"

"Maybe." She tapped along the top of the page. "He's the last Carrington to enroll in Scroll & Ivy," Isha added, standing up. "You know who you should talk to about this?"

Before I could process any of it, a heavy thud from the front door echoed through the room, followed by the metallic clank of the brass handles against the library's doors.

Malena stood in the doorway, her hair windblown like she'd run here and her eyes pulling my attention like a rip cord.

"Hi," she squeaked. A cautious half smile burst open at

either side. *That* smile, the one I'd stolen at first but had slowly become mine.

She blinked a couple of times, her lips straightening. The warm swell in my chest got rained out under the memories of the last few days, and everything I wanted to say was tangled up.

"I didn't know where to go or where you'd be..." Mal took a step forward then stopped. "It's Packham. She was a student here, and she has a house in New Harbor," she blurted between breaths she tried desperately to catch. "It's the Carrington property."

"Well." Ishani clapped her hands together, snapping our attention. "Isn't that a serendipitous revelation."

Malena's brows scrunched as she looked between us.

"She might be related to the Carringtons," I explained. It was all falling into place, days after everything else had fallen apart. "The Packham family comes up in the last Carrington journal."

"You read the last set of journals?" She paused for a moment. Then, like she was scared to hear the answer, she kept going. "So, Packham would have known about the catacombs, where they lead, Scroll & Ivy, the paintings that were in circulation and the ones on the walls—"

"She'd know exactly what to make," I cut in, unable to help myself because we'd just solved it.

"And *she* never got her key. But she may have one from her grandfather." Malena's voice rose and her words braided together—the way they always did when she was overcome with excitement. "It's not a student, it's President Packham."

Relief and anguish filled me in equal measure. Seeing her now, knowing it was over, was so much worse than I imagined.

But she was here.

I braced myself and nodded, pushing past the uncertainty. "So, what now?"

"I have an idea." Isha grinned like a maniac between us.

CHAPTER 48

Malena & Conrad

MALENA

The motor of Conrad's car hummed through the cabin. He hadn't said anything since we figured out what our next step was: heading to the gallery.

All *three* of us were going, seeing as how Isha had sort of become an integral part of the plan.

"Will this work?" I asked. The silence was killing me.

The hope that'd sprung up in the face of Conrad's excitement at the mausoleum... well, it had frosted back to what was to be expected after I'd hurt him.

"Of course it will work." Ishani popped her head over the center console from where she was smushed in the back seat. "When I called the gallery, they insisted that I come in to discuss it. They refused to confirm *anything* on the phone."

"And that makes you sure they have the painting?" I asked.

Maybe Winchester *should* have had a class called Bizarre Rich People Shit 205, because I'd heard this plan already and was still lost.

"*Oh*, they have it." Isha put a hand on the side of each

seat. "They wouldn't have me come in otherwise. Making me jump through hoops and stoking my interest with vague mentions of the piece is simply a tactic to drive up the price. Don't worry, I'll offer a few million more than it could ever sell for."

"Isha will buy it and ask for a secondary authentication," Conrad said for my benefit. The first time we went through this, admittedly, I'd been a little distracted.

"They'll do that?" I asked as I tried to push through the heaviness I was feeling in my chest. He'd read *all* the Carrington journals.

Just because I gave up didn't mean he had.

"As long as I pay that much for it and accept that the secondary authentication will damage the piece." Isha leaned back into her seat and examined her nails.

"And *you* can do that?" I confirmed, seeing just how indifferently Ishani treated the prospect of spending millions at the drop of a hat.

Sabrina was rich. Conrad was too, I assumed, given who his family was. But even so, what level of rich did you have to be to simply throw around millions without a thought?

"Money really isn't a thing I think about." Ishani shrugged. "Don't worry, this will work. And if it is fake, the sale will be void."

With that, the car became noiseless again, and about forty minutes later, we were at the gallery.

Inside the cool industrial-style gallery in SoHo, under the bright Edison bulbs, I stared up at a painting from a Berlin artist. An abstract pop-art piece.

Instead of staying with Ishani to talk to the curator who opened the gallery on a Wednesday before a holiday weekend for us, Conrad stood silently next to me. He never left me to fend for myself, even now when there was a mountain of angst between us.

"How did you explain this trip to your parents?" he asked, not looking away from the painting.

"I didn't." I pulled out my phone and tilted it in his direction. Already three missed calls, and I suspected there would be plenty more before the day was up.

"Mal." The gruff and jagged tone distilled down to concern. "Are you sure you want to do this?"

"The parents part or the potential FBI investigation about a million-dollar forgery scheme that the president of our university might fall right in the center of?"

A chuckle broke the serious look on his face. "Both."

"I'm tired of doing what I'm *supposed* to do. And I'm done with all the pretending," I admitted. "It isn't worth it."

I fastened the last few buttons on my sweater. The downright inhospitable gallery may as well have had the air conditioning on. Conrad took a couple of steps closer, shrugged off his coat, and threw it over me. The cedary scent, the rich silk lining... I'd missed how it felt around me.

"You probably won't get a recommendation from Packham after this," he teased lightly.

This revelation threw everything Packham had done for me into a blurry state of disorder. Probably similar to the one Conrad was in with me.

"She already pulled the article, so I'll figure it out," I told him.

Packham specified that I kill the article for the *paper*. But it could still be my submission for the Keller Award. Packham wouldn't like it, but I didn't care.

"What do you want from this?" he asked cautiously.

"What do you mean?" My heart skipped, hoping the strained air between us might finally loosen.

He opened his mouth and closed it. "The article," he clarified. "Packham pulled it, so what do you want?"

"I want to see this through."

He nodded, and the faint sound of Ishani's block heel booties echoed through the industrial gallery's high ceilings, ending any chance of him opening up further.

CONRAD

"I'll have the newest edition to the Roy art collection next week," Isha announced as she walked out of the gallery offices with quite possibly the world's worst timing.

She tucked some files beneath her arm and clasped her hands together.

"They had it?" Malena asked.

"Mm-hmm. Your stunt with the fire alarm worked." Isha nodded. "The authentication should come through in a few days. A bit of damage to the bottom of the piece, which hurts its value but adds a bit of character." She looked from me to Malena. "I'll send the results to you both."

Malena pulled herself out from under my coat when we reached my car. She handed it to me and looked at Isha. "You can have the front seat, you're taller."

"Lucy is meeting me at the Roy house on the Upper East Side." Ishani put her hand up. I knew she was lying because the McMaster Thanksgiving was very much mandatory, and Isha should've been on her way to her *London* house as it was. "Why don't you two head back together?"

Just as she said it, a black car pulled up to the curb. And before Mal or I could argue, she was being ushered into her seat.

Another, less awkward silence fell between us until Malena's phone buzzed in her hand. She looked at it, hit ignore, then pushed it back in her pocket.

"Do you need to get that?"

"Nope."

"Mal." My voice softened. I didn't like that we were in a

place where she was made to choose, and I couldn't blame her for picking the path of least resistance. More than that, I didn't want to see the blood drain from her face like I had a week ago. I *couldn't* see that look again. If it meant I had to be the one who hurt, then I would be. "If you need to get back—"

"I meant it when I said I wasn't lying anymore." Malena's voice was steady, her gaze fixed on me. The orange afternoon light sparkled in her eyes. The sincerity hooked itself between my ribs, an invisible string that pulled me back to her. "I told them I was out and turned off my location settings. I'm not giving up anything else for them."

Hope, stupid and persistent, flickered in my chest, and an idea took hold in my head.

I took a step closer and threw my coat back around her. I loved seeing how it flooded her frame. Holding the wool fabric at either lapel, I drew her forward and she came without any protest.

"If there's no rush to get back... want to see if this article might be something bigger?"

Of the many things being with Malena did to me, the greatest one had to be refusing to simply accept less than what I deserved.

Her cheeks a little flushed, she looked up at me. "What do you mean?"

I wasn't ready for this day to end. I wasn't ready for any of it to. "I'm feeling ambitious."

"Oh no," she teased in a quiet laugh.

She rocked onto her toes then back to her heels—hesitant or cautious, I wasn't sure. But if she wasn't going to give up on what she wanted, neither was I.

"I'm taking you somewhere. And you're going to have to proof something for me in the car."

CHAPTER 49

Conrad

The next twenty minutes were filled with a different type of tension. A slow burn that moved like a flame patiently flaring down a wax-covered wick.

It was like that day after the race in Boston: the air sparked with the anticipation of something new.

"I can't believe you rewrote this whole thing." Malena held my laptop in one hand and scrolled with the other.

While I drove, Malena read the article and did a quick proof. Now on the sidewalk, she was still reading it and not looking where she was going. I steered her into the washed limestone mid-rise building and the doorman pointed us in the direction of the private elevator.

"Well, this last bit needs to be added in," I told her. It was the part where we solved the whole damn thing.

The "myth of meritocracy" version Malena sent me had no mention of everything we found together. And someone *had* to write our story. I couldn't let it go.

"I added it in the car." A smiled curved up her cheeks. Standing in front of the elevator, she saved the document and closed the laptop. "Con, this is great."

"I love that my ability to complete basic human tasks astounds you."

She finally took a look at the towering archways in the marble lobby. My brother Barrett lived in the penthouse of a building on Central Park East. The interior of its lobby resembled a decadent Italian renaissance palazzo. "You haven't told me what we're doing here."

She crossed her arms around the laptop protectively, holding it against her chest.

"Just because it can't be in the *Winchester Daily News* doesn't mean it's not newsworthy."

Her eyes, wandering the soaring gilded ceiling, boomeranged back over to me.

"I know a guy," I added.

Barrett also happened to be in charge of print media at my family's company, and one of the many facets under his control was the newsroom. The news media arm of Hastings Media was its original purpose before it expanded into everything it was today.

"Con." Her mouth hung open in disbelief.

"As much as I love hearing you say that..." I leaned in just as the elevator dinged. Her breath hitched and I wrapped one arm around her waist. "Let's handle this"—I tapped on the laptop she held tightly against her body—"and then we can get to *that*."

With her teeth pressing down on the corner of her lower lip, she smiled as I pulled her into the elevator.

STANDING in Barrett's home office, a menacingly dark room with no pictures and a sleek walnut desk, was like seeing the ghost of Thanksgiving future I was trying to avoid.

It was depressing as hell.

"Should we apologize for interrupting?" Malena said under her breath as we watched him read over the article.

I glanced down, noticing she was twisting her fingers together, and took her hand in mine, giving it a reassuring squeeze.

"Interrupting a holiday week for work?" I whispered back. "He'll throw me a bigger parade than the abomination that'll march down Park Ave in two days."

Malena's silent laugh rumbled through her shoulders.

"How long have you been putting this together?" Barrett's monotone cut between us.

Mal and I looked at each other. "All semester," Malena answered.

"And this is all true?" Barrett asked brusquely, not looking up from the screen. "You have sources to back it up?"

I had half a mind to hit him for how he was speaking to her, but I knew Mal didn't need me coming to her rescue.

"We'll have confirmation in a few days—an authentication report from the gallery," Malena supplied firmly.

"And the Modiste Gallery will probably keep it quiet because it's a major scandal," I added. "So you'll have time before word reaches the public."

If Barrett was on board, one of the largest news outlets in the world would break the story. Our story.

"It'll require a thorough fact-check." Barrett finally looked up at us, steepling his hands in front of his face. "And edit. Probably needs a few days before it's ready."

"So...?" Malena asked cautiously.

"Front page next Tuesday." Barrett leaned back into his leather chair and a rare smile graced the depressing room. "Gives my team a week to rally. Send me any evidence you have, and I *need* that authentication report."

"Okay." She stayed stoic, but the excitement filled her eyes.

He stood up and adjusted his tie, then looked directly at

Mal. "Miss Amin. My accounting team will be in touch regarding your freelance fee."

"Oh." Malena nodded eagerly, but just as she was about to say something, she tapped her fingers inside her pocket. She glanced at her phone, and whatever it was she found stole the sparkle from her eyes. "I'll get that to you." She looked at me and her voice lowered. "I should take this call."

My heart sank seeing Malena walk out of the office down the hallway we came. This time because I knew her next steps wouldn't be easy, no matter how good this news was.

"What about my payment?" I pushed my hands into my pockets and plastered a grin on my face.

"Have you already run through your substantial trust?" Barrett pointed to the door, dismissing me. "You've surprised me twice in one day."

I shrugged off the dismissal and walked out into the hallway, where I was met with Mal's absence. I kept going till I got to the private elevator landing, and that was where I heard Malena's hushed voice.

"Do whatever you feel like you need to do, Mom," she whispered harshly before jabbing at the screen and stowing it back in the pocket of my coat still draped over her shoulders.

I reached her in a single stride, disappointed that the reconciliation I was hoping for would probably have to wait. "Why don't I drive you home?"

"I really *don't* want to go there right now." She took a step back, her eyes dropping to the floor. "Sabrina invited me to Thanksgiving. Her parents' house is only a few blocks away."

"Mal." I looped my arm around her waist, a protective kick in my chest that I couldn't ignore this time propelling me forward. I couldn't put my finger on it, but seeing her this anxious worried me. She *looked* fine, but I hated thinking of what was going on below the surface. Maybe one day she'd tell me, but for now, I would do everything I could to support her. "You can come to my place. It'd be just us."

She looked up at me and the corners of her mouth dropped.

"Try not to pity me," I added playfully. "I was planning on going to the Rutherfords'."

"Con, I..." She stared down at her hands as she twined her fingers. "I've already done enough damage." She let out a deep sigh. "I don't want to intrude on your holiday. Why don't we figure things out when we get back to campus?"

"Look, Mal." I lifted her chin gently. "I don't need to figure things out. I want to date you. I want to be in the real phone, in your real life." Her lips quivered and she opened her mouth, but I continued. "I deserve that. And I've never wanted to deserve anything as much as I want to deserve you."

She nodded, her eyes becoming glassy. "I never wanted to lie to you. Or about you."

"Then don't." I leaned my head against hers, completely forgetting to press the button on the elevator. "Ever again."

"I won't." Both hands on either cheek, she drew me in.

"And I want the real Malena, every single fucking day."

She raked a hand through my hair. Her fingernails scraped against my scalp, sending tiny sparks down my spine. "You've always had her."

My next breath faltered.

Unable to wait any longer, I leaned in and pressed a kiss against her lips. A sigh shuddered down her body and she kissed me back, moaning softly as I tilted her head for better access.

In a few short months, Malena had spindled around my entire world like ivy. Climbing so high and spanning so completely that there wasn't a single portrait of my future that didn't have her in it.

CHAPTER 50

Conrad

Unsurprisingly, Malena loved the library in my parents' house. I hardly ever spent time here—I'd been away at boarding school for most of my teenage years and we spent summers in Newport. My room was nice, but it looked like a page out of a catalogue, like a hotel room. The only parts of the house that ever felt warm were the salon and the library.

One of the large double doors opened and in she slipped, closing it behind her.

"That was Sabrina." Malena walked back to where we'd sprawled out in the middle of the room. We came here straight from our meeting with Barrett and ordered takeout. "She was just checking in."

On one side, expansive windows let in the city lights and on the other stood walls upon walls of bookshelves. She put her phone back on the table and picked up the novel she'd selected.

"No threats?" I asked lightly as I stretched my arm out along the back of the tuxedo couch and kicked my legs up.

She opened her mouth just as her phone lit up—another text from her mom. She leaned forward and flipped it over.

"Mal, I..." I paused. I cleared my throat. "I don't want you to have to blow up your entire life to—"

"It's already in pieces." She turned to look me in the eye. "But now I have the chance to put it back together the way I want."

"I can *finally* make a résumé, if that helps. You know, I did just help uncover an art forgery scheme." I ran my hand up and down her side. "I can use it to impress them. I'm Conrad Hastings, after all."

She laughed, and the sound warmed my chest.

But her smile faded as quickly as it appeared.

"Look, Con." Her voice became serious. "My parents have a very narrow view of what I should do with my life and who I should surround myself with. They want me to follow *their* plan, and I don't know if that will ever change."

She pressed her lips together, the corners wavering. Her eyes fluttered down and she twined her fingers in her lap.

"They're not going to like me," I surmised, then nudged my hand between hers and stroked my thumb over her knuckles, back and forth. "We'll figure that out."

She looked up, her hand squeezing mine, and her smile held this time. "I'm only telling you that because I want you to know that what happens with my parents doesn't change anything for me. For us."

Relief moved down my body. "I'm not going to lose you?"

Like she was trying to physically prove that fact, she slowly swung a leg over mine, straddling me, and laid both her palms on my chest

"Not a chance." She shook her head and smiled. "Unless I get thrown in jail for murdering Gemma."

Bright and funny, the Malena I knew sparkled through the gray day.

I chuckled. "I knew that bothered you."

"Yeah, well..." She played with the fabric at my collar. "You're *mine*."

"Have been for some time, Mal."

"And I'm yours."

"Good." I leaned forward, my hands spanning over her thighs, and said, "Remember what you promised—the real Malena, every day."

"That's the thing, Con. I can't help but be myself around you."

"Yeah?"

"It's always come naturally."

I wrapped my fingers around the back of her neck, gentle but leading. Because a part of me couldn't believe how I felt. How close I needed her. In every single way. "Come here."

I pulled her into a kiss, unhurried.

Her lips melted against mine and she hummed softly. Warm and sweet, I deepened the kiss, wanting more of her taste.

Flushed, she pulled away a fraction of an inch.

"Where's your room?" she whispered against my lips.

I took her hand and led her down the long hallway, where I was hit with the realization that with Mal, the space I'd resented for years no longer felt cold and lonely.

"I missed you," I whispered against her lips as I kicked the door shut behind us.

"It's only been a week."

I stepped her back to the bed, my hands spread over her back, and pulled her out of her sweater then her tights. Her nimble fingers undid my pants and soon we were tumbling toward the mountain of pillows that sat along the top of the bed.

Her nails gently scratched against my scalp.

Laying her on her back, I dropped kisses down her body,

stopping at her breasts for a few languid strokes around her nipples.

"Con..." she whispered, her face already flushed.

I moved down her body, making my way between her thighs. I looped my index finger around her panties and dragged them down her legs.

I wanted to savor her. Every part: the soft moans she let out, the tiny hitches in her breath when I grazed my teeth against her skin, the electricity her nails sent down my spine when they dug into my back as she chased her climax.

I wanted to feel it all, and I wanted to make it last forever.

She whimpered as I spread her legs open and tried to maintain some restraint. She was already so wet that it took every patient fiber in my being not to bury myself there immediately.

"Mal." I released a tortured groan. I leaned in and gently ran my teeth across her clit. "Fuck, you're wet."

She curled her hand around the bedsheet and her breath caught in her throat, rewarding my patience. I *loved* that sound.

Lapping my tongue over her clit again, more firmly with each stroke, her hips began to move in time with my mouth, begging for more friction.

I sucked with more voracity, alternating between hard presses of my tongue, and before long, her thighs began to tremble.

"Con..." Her legs shook around me. A few unintelligible pants and moans slipped through her mouth as the climax broke over her. "Kiss me."

Stray tears rolled down her cheeks and the final tremors of her orgasm rippled through her body.

I took a second to roll on a condom then kissed her, pushing myself into her at the same time. Inch by inch, she moaned into my mouth. I didn't move, taking the moment to enjoy just how perfectly we fit together.

Sweat misted off her forehead, her eyes connected with mine, and staying still became impossible.

"Fuck," I groaned, then kissed her deeply as I thrust into her. She rolled her hips in tandem. "That's it, Mal... Fuck."

Her tight pussy teased me to move faster, but I held back, keeping the sensuous pace. My muscles, my jaw, my teeth all held taut as I fumbled for control. I lingered, gliding in and out, and took my time relishing the slick pulses around my dick.

Her mouth hung open and her breath stuttered with tiny hitches.

"Harder," she begged.

She arched up from the sheets and a cry broke through her deep-red lips. I sank in even deeper. *Fuck.*

My patience finally slipped. I couldn't hold back anymore; I needed all of her.

Pushing into her with more force, the frequency of her breathy moans kicked up.

My fingerprints became bruising on her hips, gripping them tight while mine snapped forward and back, plunging deeper and chasing the high only she could give me.

"Con..." She writhed on the plush sheets, her hair splaying out around her beautiful face.

She closed her eyes, her body becoming rigid, and I pulled her into another kiss as she climaxed. Swallowing all of it.

Her walls clamped against me. In a blinding flash I came undone, deep inside of her.

"This is what I want," Mal hummed into my neck as I pulled her in close, intertwining our bodies.

The hardest thing I'd ever do was be good enough for her, and I'd never wanted anything more.

CHAPTER 51

Malena

Sunlight peeked through the curtain grommets, filling the room with the occasional bar of light.

I woke up to one missed call and a few texts. Surprise lifted me when I realized they were from my sister. I leaned on an elbow to read them.

> Avani: Okay, so you should probably come home

> Avani: I got in last night and had to convince them not to file a missing person's report

> Avani: Now Mom has decided she's 'done'

There was an eyeroll emoji at the end of the last text.

While Avani and I were very different people, we'd grown up in the same house. She knew what I was up against, and I hoped she'd at least hear me out when it was time for me to face my parents' judgment.

I sat the rest of the way up and texted her back.

Me: Okay. I'll be home later.

The sheets rustled behind me, and a finger ran down my spine.

I looked over my shoulder to find Conrad with one arm tucked under his head, the other continuing its slow journey up and down my back.

"I'll drive you home," he said through a yawn, smiling at me, looking all sleepy and adorable. "Are you going to be okay?"

I nodded. "I need to be brave."

I reached forward and placed the phone back on the nightstand.

"The Mal I know is fearless," he encouraged, rising up to brush his nose against my cheek.

"That's because around you, I don't have anything to be afraid of," I whispered. Around him, I felt *safe*.

I closed my eyes and leaned back into him. I'd had my share of sex, *good* sex too, but with him, it was the first time I ever understood what it felt like when there was connection that went beyond the physical. It was a feeling I never wanted to give up.

He didn't say anything, simply pressed his chest against my bare back and wrapped me in his arms. He dropped a few sweet, featherlight kisses on my neck.

"Mal." His voice deepened, becoming serious. His thumb ran over the healing bruise on my arm, now visible with the low light of the morning sun. In all the emotion of last night, I'd forgotten it was there. It no longer hurt and had gone from that awful black and blue to a less daunting shade of pale green. "What's this?"

"It's nothing."

"It's not nothing." Concern flickered in his eyes. "Why don't you stay with me this weekend?"

"It's fine, *really*." I wasn't scared to go home, just hesitant. Until now, I siloed that part of my life off to where I could rationalize it. The smacks, pinches, little physical means of intimidation were never *that* bad. I wasn't *injured*. But even if it was small, it was still unacceptable. I saw that now.

"If I don't want to stay the whole weekend, I'll go to Sabrina's," I added, turning to face him.

One day, soon, when it all wasn't so fresh, I'd be ready to talk to him about it. Because I wanted him to know everything about me, even the things that were hard to share.

"I'll get you if—"

"No need. Sabrina will send someone for me if I need it," I interrupted. "Just because you and I are dating doesn't mean she's *not* my knight in shining armor."

She and Cora were my lifeboats, and I was theirs.

His laugh was light and a little forced. "Okay."

"I can take care of myself." I pressed a kiss against his lips.

"Yeah..." His fingers laced into my hair and he moved them back and forth, sending pleasing static down my neck. "I know."

MOM TOLD Avani that she was worried that I was an addict, or an escort, or any number of ridiculous accusations for only having the tiny piece of evidence that I was kissing a boy on the street.

And had a secret bank account.

And had gone to Paris.

And lied to them for years.

And kept a burner phone to *help* lie to them for years...

Admittedly, it didn't look great.

"Well, you ripped the Band-Aid off." Avani turned her coffee mug in her hands as she sat squished next to me by the slightly frosted bay window in our kitchen. Mom and Dad had been out all morning, and the house was eerily—blissfully —quiet. "Making them confront your sexual activity head on, brave."

I had just finished telling her the story of what happened. The version my mom told Avani had taken a lot of liberties with the truth.

"They couldn't seriously believe I was still a..." My voice lowered because I realized my sister and I never talked about this stuff: boys and sex and everything normal sisters bonded over.

I was open with Cora and Sabrina. They were more my sisters than my own because I always assumed "perfect Avani" would shame me for my choices. At least now I didn't have to muster the courage to bring it up, it was already out there. And while she seemed blasé about it all, I was anxious.

"They live in delusion, Mal. But..." Avani moved her mug to the side. "I hope you're not doing all of this for a guy."

My overly tired nerves crackled to life. She'd said it with care, but all I heard was judgment.

I was doing this for *me*. I was simply choosing to live my own life.

"I'm not," I snapped back. But the fact remained: in a life filled with people who wanted me to be a Malena that fit *their* expectations, Conrad only ever wanted the real one, he only ever expected the truth. And I refused to lose him. "Not all of us see the jail cell Mom and Dad created and willingly lock ourselves in."

She was their happy little soldier, which made me the problem any time I voiced some dissent. I didn't need to hear her concerns to know what they were.

The window at her back rattled with a strong gust of wind, the sound slicing into the silence.

Her shoulders fell and she let out a quiet sigh. "Sorry," I said, guilt whistling in my ear. "I shouldn't have said that."

"It's different for me, Mal." She glanced out at the gray sky. "I wasn't perfect in school; I couldn't also be the rebel. Doing what they want... it keeps the peace."

It was like we were collecting points and the ones she lost academically, she made up for by being agreeable and doing what they wanted. It was no way to live.

"You didn't screw up," I defended. "And is it really peace if you're quiet out of fear?"

A tiny smile inched up her cheek. "I guess not."

A gentle melancholy blanketed the kitchen and suddenly I felt even worse because I'd done the exact thing to her that I worried she'd do to me: judged her for her choices. I was angry at her for choosing the path of least resistance and being okay with it. I resented her for it because I couldn't find a way to do the same.

"Besides, *you* didn't have the convoluted idea to create a burner identity," I added.

She harrumphed a laugh. "Impressive, by the way." She tipped her coffee cup in my direction. "I guess I never prepared for the future quite like you did."

I looked down at my lap. I'd been avoiding this part because it was terrifying, but if I wanted things to change, it had to be done. "I don't think I'm gonna come home anymore. Not for a while, anyway."

I didn't want to live a life without my family. But I couldn't keep subjecting myself to this. Not when I was always going to feel like a blemish that needed concealer.

I looked up when Avani didn't say anything. Her eyes were wide.

"I hate feeling like my world will come apart if I tell the truth. And I can't just pretend the occasional smack is okay," I explained. We didn't dwell on that sort of stuff, but it burned a hole in my heart. "I know we don't talk about it, but I need to. Because if we don't, it won't change."

And I needed things to change.

Avani nodded.

"I can stay with Sabrina over the summers, and from there... I'll figure things out," I added.

"I'll be back on this coast after residency," she encouraged. "And I'll talk to them."

I couldn't help but laugh. "I'm *sure* that will help."

Though... it probably wouldn't hurt. The words could be the same, but if they came out of Avani's mouth, my parents tended to listen.

"I mean it, Mal. They've never had a reason to look critically at their own behavior." She put her cup down, then scooted over and wrapped one arm around me. "Now they do."

"But until they do..."

"Keep your distance." Her hold tightened. "And anything you need, you tell me."

I nodded, looking down at my fingers on my lap because the next question got caught in my throat. I paused and took a hard swallow before managing to choke it out. "Will you still do holiday stuff with me?"

That was what always flashed in my head when I justified my mom's actions to myself. Or my own actions in lying. It was justified because I wanted part of my life to stay as it was.

I thought about Holi, Diwali, Navratri, each one celebrated *alone*. I loved my culture; I didn't want to lose it. My whole life, my family had been my connection. But I was finding new roots there too. Maybe ones to nurture and grow while my parents—hopefully—changed.

I looked up and her eyes were glossy. "If they don't change, they lose us both, because I'm not doing any of it without you." Avani sucked in a deep breath and smiled, nudging me back so she could look at me. "Now, tell me about *him*. We probably have another hour before they get back and we all have it out."

Surprisingly, we never actually "had it out."

The next three days in my parents' house were the quietest I'd ever experienced. My mom barely said more than a few words to me; she was probably expecting me to do what I always did: apologize and let it go.

But I didn't, so this Thanksgiving weekend became the world's longest game of chicken.

I spent most of it reading, like I did every extended period at home. I did try to spend some more time with Avani because the prickly undercurrent between us was gone. One I now realized was a hushed umbrage.

We all sat down to eat dinner, dosas: her favorite. It was quiet up until Avani broke the silence.

"*My* sister is going to be on the front page of the *New York Herald*," Avani mooned. "That's pretty cool."

"Why don't you focus on residency," Mom interrupted, looking at Avani with a frown. "So you don't have any more problems like you did before."

Avani shifted back in her seat, looking at me and then squeezing my hand under the table.

"Malena, whatever you are doing, think about your future," Dad said calmly just as my mom opened her mouth. "You have medical school, then you can figure out"—he shifted uncomfortably and gave my mom a sidelong look— "everything else. We're strict because we know what's best for you."

How could they possibly know what was best for me when they didn't even know me?

"I *am* thinking about my future," I answered, voice just as calm.

"Fine. Embarrass your family, disobey your parents..." My mom didn't look up from her plate. "After everything we've sacrificed for you, are you not ashamed of yourself?"

The words registered with clarity between my ears.

And I wondered when the debt of my existence would *finally* be repaid.

It didn't happen when I was at the top of my high school class, but maybe it would when I was at the top of my college one. Or when I graduated med school. Or when I married the *right* guy and had the *right* type of family.

When would it end? And would I even recognize myself when it did?

I couldn't help but smile, because it ended now.

"I'm only ashamed that I lied. I'm never doing that again," I admitted.

This entire episode was the disaster I expected. But instead of the earthquake, it was like a volcano. Searing, eruptive, and chaotic. But the white-hot lava that destroyed everything in its wake would cool. And on that I would build something new. No lies this time.

My mom shook her head. "Then you'll be honest, and you'll be alone. See how far you get."

"Mom," Avani rebuked quietly.

I glanced up at my dad who just sat there, letting it all happen.

"Aren't you exhausted?" I asked my mom honestly. "Living in fear that you'll be judged, so you just don't live at all?"

I pitied her a little. The constant need to judge and the fear of being judged was its own prison. I couldn't make it through college like that, how had she gone her whole life? Maybe she had to, for survival here in a new place when she immigrated. But it didn't mean I had to suffer the same fate.

"I can't live like that," I added. "I don't want to argue, I just want to live my life."

My mom's stone facade held. "*Selfish.*"

I looked down at my own plate because a little piece of my heart—the part that was holding on for dear life—frayed even further in that moment. It was the hopeful bit that thought maybe she'd put aside her own pride and love me as I was, without conditions.

Maybe she'd never understand, although that dying part of my heart hoped she did.

Later, I'd get back to school, and at some point, they'd realize the game of chicken wasn't a game. But that was fine because I wasn't scared anymore.

The scariest thing that could happen *did* happen. And I was okay. Mostly.

I had my sister and the family I'd made on my own. I'd figure it out. If my parents wanted to be actual parents, they could figure that out too.

CHAPTER 52

Malena

President Packham's office was always neatly kept—books stacked on the shelves, never a painting or framed diploma askew. On Monday morning, when I got back to campus, the authentication report came through. We were right.

Wrapped in a deep red peacoat, she stood looking out the multi-paned window at the center of the room. From this viewpoint, I could see the quad still blanketed in the thin layer of snow that'd fallen over the weekend.

I cleared my throat and knocked on the doorframe.

"Malena." She looked over her shoulder then turned around. "I was just leaving, can this wait?"

"No." I crossed the room to her desk but didn't sit down. "I think you need to hear this."

She blinked in surprise. "Okay."

"I..." I twisted my fingers, feeling my pulse beat in every one of them. "I wanted to let you know that I won't be publishing that article Professor Fulton told you about in the *Winchester Daily News.*"

"*Great*," she said tightly. "Is that all, Malena? I have a busy—"

"I *can't* publish it there because the feature turned investigative, and we stumbled on what looks like a forged Van Holden painting that was being sold through the Modiste Gallery in Manhattan." There. I said it.

She froze. "Malena..."

My nerves wore down, and that feeling of telling a story took over. "We had a piece go through a rigorous authentication process and the report came back this morning, confirming it's a fraud. The buyer won't have to pay for the piece, but the seller... well, I'm guessing the gallery has to report the seller to the FBI."

Her face paled. "Why are you here?"

"You gave me a warning. I'm only returning the favor. The article with all of our findings comes out tomorrow morning in the *New York Herald*."

She'd looked out for me over the years; maybe it was my own mommy issues, but I felt like I owed her this much.

"I don't know what you think you know," she stated calmly, folding her hands in front of her, stoic as always, "but I'm sure there are things you missed."

"I know everything. Your grandparents, the Carrington money, and the house off High Street. They made their money in shipping, right?" I asked genuinely. Maybe I wanted to give her a chance to explain because I knew how tricky the truth could be_I used to be a liar. "I'm not wearing a wire or anything. I just... I know how nice it feels to finally stop lying."

A faint smile wisped across her face. "I hope this means you're considering a path outside of medicine. Because I can't help but be a little proud."

"I am." I took a few more steps forward until I was lined up with her at the window. "What happened? I mean, it doesn't matter what you tell me now..."

Lines formed and vanished on her forehead. A few beats of silence passed.

"I grew up surrounded by art. My grandmother taught me to paint, she told me that we were artists by blood but shipping magnates by trade. Her father painted with 'the greats.'" She paused here to hook her fingers into air quotes, then huffed a laugh. I was itching to ask her who *the greats* were, but I knew it was neither the time nor place. "She told me she lived like a princess when she was young." She turned and opened her desk drawer, revealing a familiar brass key under its false bottom. "I found this key in my grandmother's things after she died, apparently it was her brothers'. They were Carringtons. She married Victor Packham, one of the wealthiest men in London. He mismanaged both of their fortunes, which was why, as you probably know, the Packhams never made Scroll & Ivy history."

"Would you have punished me in order to stop this from coming out?" I asked.

She quirked a brow. "Yes."

"So I did the right thing," I told myself under my breath.

"Depends on who you ask. Life may seem simple in college, but the real world is brushed with varying shades of gray." She buttoned up her jacket and tied the two tassels resolutely. She knocked on the hardwood desk as she walked past it, then stopped at the threshold. "But it's hard to live one life when you *know* you could have lived another."

She left with that eerie warning to a trap I narrowly missed myself.

If I ever needed proof that I made the right move in taking control over my own life, she was the living embodiment. I didn't want to spend my future weighed down with the ghost of a life I *could* have lived.

A few moments later, I made my way out of Packham's office, where a set of blue eyes awaited me.

That gorgeous, tingle-inducing half smile pushed up one cheek. "Holmes."

Delight filled me. "What are you doing here?"

When I returned to campus last night, Cora was back from San Francisco too, and I filled her in on everything she'd missed. We spent the night watching movies, and I needed that time with her, but I planned on catching up with Conrad this evening.

"I got the same email from Barrett." Conrad stood from one of the leather chairs outside of Packham's office. "I knew you'd come here. I figured I'd wait for you to say whatever you needed to."

"So you followed me?"

"Always." He closed the few steps of space between us. "You have a tendency of running right into trouble."

"I do," I admitted. "It ran me right into you."

"I never said I didn't love it." He looped both arms around me. "Are you okay?"

I nodded. "I will be."

"Wanna get some lunch? Isha and Lucy are talking winter break plans."

It was sweet—and I could definitely see this being his way of trying to make me feel safe and included, since *home* wasn't an option right now.

"Sure, but I should warn you, I already decided I'm going to California with Cora for winter break."

He pressed a kiss on my head and nodded in the direction of the exit. "Then I should warn *you*, Isha has a way of negotiating that makes you agree to things without realizing it."

I smiled and leaned my head on his shoulder.

Today was a little easier than yesterday, and I hoped the trend would continue, because the path forward was daunting, but it was worth it.

CHAPTER 53

Conrad

Three days after Malena confronted her, President Packham resigned. The article was all anyone could talk about.

I picked the paper up from the coffee table in my condo.

Poisoned Ivy: Two upperclassmen at the prestigious Winchester University unravel a forgery scheme

My eyes fell to the byline. **Conrad Hastings & Malena Amin**

Even though Malena was excited about the article, the reality that her life was going to be different weighed on her. But, with every day that passed, she got a little closer to herself. And she was becoming more okay with the uncertainty.

I was about to pick up my latest paperback and settle on the couch for the morning when a knock came at the front door. I glanced at the clock—it wasn't Mal, she had a meeting with Winchester's administration and I planned to meet her later when it was over.

I opened the door and was met with a face that was stoic to the point of looking like a statue. "Dad?"

Deep circles dug under his eyes. "Hello, son."

Without waiting for an invitation, he maneuvered around me and walked inside.

"Come on in," I muttered dryly.

"The Winchester alumni group at the Augustus Club received an interesting call." He stood in front of the coffee table, glanced down at the paper. "A door in the catacombs needed to be resealed." He looked back up and held my gaze. "It led into the Amherst Building's basement."

The Augustus Club was a members-only club in Manhattan. My family had been members since its founding, and the alumni group he was referencing happened to fund Scroll & Ivy.

"Weird."

My dad took a seat on the couch. "It is, isn't it? Considering those tunnels were the same ones used to move the paintings."

"Weird," I repeated.

"It's taken care of, in case you were worried."

"I wasn't." I *was* a little concerned with why he was here, but he looked different. Like maybe someone else's success managed to humble him. Or maybe he'd received the divorce papers.

"I'm not here to reprimand you." He leaned forward and lifted the paper. "Quite the opposite. I've been fielding calls from politicians to Nobel laureates congratulating me on my son's accomplishments. And Hastings Media's circulation projections jumped this week, you know."

My entire body filled with a feeling I was getting more familiar with. Pride. In myself.

Malena was right, it was a little addicting.

"That was all Malena," I confessed.

"Yes, well, I had a feeling it wasn't a sudden burst of productivity that had you investing your time in the family business." He set the paper back down. "Either way, looks like you're finally taking our name seriously. I'm proud of you, son."

I grimaced; I couldn't help it. "That's nice, Dad."

"You could be a little more accommodating, I am trying to—"

"Get on my good side because Mom is going through with the divorce?"

Another sharp silence fell over the room. I had a feeling that was the real reason. He needed some good will on his side, and I was the only one she liked.

He shifted in his seat. "I came here to tell you in person. I'm going to be spending the next year or so overseeing the London offices. Your mother asked that I go."

Oh no, were these the consequences of his own actions? I grinned. "Did she?"

"Yes, and I can't seem to get her to rethink this divorce, so I will respect her request." Regret laced the last few words.

Good. I hoped it hurt.

"I'm sure your mistress will be *so* pleased."

His jaw flexed. "This summer, Barrett will be taking over all operations at Hastings Media."

My brows jumped. My dad was painfully predictable. One thing he loved to do was toy with my older brothers, let each think they had a chance at leading but never give up even a shred of his power. I never actually expected him to pick a successor. I'd honestly always assumed Tripp would just have him killed. "Okay..."

"It would be a good opportunity to learn about the inner workings of the company before you go to business school in the fall."

"So, you..." I muttered in confusion.

Was he... *trying*? He'd picked a successor, he was being agreeable toward my mother. Was he... apologetic?

A part of me basked in this, watching that man finally get what he deserved.

"I'm here hoping you'll do it. But it's your choice. Spend the summer there or gallivant with your friends like you always do."

No threats.

Bewildered, I wondered what I wanted. As much as I hated to admit it, the idea of a summer working there—knowing he wouldn't be around—didn't sound terrible.

"Someone should probably keep an eye on Barrett," I mused casually. A curt smile shoved against his cheeks. I didn't want or care for his approval, yet having it felt admittedly nice. "I'm sure somewhere in Manhattan, Tripp is plotting his murder."

The lines along his forehead dug even deeper and he barked a laugh that spilled over into a rolling chuckle. He coughed and cleared his throat as he stood up, transforming back into the slab of granite I was used to.

He didn't say anything, just gave me an oddly affectionate pat on the shoulder and walked to the door.

"I don't know how to be anything other than *this*." He stopped in the doorway. An acknowledgement that he was never a father, never a husband, not even all that good of a man. That he was the person his father raised him to be: the Hastings Media heir. It felt like advice as much as it did a warning. "But I hope you do."

THE ADMINISTRATION BUILDING loomed like a gothic cathedral in the gray December sky. Snow coated the sidewalks and grass in a thin layer of white, and while the heavier snowfall had begun to die down, a few flurries still peppered the air.

I caught Malena right as she was coming down the steps.

"When were you going to tell me that I was the lead writer on the byline?" I threw the scarf I brought with me around her shoulders and looped it twice.

"I wasn't." She looked up at me impishly. "You'd have tried to be chivalrous or something and stopped me. Come on, Con. Admit it: none of this would have happened without you."

"I'm sure you would have found a way to blackmail James."

"Probably. But you're cuter." She tugged at my jacket. "I mean it. I wish you could see yourself the way I do."

"Handsome, right?" I brushed my lips against hers.

Her voice distilled down to a serious note. "Remarkable."

My heart stumbled and I didn't know how to respond to that. So, I kissed her. Deep and slow.

"Con..." She pulled away, her cheeks and the tip of her nose a little red.

Our breath mingled together, making a tiny cloud in the cold air.

"Sorry." I leaned my head against hers and kissed her again, a quick one this time. I kept forgetting the no-PDA-around-faculty rule.

"No, you're not."

"Nope." I circled my arms around her waist. "How was the meeting?"

Malena met with the heads of Winchester's administration board to discuss the article. She'd insisted on going alone, but had recorded it for an added layer of protection. They'd assured her it wasn't punitive, rather congratulatory, and a way to find out if they needed to cover their asses for any future articles.

"Great." Mal practically glowed. "They *did* ask that the next time I discover a forgery scheme at the school, I go to them first."

"And you said..."

She jutted her chin up defiantly. "I'd consider it."

I chuckled. "You're sort of a big deal, you know. That article is making waves."

"Oh, I know." She lifted to her toes, excitedly tapping her hands on my chest. "I submitted it to the Keller Committee."

Relief moved down my body. Originally, all of this chaos was in pursuit of that award. "Really?"

"Yeah, I submitted the article as my piece, hoping they wouldn't mind, or at least make an exception. They accepted it." She linked her arm in mine, and we walked over to the café where she was meeting Cora. "*And* I've decided to take the writing seminar over the summer."

"How did you get all that done in one morning?"

She laughed, light and joyful. "I stopped by the paper on Monday to see if it would even be possible. Dillian knows one of the lecturers and got me in last minute, under the condition that I complete the prerequisite assignment. I only just found out."

The realization that we'd be together in the city for the summer hit me all at once. "If the Alders' house gets stuffy, you can stay with me in the city."

She looked up at me, her eyebrows almost at her hairline.

"I'll be working at Hastings Media."

If you could distill the words *I told you so* into a look, it was the one currently on Malena's face.

"That ne'er-do-well reputation is done for," she teased.

Yeah. So was I. The second she barged into my life because I stood between her and something she wanted. And, fuck, I was never so grateful to have been in the way.

CHAPTER 54

Malena

My dad sat perched across from me at our kitchen table, his hands folded and an expression I couldn't decipher on his face. Against my better judgment, when he showed up at my door unannounced, I let him in.

It'd been a couple of weeks since everything went down over Thanksgiving weekend. I was a week out from finals, and I hadn't heard from my parents.

"So, what's up Mr. Amin?" Cora called from the living room, where she was pretending to read her book.

When she heard the door open a few minutes ago, she meandered out of her room and planted herself on the couch. Now that Sabrina and Cora knew the full extent of what my home life looked like, I knew she wouldn't be leaving.

My dad glanced over his shoulder and gave Cora a polite smile before turning back to me. He tapped his fingers along the folder in his hands.

"I wanted to see you and give you this." He handed it to me. "I stopped by the bursar's office today."

Inside were two sheets of paper letting me know that my tuition was paid for next semester.

My nerves hissed.

"You think this fixes everything?" Was this some backward way of bribing me into compliance? I was supposed to forget everything that happened? "That I'll just go ahead and do what you want?"

"No," he answered resolutely.

"I'm just going to forget all the abuse over the years?"

He flinched because I named it. I said it out loud where someone could and would hear. We weren't the type of family that talked about the ugliness. We yelled about it and someone —me—always knuckled under.

"Well, fine, it's your money." I wasn't too proud to take it, but it wouldn't be in exchange for anything. "You can pay for it, but it won't change anything until *you* change." Every demand I should have made over the last few years came flying out of my mouth. "If that's not okay, then don't—"

"We are your parents," he said, his lips curving down. "We will always take care of you."

My steadfastness wobbled. The words cracked down my sternum because I was still their kid. Despite everything, I still ached for them to want me.

I sucked in a breath to keep the tears at the corner of my eyes in place. "Okay."

The room went still again.

"Getting you girls everything you needed... that was all we could see for a long time," he explained. "We did what we thought was best."

"Best for who?"

"For you. To protect *you*." He said it so sincerely that I was sure, on some level, he thought that's what he was doing.

"Everything I know about living, working, being a good friend, a good partner—" My voice hitched "Although that last one needs some work. All of that, I've had to learn by lying to you," I told him bluntly. "In *protecting* me from the world, you made me unprepared to ever face it."

The words landed heavier than I meant for them to, but they had the intended effect. The lines in his forehead sank deeper and his shoulders slumped.

"That wasn't the intention," he said quietly. I still couldn't know if that was true because controlling me was pretty convenient for them. "And I don't want to fight, Malena." He steepled his hands together. "I just want you to know that you *can* come home. You can always come home."

My lips wobbled. "Mom doesn't—"

"Mom is going to do better," he promised. "So will I."

President Packham was right. Life was shades of gray. Right and wrong were fuzzy.

As a woman, I felt for my mom. I understood what she was *trying* to do: set me up in the best way she knew how. She was trying to make me perfect by *someone else's* standards. She stole parts of my girlhood because those were probably the parts stolen from her and she didn't know any better.

As a daughter—the person subject to the temper, the judgement, the unrelenting weight of her expectations—I was angry. Angry with what would have happened if I hadn't stood up for myself. I came too close to living the wrong life because of her.

Maybe one day that anger would distill down to something less volatile. Maybe I'd have a daughter of my own and I'd know how *not* to treat her. Maybe we'd be able to have a relationship, a real one.

I hoped for it, but I wasn't leveraging my own happiness to get it. Not anymore and never again.

"I hope you do. But I'll wait to see proof before I come home."

"Okay." He stood and nodded, walking to the door with

his hands in his pockets. He paused at the threshold. "I *do* want you to be happy and safe. We just might have different ideas of what that is."

That was probably as close to getting some sort of agreement with what I wanted.

"I'll be fine, Dad." I tapped on the headline on the paper. The one Cora refused to move from the kitchen table. There was also a copy on the coffee table and a stack of at least thirty in her room. "Turns out, I'm pretty resourceful."

His chest puffed up proudly and he looked down at the paper. "I know."

CHAPTER 55

Conrad

Malena followed a few steps behind me into the Scroll & Ivy's mausoleum. She'd been patient up until we got into the library, but once she passed through the doorway, she started guessing at our reason for being here.

"It's another path in the catacombs, isn't it." Malena snapped her fingers. "I knew there had to be more."

"I already told you it's not." My voice dragged, suddenly feeling like what I wanted to show her wasn't going to hold up to all the ways her imagination churned.

I walked over to the bookcase and pulled out a journal. One that wouldn't be complete until next semester, but I wanted to show her this before I told her how I felt.

"I wanted you to see this." I handed her the leatherbound journal.

She took it and ran a finger down the spine. **Hastings, 2025.**

Her face brightened.

"This is..." She walked over to a wingback chair and sat

down. Flipping to the first page, her eyes scanned over it once. Then again. She looked up at me like she'd just discovered something, and her eyes filled with delight. "Con, this is the story. Our story."

I was finally able to put what I felt about her into words. A lot of them, actually.

"We had to leave some stuff out of the news report," I reasoned.

I didn't have a journal for her since she wasn't a member, but I couldn't let *this* story get lost. Our story. One that would sit in here for however long this place was around, and I liked the predictability of it. The story of how we met and became everything we were now was written down and tucked away here for good.

"You can read it later." I leaned down to close the journal, realizing now that she was going to sit here and read through the nearly thirty pages I'd filled.

"I'm a fast reader," Mal insisted, putting her finger up and dodging my attempt to take the journal back.

"Mal." I splayed my hand over the pages. "I promise you can read it whenever you want."

She held it to her chest, then looked up at me cautiously. "Okay, I'll stop. But can I take it with me?"

"Give it to me or Sabrina when you're done?"

She nodded, carefully storing it in her bag, then came to stand in front of me.

"You wrote a story." She beamed, curling her hands around my sweater.

"Yeah." I leaned in and brushed my lips against hers. "Because my blank journal ended up in my backpack..."

"Huh. A mystery." Her brow crinkled and she gave me a knowing grin. "I've read your writing, and I thought maybe you needed a nudge."

"I think I did," I admitted. "And now our story is here, with Isha's and James's and everyone else's," I reminded her. Because for the next while, she was going to go through a lot with her family. She'd need to seek refuge with another—the one she built. But, if she needed anyone else, I had a family that wasn't the one I was born into and she was welcome to it whenever she wanted. "This is as much your story as it is mine."

"I know." She took a deep breath, her eyes shimmering with a glassiness that she blinked away. "I'm glad it'll be in here." She gestured to the towering bookshelves. "*After* I finish reading it."

We'd read through countless of these journals. Most were similar. Parties, classes, stories that would be told a hundred times between friends for years to come. At first glance, relatively mundane. But the simple act of writing it all down was choosing something versus doing nothing. Accepting the world in front of you or making it into what you wanted.

It wasn't until Mal that I realized I wanted to happen to the world; I didn't want it to happen to me.

"I was thinking..." Mal smoothed her hand over my chest. "Switzerland this winter break..."

I pulled in a quick breath. Isha tried with no luck to convince her to come along. "Yeah?"

"Can Cora and Sabrina come?"

"Of course." My thumbs swiped up and down on either hip. "The house in St. Moritz is huge."

Finals were in a week, and after that it would be a month before the next semester started. I wanted to spend winter break with her, but I didn't want to push.

"Good. Because they're my family, and I love them. So..." She paused. "I want you to spend time with them."

Now felt like the perfect time to tell her. Because in the

time we'd been together, we'd been through enough that made me sure of how I felt.

"Can I tell you something?" I asked, tapping my fingers along her waist.

"Sure." An upward inflection curved the end of the word.

The pins and needles were back and, *fuck*, I hoped they'd never go away.

"I didn't think I'd ever be any good at this, but you make me want to be." I swallowed hard against a dry throat. Suddenly everything I'd been able to write down in the journal was lost to me. "So I *will* be."

"You already are." She pushed her fingers through my hair.

"And I... I like who I am when I'm with you," I admitted, taking her hands in mine. With a steady cadence, firm and unwavering, I went on. I didn't want her to doubt any of it. "Malena, I love you." The words settled in the narrow space between us. She raised her brows, and I didn't know what that meant, but dread set in. "You don't have to—"

"Con," she interrupted. My panicked gaze met her steady one. "I've spent a lot of time wishing I was more of something or less of something else." Her next intake of breath was shaky. "And that's on me. But being with you makes me *want* to be radically myself. And it's a kind of peace I've never known before." She blinked a few times, clearing the mistiness that coated her eyes. She straightened a bit and smiled, her hands pulling on my shirt. "I love you too. I just wanted you to know that first."

Relief moved down my body.

I leaned my head against hers and laid a kiss on her lips. Then one on her cheek, then a few down the column of her throat before wrapping both arms around her.

With a soft hum, she pulled away. She looked around, then over to her bag where the journal was. "All of this... it's really sweet, Con."

"Get used to it." I brushed my lips against hers. "I'm working to get some of those annotation tabs in our story."

Mischief glinted in her eyes. "Take me to that ladder and you'll *definitely* get a few."

Epilogue
MALENA

The summer was a welcome reprieve.

After Conrad's graduation, I stayed in the city with Sabrina. But since my writing seminar started the week after the Fourth of July, Conrad and I decided to enjoy the beach in Newport for a week.

A warm, salty breeze swept off the ocean and through my sheer cover up as I typed up another chapter, coasting along a burst of creativity.

I smiled as I read back the last few pages, stunned at the words I'd placed so neatly on the page. Before I could dive in again, the slide from the glass door pulled my attention and a newspaper was placed over my laptop screen.

"The plot thickens." Conrad leaned over the back of my lounge chair and braced a hand on either side of the headrest. "I picked this up when I was at the store."

Former Winchester University President cuts deal with FBI White Collar Division, avoids jail time for the 'Poisoned Ivy' Scandal

I smiled. It wasn't a secret to me—I'd been there when Conrad reviewed it and helped Barrett oversee its approval process at the paper last week—but it was still an interesting end to our saga.

"It was Abby, the librarian," Conrad confirmed.

"She came forward?"

Conrad nodded. "That was the second voice we heard in the closet that day. Apparently, she and Packham knew the authenticator at the gallery—a former Winchester alum—and all three were in it together with the art dealer that brokered the sales. He used the dormant Lancaster account to evade suspicion. The FBI traced all the money."

"Wow."

Maybe it wasn't the end. Either way, Conrad was enjoying the summer more than he expected, and it brought me a surprising joy to see it. To see him finding delight and success in places he assumed he never would have.

"So..." Conrad pressed a kiss on my hairline and took a seat on the chair across from me. He tapped my screen. "How's the short story going?"

"Amazing." Practically giddy, I worked on the writing seminar's pre-lesson assignment with so much ease that it didn't feel like work. We had to write a ten-thousand word story, in any genre, which we'd revisit at the end of the summer.

The only person more excited about it was Conrad, who insisted on reading every draft.

"And the *other* document?"

"My pro/con list?" I saved the file and tilted the screen down a bit.

The sea breeze whistled between us.

"That's the one."

"I'm leaning toward a gap year," I finally said out loud. Avani called a friend at the Winchester General Medical

Center, where I interviewed for a part-time research position. I could work there and spend my free time writing and figuring out what I wanted to do long-term. After next year, once I graduated, that felt like a good plan. The right one for me. "I hear back from the research team in a week."

I wasn't ready to sign up for a life of *anything* until I got to experience more of it.

"You'll get it," he said like it was a fact. "Did you tell your parents?"

I shook my head. "Avani did."

I got the occasional call from my dad over the last few months, checking in without any expectation of me seeing them. It felt like progress. And when we got here, I met Conrad's mom, who was kind and doting. It made me ache to see my own, but I wasn't ready yet.

"Do you want to go and see them?"

"No," I answered immediately. What I wanted was that feeling of safety I had every day when I was at Winchester. The corners of Conrad's eyes fell, but he nodded. "Not yet. But once Avani's back for good, I think I will."

Avani would finish her residency this year and then she'd be starting her job in New York. She'd been talking to them more, making sure they understood what they'd done to push me away. Maybe with her around, it would be easier to see them. I hoped they were actually going to be better. To work on their obsession with what other people thought, to make amends for the pain they caused. I knew it would take time, but I was willing to wait.

"Well..." He tucked a lock of hair behind my ear. "On a brighter note, you'll be close by when I'm at business school."

I smiled. Conrad would be at Winchester's business school, so for now, not too much would change.

"I may turn on a dime," I warned. "Who knows, I could be going to med school the year after. Or going for a master's."

He grinned. "Where you lead, I follow, Holmes."

I took a sip of lemonade from the glass sitting on the table beside me and relaxed into this feeling.

These days, I was filled with an ease that came with no pretenses.

I was myself.

All the time.

"Okay." He stood and gave me another quick kiss. "I'm going for a swim, you write."

I nodded as he walked back inside to get changed. Then, I looked at the words I'd assembled on my laptop.

Maybe this would be my first assignment for the seminar and after that it would live on my laptop forever. Maybe I'd turn it into a full-length novel and publish it. Maybe I'd see it in bookstores. I didn't actually care about the outcome.

What mattered was that *I* decided what I wanted, who I wanted, and how I wanted to go about getting all of it. It was so simple I wondered how I ever let myself believe the two-Malena system would work.

All the lies kept me stuck in the web, and now, with the truth, I was finally free.

THE END

Sabrina Alders is American royalty. She lives her life in "by the book". A semester abroad in close proximity to her broody Secret Service agent just might be enough to make the American Princess break a rule.

Pre-order *Gilded Lily* Now!

Bonus Chapter

Want a swoony (and spicy) chapter in Conrad's POV? A bonus chapter is available at:
Bonus Chapter HERE!

Acknowledgments

To my readers, thank you for continuing to support my work. Writing is the greatest catharsis I have ever experienced, and it's possible because of your love.

To my wonderful husband, who saw the weight I spent my life carrying and refused to let me carry it alone. I could write a book (and I have) about all the ways I love you, but for now: heart, sunshine, world.

Dimpy & Lenny: The names and scenarios were changed slightly to protect our wilder days, but I think the general feeling remains the same. Thank you for loving me as I was, not under the expectation that I would change into something different. At the same time, thank you for being so wonderful that I wanted to become better, so that I could be a better friend to you both. Thank you for giving my wary and insecure heart a safe place to grow. And finally, thank you for giving me a space to learn to love every part of myself, unapologetically. Seventeen years later, here we are. I love you so much.

To all of my friends: Thank you for being all of the love and support of a family for all the tough years when I really needed one. Levina, Angella, Jen and Kerri— thank you for being my cheering section.

To my family: Therapy. Am I right?

Pri, there is nothing quite like having an older sister. If you read any of my books (and you promised you wouldn't!) you'd know that I spend a lot of time writing sisters and sister-figures. Occasionally, I mourn the time that was lost in misunderstandings created by different approaches to an impossible set of expectations. But that makes this time, when we finally found our footing, truly amazing. I am so thankful to your patience, understanding and humility while I found my way. We may have gotten it wrong a lot, but we were always moving in the right direction — back to each other.

To the rest of my giant family - Thank you for supporting my stories in all the ways you do. Vulnerability has always been a challenge for me, but your love has made it easier. And Dhara: thanks for screaming reason at my mom (only for her to ignore it), it was a lifeline when you didn't know I needed it.

Kimberly & Aimee: Thank you for continuously supporting my work and giving me the opportunities I could never have imagined. Your encouragement has been a lifeline.

Britt: I send you these stories in rough shape and you take those fragile words and help give them strength. Thank you for being so careful and loving with these stories.

Shaye & Linds: I'm fully sobbing now. I can't believe we're here. Too many things to thank you for, but as always, don't ever leave me.

About the Author

Ava Rani is a USA Today Bestselling author writing flawed characters with real problems in a (slightly) idealized world.

The daughter of two immigrants, her Indian-American roots peek out in different ways in her novels.

When she's not writing, she's working in the field that was her first career-love while being a wife and mom to an adorable kiddo and labradoodle. With hobbies from gardening to studying to being a sommelier, she's always looking for her next delicious treat.

For more: Visit Ava's Website

Also by Ava Rani

THE BIOTECH BILLIONAIRES

High Stakes, High Society

THE SPARE

THE HEIR

THE CHARMER